THE BLOOD OF KINGS

Angela King

London, October 1559

Dear Friend,

I have gathered together all that may be discovered about the Tudor boy, set down for your consideration and contained herein.

I trust this is a true and honest account of the affair but clearly the origins of his treason must remain concealed.

I rely on your discretion in this matter.

Padruig
Master of the Company of St. Thomas

LONDON, JUNE 1559

Aalia came in June, when the tides were low, and the city reeked of vermin. Brought on a caravel commissioned by the Company of St. Thomas, she meant to betray a promise. The caravel called *Cornucopia* flounced up the Thames like a harlot, bloused with bright-painted sails and long, shimmering pennants. As the river-pilot boarded at Greenwich, a band of minstrels started hammering out tunes from her deck, none vaguely virtuous, and while the gaudy little ship wove her way towards the Pool, barely a wherryman working the Thames wasn't tempted to raise his oars and let the grafted labours of everyday skip to a different beat. For the devil owns all the best tunes.

Rumour ran ahead of the tide. Before *Cornucopia* could reach her final mooring, merchants gathered at the Foreign Wharf, eager to discover what St. Thomas had brought to trade. A boat from the East was bound to carry barrels of spices or pepper, or bolts of fine silk brocades for the spendthrift ladies at court. Nothing bad ever came out of India.

After *Cornucopia* nestled against the quay, the ribald music played on. Turning heads, distracting souls, drawing easy legend. Two figures swathed in clotted cloaks watched from the caravel's deck, bare heads bent together under the timid English sun.

'You've stirred up a festival, Aalia.' Tall, fine-featured, the gentleman nodded his raven head and smiled. 'Is your voice wrung dry with singing?'

Hugging her thin bones, the girl looked away.

'I can bleat 'til dawn, if necessary, Georgiou, but I wonder at this audience? We've barely stirred their stolid English souls. I fear we're hosting a wake.'

'Did you ever see such a city?' He pointed above the wooden shore, to the spires and towers, the clustered roofs and pied buildings.

'I like Venice better. The air's too sombre here.' Her gilded head didn't turn.

'They say the English smell of fear, but Piatro says that's because their clothes are sweated and stale.' Georgiou laughed, pinching his nose.

'Well, it can't possibly come from dancing… who can resist such a jig? But, see… they're so boned and padded, they can barely bend, never mind hop, skip, and jump.'

'That's actually the second encore.' Georgiou ignored her pouting. 'Though it will hardly please the London Master of St. Thomas. Padruig warned we must creep into England like mice.'

'He confuses us with rats, another good reason we shouldn't bide by his rules.' She tightened her boyish hands into fists. 'Why hide? We need to be noticed, or else we shall fail.'

Georgiou leaned across the rail, unwilling to soothe her spite. When they left India, he'd dragged her on-board, spitting like a cobra. Despite everything the fool had done, Aalia kept faith with her brother. William, the golden boy. He'd been Georgiou's idol, too, except the measure of his betrayal cut him to the heart.

A pennant grazed his face, and he turned from gazing at the city, nodding instead at the shuttered hatch which let below deck. 'Piatro's anxious to know how you persuaded our good Captain to raise every flag and banner in *Cornucopia*'s store?'

'Bribery. It oils the wheels of avarice.'

'That old river-pilot warned we'd have to pay a fine for raising pennants we've no right to. He thinks we're probably pirates.'

'Horrible little man… officious true, spiteful yes, but lacking the artillery for a proper battle. I wonder if William has come.'

Georgiou ran his memory across the faces lining the wharf. 'Your brother made clear he didn't wish to be followed. He'll hardly come to greet you.'

'Verily… isn't that a lovely English word… I'll catch him by and by.'

Cornucopia's Captain bellowed out orders, as ropes crashed and pulleys creaked, and the last torn sail crashed stiffly onto deck, carpeting the busy troubadours. In a sudden warp of silence, bare-footed sailors crisscrossed the decks, nodding deferentially as they passed between the grey-cloaked servants of St. Thomas.

In *Cornucopia*'s comfortable belly, two fellow travellers ignored the banded celebrations announcing a new port of call. Piatro Kopernik, silk-tongued merchant of Danzig, was so imbibed with India, he assumed Mughal style, and Andreas Steynbergh, owl-eyed doctor and alchemist, who rarely ventured anywhere without the promise of a new discovery. They'd remained in their quarters because Piatro was sick, too sick to move from his bunk, and Andreas served as a willing nurse, Aalia's moods being better viewed at a distance. A gifted child but difficult. Sometimes, when she sang, her voice held a majesty that could charm a lion from its lair. God willing, this time it would.

Draped across the bunk lay a dull woollen cloak. Andreas pulled at its folds until he found the simple, black cross which defined the ancient Company of St. Thomas. In their name, his good friend, Otar Miran, had commissioned their Portuguese captain and twenty experienced hands, promising a generous dividend should they happen to drop anchor in London before mid-summer's dawn. They'd succeeded with one day in hand, the mission being urgent and St. Thomas's pockets deep. But when they'd left India at the tail-end of November, they had no way of knowing Mary, Queen of England, was already dead, never having given birth to an heir. Nor did they know her half-sister, Elizabeth, was already crowned in her place. While a season of feting drained every tavern of its living, *Cornucopia* raced frantically towards England, because St. Thomas's most dangerous secret was about to be revealed, and the name of that secret was William.

SANCTUARY – 1st Disclosure

K nowledge is fundamental to the principles prescribed by the Company of St. Thomas. Everything must be proved, before it can be accepted as truth.

Padruig fetched a second jug of ruby-wine and braced his mind to listen while the old river-pilot rambled out his news. They were settled in the white-walled study which encompassed Padruig's life as Master of St. Thomas. His sanctuary. The hub of his working life during most of his adult years.

Aalia had come, despite everything he'd warned. Otar had set the girl to find William. Padruig braced his mind, despite the pounding beat of his heart.

Pilot Solomon had been his willing confederate since old King Henry's day. The man was mean of stature, and meaner yet of spirit, but as Master of Trinity, he earned his living piloting every manner of vessel along the busy Thames. For a nominal bribe, he brought Padruig word of their landing. Except he'd a mariner's gift for spinning out the telling.

The Pilot squeezed his back against the chair and sighed. 'The lines on that caravel... *Cornucopia*, they call her... cut through the water like a seal pup, like silk under sail, but we was near calamity before they fetched up anyone who spoke proper English.'

Gorging back his wine, Solomon held out the empty cup, marrying Padruig's level eye. 'I was stood on the deck, waving me arms like a lunatic, afore I could get them to steer where was needed. That blasted music didn't help... almost brought the whole blooming river to a halt. 'Ad to put me foot down and tells them straight… find me someone who speaks my tongue, or I'll take my leave here and now!'

'And that's when you met my ward? Aalia?' Padruig re-filled the Pilot's cup.

'Course, if you hadn't warned me what to expect, I'd have got confused… not many with that colouring comes from the East… and me apprentice, Drake, was smitten, poor lad.'

'I'm grateful you thought to bring the news so swiftly Master Solomon. My steward will pass you the fee, as promised.'

The Pilot wouldn't be hurried. Draining his cup to the dregs, he smoothed his grizzled chin. 'Not saying you should worry, Master Padruig, but they've hardly come in with discretion. They were weighted with more flags and pennants than Her Majesty's royal barge, and then, there was the music… like of which I never 'eard, least not since last Lord Mayor's Parade.'

'Noted, Pilot Solomon.' Padruig stood at the door, willing his guest to leave.

'You still serves the best Burgundy on this side of the channel Master Padruig.' Solomon began to shuffle from his seat. 'But you needn't think it my fault if half London knows she's come.'

'That need not concern you my friend.'

Padruig's steward caught his eye, as he began to steer Solomon outside. Though he'd trained many apprentices over the years, Gull was proving the most intuitive. It fell to Padruig to teach St. Thomas's novices to respect the company's rules and act within its customs. From tentative beginnings, succouring to the needs of crusaders during their long journey to Jerusalem, the Company began to broker in the rare and the impossible, but few had Gull's instinct for the business which made St. Thomas unique—the lucrative trade in secrets which brought jeopardy to their door.

Padruig sat drumming his fingers on the neat-laid pile of papers overflowing the desk. Afternoon sunlight fanned shadows across the lime-washed walls. Aalia could never succeed in tempting William back inside the fold. Otar pandered to her gifts and failed to see, as Padruig could, the risk of bringing this misfit girl to England.

It wasn't that he feared her coming but how could he trust his company, his life, to this precocious daughter of stained destiny.

How God tested his soul.

Padruig never waivered in his service to God or St. Thomas, but since the fateful day he went against his principles to conceal the birth of an ill-timed heir, he rarely knew true peace. Preserving that babe sealed his destiny. Too late he learned the mantra, *'When a good-friend comes a-begging, it's kinder to show him the door'*.

Fate had a habit of twisting truth. To keep William's birth a secret, many good men gave up their lives, and Aalia became Padruig's charge, if not his eternal penance. He swore to keep both children well-hidden, and St. Thomas's ventures in India offered safe refuge until the hand of destiny intervened. Since learning of William's rebellion, how the boy sought revenge for the decisions which framed his life, the first thought in Padruig's mind was the promise he had given Aalia's father. He would do everything possible to ensure the girl stayed safe.

It had been Otar's choice, allowing her to share William's nursery, but they should have foreseen how the two would grow inseparable. When Padruig ordered Otar to raise the boy out of sight, he couldn't explain his reasons without breaking a solemn oath. Better live in ignorance than beg a traitor's death.

Padruig was still mulling the past when Gull returned, soft-footed, to collect the tray.

'The Pilot likely exaggerated, Master.' The lad said it gently.

Padruig looked up in time to catch his frown. 'Aalia has come after William.' He picked up a pen and stabbed the nib in thick black ink. 'All we can do is keep St. Thomas's principles and reason with our heads, not our hearts!'

Gull trimmed the candles and pegged the shutters closed. Leaving the Master to his business, he stopped briefly at the door, nodding silent agreement.

The lighterman who collected Solomon from the Old Temple's sheltered landing spurted bold-eyed gossip as he ferried him up to the bridge. Weighing the purse, he'd collected from Padruig's steward, the river-pilot pondered why his friend had appeared so troubled. St. Thomas had long anticipated *Cornucopia*'s coming, and the Master steered his company with utmost discretion, unlike those Merchant Adventurers, a company of gold-hungry adventurers who lacked any notion of tact. It was rumoured throughout the city Queen Elizabeth's new council favoured the tides of change, and if ever Dick Solomon was made to name a company who'd best embrace the future, it would have to be St. Thomas.

Passing through the forged steel gates which bounded the legal wharf, the pilot's eye went straight to *Cornucopia*. Stripped of her sails, she sat easy against the tide. Her musicians continued to play, and some folks on shore were dancing.

Solomon laughed aloud. Whether by charm or bewilderment, the brazen little caravel had stolen the best mooring on the wharf, though it was promised to another, greater ship. Except he'd seen the heavy-hulled *Hanser* grounded on a sand-bank, unable to shift until the next high tide. Whatever means *Cornucopia* had used to gain the coveted dock, it wasn't on the orders of the latest Master of Customs. Sir Andrew Mortimer couldn't afford to offend the worthy merchants of Antwerp; the man might be a fool, but with the Queen's sombre council keen to raise taxes, he had to beggar respect.

While a pilot going about his business might have many suspicions about a caravel coming from India, he'd leave that arrogant official to discover those secrets for himself. A pilot's work began and ended on the river. He climbed into his wherry, grizzled face rapt, settling down to sleep, while his young apprentice, Francis Drake, set the oars into the rowlocks and steered under the pungent, green belly of *Cornucopia*'s hull. As they cleared the driftwood shadows, the young man lifted his fustian head and gazed towards the music. Aalia's crystal voice seared above the harmonies.

'She's got the voice of an angel.' Drake said, heart laid bare in steady, blue-grey eyes.

'Perhaps?' the Pilot croaked. 'But not any angel of the Lord.'

SANCTUARY – 2nd Disclosure

Rule by reason, not by force.

Being it was mid-summer, and this was England, Padruig liked to mark the close of day before it sank into night. Standing on the Old Temple's corbelled roof, above the open courtyard which lay at its ancient heart, he watched the fiery sphere fuse crimson across the wide river. Witnessing such glory gave him a better sense of the Almighty. As Master of St. Thomas, he tried to steer by His principles, and should there ever come a time when he couldn't choose right from wrong his role, his service would be at an end.

Padruig could no more put his faith aside than fail to serve his Company, but William's presence in England meant his principles were torn. St. Thomas's intricate network was used to smuggle the boy out of England, and he feared the coming storm if their part should be exposed. They must bring the lad to heel… otherwise? That was something he dared not consider.

Padruig was descending the dark outer steps when he heard the entrance bell chime. Anticipating the arrival of his guests from India, he returned to his study to collect the lists of duties he'd already prepared. He trusted these associates would readily bow to his authority, but hearing Solomon tell of the caravel's blatant pageantry more than unsettled that confidence. There could be little doubt who was responsible for the troubadours. Otar often wrote of Aalia's talent for music, so, clearly, it was the girl who'd flouted his instructions. Padruig's way, St. Thomas's way, was to act with utter discretion.

He expected to greet three men and a girl, rampant with excuses, but Gull escorted a solitary middle-aged gentleman into the room, capped in straw and swaddled like a peacock. Padruig set aside his annoyance to embrace his flamboyant friend.

Andreas Steynbergh peered awkwardly through gold-rimmed spectacles and sank the cup of wine Gull handed him without drawing breath.

'Piatro's too sick to leave the boat, and I couldn't find Aalia or Georgiou.' Untying the bindings of his cloak, he handed it to Gull. 'So, I decided to come alone... no... I know... it's hardly a potent beginning, but I think we're likely deceived!'

Padruig had befriended the German polymath during his student years at Padua, not long after St. Thomas took them both under its wing. During years of service, they'd fulfilled extremely different roles, and Padruig respected Steynbergh's restless curiosity, though it sometimes brought them trouble. Since their last meeting, his thatch of chestnut hair had peppered grey, but his deep-brown eyes still burned with childlike intensity.

'Apart from Piatro's illness, all is just as I feared?' Padruig pulled open the shutters, letting the night air cool his face. 'Surely Aalia must come to the Old Temple, or where else can she go?'

Andreas squeezed his eyes thoughtfully. 'I suppose William remains at large... pursuing dreams of treason? We hoped Tom might find us soon after landing... but he'd have struggled to get close with the weight of crowds packing the quay. I see you've heard... rather a novel means of making port, but Aalia likes to be... original?'

'Rather a foolish means, when you're warned to be discreet. Who on earth sanctioned such a display? And where... or maybe I shouldn't ask... how did she find these musicians?'

Staring into the empty hearth, Padruig cursed Otar in silence. Why didn't he heed the warning? William could go straight to hell, but not Aalia; this was never her fault.

Andreas tapped Padruig's shoulder, bringing his thoughts to the present.

'We must only count ourselves fortunate she failed to bring the elephant.' He laughed. 'Captain Marron wouldn't accommodate the beast however much she argued. He first refused to carry the troubadours, too. Five Venetian musicians assigned without authority… didn't Aalia travel with Otar when he paid his last visit to the Doge? Well, that first day, we moored on the Tagus to board fresh supplies, these troubadours appeared, saying they'd been promised a commission. Piatro tried to turn them off, but… you've probably heard she can be wilful… although, I must admit, it's hard to think of any better means of attracting her brother. Music is one passion they share. She thinks to draw him out in the same way a magnet compels iron.'

'This isn't one of your experiments, my friend. Need I remind you how William's presence in England compromises the work of our Company? We promised to keep the lad hidden. I thought he was settled in India. Wasn't there a woman in Goa?'

'Yes, it's true.' Andreas stared at the ceiling. 'I remember with joy the day Otar declared him married! Whatever his new friends used to tempt him, William failed to disclose his plans to anyone, not even Aalia, before he left home. None of us had any inkling where he'd gone, until Otar received your message.'

'Thank goodness Tom Hampden had the good sense to come straight to me. Few men would remain so diligent after twenty years.'

Andreas sat, hugging an empty cup. 'You know Tom better than I do, Padruig. We rarely met, once William outgrew the nursery. I remember he was confident the lad would settle to a role with St. Thomas, but there were rumours… Will had a mind to go chasing rainbows. Have you any recent news what he's doing?'

'Tom's last report describes a devoted following among the lower ranks of Bankside. The lad's hard to track, because he moves his lodgings daily for fear of being detained. Neither has William seen fit to visit the Old Temple, but Tom prefers to remain out of sight and send messages in cipher. Having served King Henry's court, he understands the value of discretion. Perhaps you can explain how William's head was so easily turned by these strangers spilling lies?'

'It wasn't the lies but the promises! William's head is easily turned, and he's never been known for his reticence. Dear friend... you may rest assured we won't fail you... or the lad.' He jumped from his seat in a swirl of lurid colours.

'Andreas, I do not doubt Aalia will draw out her brother, but I fear she is far too reckless, a bright flame burning where there's no want of light. We have to apply caution... but what is done is done. It can't have been easy for Otar, letting her out of his sight, particularly after the last fiasco.'

'Oh! She's older now, and we found means to temper her gifts. You'll like him; he's called Georgiou Blemydes. Has Byzantine ancestry but Indian-born... like so many of that race, his family fled Constantinople and settled to trade in Goa. He's a fine young man... trained to Otar's impeccable standards and exceedingly quick-minded. I'm sure he's capable of containing her passions.'

Andreas smiled, holding his pewter cup to be refilled. But Padruig was not smiling, as he poured the dregs from the jug.

Pared by a silver moon, *Cornucopia*'s tangled decks were silent. Spent sails draped from the lower beams, pegged in awkward shadows, where mariners lay asleep. Tiptoeing between spooled hazards, Andreas worried for his patient, but it had been good to speak with Padruig. Too long they'd been strangers. Queen Mary made England impossible for any who embraced Calvin's creed. The burnings seemed to have robbed Padruig of his former zeal, but then, a lesser man wouldn't have been capable of steering the Company through those stormy years.

God Bless Queen Elizabeth. The woman seemed determined to deny the Pope his authority. He heard the priest had taken to his bed on finding himself deposed. A woman was defender of England's faith. Or was it the faithful? Kopernik would know. Their long-boned merchant took great pride in knowing every pernicious detail of every legal official who traded within the known world. He could even speak Flemish, if forced.

Andreas ducked his head to go below deck, when a loud English voice drew his attention. Seeking the cause, he found a squat-faced officer shouting from the wharf, brash badge of office on his upper arm.

'You've no permit to anchor here. This mooring's promised to a Hanse vessel.'

Aalia stood on the yardarm, wrapped in her cloak, barely distinguishable from the rigging. She turned when Andreas approached, and her hood slipped, bright hair silvered by the moon.

'Just where is this vessel?' Her silk-sweet voice was soft.

'Sir Andrew Mortimer orders this vessel removed, immediately.' The official threw out his arms, disturbing a pile of broken baskets. The clattering echoed into the night.

'No chance of waking the crew. They've had little rest since Christmas.' Aalia shook her head. 'Whatever this Mortimer demands… unless you'd like to rouse them?'

'The tide is rising,' the officer yelled. 'Fetch your Master. He can take up ropes and steer to Bear and Young's, without putting up sail. That's where Portuguesers are meant to moor.'

Aalia crossed the deck and peered up and down the black river. No boats were waiting midstream. Andreas caught her smile. *Damn.* In this mood, she'd keep the simpleton arguing all night. Having made a habit of withdrawing from any confrontation where his intellect wasn't best served, he went to fetch the man who matriculated in diplomacy.

Piatro Kopernik was propped in his bunk, mink-brown head tipped sideways, as he tried to hear what was boiling on deck. Andreas took a copper lantern from its hook and held it near his patient. Piatro's skin was damp with the grey shroud of sickness. During six months at sea, the Pole had worked his fingers and his tongue to the bone, only to fall victim to fever the day *Cornucopia* sailed into the marsh-ringed Thames.

Andreas laid his hand on Piatro's brow and pretended to shiver. 'I suspect the Hanse merchants took their woes to this man Mortimer after trading was forced to foreclose.' He held the heavy eyes and shook his head.

'Aalia wouldn't be warned that plying the docks with music wasn't our best means of gaining friends. In London, trade is king.' Piatro reached for his cloak. 'Nor can we allow the harbourmaster to search the hold. May I take your arm?'

Andreas steadied his patient, as he stooped to clear the beams.

'In this mood… she's mocking their petty rules. Perhaps it would have been wiser if Otar had kept her in India.'

'Is that what the good Master of St. Thomas said?'

The physician gave the breath of a smile. 'He actually suggested we've had six, long months to tame her!'

Piatro stretched to climb the ladder. 'Aalia knows better than to strike an officer of the state, but after so much time at sea, I thought she might relish some responsibility.'

It took an hour to negotiate, of making promises he sincerely hoped they might keep. Finally, in desperation, Piatro offered the fastidious little man a barrel of their best Port wine. That tidied the frayed ends of protocol. While he dolefully promised to sign whatever documents the sycophant thought necessary, the single comfort Piatro craved was an ice-lined bunk in which to cool his burning skin. Imagine what a rich man might pay for such a luxury. Andreas must take note; here was a scheme which could more easily turn a profit.

SANCTUARY – 3ʳᵈ Disclosure

The first principle of discovery is observation.

The sable waters of the Great Tower's moat lay pock-marked by torchlight. Two shadowy figures ran along the wooden jetty linking the forbidding fortress to its pooled fiscal port. Georgiou and Aalia ducked inside a low-arched tunnel, which cut through the tall timber warehouses, then waited in darkness, as the night-watch passed by. Having been goaded by the river-pilot for being a *devil-spawned foreigner,* Georgiou welcomed the anonymity of the Company's heavy-hooded cloak and touched the black-stitched cross of St. Thomas laying proudly over his heart.

Georgiou had always been a foreigner, even in India, the country of his birth. Being an outsider provided the spur which drove his juvenile ambitions. He hated the Portuguese for stealing his father's lands as much as he hated the petty Indian warlords for failing to beat back Portuguese invaders, and only joined St. Thomas because it traded beyond Portugal's ruthless grasp. The Syrian showed him loyalty grew from a different seed than fear, Otar being easily the wisest man Georgiou had ever known. His love for William and Aalia ran deeper than blood. Watching them driven apart made Georgiou hate another breed of men. Jesuits. Who lured men with their lies.

Torches flared, as stragglers hiding from curfew joined them in the alley. Aalia kicked at a stumped pile of rags and a furry bag of bones jumped to its feet, wagging what was left of its tail. Beneath its filthy paws, the rags shifted to exhume a human face, crusted with age and scowling.

'You could have brought me supper.' The beggar reached out a filthy hand.

'All we've left is olives, and you never suffered such delicacies.' Aalia bent to stroke his dog.

'Last time we met, you owned two legs?'

'A matter of expedience, and besides...' The man shuffled awkwardly, tossing aside the rags. 'Able men don't beg.'

'And there was I, hoping we could walk through the city together. I'm tired of boats and water, and you promised to show me your home, Tom.'

The beggar stretched, leaning his buckled frame hard against the wall. 'London's changed beyond my knowing. Everyone's afraid, wondering what this next queen will bring. Nobody dares speak their mind... and I'd forgotten what it's like to be cold.'

Georgiou helped sift through the rags until they found a scrap large enough to make a rough cape. He'd known Tom almost as long as he'd known Aalia. Being William's devoted servant, he never left his side, happy to serve in whatever role was needed, whipping boy to guardian angel.

Georgiou held his old friend's arm. 'It's good to see you my friend.'

Tom's walnut face was deeper incised, and his soft brown eyes doused of their usual fire. 'And it warms my heart to welcome you both. William's biding his time, quietly gaining support. You'd hardly recognise him... dressed like an Englishman.'

'Perhaps he's changed his mind?' Georgiou spoke gently. 'Now England has a new queen?'

Aalia laughed. 'William isn't dallying with a new hobby, but truly believes he's fulfilling his rightful destiny! The Jesuit, did he know it, woke a dragon not a lion.'

Tom rattled his begging bowl, as a passing stranger spat. He pulled Aalia into the shadows and swore. 'Better whisper such things in Urdu. William's stirring sedition.'

'The streets are not safe?' Aalia bowed her head meekly.

'We are not safe. Understand this. William pursues a highly contentious path, and unless we tread carefully, we risk being condemned by association. Give them cause and an English court will bay for hanging… if we're lucky. Remember, they like a good burning, because beheading's reserved for the rich, not nameless bastards like you and me.'

'Or William?' Aalia took Tom's filthy hands and laced them in her supple fingers.

'Especially William,' he whispered, levelling her stare.

They followed Tom back along the empty wharf and waited behind tall iron gates while he stowed his dog and meagre belongings. When he returned, he'd scrubbed his face and changed out of his stinking rags. Dressed head to toe in faded buck-skin, he was more their familiar Tom.

Crossing through the custom gate, they entered a labyrinth of narrow streets where crowded dwelling-houses were marked at every corner by a soaring spire or tower. Street lanterns danced shadows across the cobbles and scored the sturdy undercrofts supporting wooden-framed buildings. Occasionally, through an open gateway set between high red-brick walls, they caught the glinted opulence of diamond-paned windows. It was by far the largest city Georgiou had ever seen, and he walked beside Tom in silence.

Aalia skipped ahead, eager to run free after months of sea-bound confinement. Georgiou never let his attention slip, guessing how she would feel if they met her brother. By leaving the boat, Georgiou had broken his pledge to Piatro. Not because he wanted to disobey orders, but because, like Aalia, he needed to hear from William's own mouth where his allegiance now lay.

'We're heading up to Coleman Street.' Tom pointed. 'There's an alehouse called The Windmill; it's one of William's favourite haunts but not a place for women. I'll take Georgiou inside, and if we find your brother, I'll fetch him outside.'

'I can pass as a man!' Aalia threw back her hood.

Tom ran his fingers gently through her close-cropped crown and swore.

'Am I being chastised?' She pushed his hand away.

'Tom knows you as a lady.' Georgiou spoke very carefully.

'Tom would like to know what you've done with your beautiful hair.' He scowled.

Aalia tossed her head. 'Piatro didn't need much convincing. He said it spared his responsibilities, leaving small need for a chaperone.'

'She shaved her head the day we sailed.' Georgiou ignored her tiger-smile.

Tom spat into the gutter. 'Me… I'd like to wring Master William's neck for all the trouble he's causing.'

Reaching the Windmill took longer than Georgiou expected. London's maze of rough-paved lanes had a disconcerting habit of turning into blind alleys. Packs of scrawny dogs scavenged in the debris, and dirt-carts rattled across the cobbles, filling the air with foulness. Tom explained how Londoners preferred their cruder chores cloaked in darkness, and the buckets of filth were emptied onto barges to be ferried down-river then dumped on Kentish marshes.

While they walked, Georgiou mapped the city in his head in the manner he'd been taught. If anything happened, he must be able to find his way to the boat. St. Thomas had trained him as an engineer because he enjoyed clarity, and mechanical disciplines satisfied his sense of order, but this city didn't have clarity. It muddled together without any real plan, just like his home-town in India.

'How many churches have you counted?' Aalia waited near a high, stone wall which was almost concealed under a geometric cladding of scaffold. Retracing her steps, she walked backwards in order to view the roof.

'Eleven so far. This being a Christian land, we should expect to find many churches.' He followed her gaze, tipping back his head. 'I think this is a new church being constructed?'

'No, it's a very old one being mended.' Tom caught up behind them. 'St. Katherine's got hit by lightning two years prior. She lost her steeple in the fire, and they're working on repairs, except the money's wanting.'

'Then you'd hardly expect a need to work into the night.' Aalia's hood slipped, as she peered to see the tower. 'Or perhaps they've posted a guard.'

'I can't see anyone.' Tom squinted into the shadows.

'Aalia has the eyes of an eagle.' Georgiou watched the broken roof-line, but nothing appeared to move. 'Perhaps the gargoyles came to life?'

The tormented carved figures writhed in the masonry, and seeing the ugliness in their forms suddenly made him shudder. 'We've nearly reached the inn,' Tom said, patting him on the back. 'You two need feeding. Empty stomachs make wild imaginings.'

'I blame the olives,' Aalia said, replacing her hood and following behind almost meekly.

Despite Tom's confidence Aalia's brother was not at the Windmill. Georgiou hoped they would find him downing a cup of ale or gaming, perchance even fighting. His passion for hot debate usually marked him out, that and his unusual height. Though, in India, most remarkable was his thatch of copper-gold hair.

The low-beamed room was packed, despite curfew. Spent ale clogged the rushes and stuck to their boots. Aalia pinched her nose and pulled such a face Georgiou wanted to laugh. Shaking his head, Tom marched to the farthest corner where a bevy of men were huddled around a table playing cards. Shuttered piles of copper and silver coins marked the winners and losers.

Tom trapped the dealer's hand, forcing a grunted answer. William was hard to forget, especially if you knew who to ask. Tossing a couple of angels onto the table, Tom dragged Aalia back to the door, while the men scrambled to reach the gold coins.

'They haven't seen William since last Friday, though he rarely misses a night. Usually comes with a handful of Spaniards and a "monkey."'

Aalia laughed. 'William's never had a pet.'

'They think the lad's lost far more money than his friends can afford. And they were keen to add the younger Spaniard drinks but never gambles. Sounds very like that bastard Alvaro de Manríquez. Thinks he's God's personal envoy. They'll be keeping your brother hidden, if they know his friends have arrived, and there's barely a mouse in this city who hasn't heard tell of *Cornucopia*. The boat which sang its way from India.'

'I'm touched.' Aalia smiled. 'Best inform the whole country than sneak like thieves in the night… they'll have posted spies on the wharf anyway. This Jesuit is said to leave nothing to chance.'

In the hollow streets, a final curfew rang. Aalia was half a league ahead, flitting through the lazy arc of night-lamps, when she stopped and pointed skywards, a finger to her lips. Even before they could reach her, they heard a deep, grumbling sound, like a mill-stone sloughing grain, except it came from the scaffold-clad tower of St. Katherine's.

The noise stopped, and Tom suggested they hurry back to the boat or risk being arrested by a night-warden. Georgiou nodded, and without further discussion, they continued along the unlit lane and almost reached the next crossroads before either realised Aalia was missing. Retracing their steps at a run, they returned to St. Katherine's, where she was halfway up the scaffolding, cloak billowing out like a sail. Hollow-mouthed, Georgiou stood watching, while Tom swore softly in Urdu.

Aalia crawled sylph-like onto the parapet and then waved down at them.

Georgiou started to follow, climbing onto the platform, while Tom went to find a safer means of getting inside the building.

It soon became apparent how Aalia reached the roof so quickly. Between each level, the masons had fitted ladders, except they couldn't be seen from the ground. On reaching the highest platform, Georgiou had to slide across a very thin beam in order to reach the angled roof, but once he climbed to its apex and lifted his head above the ridge, he found Aalia lying on the opposite side, peering over the gantry.

He slid down the roof until he lay on the platform beside her and then stretched to see what caught her attention below. The square, cobbled yard was clogged with rough piles of stones and barrels of mortar, and tucked against the opposite wall sat a long, sturdy bench laid with masonry tools. Everything in the yard shimmered with chiselled dust because the stark arena glowed in the light of a myriad torches.

Gathered around a gaping hole near the centre of the yard stood a circle of chattering women in round-hooped skirts and petticoats in a bouquet of crimson, azure, and gold. While most women had their hair drawn into box-like frames, in that peculiar English fashion, one hooded in an ermine-edged cape stood slightly apart from the others.

Aalia pointed to the far end of the platform, where a tiny stone portal led into the main body of the church. Finger to her lips, she drew him along the ledge and crouched against the stone wall.

'There's a banquet laid inside… tables heavy with food and wine. I think it's some celebration, despite the ruinous state of the church. Tom always warned me the English are mad.'

Tom's face appeared at the portal. He climbed awkwardly through the frame and squatted down beside them.

'I heard that the masons uncovered some fancy Roman pavement, an image of Medusa made from tiny squares of glass, and that the elders of St. Katherine's charge honest citizens to take a peek.' His voice was a grunted whisper.

'Strange anyone would want to come at night.' Georgiou shrugged.

'Better be devilled by moonlight!' Aalia whispered rakishly. 'The casting of fear comes easy with Medusa. Nothing compels fright better than writhing snakes for hair. Night-hours likely raise the fee.'

'The women certainly look wealthy. I don't doubt they paid a premium to come in the witching hours.' Tom shuffled towards the portal, except in that same moment, the grinding noise sounded again.

The women didn't seem to notice. Tom began to climb towards the broken tower, and Aalia went to follow, but he pointed back to the platform, ignoring the pouted lip. Georgiou moved back across the roof, taking the same route, he'd come so he could approach the tower from its opposite side.

Obeying Tom more than he might have hoped, Aalia scrambled through the levels until she lay on the lowest platform, hoping that women wouldn't note the slight disturbance of dust. The yard was bordered by a range of outbuildings, but only the church was clothed in scaffolding.

Just below her roost, she could see a box of light thrown from an open door. An elderly man in long, black robes swept out from the entrance and walked to the edge of the hole. Despite stretching as far as she dared, Aalia couldn't hear what he said until, reaching a critical chapter, he raised his voice an octave.

Rounding on the women theatrically, he took two torches from their brackets and handed one to a younger man, also dressed in black, who came to stand at his side.

'The Romans, we may be sure, made the city of London their capital.'

The men waved the torches across the hole until they flared, illuminating a shimmer of gem-like colours. The women applauded politely, and the older man continued, weaving a story that meandered far from its subject, though it received their bated attention. While he was talking, the younger man shuffled backwards until he stood at the edge of the yard, next to a dark sheath of alley.

The circle of women drew tighter, voices rhyming above the fragrant rustle of petticoats. The lady in ermine raised her satin arm and barked out a string of questions. The movement dislodged her hood, revealing a mass of copper-gold hair. Catching the young woman's eye, the old cleric seemed to flounder and turned to seek his assistant, except the young man wasn't at hand. The copper-haired woman laughed, voice reed-high, gloved hands flashing with jewels. The man bowed, and everyone applauded enthusiastically, causing the torches to flicker and dance.

High above her head, Aalia heard the grumbling sound again, except this time, it crescendoed with an intensity very like thunder. In that moment, she knew what was coming and screamed, as only a soprano can scream. Wringing out her lungs with the warning.

Mortar and stones cascaded from the roof, leaping and smashing through the quivering platforms, churning beams and rubble in spewed momentum. Aalia leapt inside a deep-cut niche, just as the scaffolding bucked, twisted, and finally collapsed. Wrapping the resident statue in her arms, she waited for the turmoil to end before kissing St. Katherine's cold, carved cheek.

Blind deathly silence.

Wiping dust from her eyes, Aalia peered into the darkness. Tying her hood across her mouth, she climbed down the wall, gripping with her fingertips and toes. It proved very hard to breathe. With every torch extinguished, the broken yard shifted in clouds of opaque black, but bursting through the nothingness came a sudden rush of screaming, which Aalia held as a good sign, for the dead are generally silent.

SANCTUARY – 4ᵗʰ Disclosure

Gold may purchase the key but will not unlock every door.

By the time Georgiou found her, choking dust and cloakless, Aalia was halfway across the shattered yard, crawling on her knees. He found a broken lantern and guarded its limited light.

The screaming fell to an occasional whimper.

'We saw two men… They dislodged a stone beam from the tower and used it to unleash this devastation.' Georgiou wiped his face on his sleeve. 'Tom's giving chase.'

Aalia, her voice raspy, turned to look where he pointed. 'The mason's going to be furious having all his best handiwork spoiled.'

'You're not hurt? You screamed like a banshee.'

'Singing is just applied screaming… something I practise every day.'

She coughed. He lifted the lantern to study her face and noted she was shaking but knew better than to empathise. Aalia would judge him weak.

'If you're not hurt, we'd best see what can be done?' He angled his head, hiding his worry.

Molten mortar hung in pale shifting clouds as they began to search for the injured. Broken timbers and fractured stone tested each tentative step. Medusa was tombed in her grave once more. The spooling light revealed the young cleric buried deep under debris. Aalia gently wiped his face with her cuff. His eyes flickered, and he groaned, unable to move, his lower torso trapped beneath a huge, stone lintel.

Georgiou rolled a wooden beam and used it for a lever. Working slowly, he pushed down with all his weight until Aalia could drag the trapped man free. Every movement dislodged another fall of scree.

'We need more light! Try inside the church... but take care as you go.' He released the lever, and its weighted thud echoed across the yard, charging yet more dust.

When the scaffold collapsed, it acted like a dam, walling entry to the church. Aalia crawled over the broken spars until she reached the side-door which had been wedged open. Aside from a river of rubble spilling through the door, the elongated, pillared hall barely stirred with any distress. The women were clustered in a corner, beside the bench where their banquet had been laid. They seemed remarkably uninjured, though their finery was filthy and torn.

Ignoring them, Aalia went towards the altar, searching for the vestry where candles would likely to be stored. She almost tripped. Lying across the aisle was the old man, blood streaming from his forehead. Touching his arm, she knelt at his side.

'You were the one who screamed?' he said.

She squeezed his hand.

'I was with friends... we heard a noise and stopped to investigate... we're looking for those injured and need lanterns. Shall I find them in the vestry?' Tearing a strip of linen from the hem of her tunic, she used it to stem his wound.

'Where's Paulo?' Trembling, he pushed her hand aside.

'Is Paulo the young cleric? Georgiou's taking care of him. Your friend is hurt but breathing.'

The old man closed his eyes and began to pray, mumbling automatically.

This was no time for praying, Paulo needed corporal light.

One of the women came to stand at Aalia's side. A small, doe-eyed woman, she'd lost her head-dress and her brown head was crystallised with dust. She smiled at Aalia and seemed about to speak, except the woman with the ermine cape arrived. Arrogant, suspicious, she stood with her fine jewelled hands fixed on her wide padded hips. In the flare of limited light Aalia noted her pearls, glowing like winter moons strung on a sultan's promise. Worthy of an emperor's ransom, Piatro would be impressed.

'And who exactly are you?' The woman's tone was pin-sharp.

Aalia met fox-amber eyes and bit back on her temper. 'Hardly crucial… but my given name is Aalia.'

Her mind raced. Georgiou waited on her return. She must fetch candles, but this stupid woman barred her way. Losing patience, Aalia reached to push her aside, except the doe-eyed woman stepped in front, arms outstretched. Nodding to her copper-haired companion, she caught Aalia's hand and led to a narrow door tucked beside the altar. Taking a heavy key from a hook, she turned it in the lock, and lifting the altar lantern, drew Aalia inside the tiny room. Together, they raided the store of candles, and while they worked, the copper-haired woman arrived, watching in silence.

The vestry had a shuttered door which led into the street, avoiding the chaos of the yard. Aalia ran outside, skirting the building, except the copper-haired woman trailed behind.

Georgiou had moved Paulo beyond the shifting debris, and Aalia met them in the narrow alley. Lighting a ring of candles, Aalia bent to examine the young man's injuries, ignoring the woman's eyes on her back. Scarlet blood pumped from the wound in Paulo's leg, and Aalia knew it was urgent she stemmed the flow quickly.

Unwinding her belt, she tied it tight above the wound. She'd watched Otar save lives in India by binding a limb to stay the loss of blood, but never had need to test her knowledge.

Without a word, the woman took the lamp and held it above the injured man. Hawk-like she watched as Aalia took out her knife and cut thin strips from her tunic to bandage the wounds. Georgiou brought two thin blades of wood. They used them to splint Paulo's leg, and all the time he screamed, but they had nothing to ease his pain. Finishing the knots, Aalia leaned back on her heels, meeting the woman's bleached face. Lamplight haloed the copper-red hair. She was younger than Aalia had first thought, but her gaze was entirely disquieting.

'Why did you come?' The reed-thin voice wasn't doused with fright.

Aalia slowly released her breath. 'We happened to be passing… God knows we've better places to be.' She bent to sooth the poor man. He needed a physic. And soon.

'You have an odd way about you, boy.'

Long, jewelled fingers bit her shoulder like a vice. Otar would advise caution. Aalia let out another long breath and met the woman with absolute honesty.

'We heard a strange noise. And I was born inquisitive.'

Georgiou caught her eye and gestured towards the alley. They must slip away before any wardens came, and more questions were raised.

'*You* were the one who screamed?' The woman's tone was scathing.

'Instinct. I shan't apologise.' She raised her chin defiantly.

Paulo groaned. She bent closer, laying her hand on his brow.

'We've bound your legs. There's nothing to fear but the bone-setter.'

Finding sudden strength, he raised his head. Opening his eyes, he met the copper-haired woman peering into his face. His head dropped back, and Aalia saw fresh tears.

If only she carried one of Andreas' poppy-seed potions.

Yet, the woman persisted, thin face blanched in lamplight, white skirts mired in blood. 'You have other friends?' The amber eyes were blazing.

The doe-eyed woman had been watching from the shadows, arms folded across the rigid cage of her bodice. She'd busily set a line of candles from the yard to the street.

Aalia straightened her back in readiness to run. 'Our other friend has chased after the culprits. Georgiou doesn't have much English, and Tom knows the city best.'

'Not well enough.' Tom ran into the candlelit alley, chest heaving at each gulping breath. 'They planned their route with care, I…'

The copper-haired woman turned her head.

'Your Majesty!' he said, dropping to his knees.

SANCTUARY – 5th Disclosure

The Company of St. Thomas does not train warriors, but soldiers.
Our duty is to defend, not fight.

The sombre gentleman who had arrived soon after with a retinue of well-armed servants wouldn't allow any of them to leave until they'd answered a ream of discomforting questions. A tall, broad-shouldered man, with steady grey eyes, had reached St. Katherine's swiftly, having been dining just a few streets away. The doe-eyed woman, who the Queen called Meg, knew exactly where to find him, because she was his wife. Even before the debris had settled, the practical Countess had sent a servant with a message for her husband, Francis Russell, the second Earl of Bedford.

Surveying the fractured scene, Bedford scrambled over broken stones and splintered wood in order to enter the church. Disregarding everyone, except the white-faced, young queen, he nodded his head while she explained all that had happened. Her clarity was startling, laying emotion aside.

'We must count it a miracle you weren't hurt.' Bedford steadied her trembling hand.

'I should prefer to forget the whole matter.' Her voice lowered. 'Cecil advised against this visit, and very few at court knew of it!'

Bedford drew his mind to order. This wasn't born of chance. He must begin a wider enquiry, but first, he summoned the man called Tom, who'd apparently chased after the would-be assassins.

'Her Majesty tells me you saw these madmen?'

'It was hard to see in the dark.' Tom didn't flinch in his answer. 'One was a good bit taller than the other, but they was both agile brutes and sure-footed... must have planned their escape knowing they'd likely be chased.'

'And you failed to catch them?'

Tom nodded his sandy head, bending a worn, woollen cap in his hands. 'They went south, towards the river, and separated when they got to St. Olave's. I chased one halfway down Tower Street, but he disappeared at the crossroads.'

Bedford weighed his story. Whoever calculated this mayhem wanted it to seem entirely accidental. Without this man's observations, they would hardly have known any better, and Bedford daren't consider the consequences if the plan had succeeded.

Leaving Tom, he went outside, looking for the girl his wife had described as a God-given misfit. Aalia remained in the alley, supervising Bedford's servants while they lifted the injured man onto a cart. Her boyish clothes were marred in blood and filth, but her eyes held his with a sureness he found startling.

'Where are you taking him?' she demanded.

'To the hospital of the Savoy.' Bedford frowned. 'The Queen tells me you were *just passing,* but can I ask where were you going at this late hour?'

'It's our very first night in London. Tom was taking us to meet... some of his friends, except they weren't where he thought they should be, and we were returning to our lodgings...' She bit her lip.

'You've travelled from Scotland?'

'No. Why Scotland?'

'Your accent, a peculiar rounding of vowels... Where have you come from?' As he spoke, Bedford felt a shower of stones stutter from the roof, just missing his head.

The girl didn't move. 'We arrived today, on a boat from Lisbon.'

She spoke carefully, which made him wary, though her tone fell gentle on the ear. While his servants went with the pallet, Bedford grabbed her arm and pulled her towards the church. He'd ordered his men to clear a path, and caught on a broken spar, hung a torn grey cloak. He recognised the badge, even before he shook it from the debris and held it up to the light.

'This cloak bears the cross of St. Thomas. Do you know anything of this?'

The girl nodded uneasily, but didn't answer his question. Throwing the rag across his arm, he led inside the church, intent on asking more questions, but Aalia went straight to tend to an elderly cleric, who sat with a bloody rag to his head. Tom came to join her, standing protectively.

'Is this your cloak?' Bedford shook it open, pointing to the badge.

'No! That's Aalia's, but we all belong to the Company of St. Thomas.'

Bedford caught a flicker of apprehension. This wasn't the whole truth. 'I know of them.' He didn't mean to shout. 'Although highly respected, that doesn't mean I can trust you.'

Tom bowed meekly. 'Master Padruig will gladly confirm what duties have brought us to London.' Then, without further prompting, he meticulously explained everything that happened from the moment they had arrived at St. Katherine's.

Bedford didn't interrupt, even when Tom described the moment the attackers levered great beams from the tower, engineering a deliberate fall of masonry. It confirmed his worse fears; they had intended to murder the Queen.

Bedford remained silent for a very long time after Tom finished. Why should he doubt this man's account? But knowing he must be absolutely certain of everything which had taken place, he set out to look for the third member of their party. If his story tallied, he might believe the tale.

Black mane hazed with sweat, Georgiou was waiting near the altar when Bedford managed to corner him. He'd been helping take the ladies to the safety of the street. He wore a dark blue tunic and loose leggings, very like Aalia's, but his dark bronze skin and black almond eyes were markedly oriental. Then, Bedford remembered the news he'd heard earlier that evening, of a ship arriving from India.

Before Bedford could ask any questions, Tom intervened, explaining his friend Georgiou spoke hardly any English. Ordering him to stand where he couldn't infect the foreigner's testimony, Bedford tried various tongues before discovering the young man spoke excellent Spanish. Being equally familiar with that language, he listened closely while Georgiou gave his account. There was little which didn't tie neatly with the others. Perhaps he should accept these strangers acted in complete innocence and saved the life of the Queen. Yet, Bedford was sure they were not entirely honest.

Permitting them to depart, he withheld his suspicions, thinking he would discover more about them at the docks. Meanwhile, he offered an escort, needing to be sure they returned safely back to their ship.

'Thank you, sir,' the girl replied, smiling. 'But we've a perfectly good guide in Tom, and hardly wish to stir more interest.'

It appeared a sound objection, and Bedford didn't insist. He'd already set a man to keep watch, because he owned a diplomat's instinct for deceit.

SANCTUARY – 6th Disclosure

Comply with the law, unless you doubt its purpose.

It began as all rumours do, with a whisper. Half-truths spun in mischief, rung by lesser souls, courting a moment's fame. By the time Padruig's favourite novice appeared, fresh from the baker's door, news had spread like wild-fire from St. Katherine's to Fenchurch Street and up to Temple Bar. Last night, some assassins had made an attempt "to murder our new Queen."

Listening to Gull's sombre report, Padruig wondered sourly how fewer might have cared had the victim been bloody Queen Mary. Then, he chastised his soul immediately. Following the winter of that bitter queen's short reign, London's canny citizens had been keen to cast aside her vehemence and opened up their hearts to a fair-minded queen. The Pope might claim she was merely King Henry VIII's bastard, but Princess Elizabeth was born of royal blood. Already she'd made a pact for peace at the Treaty of Cateau Cambresis, and Henri, King of France, had promised to ensure Calais, bastion of English pride, was not irreparably lost, as long as England behaved.

Instead of taking breakfast, Padruig rushed back into his study and, binding down blind panic, penned a list of what his Company must do if any assassin succeeded. Elizabeth hadn't even been crowned a year; her death would lead to a crisis. England possessed no heir; no *legal* Tudor sibling waited in the wings. William was right in biding his time. Given the right proofs, there'd be little need for a coup, and meantime, Elizabeth's religious changes were igniting her enemies to act. Padruig's concerns extended as his list grew ever longer.

'The walls could do with a fresh coat of lime.' There was no knock. The door to his study swung open, and there was Aalia, culpable as dust in sunlight.

She'd recently bathed. Despite the borrowed shirt and limpet crown of hair, her manner had the quality of a finely-honed knife. The child had become a woman. Otar's precocious ward, raised on the premise she deserved to share in the advantages shown her brother. Allowing such freedom had failed to harness her spirit. Feral, just like her mother.

Padruig laid down his pen and set aside his presumed troubles to pursue those closer at hand. 'Why? Are you offering to help?'

'Me? I may be sharp of mind and fleet of foot, but I lack diligence.'

'You've been reading my letters?'

'Otar's teaching me ciphers and lets me practise on your reports.' Having stalked the periphery of his chamber, she returned to lean against the desk.

'I will trim my comments accordingly.' He stood up, anticipating the effect of his unusual height.

'Now I know why you chose the old granary for your quarters. It can better accommodate your crown!'

Padruig bent and kissed both cheeks. He would treat her as she deserved, like a long-lost child.

'Welcome to the Old Temple. The porter informs me you came hammering at the river-gate in the middle of the night. I was also informed *Cornucopia* anchored long before nightfall. It doesn't usually take half a day to reach here from the legal quay.'

'A small excursion… Tom's idea. He said he knew where William might be found, and isn't it Company policy to strike while the iron is hot? However, the iron anticipated our arrival and sought entertainment elsewhere. That's William—never where you want him to be.'

Smiling failed to divert his attention.

'And the porter also mentioned there was a quantity of fresh blood on your clothes.'

'Oh, that was not mine. I'm whole and elaborate.'

'Much is obvious. And may I add, I prefer the truth above excuses.'

'And there was I hoping your elevated principles were mere legend.'

Padruig folded his arms, silently praying for patience. The girl was no less biddable than the last time they'd met. What age had she been, nine or ten?

But something had changed. Mistaking his hesitation, she meekly took up a stool and set it on the hearth-rug, then proceeded to give a thorough account of everything that had happened at St. Katherine's, blanching only at naming her part. Her tone was such she might have been reporting on the weather, which was refreshing, given Otar had warned how she liked to dress reason with legend.

The least of actions could steer a wide reaction. Like tossing a tiny pebble across a mirrored pond, the contour of its wake ringed in finite tracings. Aalia had acted in good faith, but saving the life of Queen Elizabeth had repercussions outwith and beyond his control. Padruig's rules dictated the Company must act with utmost discretion, but Aalia wasn't to know the real reason he despaired. God willing, she should ever know.

And then, he remembered Tom, who ought to have known much better.

June had been hot. Festering in gullies and shallow filth-strewn rivers came the cloying scent of death. But Tom had lived too long to fear death, had fought too many battles. Not that it meant he liked it, especially when dying happened young. The previous week, he had stood helpless, as a beggar-boy jumped from the bridge. His dog had yapped, while half of London stood gawping, and a pathetic lost child swirled in the flotsam. With barely a spare morsel for the living, who cared twopence for the dead?

'I blame you, Tom.'

The Master's soft presence interrupted Tom's thoughts. He'd chosen to wait in the kitchen garden, to feel the midday heat on his bare head and pick his fill of sweet, ripe strawberries.

'Why not come to me as soon as you found William?'

The Master looked no different, even after twenty years. His hair was no thinner, still the colour of sand, and no spare flesh lay on any of his angled bones. But the steel-eyed authority, the closed emotions, came new to his memory.

'Because I didn't want William or any of his associates to think of coming here.' Tom squared his heavy shoulders. 'And because I understand how you can't afford to be kind.'

'If I'd known any of this might have happened, I'd have smothered the boy as a babe. I thought he was settled in India.'

'Ten times so, but times change, and older doesn't always mean wiser.'

High in the soft English sky, swallows swooped and dived. From the street beyond the high walls came the distant cry of a tinker. '*Any rags or bones?*'

Tom sunk into the soft earth, wishing he was anywhere but under the Master's knowing eye.

'Does Aalia have any inkling of the truth?' Padruig finally asked the question.

'No. At least I think not. And Otar would never break his vow.' He held the grey eyes level. 'Jesus... I curse the day I brought the runt to you. Knowing what we know is tantamount to having a death warrant. Do you think I'd be so ignorant as to tell a living soul, never mind Aalia?'

'She's bright, intuitive, and apparently reads Otar's letters. You're certain she doesn't suspect William's claim might be true?'

'Oh, she heard William boast. What his new friends promised... blood, power, and a throne. For God's sake, he's never been shy of mischief, and anyone lacking a title always holds the dream of finding fortune. But Aalia believes it's a fool's whim, though now he's arrived in England, there's no denying the boy inherited his father's looks...'

'There are still men alive who would put their trust in another fatal pretender and spill good English blood defending his unworthy claim. My fear is the men propelling William to take the English throne possess any sort of tangible proof. We need to know exactly who's steering this mischief. Otar wrote the man who had first approached William in India was a Jesuit?'

'Alvaro de Manríquez, fights like a mercenary and acts like he's God. Comes from Catalan. Son of a noble family and full of Catholic fervour, but he can't be acting alone.'

'You've met?'

'Faced up to him in Diu… not long after that, he tried to have me killed. Like I say, shifty bugger, sends others to do his mischief. Once he discovered I was following William, he sent a pair of assassins. Obviously, I survived, but they gave me a festering wound, and when I finally got to Portugal, I'd fallen a month behind. Thank God for your agent in Lisbon, or I really would be crippled.'

'He had sent word you were injured, but when you didn't call at the Old Temple, I feared the very worst. Had you not sent that first message, I wouldn't even have known William was in London.'

'The Jesuit is like a snake in the marsh; rarely do you see him, but somehow, he knows where you are… and meanwhile, he plots and plans. I hardly wanted to allow him another chance to strike and staying hidden was easy, once I found friends in the city. Between us, we've learned Alvaro's taken a post as secretary to the new Spanish ambassador, De Quadra. He's got rooms in Durham Place.'

'Good, in fact, excellent work, Tom.' The Master's thin face relaxed. 'I hope this will help us determine exactly who conspired to bring William to London. And you can return to India as soon as *Cornucopia* sails.'

'India! I'm not going back 'til it's over, one way or another.'

'Apparently, Aalia will attract William like nectar draws the bee. This ends here. I'll not put you at further risk, Tom, not after everything you've done.'

'You mean I'm being discharged?'

'Perhaps you're tired of India?'

'Only the dead tire of India... but everything I hold dear is presently here in England. And there's something I need to tell you about last night.'

'Aalia gave a highly detailed report.'

'But she didn't know one of the men I had chased works for Alvaro.'

'You're absolutely certain?'

'Even in the dark I could see he had no ears, same as the man who struck me down. And he favoured his left hand. When you think it's your last breath, you don't forget such details. I'd swear on my brother's grave it was him.'

'You understand what this means?'

'Why do you think I held my tongue? What better means to speed this conspiracy than bring about the death of the Queen? Alvaro is that breed of fanatic who'd readily marry fate. If he devised this accident, and I don't doubt he did, he'll be planning to try again and cursing Aalia, no doubt. Whether William knows it or not, he's entirely implicated.'

'I didn't expect them to act, unless they'd sound, legal proof. I can only speculate this ruthless attempt on Queen Elizabeth's life means they are ready to announce William as Henry's legitimate heir.' The Master rested his heavy hands on Tom's broad shoulders. 'They would need an army to suppress the subsequent rebellion... so we must assume the Jesuit has Spain's support, because you and I both know there's nothing whatsoever that can prove this boy's bloodline. Of that we made absolutely sure.'

'Then I can stay?' Tom began to get up.

'As long as you answer to me and not the girl.'

'I promise.' He winked. 'But let's not tell Aalia just yet.'

Tom picked another big handful of strawberries and, licking stains from his fingers, left the Master to gather his thoughts. How could he confess to one token which lay unconfessed? A trinket given in trust, from William's dying mother. Like a bond-slave, it remained where it had lain for twenty precious years, tight around his neck. Perhaps he should pass it to Aalia, on the promise she'd keep it safe, without need to learn its history. The girl had a gift for gathering secrets.

Later that same afternoon, intent on finding clarity from vague and muddy waters, Padruig invited all those who had arrived on *Cornucopia*, and Tom, to attend him in the library.

Almost four hundred years had passed since the Company of St. Thomas had earned its Charter from an Angevin king. From tentative beginnings, their business slowly expanded, as they brokered for trade in every land between Constantinople and Europe. During those early years, one founding principle underscored every penny of profit—a compulsion to preserve wisdom from the fires of ignorance. As rational as they were far-seeing, the company garnered knowledge, regardless of faith or nomenclature, and constructed the Old Temple as a fortress to protect their treasure.

For this single reason, Padruig held the library sacrosanct. As an infinite storehouse of wisdom, its very scope ordered the need for discretion. While the Company gave permit to scholars it could trust, Padruig was ever mindful how this store of understanding remained inestimably fragile. It was solely his duty to preserve its contents.

Lining the high partitioned walls were a thousand books. Lines of dusty works bound in wood and tooled in gilt Morocco-leather; worn bindings hinged with metal locks; blackened heresies written by devoted monks; ancient Arabic scripts drawn on parchment scrolls, fitted inside tooled leather boxes. Bowing the more recent shelves were the products of Europe's new presses, ordered into categories denoted by language and discipline. Even in mid-summer, with the shutters open wide, the room suffused the musky smell of vellum, despite Gull's fresh-laid rushes.

The Master gathered his confederates in the sombre-walled room. Grotesque shadows shifted under the pendulous arc of oil-lamps, as Padruig considered each solemn face sitting around the leather-topped reading table. He wished he owned the capacity to see inside their souls.

Closest was the merchant, Piatro Kopernik, mink-head bowed and clothed like a sultan, despite the effects of his fever. The Pole had good sense for business, flawed by his aesthetic tastes.

Seated at the opposite side was his dearest friend, Andreas. Cocooned in a peacock cloak, he bent to a nearby shelf, unable to keep his curiosity in check. Aalia sat next, making puppet shadows dance from her supple fingers. The fierce-eyed, young man on her other side was the only stranger. Otar wrote praising Georgiou's virtues. Born in Diu, he noted his courage and integrity, but Padruig couldn't help observing how his attention rarely wandered far from Aalia. This attachment to the girl might prove difficult.

Finally, there was Tom Hampden, the servant who'd suffered the burden of his duty with loyal determination. Tom stood quietly, eyes half-closed, waiting.

'I don't believe I need to introduce myself, or explain why we're meeting here today. Knowing how far you've travelled, I must assume you're each prepared. We must prevent this crisis from becoming a tragedy.'

He paused, studying their faces. They were all disciplined in the ways of St. Thomas—a discipline based on reason. He rested his eyes on the girl, pacing his words with care.

'Unless we act together, unless we stop William's ambitions, I hardly need tell you how badly this will end. He can destroy everything we love and respect. I've prepared a list, based on Tom's observations… everything we know of William's activities since he left India. From this information, I must concur with Otar's first warning that the boy's new master is Spain.'

'Was there ever a chance it was anything else?' Kopernik sat draped in his chair, eyes leaden as stone.

'For those who know India better than England, it might help to explain our concerns?' Tom moved into the ring of light.

'Yes, a pertinent point, Tom, though we can hardly spare the time it would take to sift England's recent woes. Perhaps it's best explained by saying Europe is suffering from a crisis of faith.'

'But surely these are Christian lands?' Aalia looked up, a pretence of innocence in her eyes. 'Each God needs a temple, but in India, we prefer the lesser gods—far less demanding and more tolerant of play.'

'Ignore her,' Andreas said, shaking a finger at her smile.

Piatro rested his chin in his hands and sighed. 'Having a surplus of gods does not make India superior.'

Aalia put her palms together, as though in prayer. 'I righteously agree, but there's liberty in owning the right to choose.'

Padruig continued bluntly, 'In Europe, religion walks hand-in-glove with power. Until the monk Luther denounced its misuse of power, Rome steered the policies of virtually every Christian land. When England broke from the Catholic fold and proclaimed its monarch Supreme Head of the Church...'

Kopernik interrupted, 'Marriage, or more specifically divorce, was the true reason Henry Tudor decided he didn't need the Pope. I agree with Aalia; it merely diverts those in power from filling their souls to filling their pockets. I hear they burn anyone who doesn't embrace the latest decree.' He turned awkwardly to Georgiou. 'Do you want me to translate?'

'No, I listen well. It's speaking the language which defies me.' Ruffling his fingers through the mane of coal-black hair, Georgiou glared at Padruig. 'The Portuguese brought such burnings to Goa. You do not need to explain how Christians can't agree; my mother's people have been torn apart by brutality.'

'She is of the Thomasines? Otar explained in his letters how he had tried to intercede, but these men act out of ignorance, they do not understand this faith is equal to their own.' Padruig flattened his hands on the table. 'Since Elizabeth was anointed our queen, she made clear she prefers the path of tolerance. But her policies are distinctly Protestant, and there have been no burnings since her half-sister, Mary, died. Many powerful nobles want England to remain Catholic, and seek only an opportunity to displace Elizabeth.'

Then, Padruig remembered something else Otar had written. 'Is William very religious?'

Without exception, they exploded into laughter.

'William loves to win and will use anything to hand, be it religion, a woman, or his sword,' Kopernik answered, glaring at Aalia, who'd coloured from collar to fringe.

Tom bent and whispered in her ear. Turning from Piatro, she smiled.

'Our task is to find the boy before he does more harm,' Padruig spoke carefully. 'Because… make no mistake, the reason William has come to London, the reason he has broken all ties with his friends… is because he intends to have himself declared legitimate King of England.'

The room fired like a field-gun. Aalia slammed her fists hard down on the table while Tom, scarred knuckles white, placed his hands on her shoulders and locked eyes with Padruig. Arms flaying wildly, Andreas tried to speak, but Kopernik, the merchant, the negotiator, shouted loudest, bass voice grating with fever.

'William is base-born. Nameless. What are you saying? He's one of King Henry's bastards? What idiot plucks a man from the crowd and names him a true-born king?'

Aalia bit her lip. 'I can't believe my brother is fooled by such precarious lies.'

Padruig could see her unshed tears. The knife-edge swung at treason. Unless he could make her understand, she would judge him as an enemy. Yet, he couldn't tell her the whole truth. At least not today. Hopefully not ever.

He spoke quietly. 'Tom has learned enough to know William is fully complicit with this treason, and surely, it would be ignorant to assume a Spanish Jesuit plucked your brother from obscurity because he bore a passing resemblance to English royalty? However, in order to deter the boy from taking this path, we must disprove their lies and untangle the lure. What made William trust he's legitimate heir to the Tudor throne.'

Aalia put out her hands. 'There are clowns a plenty who act on such likeness... What if this is meant as a surprise... contrived to entertain the new Queen?'

Her eyes betrayed she dealt in lost hope. Tom bent forwards, to see her face. 'William has become the tool of desperate men,' he said gently. 'But Otar would never have let you come, if not convinced of his purpose.'

Padruig nodded. 'What I want to make clear to everyone is we risk an equal chance of being condemned, if we fail to curtail this plot before it is hatched. And the penalty for treason is not a quiet death.'

'Why now?'

Aalia put the question Padruig feared most, though he'd weighed the answer too many times.

'This plan was likely hatched during Queen Mary's final illness. Philip knew his wife was dying, and De Feria, his ambassador, was charged to manage Spain's interests in England. It suited both France and Spain to remind the world in Catholic eyes, Anne Boleyn's daughter, Elizabeth, had no legal right to the throne. De Feria needed to find England an alternative heir while Spain still had status, except Mary died before he could succeed. Need I remind you... when William left Goa, this queen was still alive? But there's something more we must consider. While gathered to sign the Treaty of Cateau Cambresis, France and Spain made a secret contract promising they would do everything in their power to restore England to the Catholic fold.'

'Can we ask how you know this?' Piatro studied Padruig's face.

'Our Company survives by harnessing such knowledge.' He said it simply.

Piatro smiled slowly and leaned back in his chair, pale face deep in thought.

Tom released Aalia's shoulders and stepped back. He spoke each word deliberately. 'Which brings us to the man who tempted young William to England. Alvaro de Manríquez is a member of an order of priests who think themselves God's appointed foot-soldiers. We assume he acts for Philip of Spain, and so far, there's little to disprove it.'

Andreas fixed his eyes on Padruig. 'It's difficult to denounce shadows. Might I suggest, thinking as a lawyer might... they will require some written legislation to finally impose their scheme; documents, letters, whatever will steady the law. Presenting William as Henry's legitimate son requires more than agreeing to a likeness. It might help our case to discover if they've created any such documents.'

'Exactly my point, Andreas. Tom has spent his time in London observing William and keeping note of his activities, but together, we might keep better watch on Alvaro. We need to discover his liaisons. Now... are there any other suggestions?' Padruig resumed his seat.

'Since I brought William to you as a babe in arms...' Tom began.

'I hope you're not about to admit you kidnapped the son of an English king?' Aalia was smiling. 'Because William always believed he was better than a bastard.'

Padruig steadied Tom's eye, thankful the girl had her back to his face.

'There's nothing shy about the lad, it's true. But I wanted to say that having known William his whole life, I'm also convinced he thinks on this as some sort of game. We are his friends... we need to show him how much he is being manipulated. Otherwise, I need not warn how it will end.'

'And what would have happened if the Queen had been killed last night?' Aalia leant back in her chair.

For Andreas and Kopernik, it was news. Padruig waited for the shouting to subside before asking Tom to give account. While the old servant explained how they'd rescued the Queen of England from assassins, Padruig was able to study their reactions. Kopernik shook his head and finally laughed, but

Andreas waited until Tom finished before looking at Aalia and tutting.

'Speaking as an outsider, I'm only thankful England's affairs are not my responsibility. I wonder how much they're prepared to be without a sovereign.'

Before Padruig could render an explanation, Kopernik's head came up.

'Yes! Doesn't that beg at the door of coincidence? Who other should gain if Spain wasn't behind this attempt to murder the Queen of England?' He pointed at Tom. 'I hear France is also claiming the English throne?'

Padruig tried to offer clarity. 'France has the closest legitimate alternative in Mary, Queen of the Scots. Being the grand-daughter of Henry VIII's sister, she has Tudor blood, and as wife of the Dauphin of France, she's a puppet of their regime, but we must also consider England recently took a solemn vow they would not offer any assistance to Scotland's Protestants or France has open permit to cross the channel. Already they've sent troops into Edinburgh, and there's word a fleet is anchored at Honfleur only waiting orders to sail.'

Piatro and Andreas both nodded. Padruig realised he'd underestimated their grasp of Europe's bickering. 'You've clearly heard how the Scottish Queen quartered her coat of arms with those of England? Much has been made of France's ambitions, but…' He considered his words. 'But William remains the focus of our concerns. Bring him to me, and the company will protect him. The reason I called you together was to discuss our best means for resolving this matter peaceably. Before you leave, I would like to discuss your various responsibilities. I need to draw up a secondary list of who's doing what. Perhaps I could begin with Aalia?'

Later, when the shouting ended, and Kopernik drooped feverish in his chair while Andreas and Georgiou fled to the kitchen in hopes of being fed, Tom went in search of Aalia. He found her in the grass-paved courtyard which lay at the Old Temple's heart.

She was flat on her back, staring at the sky. 'Where's your faithful hound?' She spoke without moving.

He crouched on the grass beside her. 'The dog? Left in my sister's care. He's no natural beggar, started biting the hands of charity.'

'From where did you fathom a sister?' Aalia laughed.

He caught his tongue. The girl had an instinct for things untold.

Echoing from the narrow streets beyond the tall limestone walls came the layered sounds of London. Bells and boasts, beggars all. And Tom wished, more than ever, they were safely home in the sacred bluster that was India.

SANCTUARY – 7th Disclosure

Knowledge without experience is as a candle without light.

The following evening, ignoring Padruig's judgement, Aalia and her minstrels rattled out tunes from the legal quay, ringed in blazing torches and set on a makeshift stage just behind the ropehouse. They performed a formidable repartee, unaware that high above the common press and flanked by her most favoured companions, a copper-haired woman leaned from the uppermost gable of the Company of Merchant Taylors warehouse. Given the Lord Mayor's complicity, Elizabeth Tudor was bent on discovering why these foreign players formed the theme of every discourse heard at court that day.

They played without artifice, tight-wove madrigals woven in voices smooth as velvet. Under the restless flame of makeshift torches, it was hard to discern their features, but anyone would know Aalia by her buttercup hair. As the songs delved into themes of love and hope and death, each tapered chord extended their exquisite range, nurturing passion with the precision of a knife.

Listening from her eerie, the young Queen understood why Cecil would have such things banished. Drying her eyes, she slipped away discreetly. Her compact guard proved useful in parting the crowds who packed the length of the wharf. Having declined the use of heraldry, she was comforted it didn't rain.

Before the last minstrel fell silent, Andreas Steynbergh went back to attend on his patient. The decks of *Cornucopia* were empty except for the night-watch. Music tempered the night, as he stepped below deck to the rhythmic creak of rigging. He liked boats, liked the fall and rise of the tide, liked the boundaries of his life to be unsettled and impermanent.

Kopernik was stretched on his bunk and shivering, despite his many blankets. They'd shared the same tiny berth since coming on board, but it was Steynbergh's discoveries and specimens which spilled from every corner, and he was only thankful the Polish merchant remained tolerant of his passions.

His patient was fingering a torn scrap of paper but screwed it tight in his fist when Andreas appeared. Aside from his many duties, the task of paying the musicians, and consoling their differences, fell to Piatro's management.

'Don't you like what you hear?' Steynbergh took his patient's hand and patted it gently.

Kopernik pulled away sharply. 'The vision was Aalia's... if they deign to play together with some semblance of harmony it says more for her charms than my pocket. She has a talent for steering lost souls, but the fact England is enchanted by these Venetian canticles is down to sheer bloody-minded luck.'

'England is not, as you first suggested, such fallow ground for sentiment? No wonder my old friend Otar worries for his *little cuckoo*?'

'It is just beginning, Andreas! Master Padruig is right to be cautious. Certainly, I would prefer to keep my head firmly where it belongs, on my shoulders. Aalia is reckless... Damn... they've decided on an encore. Is there any news of the brother?'

Andreas tilted his head, marking the tune. 'Sometimes, I think she has no need of sleep! Tom has been extremely thorough. Padruig makes copious lists and hopes to keep London ignorant of William's intrigue. Aalia's made her presence known, so there's little we can do except wait... and hope the waiting bears fruit.'

'While we must bear the fear?'

Andreas kicked off his shoes and stretched onto his bunk. 'Sleep, my friend. Tomorrow you will feel stronger, and our problems fully surmountable.'

Sleep didn't come. Far into the night, the weathered timbers of the caravel throbbed to the beat of Aalia's rhythm-filled mutiny.

Next morning, Piatro Kopernik woke early to find both Andreas and his fever were gone. Having shunned his responsibilities long enough, he dressed with unusual care, robed in Eastern habits.

He went first the Customs House, but the person he had hoped to meet had not yet arrived. Sir Andrew Mortimer had earned a turgid reputation, despite having held his position for less than three months. Waiting at the makeshift entrance to his office, Piatro decided he would easily sway the man with a show of his company's wares.

Piatro had only recently learned the value of patience. Despite his illness, despite Aalia's misdemeanours, he'd made it his business to discover all he could about London. He knew, because he overheard pilot Solomon telling Aalia, a fire had razed the old Customs House to the ground. The pilot proposed it was arson, because locals were jealous how Hanse League merchants paid less duty than their English rivals. There was great hope amongst the higher guilds that this new queen would see fit to reform the scale of tithes and taxes in favour of her countrymen. But not too soon, Piatro thought, or his family's trade in Danzig would suffer.

A beggar shuffled past, and he thought of Tom, wondering why Padruig so dreaded the consequences if William managed to succeed. Agreed the brat had much to answer for, but he sensed Padruig's fear ran deeper than that of a diligent Master of a highly respected trading house. Surely St. Thomas could prove they didn't spur William's crazy ambitions? Whatever risk William posed for the company, it was obvious Aalia didn't recognize why Padruig was so afraid. For all her bright anomalies, she always braced the truth. The fact Piatro owed his very life to St. Thomas, to their generosity of spirit, had stirred in his heart a loyalty which had dissembled his former creed. Following a lifetime carved from misfortune, he set aside his more predatory enterprises to devote his talents to a company which respected resourcefulness. That they could also provide him with flawless specimens to trade meant his loyalty was fully assured. Or else Piatro Kopernik couldn't finance his trade in diamonds.

Such minuscule cargo was hardly a matter for open dialogue. He'd learned caution went hand in hand with discretion, but this bright, summer morning offered an excellent excuse to explore the opportunities of this fabled city. Had they been in Antwerp, or even Venice, his first meet with potential buyers might have been at the merchant's Bourse, but London lacked a formal exchange. Padruig suggested there was no better place to broker his wares than the guildhall of the Worshipful Company of Goldsmiths. Except he suspected he would be better received if the Master of Customs introduced him to the Master of Goldsmiths' Hall. Piatro knew his flawless gems wouldn't fail to attract buyers once he prised open those fabled doors in Foster Lane.

After less than half an hour waiting for the absent Master of Customs, Piatro decided he was bored and returned to brood on board *Cornucopia*. Aalia and Georgiou were just leaving for the Old Temple, and hearing of his dilemma, they offered to help him find the Goldsmiths' Hall. There was a time he might have suspected his integrity was in question, but St. Thomas had been forgiving of his indiscretions as long as he provided a profit.

St. Thomas preferred to run with the precision of a well-oiled clock, but it was their capacity for taking risks, for exploring new markets, which attracted men such as Andreas Steynbergh, a genius of no small notoriety. Piatro understood his role, and was glad of the opportunities offered, but had no illusion that the Company weren't mindful of his weaknesses. But then, Aalia was also a misfit who didn't fit the Company mould, and Georgiou was ever her servant, because he had worshipped her like a lapdog since the moment they first met.

Georgiou had made a coarse map marking the way to the Old Temple, but once they reached Cheapside, they soon discovered the ancient hall of the Goldsmiths' craft. It was set behind St. Paul's, well-placed for sacred commissions as well as London's thriving trade. Among its smiths, jewellers and gravers were craftsmen trusted at court, men who would undoubtedly crave Piatro's rare merchandise for their more lucrative commissions.

His knock was answered by an anxious porter, and Aalia and Georgiou left him there to pursue his favourite passion, the cut and bargain of trade.

During the morning, Aalia had been nursing what might have been a quiver, except its leather cap was neatly laced over a tight-bound roll of vellum. Georgiou teased her in Urdu, but Aalia enjoyed her secrets, and he couldn't spur her to explain. Leaving Kopernik at the Goldsmiths, they turned back into Cheapside, where the smell from a pie-shop oven was stoking midday business. Dozens of hand-carts and wooden-framed barrows blocked the street outside. Weaving in-between, Georgiou looked up and down the long street suddenly concerned they were lost.

'You're sure this is the direction?'

'We head west towards the Ludgate. I know it's probably easier by wherry, but Tom drew a map of our route, and I thought you'd appreciate the walk.'

After months contained at sea, it was indeed bliss to walk on solid land, even though surrounded by strangers in strange clothes. As the road began to narrow, they had to squeeze under the eaves of a great beamed gate-way, while a heavy ox-wagon crammed the whole width of the road. Despite the large escort of purposeful guards clearing people from its path, the team of beasts ambled forward very slowly, the metal-rimmed wheels sparking against the cobbles. In its wake, it left a sharp pungent smell, and a drunken tinker cursing the temper of his donkey.

Georgiou stepped back into the street deep in thought. Hadn't that very same tinker been waiting at the gate to the wharf? But Aalia pulled him onwards, describing their route in English, which still required every effort to translate.

After crossing a stone bridge which spanned a stinking, mud-dammed river, she turned left into a moss-lined vennel, whose entrance lay almost hidden between high, bare-stone walls. Georgiou could see the waters of the Thames glinting at the end of the passage, but before they reached the river, Aalia pulled aside a tangled curtain of ivy to reveal a low arched entrance, barred by a latticed gate. The steel bar wasn't locked, and the gate swung smoothly open onto a short flight of worn sand-stone steps. At the bottom was a black studded door embossed with St. Thomas's cross, its copper pricked with verdigris.

Aalia tugged on the bell-chain, and while they waited for an answer, Georgiou tried to map the building in his head, mindful of his obligations to the Company and worried he might be tested. It wouldn't be the first time. He was regretting he hadn't brought means to make a sketch, when the door opened wide, and they were admitted by Padruig's young novice. He made them wait without ceremony in a long, musty hall, whose starkness was augmented by a complete lack of furnishings.

Georgiou leaned against the wall, arms folded, holding the novice in his best sullen glare.

'It's like waiting for God.' Aalia removed her cloak, smiling from a halo of dandelion hair. 'It's Gull, isn't it?'

The novice blushed, pushing his tongue against his teeth. 'The Master has engaged someone to help...'

'And where is the Master?' Georgiou interrupted.

Gull steadily ignored him. 'And I have another friend, less qualified but extremely keen nevertheless. They'll both be arriving from the water-gate. We don't use this door very frequently, as you may have guessed.'

'Your talent for intrigue is irresponsible, to say the least, Aalia.' Padruig arrived, silent-footed, from the depths of a long dark hall.

'He sounds like God, too, don't you think?' Aalia laughed.

Gull bowed his head meekly, while Padruig stood glaring, but Aalia faced him triumphantly.

'At least my intrigues have born fruit. This morning, we received a royal warrant promising us freedom to trade.'

'A warrant any responsible trader might be granted without drawing notice from every jealous eye. If you continue in this vein, I will keep you under guard. I've accepted your minstrels, but I will not have this Company indulge in frippery.'

'Don't fret, Master Padruig, the officers of St. Thomas are deaf to music's charm, except perhaps Andreas? But if luck should steer my stars, I might show more profit than our merchant.' She spun on her heel, tossing the quiver to Gull. 'So? Where do we assemble?'

Leaving the Master behind, Gull took them through a labyrinth of white-washed halls and corridors until they arrived at a neatly laid kitchen garden. Aalia bent beside one of the rows of shrubby plants, and Gull knelt smoothly beside her, his manner suggesting this was a matter of some pride.

'Mostly we grow vegetables, but the herbs are used to make infusions for healing. With the monasteries closed and lay brothers scattered, there is little to help the sick, except worthless potions bartered in the streets.'

'No hyacinths for the soul?' Aalia broke off a tiny sprig and squeezed it between her fingers.

Bending to smell, Georgiou wrinkled his nose.

'That's lavender not hyacinth.' Gull corrected.

'A poor substitute but purple and sweet, unless you have oriental lineage.'

And the novice glowed in the warmth of her smile.

Tucked into the outer wall rimming the kitchen garden was an unadorned, brick building. Gull explained the annex could be accessed from a river-gate without passing through the Old Temple. It fitted well to their purpose, because one long wall consisted almost entirely of glass windows, flooding the room in sunlight. Otherwise, the room was simply furnished with a plain, oak table, a collection of three-legged stools, and a long, low settle stepped beneath the windows. The beams above their heads were hung with green-grey bunches of herbs, and the potent scent graced each and every movement.

Also furnishing the chamber was a compact gentleman who rose to his feet as soon as they entered. Clothed in dark formal robes frayed by age, his round, polished forehead was dissected by a pair of thick Venetian lenses. Removing his cap, he watched quietly while Gull untied the laces of Aalia's quiver and tipped out the sheath of papers rolled inside. He then helped lay them flat on the table, resting a paperweight at each corner. As the gentleman stood transfixed, Aalia gently took his right hand and brought his fingers to rest on the vellum. Sliding the spectacles onto his nose, moments passed into minutes while he examined the manuscript in silence.

'This is incredible, so precise. Such detail? I presume these charts are Spanish?' He spoke with a thickly broken accent, proving English was not his birth tongue.

'Yes, and highly accurate. Georgiou can vouch for every ripple and tide.' Aalia pointed. 'We must quarter the work in order to succeed, that is, if you have no objection for helping our endeavours? We hardly want to lose precision, but I promised to get them back to the navigator before dawn, otherwise he will be in trouble, and he's done a very great service in lending them to us.'

Padruig came into the room carrying a wicker basket. 'May I apologise for Aalia's eagerness,' he said. 'And begin by introducing Thomas Gemini? He comes from the Low Countries, and has better experience of making charts than any one of us.'

Placing his basket on the table, he took Gemini's hand and turned. 'Aalia might be impatient, but has every skill required to assist.'

'I daren't enquire how she came to *borrow* such precious maps.' Gemini nodded, gentle hazel eyes made grotesque by his lenses. 'But I sincerely hope we can do them justice. Gull tells me he has found another pair of qualified hands?'

'Yes. I believe he's just arrived. As soon as everything is ready, can you fetch your friend from the jetty, Gull?'

The Dutchman removed a set of finely engineered, brass instruments from a large, leather pocket tucked into the lining of his coat. Aalia fingered the incised maker's mark as he laid them on the table, and Gemini smiled benevolently.

'I make my own instruments. I'm partial to precision, and this is very precise work, particularly the mermaids. I suppose we must transcribe them, too?' His eyes twinkled.

'Ever the omnipotent mermaids! How better to lead a navigator astray?' She laughed, rolling her eyes playfully.

Gull took a selection of brushes, charcoal, pens, and glass-stoppered bottles of thick, black ink from Padruig's basket and set them on the table. Folio sheets of good linen paper were already laid out.

'The clarity of detail is excellent, but the text doesn't seem to make sense.' Georgiou stalked the periphery of the table, stabbing a finger at the letters.

'It's a cipher. I have the key, but we'll have to work on that later.' Aalia brought a stool to perch beside Gemini. Gold head and bare, they started work, pricking tiny needle holes through the chart.

Gull returned soon after steering a square-shouldered youth by the hand, because the neat, round face was spliced by a blindfold. Gull removed the mask, and the young man blinked into the light.

'This is Francis…' Gull began.

But Padruig interrupted. 'Solomon praised your ability with maps, and I'm sure you appreciate how we need to copy these charts quickly and in complete secrecy, but you might prefer, for your own wellbeing, to remain anonymous.'

The lad smiled benevolently. 'My name is Francis Drake, and I'm most obliged to be of assistance.'

'Welcome to the Old Temple.' Aalia narrowed her eyes. 'If you have any doubt, now is the time to declare it. No? Well, come and help us stir this mischief.'

Francis bent to look closer, then traced a line with his finger. 'But, surely, these are the Spice Islands?' He looked up, round face beaming. 'I've heard mariners talk of them, but never thought I'd see such detailed charts.'

Padruig glanced at Gemini, eyebrows raised. 'The Company of St. Thomas are not alone in wanting freedom to trade in these waters, but Spain and Portugal think to divide the world between them, thick as thieves and...'

'Far more devious,' finished Aalia.

Thereafter, silence was their master. As they toiled throughout the day and halfway into the night, a sense of the work's significance drew them close together. Given accurate charts, any sound ship could navigate these distant shores, and St. Thomas would willingly barter them to the highest bidder in England, while keeping good copy for themselves.

By the time Padruig rolled up the final finished quarter and put the originals back in the quiver, Drake was curled asleep on the floor, and Georgiou had escaped to the kitchen. But Aalia was wide awake and discussing the ancient laws of geometry with her new friend, Thomas Gemini.

SANCTUARY – 8th Disclosure

It is sometimes more expedient to question the truth rather than progress a lie.

Despite his reputation as St. Thomas's most ruthless trader, Piatro Kopernik couldn't meet the terms London's goldsmiths were demanding. When Otar suggested he could continue in his favoured trade, as long as it profited the Company, he'd embraced the opportunity. All he needed was one enlightened merchant, with barrow-loads of capital, and he could finance the Company's venture, omniscient or not. Otar had supplied him with an unrivalled store of exceptional gems, except he wasn't permitted to explain their origins. India was a storehouse which never failed to astonish. But although the purity and clarity of his diamonds appeared to tempt the worthy gold-masters of London, they consistently baulked at his price. And Piatro wasn't bargaining lower, not with these invaluable beauties.

There had been a time when Piatro's reputation was peerless in his chosen sphere, and surely Otar had enlisted him because he respected such resourcefulness. How the old man acquired such gems might remain a secret, but being contained by the Company's rules was proving both a blessing and a curse. Operating an erudite mind, with the quick-fingered leanings of a pick-pocket, had always tooled Piatro's dealings with impractical flaws. The gems he brought to London were never destined for plebeian fingers. But then, trade without danger was only worthy of his contempt.

Aalia had spent the voyage helping improve his grasp of English, while admitting to having learned the tongue from a Scottish nurse. At the time, he didn't realise it might be significant, but now, believed it one of many reasons why he'd failed to impress the goldsmiths. Then, on returning to the boat, he received an urgent message from Padruig warning he must stay on board until further notice, implying Aalia had acted out of hand again. Ironic really, when Piatro had run away to India in order to forget an impossible woman.

By late afternoon the following day, an almost tropical sun was toasting the decks, and crazed shadows danced through the rigging. Fanned by a turn of tide, a lazy breeze rustled the upper pennants, fingering their glazed colours, while high overhead, white shafts darted across the cerulean sky, as seagulls wheeled between the spars and masts, their screaming thievery a constant and unwelcome distraction.

Cornucopia's reputation for song had quickly made her popular along the length and breadth of the quay, and Aalia blithely demanded more and better practises, despite being grounded on the ship. Sparring to her challenge, half a dozen minstrels sat bandying out tunes from the boards of the lower deck, and their rhythms stirred rapt attention from the wharf. Soon after the first reel of arpeggios took tune, requests flew up from the wharf, and the entertainment began. Heroes requited in love, mortals missing and found, battles won and lost, ageless themes on any shore, in any tongue. As Aalia's musicians accepted each challenge, the fast-growing audience roared their approval.

Skulking on the upper deck, propped against bales of spare rigging, Georgiou did not approve. He watched the gathering audience in company with Piatro and Andreas, arms firmly folded.

'Grown men should not allow music to cloud their duties,' he growled.

Andreas patted his arm. 'You lack sleep, my friend. What time did you return? I heard the watch complaining.'

'Aalia wanted him to dance a jig.' Georgiou's face lit with the memory. 'And the noise brought Captain Marron running.'

'Your heathen heart lacks grace.' Andreas leaned his back to the rail. 'Do you prefer the temple monks with their monotone chants? Aalia knows how to bend each note to her bidding.'

Georgiou pointed to the neighbouring boat, a big Flemish galleon which overshadowed *Cornucopia*. She was set ready to sail on the next high tide, but every able man sat perched along her beams, straining for a better view of the musicians.

Piatro looked up, but he wasn't smiling. 'And make fools of weak-minded men! But at least take pleasure from her mastery; such minstrels cost the Company too dear to willingly ignore their talents.'

'Music destroys the soul as surely as poppy seed.' Georgiou refolded his arms and squared his back to the performers. But then, turned his head curiously when the applause turned suddenly to jeering.

Straining from the lower deck, Aalia was trying to take a folded paper from the hand of a crimson-coated warden reaching from the wharf. Piatro couldn't see the soldier's face, but while their soprano was diverted, the violins spun out the reel of a fast-paced jig.

'A layperson may find it alluring, but the harmony lacks structure, and together, they make a noise which I might kindly describe as vulgar.'

Clambouring from the lower deck, a stranger's head appeared. Drawing himself up to their level, ignoring the ring of surprise, his smile had the charm of a tiger.

'Quite frankly, I believe it's better called a cacophony,' he added with authority.

Georgiou drew his knife, but Piatro put up his hand. Stranger the man might be, but his bearing set him apart, that and the mouth-watering rubies embroidered over every inch of his powder grey doublet.

With tiger-smile fixed, the gentleman raised exquisitely gloved hands in mock surrender, nodding to Piatro as if to a friend.

'You're preaching to the converted.' Aalia had climbed up through the rigging to pitch just above their heads.

'Don't let me draw you from your acolytes. The day is young, and I'd prefer to hear the extent of your repertoire, if I'm to judge fairly.'

Aalia didn't move. 'Then I suggest you don't enquire of my friends. They've grown deaf to my talents.'

'My dear sir, I must apologise.' The gentleman pushed Georgiou firmly aside. 'But I'm curious about savages, and you appear to have a glut.'

Piatro swallowed hard, his full attention fixed on Aalia. Thankfully, Georgiou hadn't understood his meaning, but, being prudent by nature, Steynbergh stepped judiciously aside.

Aalia laughed. 'A glut of savages, what a ravishing thought? And clearly, we've ample means to satisfy such curiosity. But which of my savages might educate you best?'

She jumped down from the ropes, soft-footed as a panther, and whispered in Urdu. Georgiou's face lit with understanding, and he sprang before she could finish, knocking the stranger to his pristine knees and pressing his elegant nose hard against the deck. But despite his impressive sword, the Englishman didn't attempt to draw.

Fanned by the dearth of music, the audience lining the wharf began to mutter.

'Georgiou knows best how to tutor with practical example.' Aalia clicked her tongue and smiled. Then, she raised her voice enough that those listening from the wharf could hear.

'The savage using you as a cushion comes of an ancient line, Byzantine and proud. Whereas Kopernik here rarely shows any hint of primitive passions unless meted a tangible profit, or why else would any sane man engage intellect over instinct?'

Piatro, capable son of a long and distinguished line of Polish scholars, raised his cap and bowed, ignoring the horrified shame glowing in Andreas' face.

'Or perhaps we could count our good doctor a savage?' Aalia continued. 'Andreas Steynbergh's name is celebrated in every institute which doesn't censor rational thought. Don't be deceived. The list is very limited.'

Aalia's cheeks were glowing. She touched Georgiou's shoulder, and he released the gentleman, even helping him to his feet, although not kindly.

A deep rumble emanated from the man as he shook the dust from his clothes.

'My apologies, boy,' he roared. 'Dressed as you are, I mistook you for a savage. I am Her Majesty Queen Elizabeth's Acting Master of Revels.' He waved an elaborate arm. 'If you would kindly fetch Mistress Aalia, we need say no more.'

'But this is...?' Andreas tried to explain.

Aalia laughed, gold hair shimmering. 'The gentleman knows very well who we are, and quite assuredly found his entertainment by goading us.'

Scrutinising every word and action from their better advantage, the crew of the Flemish ship broke into cheers and were joined readily by the audience on shore.

Waiting for silence, the stranger put his hands together and clapped, very, very slowly. 'Spirited and courageous, the Queen weighed you well, Aalia.' His hooded eyes studied her, unsmiling.

'Is an envoy without manners called "Anonymous"?' Aalia spoke quietly.

'Lord Scythan.'

He paused for their response. And Andreas bent his bare head respectfully. But Aalia paid no homage, and Georgiou and Piatro followed her lead.

'Her Majesty wanted me to judge if you could actually sing.'

'You use a curious means of discovery.' Aalia's eyes held a fire which made Piatro, despite himself, step backwards.

'I see I've been remiss. Enigmatic describes you better. I can see why my mistress was charmed. I've rarely met a savage with such raw spirit.' He ran the tip of a gloved finger down her flushed cheek and whispered into her ear, 'One day, I will tame you.'

Aalia stayed extremely still, hands pressed hard to her back. Georgiou's knife was just within reach. Before she could decide, Piatro met her gaze and shook his head.

'So, we are found wanting?' She studied the stranger, as if they were alone. 'Are you a connoisseur of music Lord Scythan?'

'Of all the higher arts, I count myself an authority. Music is mere adornment, a humble abstraction.' He removed his cap and bowed mockingly.

'While I lack the intellect to argue aesthetics, I can offer a brace of songsters who are honed in lesser abstractions. Art is hardly our purpose, but I think we know how to sing.'

She grabbed his cap and pitched it over her head, then turning to face the audience, she bowed. 'Reassemble our musicians... we'll play until the sky is black, and let you judge our talents!'

The audience went wild, and their cheering echoed around the irregular arena and up into the unwary town. The tide was high, and rising.

SANCTUARY – 9th Disclosure

For every form of trouble there is a reason, if not a cure.

Since the day posed nothing better to entertain his boredom, Piatro settled near the Customs House, or, more specifically, the low-hung door which led into the office of the Queen's Master of Customs. The fat-lipped ingratiate, titled Sir Andrew Mortimer, had willingly accepted Piatro's precious gifts, but returning on his promises was yet another matter. Bribery was a practise of which the Polish merchant approved; it oiled the dusty wheels of commerce, but he'd expected the man to honour his word, and waiting outside his door, propped against the shuttered wall, Piatro was soon besotted by the constant flow of visitors.

Being Tuesday, and therefore a trading day, the length of the quay was heaving. Mariners, merchants, lightermen, and carters, any soul driven by commerce, were busy unloading and distributing cargo as swiftly as London's fiscal duties would allow. Spewing along the wharf were spent crates, crushed wicker baskets, and splintered ribs of tarred, broken barrels leaking their dregs into the foetid mud which rimmed the river below. Piatro idly totalled the legal levy on an overflowing hand-barrow, as it passed the customs gate unmarked. The carter merged smoothly with the crush of wares which funnelled into Fish Lane and headed towards the city. Creaking above Piatro's head, the huge wooden crane swung its arm out towards its next bounty, the wheel-house rotating to the chants of the men inside.

His English improving by the minute, he liaised with anyone he could engage in conversation, cheerfully debating on quality and quantity relative to investment. The Flanders master of *The Mary George* decreed his best trade came from looking-glasses, something the Master of St. Thomas might find of benefit, Piatro mused spitefully. Clearly, few profits lay wasted in London's thriving port, and he enjoyed practising his grasp of the language while keeping watch on Sir Andrew's lair.

The makeshift wooden shack containing the crown registry was port of call for all manner of gentlemen, seamen, and merchants. Not far short of noon, a distinctive swirl disturbed the legal gate, as a party of men on horseback cut through the press. The corps of militia was kitted in impeccable cobalt-blue livery, each breast baring a bright, crested badge, showing their patron came of highest rank. And when Sir Andrew came in person to greet his distinguished visitor, Piatro watched and smiled. The Queen's Master of Customs was clearly discomforted by this big-boned man in sombre dress.

'You waiting on Sir Andrew?'

Piatro had been so intent on watching, he didn't hear the lad approach. Fair-skinned and clean-faced as a virgin, he looked somehow familiar, but then, Piatro had spoken to so many this morning, he couldn't decide just why.

'Name's Joe.' He smiled a broad, comradely grin. 'Only, he'll be tied down with Lord Bedford for the rest of the day.'

Piatro measured Joe carefully. His soft leather jerkin was left untied, white linen shirt bleached and frayed. The way he held his head and shoulders made Piatro suspect he might be a mariner, but something in the cold, haunted eyes left him wary. However, the day was young, and he needed fresh company. And perhaps he'd remember where and when they'd last met.

Less than a league upriver, Tom Hampden squatted near the Dowgate. Being close to the German Steelyard, it wasn't best picked for begging; their Protestant souls barely approved of strays, but that was exactly the reason he had chosen to wait there today.

Dirt carts rattled past, rumbling down the cobbled ramp, emptying their sludge into flat-keeled barges. The stink was enough to make most passers-by cover their faces.

'Aalia seems to think your disguise quite unnecessary now she's arrived?' The Master bent over him, sleek as a lawyer in neck-to-floor black robes.

Tom raised his begging bowl and scowled at the face beneath the wide-brimmed straw hat.

'She has too much faith in her brother. Besides, her bravado is just a mask.'

'I fear, God help us, this will soon be swept out of our hands.'

'Alvaro has William believing having royal blood is enough to make him a king, although I doubt it took much pleading. You've visited the Mermaid Inn?'

'I had to see for myself. He has a growing bevy of supporters all too keen to bandy his rights. They might whisper his claim, but never dare to proclaim him king. Treason bites hard. But if the Queen were dead... that would be another matter. William doesn't know me, and there was no opportunity to draw him aside or speak privately. The Jesuit watches like a hawk.'

'There's no point discussing the legalities. Whether Aalia likes it or not, William's made up his mind he'll one day be crowned King of England.'

'Yes, Tom, he's gone far beyond our counsel. We must bait our trap and get the boy out of Alvaro's clutches. I just have to trust Aalia plays her part. Once I've decided on the final details, I'll send Gull to fetch you. Just be ready.'

It was late that same afternoon when Piatro arrived, perhaps by chance, at the door of the infamous Mermaid Inn. Steered by way of various alehouses, his new companion Joe attracted a platoon of likeminded friends, who spurred the merchant to test his mastery of the English tongue, while tempting him with ale, cards and dice. Piatro had never overcome his passion for playing against the odds.

In company with his new-met acquaintances, he arrived on the south bank of the river, noted refuge of many and wiser outcasts. The streets surrounding the stews were tangled in perfidy, and Piatro soon discovered how much the English liked their games. Even at this early hour, the Bear Gardens bayed with savagery, as men screamed encouragement to the snarling dogs, yelled torments at the underfed bears, and brawled with drunken enthusiasm, money changing hands in the shadows.

It seemed the perfect day to break Company rules. Perusing the circle of itinerant stalls, Piatro weighed his purse. A tinker caught his eye, ploughing through the market with an over-laden donkey. Hungrily, he purchased a cone of marzipan cherries, but after one bite, tossed them away. Next, he examined the delicate figurines of a wood-carver, learning with some surprise that the craftsman came from Bruges. But Piatro's satisfaction came through bargaining, and these were worth double their price. Turning a tiny carved angel in his hand, Piatro wished he could suggest a better market, but before he could continue, his new friends grabbed his hand and pulled him sturdily away, giving promise there was better amusement at an inn called the Mermaid. Leaving behind the market, they'd almost come back to the riverbank when he heard the first pitch of music. Something in the tune stirred a memory, but he didn't turn immediately, not until he realised the second chorus was in Sanskrit.

In retrospect, he should have recognised the quality of the trap far sooner, but once he entered the courtyard of the Mermaid Inn, it was much too dangerous to retreat. Joe and his friends made sure of that. William always had a gift for extending his sister's range. Place him in any arena, and he'd never fail to attract. Though his powerful frame and commanding voice did much to compel attention, Piatro always supposed it was the thatch of copper-gold hair which honed William's fame in India. Where Aalia enchanted, William compelled. The open courtyard was bursting at the seams. In fact, if you counted those peering from the double-tiered gallery, there had to be upwards of five hundred men leering and cheering his presence. The suggestion their runaway was hiding seemed suddenly cast in doubt.

Piatro was trapped. Taking rough hold of his arms, Joe and his companions proved this trap was hardly a random idea. Someone knew his weaknesses, and Joe offered the perfect remedy for six long months at sea. He recalled Aalia had been discussing mermaids with Georgiou earlier, but couldn't recall the reason. Coincidence or not, she was the one supposedly charged with tempting her whelp of a brother.

The men surrounding him made it plain he wouldn't be permitted to leave. They dragged him down to where huge, black-slimed timbers formed the inn's river foundations and made him wait, ankle-deep in pungent grey mud, until the entertainment ended.

Nightfall was cloaking the river when William finally appeared, leaning first from the ledge of the pier.

'May I introduce Master Kopernik, the merchant who makes St. Thomas's storerooms grow richer? What trade will you rupture in London, Piatro? Has Aalia lent you her pearls? Or?... No? She would never donate her private fortune.' His supple voice rang with irony. 'But I see I've been indiscreet?'

Joe laughed, pushing Piatro until he almost lost his balance. But the merchant wasn't afraid. During his long and uncomfortable wait, he'd had plenty of time to consider William's motive for bringing him here. The lad had little purpose in seeing him dead, which suggested he required some information. And information was Piatro's stock in trade.

William waved a blazing torch above his head as he waited on an answer. The sense of drama was almost as unpalatable as the marzipans.

'She left her pearls in India, Will. They were never hers to keep. And then, we fell foul of Otar's rules. When we sailed for England, we barely had means to finance any but the meanest endeavour.'

William jumped from the pier and grabbed Piatro by the shoulders, squeezing tight, until it hurt. 'Keep your confessions, my friend. I'm not interested in excuses. I just need a reliable messenger, someone Aalia considers trustworthy.'

'I'm not sure I'm ready for the sacrifice, given your recent behaviour.'

William smiled. 'Just what lies has the little witch been telling?'

Piatro tried to move, wishing his stone-cold feet would respond. 'You'll be pleased to learn Tom has recovered, and it was he, not your sister, who described his assault.'

'Sister? Aalia is no more my sister than you are, Mester Kopernik. The grand and blameless Company of St. Thomas has beguiled us both with their tales.'

'Then, go to Aalia and discuss it. I will not play the go-between.' Piatro's knees were shaking.

'There's nothing I'd like better, but getting close enough to speak has so far proved impossible. St. Thomas couldn't have guarded her better had she been confined in a cell. All I'm asking is you bring her to meet me, alone.'

'Given your recent exploits, that would be a never... But I will tell her I met you, and where.'

'I've made many new friends, Piatro. Men who can prove everything… who can show that St. Thomas breeds only lies. Aalia needs to know the truth.'

More men clamboured to join them, and Piatro half-hoped it might lead to his release, but the group of men guarding him drew tighter.

'As far as I see it, Aalia is alone in believing in you… Barely a day passes when she doesn't defend your honour, yet I wonder how she will stay faithful to a man who holds her in such contempt?' Piatro caught his tongue, having already said too much.

'Why deny my future? Didn't Aalia once flaunt everything we held sacred, thus far nobody abandoned her.' He raised his arm as though to strike, amber eyes glowing in the flare of balled flame. 'I'm not begging answers, Piatro, but just this once, examine things from my perspective.'

'You think I haven't considered your claim? William, nobody of sound mind can ever pronounce you King. No matter what weight of evidence your new friends produce, you'll remain a nameless bastard, and Henry Tudor wanted not for bastards; it was true-born heirs he lacked.'

Piatro's eyes never left William's. He took a deep breath and continued, scouring his voice of all emotion. 'These men tease you. Their only thought is to subvert this land, to lead it into rebellion. You are no more a king than God is an Englishman.'

It was more than he had meant to say, more than he should have dared, and he waited to feel the force of William's hand.

But, instead, he started laughing, and gradually, Joe and the ring of faces watching began to follow his lead. Piatro felt himself isolated, the only sane man in a crowd of fools.

'Do you think I'm so gullible I came halfway 'round the world on such a whim? The Company was paid to hide me; of that fact, I have clear evidence seen by every man here.'

The sea of heads bobbed, high into the shadows, and William's baritone voice grew in volume and power. 'St. Thomas was hired to raise me as far from England as possible, of that I have irrefutable evidence. And every man here understands the single most significant truth… that Henry's third queen, Jane Seymour, gave birth to twin boys.'

William's sonorous voice rounded on that revelation, while all the men about him shouted agreement, burning with loyal admiration. Piatro felt he was going to be sick. This had gone further than anyone feared.

But William hadn't finished. 'The Company claims I betrayed their trust, but they are the ones who betray. In these last few months, I have learned many truths, and not merely of my birthright. I can tell Aalia her mother's name, something Otar never shared.'

'Don't say it's the Queen of Sheba, or she'll never sing again!' His mind racing, he stupidly put reason aside. 'If you examine her motives, you might realise she acts out of love.'

'Acts being the potent word, Piatro. Aalia can act any part, but nothing touches her heart, or her soul. Examine her motives? I've done that a thousand times, and I know her far better than you.'

Piatro leaned forward until he could almost touch William's face. Then, he whispered, 'Perhaps I understand you better than anyone, William. I know what it is to have dreams and see them destroyed. There was even a time I might have joined you, but then I advanced… into manhood!'

'You, as ever, are her lap-dog, Kopernik.'

William held the torch closer, and Piatro felt the heat on his cheek. Finding more courage than he hoped, the merchant threw back his head and laughed. 'You want me to bring you Aalia, but are you prepared to see her die, too?'

He felt searing pain, as William twisted his arm. Good, it proved he still had morals.

'If I were truly lost, this sister would never defend me. Tell her how you have seen me… but do not dare to judge.'

And William left, swinging the torch, never looking back. All the men trailed after their idol, ignoring the foreign merchant standing clotted in mud. Piatro waded up the bank, debating whether to trudge the long mile back to the bridge or seek out a landing for a ferry. At least he still had his purse.

SANCTUARY – 10th Disclosure

No officer of St. Thomas shall suffer duress or coercion within the company providing he always acts in accordance to our principles.

For the purposes of navigating a mud-banked river, there was no better craft than a Peter-boat. Dick Solomon had taught his apprentice well. Marsh-ringed waters require a mongrel boat, one which could be driven by sail or oar, helmed by man or boy. And Francis had steered *Lydia* into many rivers and inlets without jetties where business only takes place by night. But proving *Lydia*'s worth wasn't foremost in Francis' mind, as he waited at the foot of the legal quay late on that warm summer's day.

The girl, the one who dressed like a boy, had hailed him from *Cornucopia*'s deck just as he left the old pilot at the Customs House arguing black was white.

He steadied *Lydia* as Aalia leapt from the jetty, but having the balance of a cat, she didn't need his hand. Her companion, the black-eyed, oriental one who rarely spoke, jumped into the boat behind her, then nodded to show there would be no other passengers.

It was a fine afternoon for an adventure, seamless skies hazed with the barest drift of tail clouds. The sort of weather Master Solomon favoured when he went to sup with the canny merchants of Calais. Sadly, that little enterprise had been scuppered by the 'damned Frenchies.' The old pilot used similar expletives today, when his apprentice asked if he could take leave that afternoon. The girl had asked if he could take her to the Mermaid Inn, and he had warned her Bankside wasn't the sort of place for a woman, but she wouldn't be deterred.

Lydia quickly caught the current, but he kept her steady, holding his course, always watching Aalia. Her silken hair sifted in the wind, and she smelled like wild honeysuckle. Suddenly, she turned, and he looked up to the masthead, hoping she didn't see his blush.

'You don't look like you come from Goa, miss?' A full night and day he'd wrestled with that question, and now, it burst from his traitor lips.

'Why Goa?' She smiled, and he felt his face glow brighter.

'Pilot Solomon says that's where *Cornucopia* sailed from.'

Having nothing to conceal, he held her ice-blue gaze.

'We have an honest child?' She laughed. 'India was where I once lived, but I've led a nomad's life, and nowhere is really home.' She turned to watch the shore.

'But you're with the Company of St. Thomas?' he continued.

'As a woman, I'm forbidden to have an official capacity... perhaps you should apply to their ranks, Master Drake. You show every talent they admire.'

Still, it didn't occur to desist.

'But nobody seems to know much about St. Thomas.' He'd enquired from all his friends, without learning anything, and Gull wouldn't be drawn, merely saying he should heed Master Solomon.

'And this "nobody" thinks they're a fallacy? Believe me, learn discretion if you want to survive.' She laughed, but gently. 'Once they had great influence, trading throughout Europe, but troubles with religion have seen them fade from grace. Nowadays, they prefer to trade in ideas, which is why we are highly grateful for your skills when copying the Spanish charts. There's a very lucrative market for maps, especially when the waters are uncharted! The Company of St. Thomas likes to steer with the tide, much like you, Francis Drake.'

'Some say you've come to enter the bard's contest at St. Bart's Fair?'

He'd also heard whispers she'd been there the night St. Katherine's church tower fell to the ground, and their new Queen had almost died, but held his tongue of that knowledge.

Aalia shook her head. 'Music is the sticky web which binds our deeds together. Do you play?'

He took the bait this time. 'My father would have every church in England keeping a band to beat out the devil, but I've no talent for music, although Mother gave me a drum.'

'Beat your drum loudly, Master Drake. If nothing else, it will hold your demons at bay.'

Her insight unnerved him.

Lydia reached the apex of her tack. While Francis tightened the sail, Aalia pulled up the slack. Georgiou had to duck under the boom, and she laughed, speaking in a strange, garbled tongue. Before Francis could take offence, she explained, sea-blue eyes sincere.

'In Georgiou's land, the holy men beat drums when they want to call down heavenly spirits. I've seen a yogi use a human skull for a drum... you can't get holier than that. Why did you agree to help us?'

Francis flushed. 'I didn't want to send you with a stranger.'

'How noble of you. And I'd wager you're no older than sixteen.'

'I'm eighteen!' he snapped. 'Anyway, how does it matter... I bet you're no older than me, and I've five years experience in these waters, mistress. I know the Thames as well as anyone, just don't want to spend my life here. Not like Master Solomon.' His untold dream disclosed.

'Don't look so worried, Francis. I value nothing better than sincerity. I'd trust you... even with my life.'

They pulled up to the opposite shore beside a broken jetty. Ranged along the riverbank, a line of women was gutting fish, skirts hitched high above their ankles, as they paddled in sticky mud. The sickly smell attracted flocks of squealing gulls. No other boats were moored at the jetty, not even a wherry waiting a fare.

Francis jumped from *Lydia* while the women bandied raw greetings. Aalia waved to them, laughing, but Francis blushed, trying to ignore their lewd bleatings, as he tied the painter and stowed the oars. Then, he led them from the river.

The old road skimmed the shore almost as far as the bridge. He'd ferried them south of Paris Gardens, trying to avoid the stews. Few houses lined the road, and fields lay behind, the low hill marked by a windmill. He'd been warned against the Mermaid, one of many places Master Solomon told him never to go, but it proved easy to find because its foundations rose out of the riverbank.

Pushing the door open, he expected to hear cat-calls of drunken ribaldry, but there was only silence, clothed in the malt smell of ale. But then, it was not yet noon.

'You must wait with the boat, Master Drake.' Aalia waved him away.

'But…'

'We'll not be long, I promise.'

Inside timber-clad walls, the Mermaid Inn was furnished in intimacy. Built out of the leavings of a shipwright's yard, it took the form of an upturned boat. Lining its ribbed walls were dark, panelled booths dissected by black oak struts, which kept the bowed ceiling from falling. Few lamps disturbed the shadows, and crudely formed hatches covered the windows. Aalia pulled up her hood as she pushed through the door, hoping to pass the keeper's tiny hatch unobserved.

'If you're wanting a boat, you needs to see Gunner Jack, and he won't be returning today.'

A great ox of a man thrust his shoulders through the hole, coughed, spat, and mopped his brow on a filthy leather rag.

'We'll take a table, and wait.' Aalia's voice muffled from her hood.

Drake appeared from behind and handed the inn-keeper two silver coins. 'We're not seeking work, Mister,' he said firmly.

'Long as you pays your way, I ain't looking.'

The inn-keeper winked at Aalia and handed out a jug of ale and three horn beakers. Drake steered them to a booth near the chimney, where a small child was sleeping in the inglenook, bare feet sloughed in ashes. Only one other booth was occupied, on the opposite side of the room.

Dropping onto a three-legged stool, Aalia ran her eyes over the room, searching for the person she was hoping to meet. The two men in the far stall started arguing loudly, in Spanish.

'*No tengo nada mas darte.*'

'He doesn't have more to give,' Aalia whispered the translation to Drake.

A bench rattled across the floor, and a black-haired man flew out of the booth.

Drake readied his knife, as the other man jumped from his seat and wrestled his associate to the floor. Their bodies twisted and rolled until they met the leg of Aalia's stool. Gazing down calmly, she lifted the jug of ale and doused them with its contents.

The black-haired gentlemen rolled onto his back, screaming abuse in Spanish. Then, he pulled out a knife, but before he could move, Aalia stamped her foot hard on his collar so he choked.

'*Esperaba refrescar a su sir del ardour.*' She said softly. 'Or, "that should cool your ardour," speaking for our English friend.'

Georgiou dragged Drake aside, rushing to protect Aalia from the Spaniard. Except his valour proved unnecessary, because the other man, blond hair sodden, wasn't looking for a fight. Splayed in a mess of ale and rushes, he sat blotting his nose on a small, white linen sheet. He had the trappings of elegance, his doublet being of unquestionable quality, yet his hooded eyes seemed familiar. Aalia couldn't imagine why.

The Spaniard, face powder pale, began to wave his fists wildly, but Aalia shook her head, pressing down on his throat. When he finally dropped the knife, her smile widened.

Jumping to his feet, his opponent was uncaring. 'We're restrained from our folly by Athena. Only England can supply such charming remedy. My apologies, mistress, nothing ever justifies ill manners.' His words were smothered under the handkerchief.

'Thus, wise men take the veil?' Aalia's hood slipped, loosing the wanton hair. 'As I neglected to bring my flute, a tune is out of the question. Can I presume this is Hephaestus?'

Carefully, she raised her foot. The Spaniard jumped up, spitting with malevolence, embossed leather doublet dripping ale, and black eyes dripping hatred. He glared from Aalia to Georgiou, primed like a cornered cat. But his opponent folded gracefully and knelt at Aalia's feet.

'Sebastian Trentham, your servant perpetual.'

As he spoke, he tried to grab Aalia's hand, except she stepped out of reach. With his veil removed, she remembered where she'd last seen that face, goading a tinker's donkey near the Customs House. And Georgiou recognised him too and eased closer.

'Aren't you the property of this gentleman?' Aalia pointed to the Spaniard. 'Surely it would break your bond if we shared… You already have enough troubles.'

Sebastian's lean face broadened to a smile. 'Alvaro, a goddess speaks. Clarify my title and inform her I'm not your slave?' He waited a long time, shuffling on his knees. 'My apologies, Alvaro has lost his tongue, along with his manners.'

'Perhaps he doesn't speak English?' Aalia said smoothly.

Alvaro was occupied in brushing debris from his clothes and didn't turn his head. 'Gods or mortals, we are all slaves,' he said at last, peeling strands of hair from his cheek.

'Then how can we trust the slaves will know their duties?'

Aalia waited. Here was the man she hunted, the Jesuit who had stolen her brother. He knew exactly who she was and what she wanted.

Alvaro tapped the hilt of his sword, loathing in his eyes.

Georgiou stepped forward, but before any weapon could be drawn, Sebastian slipped between them and slapped the Spaniard on the back.

'It is I who must beg forgiveness.' He smiled, and when Alvaro still refused to back down, added softly, 'Are you angry because they speak Spanish?'

Aalia matched his smile. 'Personally, I find the Latin tongues far too sentimental, but you've gained a friend in Georgiou. His English being weak, he's had poor sport eaves-dropping of late. Lying or kneeling, I sympathise with Alvaro; the English are far too tall.' Aalia gathered her hood to calm her hair.

Sebastian tipped back his head and exploded in laughter. 'Women of wit are rare as hen's teeth either side of the Thames. May I offer my hand in marriage? Uncle would be entertained. I don't suppose you own a title? He thinks on it as an inducement and may even waive the dowry.'

Unwarned by Aalia's frown, he proceeded to dictate a list of *prime virtues anticipated in a wife* until the object of his affections took a beaker of ale, climbed onto her stool, and tipped the contents over his head.

The dousing didn't deter him. 'Seriously…I haven't proposed to a woman in weeks.' Licking at rivulets as they poured down his face, Sebastian attempted to grab the pot. Aalia fell, but he smoothly caught her, still laughing.

Georgiou was glowering, waiting on Aalia's command.

'No wonder you can't find a woman who meets with your uncle's approval. Unfortunately, the only title I own is "mistress," pronounced with a capital M.' She threw down the empty beaker.

'I'm sure Uncle would burn the list on receipt of a small fee,' he said, mopping his face with his sleeve.

They were negotiating still when a troop of local militia piled through the open door, sending the whole room into shadow. Drake, who hadn't indulged a moment looking elsewhere, saw Aalia's manner change as soon as their captain crossed the threshold and stepped up to the hatch. Dressed like the others in a coarse doeskin coat, his powerful bearing set him apart, that and his copper-flame hair.

Noting Aalia's presence, he marched immediately forward, fixing her with his bold, amber eyes. Aalia froze. Drake had never seen anyone stand so still. The lanterns flared, and the room held its breath. The young man stopped a yard from his quarry. No one spoke, no one moved, not even when the young man pulled a fine gold knife from his belt and tossed it spitefully at Aalia.

The whirlwind of reaction sent the whole room spinning. Sebastian tried to jump on the man who threw the knife, but Alvaro held him back. While they wrestled, they blocked Drake's path, but Georgiou had already launched from the table. Using the power of his fall to bring Aalia's opponent to the ground, he locked him in a spiteful hold, face half-buried in the rushes.

Still, Aalia didn't move. 'You're late, William.' She struggled to find her voice. 'By Padruig's reckoning, probably six months too late.'

She loosened the knife from the folds of her cloak and tossed it clattering to the floor.

'Really, sister? And that's why he sent you? To exact my surrender?' His voice had power, even when used at a whisper.

'Infinitely better than the alternatives… I promise. And Tom sends his love. He brought you a gift from your mother, but apparently, you've been ignoring him of late. In fact, your new friends tried to murder him.' And she almost succeeded in hiding her emotion.

Aalia realised a need to breathe. The men who had arrived with William stood huddled in front of the door, unsure of their best reaction while their leader lay trapped on the floor. And Georgiou wouldn't let go, not unless she ordered him.

'To cheat or be cheated, sister? Just like Tom, you choose to play their hand.'

No other person in the room had substance.

Aalia released her breath and took another. 'The choice was never mine, or we would be playing our future elsewhere, finding a far better destiny. But then, clearly, siblings are two a penny this season.'

Knowing him better than anyone, she was already braced when he fought Georgiou's hold. But her guardian possessed the greater skill. They wrestled barely a minute, before he slid a stiletto from his boot and pricked hard at her brother's throat. A trickle of crimson blood nestled into his collar and bloomed.

Death required a mere nod.

Drake looked from Aalia to her brother, willing the blade to drop. But Aalia shook her head firmly.

William's men shuffled forward, muttering their alarm, and the movement finally woke the child from the ashes, and he ran through their legs wailing.

Pooled dust spun in shafts.

'Georgiou agrees with the Company. He'd really prefer you were dead.' Aalia picked up the knife she'd discarded, testing its weight and balance. 'But perhaps we were bred to chase rainbows?'

The room held still, spellbound by their hatred, except Sebastian was slowly easing towards the door.

Alvaro scowled. 'Call truce, madam.'

'I did not bite first.'

'Surrender to the sprat William. What harm can she do you?'

Behind Alvaro, one of William's men, grey-haired and level-eyed, took a step forward, two hands gripping the haft of his sword.

'Let me introduce my sister.' William moved to raise his arm, but couldn't break Georgiou's hold. 'And warn you how… this witch… murders without remorse.'

'Thank you, William. That should curb any further marriage proposals. I thought murder was a family trait? Except Padruig recently informed me we have no blood in common. Perhaps I should rejoice?'

Again, Georgiou held, jabbing the tip of the spike deeper into the pulsing apple of William's exposed throat. They both knew he wouldn't hesitate to kill.

'I can prove every lie with the truth, but wasn't expecting you to call so soon. Go ask the Master of St. Thomas, for he knows the entire tale, and that is why he'd never sanction our reunion.'

Her pale skin flushed. 'I'm sure he'd be touched by your concern. Sanction isn't a word he uses as often as foolish.' She stroked the blade in her hand. 'I'm of the opinion this doesn't belong to you?'

'You always kept the best toys for yourself. Call off your leech, or Alvaro will have to draw, and the aftermath will be messy.'

But the arena of cautious watchmen had over-reached its tolerance. Those at the door surged forward, while Alvaro, having better advantage, lunged forward to grab Aalia by the throat. But Drake was ready and dived towards the Spaniard unarmed, only realising his stupidity when Aalia kicked him backwards, out of reach from Alvaro's sword. In that same moment, Aalia threw her knife, and the Spaniard screamed, holding his hands to his thigh.

Pinning William's leather collar to the floor with the stiletto, Georgiou jettisoned his hold and jumped to protect Aalia. Tearing at his collar, William could do nothing to stop the oriental catching his sister by the arm and dragging Drake towards the door. As they passed the chimney breast, Georgiou picked up the grate and threw it at the gang of men blocking their path. Drake flailed his fists in earnest, but the soldiers didn't have space to move. In the subsequent blind tussle, they daren't strike out hard for fear of injuring their comrades.

Once Georgiou had pulled Aalia and Drake through the door and into the street, the pursuit of their attackers was thwarted by Sebastian Trentham. He slammed the door shut, pegged the lock, and kicked a pile of spent barrels he'd laid ready. Georgiou helped, wedging them tight, while Drake kept watch on the windows.

The shouting attracted few observers, and they ran back to the broken jetty and jumped into *Lydia* without looking back. There was no sign anyone chased after them. Perhaps William was shy of bringing notice, for his time had yet to come.

SANCTUARY – 11th Disclosure

Dispel lies, but always act responsibly.

Piatro was leaning against the rail of *Cornucopia*'s upper deck. For the first time since their arrival, he had a broadly unhindered view of the whole length of the quay as their outsized neighbour from Flanders had set sail on the morning's high tide. Fleetingly, Piatro wished he'd gone with them. It had been a mistake, telling Aalia he'd met her brother, before going to Padruig with this news. He'd spent the day fretting, playing craps with their captain using his prized ivory dice. Now, it seemed he'd underestimated the seaman, whose run of good luck left the merchant significantly poorer.

The wharf was exceptionally busy. Preparations were in hand for a formal muster of troops to demonstrate the extent of England's militia. It seemed the Queen thought to impress her foreign ambassadors with a show of strength, but gossip on the streets held that arms were seriously lacking. Those locals Piatro had questioned blamed that lapse on Spain, because throughout Queen Mary's reign, her Spanish husband had gathered more control over the nation's civil defence than was ever sensible.

A flotilla of flat-keeled boats, carrying supplies of men and arms from far-flung ports of England, had anchored in the mud beneath the castle, and a line of wagons and carts stood ready at the gates to ferry the new arrivals to their lodgings. Piatro decided the men progressing along the wharf would be better making harvest than showing prowess in the field; most of them carried wooden stakes, but few had pikes or carried anything near fear-provoking.

Weaving through the bustle, Piatro suddenly noticed Aalia's bright head, accompanied by Georgiou and a tall, young man, with a bush of straw-blonde hair. Aalia stopped and seemed to argue as both men listened intently, bending close to hear. Clearly, she'd survived the encounter with her brother, but Piatro wouldn't make the same mistake again.

'Genuflect, the glory of our days is back,' Piatro announced.

Captain Marron looked up. '*La belle dame sans mercy*. Where did you say she was going?'

'I didn't say because I didn't know,' he lied.

'Only a messenger came... from someone called Bedford.' The big man squatted awkwardly on his knees, intent on making his next throw.

'When did this messenger call?' Piatro's interest roused.

'Around noon. I asked around and discovered Bedford is one of the Queen's privy ministers. He came to see the Master of Customs earlier, and, for some reason, asked to speak to Aalia. But the girl wasn't here.'

Piatro recalled the elegant, blue livery, and Sir Andrew's worried face. 'Such a popular child. When do we get to play?'

'It isn't your throw!' Marron threw seven and smiled. 'Why does she take Georgiou when he can barely speak the language?'

'Because he doesn't speak the language! Andreas and I do not qualify on account of our cosmopolitan education.' Piatro slid the heavy, gold signet ring from his smallest finger and placed it sourly in Marron's square hand. From the corner of his eye, he caught sight of Aalia, swaddled in her cloak, jumping up to the deck. Relief had set his heart beating like a drum.

Marron handed over the dice. 'It isn't right, the way she goes without chaperones. You should keep the girl in check.'

'I've yet to be persuaded she's a girl.' He looked up and smiled.

Aalia stood over them, sea-blue eyes in storm. 'Someone paid Otar to break the mould!'

Patently, she was in a foul temper. Piatro held his tongue.

'You should be ashamed, Captain Marron, beating a gambler with his own toys. Have either of you seen our talented physician?'

Piatro carefully weighed what excuse to best use, screwing his eyes in thought. Andreas, always diligent in his duties, had gone to find the company of a woman, but he daren't tell that to Aalia. In this mood, she would likely follow.

Aalia put her mouth to his ear. 'Perhaps another master has demand of his services?'

The merchant felt his skin flood with colour. It wasn't for him to be Judas.

'What if he's testing the potency of his latest potion?' He shrugged his shoulders and turned to the Captain, thinking to beg his support. Then, he noticed the blood, a dark stain on the shoulder of her cloak.

Catching the line of his concern, she squeezed her eyes tight and laughed. 'It's no less than I'd expect with William at play.'

And Piatro understood exactly what she was saying. William had a temper, everyone knew that, but never had he hurt Aalia. That was why Piatro believed the bastard's promise. Concerned to see the injury, he tried to uncover her arm, but she brushed him aside.

'I can bind a wound,' he said, shrugging back his pride.

'It's hardly worthy of a bandage.' She turned on her heel and started towards the lower deck. 'I need to hire a wherry as soon as I've changed my clothes.'

And smiling a blatant smile, she scooped up Piatro's dice and tossed them overboard.

'We suffer to play by her rules!' Piatro stood frowning, as the gilt head disappeared. 'I wonder where she sent Georgiou.'

But Marron wasn't listening. He was stretched over the fore-rail, trying to see why everyone on shore was running towards the Customs House.

'Perhaps we should follow?' He shrugged his heavy shoulders.

Whatever was causing the commotion, the tall gates which led into the city were being pushed shut.

'Somehow, I don't think that would be wise.' Piatro shook his head.

Aalia had joined them. She'd washed her face and changed her cloak and tunic, sloughing her telltale hair inside a knitted cap.

'There's Georgiou!' Marron yelled, pointing.

Grey cloak billowing, he was running hard, ploughing through the crowds in a race to reach *Cornucopia*. Chasing behind him was a corps of men in the Bedford livery, waving their arms and shouting. Georgiou pushed through a row of carters and tried to jump a ragged pile of fish baskets, but landed awkwardly. Rolling onto his feet smoothly, he attempted to run, hobbling badly, and then, they took him down. Not gently. It became clear what the crowd were actually screaming.

'Murderer!'

Piatro grabbed Aalia, before she could storm onto the wharf. Turning to stop his hand, eyes hollow, she explained, 'I sent Georgiou to fetch Tom.'

And Piatro's heart went cold.

Within minutes of Georgiou being arrested, any attempt to board or leave *Cornucopia* was prevented by a guard of diligent pikemen. Undeterred by this barrier, Francis Drake climbed on-board by way of the heavy hawser which reached up from the surface of the river. Soaked to the skin, eyes distilled with excitement, Piatro dragged the lad out of Aalia's range, before asking him to describe everything which had happened at the Mermaid. Squatting opposite Piatro, dripping puddles on the sun-baked upper deck, the lad replied frankly, answering each question without decoration. For which Piatro was grateful; Aalia would have made him work much harder before she came to the truth.

On his return to the wharf, Francis had left the rest of the party and gone to stow *Lydia* at the pilot's jetty, before returning to collect his fee. Aalia told Francis they would all meet back on *Cornucopia* after Georgiou gathered an old friend called Tom, who she needed to speak with urgently. It was only on hearing the commotion that he'd gone by way of the Custom House, along with the rest of the crowd, his curiosity burning.

'They say that Mortimer, Her Majesty's Keeper of Customs, sent his servants to clear a pile of rubbish blocking the main gate to the wharf, but when they went to move the debris, they found a murdered beggar.'

Piatro weighed his answer carefully, not wanting more need of panic. 'It could be that the murdered man is our friend Tom. But why do they blame Georgiou?'

'They say Mortimer himself found Georgiou bent over the body.' Drake shook his head. 'And nobody listened when I said he couldn't possibly have done him in.'

'Of course, Georgiou couldn't have killed him, but it's easy to point the finger at a stranger.' Piatro found he was shaking.

'The dead beggar was an old soldier, by all accounts,' Francis added helpfully. 'Sebastian's gone after the guard. He'll tell them Georgiou couldn't have killed anyone cos' he was with us.'

'Who the hell's Sebastian?' Piatro, nerves taut, almost lost his patience.

'Didn't Drake tell you?' Aalia stepped softly behind them. 'He was also at the Mermaid and helped settle our dispute with William.' Dropping onto a coiled hawser, she wrapped her knees in her arms. 'He was arguing with Alvaro, that viperous man.'

'Sebastian is viperous?' Piatro was confused.

'Of course not, he helped us escape.'

'You return with a stranger, who you met arguing with the one man we absolutely know we can't trust. Didn't you wonder what his motives might be? They've arrested Georgiou for murder for God's sake and…'

Piatro held his tongue, fearing Aalia might break. They couldn't know if Tom was murdered, but why else would Georgiou be found gazing on a dead beggar?

'Well… he did offer his hand in marriage.'

Aalia fixed him with an impassive smile, likely the same and proper reason why her brother's temper had snapped. Piatro wanted to shake her, to loosen her self-control, but feared the final consequence, should he prise into her heart.

'Sebastian is Lord Scythan's nephew...' Drake regarded them both as fools. 'Of course, he'll be believed.'

Aalia's spun on the lad. 'Therefore, it's what Sebastian tells his uncle that should worry us!' But she didn't speak with anger, although poor Drake flushed like a school boy. Studying his face, she stretched like a cat and added softly, 'However, he did meet with Alvaro, which means we must discover who pays the fool.'

She walked over to the rail, and Piatro followed. Buff-coated wardens had replaced Bedford's guards, but Piatro could see Mortimer striding purposefully towards *Cornucopia*, escorted by another corps of men wearing the dark blue livery he'd seen so often that day.

'Aalia.' He took her hands in his own. 'I think we have to anticipate the murdered beggar is Tom.'

Her cheeks had lost all colour, and he could see the unshed tears.

'Yes, I understand. Georgiou wouldn't have waited on him otherwise. But William wouldn't harm Tom. He was clearly surprised when I told him about the previous attack and looked directly at Alvaro... Tom was certain that viper wanted him dead. But if our old friend was murdered... the killer must be someone who knew about his past.' She shook her head, gazing at the wharf empty-eyed.

Piatro put his hand on her shoulder. 'Alvaro was with you, so he can't be the culprit. It might be he ordered Tom's death, but how could we prove it?'

She continued watching the shore. 'It wasn't as if Tom was committed to begging, but he excelled at ruffling feathers. Perhaps he was killed by another beggar, jealous of having competition?'

She had an actor's smile, but Piatro knew to watch her hands. Once, he'd heard her brother complain she didn't show emotion, and she'd retaliated, "There's a season for everything," and just like now, his heart had cried.

Drake climbed from the lower deck to join them.

'This need not concern you, Francis Drake.' She grabbed his calloused hands and squeezed them tight. 'But I will explain. You remember the man I argued with at the Mermaid? The murdered beggar was his devoted servant, and William had nothing to gain from Tom's death. In fact, he could only lose by it; Tom kept secrets, even from us.'

'What kind of secrets?' The lad shrugged, round face honest.

Piatro waited, hardly expecting the truth, as Aalia avoided his eye.

'I wish I knew, but he never told me. Being back in London, worried beyond sense over William, has raked up distant memories. Which reminds me…? I must pay a visit to his dog.'

Piatro thought he'd misheard, but Drake wasn't too proud to ask.

'Why pay a visit to his dog? How can that help?'

Aalia didn't answer, her focus had fixed to the shore.

Piatro followed her gaze. The dockside crane was swinging its great wooden arm over the nearside vessel to unload a wooden box which was set ready on a pallet. It hung barely a pitched leap from where they were standing. Before he could stop her, Aalia had climbed onto the rail and into the rigging. He jumped to grab her, but caught his foot in a rope and landed heavily on both knees.

Aalia called over her shoulder as she swung onto the beam. 'Piatro, stay here. I've got to find Tom's dog.'

'I hope you've better reason for my bruises.'

Piatro watched her land squarely on top of the pallet. The men treading the crane's wheelhouse were waving frantically, as she clung to the ropes, but the pikemen standing guard had failed to notice. Then, jumping onto the jetty, she shook out her cloak and threw a salute to the crane-men. Piatro wished he possessed half her agility, never mind her courage.

'There's a man with a mighty big escort demanding to speak to Aalia.' Captain Marron's broad shadow fell across the deck. 'Wasn't she just here?' he demanded, mangling his saffron cap in plate-sized hands.

Dealing with authority was something Piatro had long ago mastered. Dealing with irate officials required a broad understanding of their protocols. Negotiating to win respect was no more than an inconvenience to a merchant of Piatro's broad experience, his perception being honed by the many underhand systems of bureaucracy encountered in every corner of the known and civil world. Thankfully, Sir Andrew Mortimer wasn't endowed with Piatro's cosmopolitan experience.

To begin, he made use of several lesser languages, while apologising his English had yet to progress beyond nouns. Next, he showed his brand of French was far too weighty with German and contrived to try his birth-tongue before settling on Portuguese. They each proved equally unfathomable to Her Majesty's honourable commissioner, but the confusion delayed proceedings long enough to let Piatro state, without any falsehood, that the girl had left the boat long ago.

By this time, he'd steered the commissioner out of sight from the prying eyes onshore and stowed him below decks, setting him inside the cabin which had been furnished to impress. Pouring claret wine from a flask of Moravian crystal, and setting Sir Andrew at rest on a coverlet of curled black karakul, Piatro could almost feel the man purring. Running an admiring finger along the highly polished lacquer of a black Chinese cabinet, Mortimer's officiousness mellowed.

'Of course, the witness might be mistaken.' He continued to trace the fine mother-of-pearl inlay possessively.

Piatro didn't intend gifting the cabinet; there were lesser gifts in his depository. It didn't take him long to learn Mortimer had formerly practiced in law, and that his new status meant he received an annual stipend of no mean sum, given the measure of his abilities. Piatro hardly needed to be over-generous with the

Company's munificence, but in taking his time, and showing a form of ingenuity barely conceived by his guest, he discovered everything Mortimer knew about the beggar's murder. By the end of their conversation, Piatro had no more doubts the victim was indeed Tom, and in ushering the preening official back on deck, was only thankful they'd managed to purchase such a store of superior wine when provisioning their stocks in Lisbon. Sir Andrew also failed to note Piatro's command of English had improved almost to the point of fluency.

But still, the odious man was in no hurry to leave.

'Never have I seen a ship of such refined comforts.'

'We are fortunate indeed. The Company of St. Thomas leased the vessel from Portuguese owners, then furnished it to fit our taste… otherwise, such a journey would have proved extremely trying.' Piatro gritted his patience.

'I believe your troubadours were honoured by the Acting Master of Revels?'

Piatro's appeased the man's curiosity by throwing his sharpest smile, the one he reserved for his darkest misdemeanours, and offered a stilted account of Lord Scythan's visit.

'There may be some further formalities regarding the death of this beggar, but I'm sure the matter can be smoothly dismissed, given the level of your sincerity.'

He patted the pocket where a doe-skin purse of Angels was newly stored. Piatro knew to nurse his hunger, a subtle transaction best despised, but experience had long proved such bribes were a necessity.

'When Aalia returns to *Cornucopia*, I will ensure she comes to thank you in person.' And Piatro promised himself should such a meeting take place, he must also be present, for Aalia had absolutely no patience with sycophants.

SANCTUARY – 12th Disclosure

To be dishonest is to steal truth; giving false witness
dishonours our principles.

The angled shadows where a jetty met the sea was seldom visited. Hidden beneath the mossy reach of London's highest tide, a stinking shelf built from rotten timbers held little to attract attention, except a one-legged beggar might sometimes use it for home, and to store his few possessions.

Crawling to find the desolate hovel Tom had once described, Aalia searched through the sodden filth hoping to recover Tom's dog. The stink of putrid detritus turned her stomach, but she could spare no time to despair. Too much must be done, and English days were eternal. Her heart missed a beat. Tom was dead.

Aalia found the dog curled on a bed of rags. She stroked its coarse-haired head and sifted through layers of damp and tattered sailcloth to gather up her old friend's belongings. She was almost ready to leave, when she heard two men arguing just above her head and shuffled closer, barely moving.

'This has nothing to do with my uncle,' Sebastian Trentham was shouting. 'But I'm willing to give my oath the man you've just arrested was with me all afternoon. He wasn't responsible for killing this beggar, no matter what your witness reported.'

'How can you be sure? He was standing over the body.' The other voice was deep and unremitting. Aalia remembered the solid bass-tone as that of the Earl of Bedford.

'The beggar's skin was cold. We've both survived a battle-field, Lord Bedford; dead men grow slowly cold. I'd lay a wager that man had been dead an hour or more.'

'This man Mortimer arrested… what do you know of him?'

'His name is Georgiou. He came with *Cornucopia* and speaks little English.'

'But he's dark-skinned and black haired, just as the witness described. And Mortimer arrived to find him standing over the dead man and covered in his blood.'

'How can you know when a man is dead, if you don't bend down and touch him? I'm certain Georgiou cannot be the murderer. In fact, you can have my word on it.'

'With your reputation, that means little. You've your uncle's flair for deception, Sebastian.'

'I overheard the girl send him to fetch their friend, someone called Tom. Perhaps that's the beggar's name?'

'What girl?'

'She came off the same boat. A misfit of a girl called Aalia.'

There was silence, as the men moved away. The little dog nestled against her leg. She stroked its head then crawled back to Tom's lair. Digging under the last of his rags, she found a small, round bowl, heavy and cold to the touch. She lifted it higher to catch better light. This was never a beggar's bowl. Its fretted sphere was spangled in jewelled glass, thin and fragile as eggshell, and pricking the golden rim was a legend, sealed with a phoenix, just like the crest on the ring Tom had given her.

'I think you'd better give that to me, young lady.'

Lord Bedford stood where the shadows touched the bank, Sebastian crouched low behind him.

'A penny, sir! All I needs is a penny.' It was far too late to pretend. Against her leg, the little dog growled sullenly.

Despite Sebastian's pleading, Bedford demanded they both accompanied him back to his house on The Strand. They could hardly refuse, given the number of men at his command, and he didn't begrudge Aalia bringing Tom's pathetic dog, except when they reached the modest gates, he instructed his porter to lock it in the stables.

Bedford's Countess was absent, fulfilling her duties at court, but he led Aalia into her needle-room, because this was a woman's sphere, and he needed to learn something of the truth without alarming the misfit girl. But he made Sebastian wait in the hall, not wanting Scythan's clever nephew to corrupt her testimony.

Meg's sanctuary was strewn with her habits. A large, hide-bound chair was set in front of the window, a well-thumbed book, with stained green binding, sat on its tapestry cushion. Beside the chair was a neat hexagonal card-table on which a child's linen bonnet lay, a sliver of needle embedded where the intricate black-work stopped half-stitched. Of late, his wife's duties meant she never had time for her favoured pastimes.

He went to the window and drew the drapes. The lamp flickered, sparking the silvered threads which embellished the embroidered curtains and gilding Aalia's boyish crown.

When William Cecil, Queen Elizabeth's secretary, had presented a concise report to the Privy Council suggesting there'd been an attempt to murder the Queen, every other man present was wary a girl could respond to catastrophe with such clear-thinking alacrity. Not one of them had actually met the girl in question. Although Bedford was troubled not least by the way Aalia dressed, he recognised genuine courage. Not once had she hesitated from acting with utter good sense, whilst the rest of the arena had lain blinded in fear. Her actions at St. Katherine's had won his complete respect despite the suspicion, then as now, she was over-cautious with the truth.

Studying her face as she perched straight-backed in Meg's best chair, he found his heart wanted to trust where his intellect preached caution.

'So, young lady, what can you tell me?'

'India is a thousand suns from England.' She was shaking uncontrollably, swaddled in the fabric of her cloak.

'Don't be obtuse, Aalia. What can you tell me about this beggar named Tom?'

'Probably little more than you already know. He acted as guide during our first night in London and helped rescue your Queen, along with my good-friend, Georgiou, who you had arrested without just cause. Any more is a mystery.'

Bedford regarded her thoughtfully. With every fibre of her being, she was trying to hold her composure. He took the beggar's bowl from its pouch and raised it until the flame of the lamp sparked its gem-bright colours. Slowly, he traced the motto with his clumsy fingers and remembered that day, long ago, when he read the simple legend.

'And you don't know how this priceless bowl came to be in a beggar's possession?'

'I never saw it before today. I went to fetch his dog. That's all.'

She smiled, and turned to look out of the window. Bedford wondered what she could be hiding.

'How long have you known this beggar?' he barked loudly.

She didn't flinch. 'You know the answer, a night and a day, no more.'

There was nothing of fear in her eyes. Nothing but the empty smile he knew he must distrust.

'Yet, you showed a great deal of faith in each other's talents during that night at St. Katherine's.' Cecil had demanded he should go and question the facts. And Bedford was willing to bring Aalia and her fellow rescuers to face a private court, except the Queen had interfered, pouring her gratitude on the misfit's timely intrusion.

'We were united by circumstance?' She said it so quietly, he struggled to hear. But her eyes never once left the bowl. 'The beggar told me he had a sister, and I wanted to take his dog and belongings back to her.'

'Do you know the sister's name?' Bedford shouted.

'Sybil, Tom said. Sybil Penne, by marriage.' She bit her lip.

And Bedford recognised the slip.

'So, you know the beggar's name?'

'He told me his name was Tom Hampden… in the event we might enter into correspondence.' She snapped out each word.

Bedford slotted the crucial fact into his private understanding, while his heart started beating above its usual pace. This girl possessed no understanding of the bowl's real significance. And if this was the same Sybil Penne who had once nursed King Henry's brood with loyal dedication, she might be more forthcoming if Aalia called to pay her respects... accompanied by his wife, Meg, of course.

'I know of a woman called Sybil Penne. Although a former servant of the royal household, she has permanent lodgings in the Palace of Hampton Court.'

Locked in a filthy dank cell not a thousand suns from the simple splendours of Russell House, Georgiou sat silently waiting. He'd learned better patience since Otar first enlisted him. No foreign emissary had been commanded to come. He'd chosen to leave India, to leave his mother, his home, to vacate the past, because the only constant in life was death. And he remembered a wizened storyteller weaving tales to the beat of a bamboo drum, and a delighted child called Aalia tucked at his side, tossing her head of golden curls, laughing. It was like seeing one of Father Xavier's angels come inside the bazaar. And his soul had quickened.

Georgiou's thoughts strayed a thousand miles from his prison, before the clatter of a bell pierced his memories. A key turned awkwardly in the lock. He looked up anxiously, but it wasn't Aalia's slight form pushing the iron-clad door, it was the Master, Padruig.

SANCTUARY – 13th Disclosure

Loyalty is honed in trust.

By the time Master Padruig had collected Georgiou, it was too late to do anything other than bring him back to the Old Temple. Leaving Gull to minister a better form of hospitality, he went to attend to the pile of letters on his desk. It was almost midnight before he went looking again for Georgiou and found him sprawled on a bench in the refectory, balancing a wooden platter piled with bread and cheese on his lap. The smooth, boyish face was covered in bruises and showing a desperate need for sleep.

The candles guttered as Padruig closed the door.

'Her middle name is never.' The soldier looked up, his eyes heavy.

'I understand she is angry. What concerns me is how she flies headfirst into trouble, without informing the rest of this Company. Why were you looking for Tom?'

'Because blood is not thicker than water. Her brother upset her.'

'What do you mean… she's met William? Why wasn't I informed?'

'There wasn't time. It happened yesterday, around noon.'

'And they argued?'

'He hurled a knife at her. Then, he told her they were no longer related.' Georgiou frowned. 'I wanted to kill him!'

'But she said no?'

'He didn't come alone. There were a dozen soldiers; Sebastian said they wore the uniform of a city militia.'

'That's how you met Sebastian Trentham?'

'He was at the inn with the Jesuit, Alvaro. Then, later, he helped us escape.'

'And saved you from the gallows, young man! We are in debt to his pleading with Bedford. Tell me what happened at the wharf.'

'As soon as we returned, I went to look for Tom. Aalia wanted to speak to him but needed to change her clothes. She said he knew secrets, things which must be explained, and asked me to bring him to the boat. There was just a pile of rags where he usually sat, so I turned them over, and that was when I found Tom's body, covered in blood. His throat had been cut. I didn't have time to look further, before men came and accused me of murder… so, I ran.'

'According to Sebastian, there was a witness who pointed you out as the culprit. Without Sebastian's testimony… well, I doubt you'd be sitting here. There are men, rivals in trade, who would like to see St. Thomas accused.'

Georgiou shrugged, splaying crumbs across the tiled floor. 'Don't apply to me; I'm just the hired hand. I look to you for orders.'

'You are the well-educated son of a respectable mercantile family and trained to a finite degree to be capable of making your own judgements.'

'But I grew up in India. How can I judge English affairs?'

'Why do you think Otar asked you to come? He has utter faith in your abilities, and you understand Aalia better than most.'

'I know William better! We trained together.' He picked up his cup and drank.

'Then tell me what you know.'

'He was always an excellent student. Intelligent, an exceptional swordsman, though his temper turns him brutal. He spoke little, unless drunk. Preferred to get his sister… I mean, Aalia… to act for him.' His fingers tightened around his cup. 'They were inseparable, until Otar took her to Venice.' He stopped to consider his next words. 'There was some who suggested there was a need to part them.'

Padruig pursed his lips. 'There's the dilemma, Georgiou. Aalia discovered where to find her brother, but failed to come to me. Now, Tom is dead, and we have lost the one person who has known William constantly since birth. Should I send the girl back to India? Indeed, I think I must, if it would save her from being killed, too.'

Nothing Aalia said seemed to deter Sebastian clinging like a limpet from the moment they left Bedford House, along with the shivering dog. Eager to please, he showed a means of getting down to the river without encountering the night-watch, slipping through an orchard of apple trees without fear of being caught. Clearly, he'd often followed the same private path.

They met Drake at Temple Bridge. He'd done everything Aalia had asked, fetching the bulk of Tom's belongings, stowed inside *Lydia*'s hull.

Aalia picked up the lop-eared dog as she jumped into the boat. Sebastian jumped in uninvited and squatted next to Drake, and the little boat lifted her nose and smoothly caught the current. Stars sprinkled on the cobalt water, sliding on obsidian ripples. Aalia reached a hand into the water and felt the coldness bite; everything was distorted. Tom Hampden was dead. Another spike through her heart.

'If William is an example of kin, tell me how you define your enemies.' Sebastian interrupted her thoughts. He was hauling the sail, teasing *Lydia* to make better speed.

'You're very proficient.' She matched his gaze, wishing she understood why he so wanted her approval. Georgiou would tell her to be highly suspicious, but looking in his eyes, she read nothing but sincerity.

'Surely that's why you invited me!' His shadowed face split in a smile.

'I don't recall offering any invitations?'

'And I'm always proficient on principle.' His smile beamed even wider as Francis let him take the helm.

Sebastian proved a natural steersman, as the river carried them under the city's gabled silhouette, past the molten midnight labyrinths, the splintered wharfs and jetties where wherry-men slept in their boats, rocked gently by the tide. They made faster pace after Kew, where the river narrowed, taking turns at rowing when the light wind eddied and failed. Once out of the city's reach, there were few other boats to avoid, and the banks became haunts of tall, spiked rushes, and long, willow fronds spinning in silvery ripples, and night owls screeched at their prey.

When the moon slipped behind broken clouds, Francis showed an aptitude for piloting by starlight, although, as he modestly explained, it wasn't half as bad as navigating a London fog. Under an hour later, they were passing a low-roofed village when a crisp bass bell struck the hour.

'That will be St. Nicholas's in Chiswick. We're just about half-way,' Drake announced. 'But better keep *Lydia* mid-stream for fear of getting hooked in fish traps; there's far too many to count and none of them lawful.'

Sebastian was still at the helm. 'We'll pace ourselves 'til dawn,' he said. 'You can't expect a civil greeting if you call before sunrise, and I don't know how we're supposed to get inside Hampton Court Palace without some letter of invitation.'

Aalia was half asleep, nursing Tom's shivering dog, when a long-keeled boat, sleek as it was silent, rammed into *Lydia*'s side. Sebastian catapulted backwards, landing in the water with a heavy splash. Aalia reached from the side to help him climb back, just as the untethered boom swung, catching the side of her head. Ducking with the blow, she still managed to hook the beam, before it swung back on its axle. Timbers creaked and crashed, and the broken boat swayed wildly. Francis leapt to steady the rudder, as Tom's dog cowered at his feet but not a word was spoken.

The collision wasn't accidental.

The attacking boat was twice the size of *Lydia*, baring down on them with four burly pairs of oars and a sharp, steel-edged prow. There was little they could do but watch when the water-born battering ram made its second strike, because the weight of water pouring into the damaged bow had rendered *Lydia* helpless. As the two boats collided again, a pair of black-robed men, faces half masked, jumped into *Lydia*'s sinking hull. One trapped Drake by his arms, while the other tried to grab Aalia, but ducking smoothly beyond the man's hold, she used the mast to steady herself while she tried to unbuckle her knife.

Sebastian reached over the side and took the man holding Drake from behind, dragging him backwards into the river. Aalia held tight as the boat tipped and rolled. Marking his man, Drake picked up an oar and began a wild swing, however the man folded, screaming like a banshee. Though robbed of its mark, the oar kept to its trajectory, striking Aalia's head as she bent to remove her knife out of the attacker's shoulder. She fell on top of the wounded man, steeped in the water which was filling *Lydia*'s hull.

Before Drake could swing again, the man scooped her into his arms and rolled sideways into the water. Grabbing the oar from Francis, Sebastian struck the water fruitlessly then dived back into the blackness, a silver-ringed wake marking where he dropped. The other boat circled once, dragging their comrades from the water. Then, they left, shadows gloating in moonlight, sliding downstream silently, just as they had come. *Lydia* was sinking fast. Drake held tight to his broken boat, staring into the cobalt water, wishing he knew what to do. An orb slaked the surface. Drake let out a cry. Surely it must be Sebastian, but then the moon ducked behind clouds and clothed the river in black.

Darkness heightened sound. The frantic wing-beat of a heron taking flight, the whispered stirrings of a hungry owl, and then, a different, mortal sound. Drake peered towards the flat sands of the river-bank, and a movement caught his eye. Sebastian, carrying Aalia in his arms.

Then, *Lydia* finally sank.

SANCTUARY – 14th Disclosure

Be wary of blind faith, it binds the needs of idle minds.

Padruig's temper rarely passed beyond his control. As a young man, the opposite might have been true but age, or more likely, a lifetime of service to St. Thomas, had taught him better restraint, at least until Aalia had arrived.

Striding on-board *Cornucopia*, he'd just learned, in collective monosyllables, the complete dialogue of Aalia's disobedience, up to the point she was currently missing. Kopernik's face couldn't blush a better shade of scarlet if painted with mordant dye.

Brought below decks, into the low-ceilinged cabin where Sir Andrew Mortimer, Master of Customs and Excise, had established his final price, Padruig was blind to its elegance. The inlaid black lacquer furnishings, the delicately carved Oriental wood, the hoarded luxuries St. Thomas had carefully sourced and carried from India to England, stirred no aesthetic bliss as he listened to the Polish merchant expand on his copious failings.

The revelation this trail of disobedience began with an undisclosed outing to the South Bank. That the shrewdest merchant in the Company's employ had failed to weigh William's bargaining with any measure of reason, made Padruig so very angry, he wanted to beat Piatro for stupidity but landed his fist on a side-stool instead.

The sharp, stabbing pain brought him back to his senses. Aalia's life mattered far more than that of her arrogant brother. He'd failed her father; he would not fail the child.

'Otar must have explained the exacting scope of your duties.' Padruig fought to keep his voice level. 'I might almost think you acted perniciously when you told Aalia where William could be found.'

Kopernik bowed his uncapped head. 'Since we left India, she nurtured one hope—that if she had the chance to speak to her brother alone, to malign his reasoning, he'd redeem his wayward ways. I knew it was a fool's errand, but promised if it was within my gift, I'd offer that opportunity and...'

'You knew! Yet didn't send word or provide adequate escort? I had great faith in you, Piatro. Of all men serving this Company, I thought you possessed the acumen to anticipate danger... you were employed to bargain with reason.'

Kopernik crossed the cabin and knelt at Padruig's feet, opaque, jade-green eyes almost meek. 'Aalia said you wanted William dead.'

'And you believed her? What kind of man would I be if murder was my only remedy? I want William placed where he can do no harm. Otar even suggested Spain's American colonies, but I remain open-minded, as long as we take him out of England.'

'I'd rather see the lad in hell.' Captain Marron squeezed under the hatch, huge arms loaded with half a dozen rolled charts.

Padruig closed his eyes, furious at the big man's intrusion, and took a deep breath before replying. 'That's not our decision to make, though I find the thought attractive. You are ready to sail on tomorrow's noon tide?'

'We've a depleted crew, far too many temptations in this heretic land... I've enough steady hands to take her down-river, but not into open sea.'

'That's as far as need be at present, you can trust Solomon's apprentice.' He met Kopernik's bewilderment. 'Despite your generosity, I'm worried *Cornucopia* will soon be impounded by the authorities. Mortimer has been gossiping about the rare furnishings, and even before Tom's murder, questions were being raised about the nature of our trade. They don't trust a caravel coming from the East, without even a hint of spices, and Aalia's troubadours have merely made bad matters worse.'

'I presumed the Company would be gladdened by her enterprise, particularly since they've been invited to sing at court?' Marron tipped the charts onto the polished onyx table, prior to meeting the level gaze of two pairs of curious eyes.

'When did this happen?' Kopernik spoke first.

Marron's long smile showed the cunning of a wolf. 'The messenger came when Meester Piatro was away at his business. Gold and silver tabards and faces primed with pomp, but she agreed, at least that's what I thought she was saying, to perform at Whitehall during a banquet for some French hostages, which, I think, takes place after sunset on Saturday night.'

Padruig raised his eyebrows to Piatro's steady gaze. The Captain was enjoying their astonishment.

'But where are the minstrels? I haven't seen them since yesterday, on or off the boat.' Kopernik spoke with composed patience.

'They're earning their keep at The George, just across the river. The lutist, the blond one with the earring, he came back to collect Aalia, and was livid she wasn't here. He said English generosity was such he could even start to like the place, but a primed and pretty soprano would better smooth their path to fame.' Marron grunted at the memory. 'And nobody seems to know where Aalia's gone, apart from saying she needed to find Tom's dog.'

Padruig stood up so quickly, he nearly caught his head on a beam.

'Well, then, Piatro, may I suggest we go immediately and find her?'

SANCTUARY – 15th Disclosure

Value instinct, but never ignore reason.

'Can a pauper be re-birthed in finery?'

The girl's bell-like voice brought Guy out of his thoughts, and he turned from the moonlit garden. Closing the window, he quickly crossed the room to where his patient lay.

Except her eyes remained stubbornly closed.

'I regret not.' He bent close, thinking to stroke her hair.

When Sebastian had awoken him in the middle of the night, his patient had appeared dead to this world. A body so fragile, so slight, Guy's first fearful thought was his student had discovered a drowned child. They had dismantled her sopping clothes, loosed the stubborn knots, and found therein the woman. Having no other female at hand, they daren't strip the sinuous veil of undergarments but wrapped her in a thick woollen blanket drawn from Sebastian's bed.

She stirred, round berry lips pressed into the shadow of a smile. Time to introduce himself. She was, after all, at every disadvantage and most likely terrified.

'I am Sebastian's tutor and friend, Guy Yates.'

Her eyes opened, deep as an ocean, and caught his startled gaze.

'Asclepius deliberating? Or perhaps this is a dream?' She lifted an arm and carefully rubbed the contorted lump which split her smooth, round head. 'And 'til the room stops spinning like a dervish, I'm trapped in Midas's parlour. You're going to warn me I must mend my ways.'

Not the words he might expect from a street urchin. Sebastian should have better explained before he left, but then, he'd never have brought a guttersnipe into his uncle's elegant house. Guy studied the room for the first time in years, gathering details of clustered opulence. It had long ago become too familiar to consider remarkable.

She threw him a rascal-smile. 'Better point me towards my clothes so I can sink back into reality.'

He wondered if she actually read his thoughts and watched, unmoving, while she tried to stand, grasping the blanket round her thin, white shoulders. Fingers shivering, arms and legs inept.

Neither did he help, as she sank back into the day-bed, its fine blue damask cushions ringed black beneath her head. Lord Scythan, Sebastian's uncle, would be furious having water stains on his precious furnishings.

Gently, cautiously, Guy stroked the furrow of her cheek. There was no response.

'The blow to the head was heavy, little one. And you were very, very fortunate to have Sebastian pull you from the river.'

SANCTUARY – 16th Disclosure

Consider every option before entering a dispute.

The Earl of Bedford understood he'd failed in his duty. His sovereign had committed him, ordered him, to organise a Great Muster on the low green hills above Greenwich on the first Saturday of July, barely a week from today. His responsibility was to try and persuade the foreign emissaries, the spies, the men who wanted England in their pocket, that his country had sure and ample means to defend its wide-flung shores. But the awful truth was evident as soon as the detailed lists and scribbled reports began to land on his desk, not even the Queen's able secretary, William Cecil, could conjure enough of an armoury to deter an imminent invasion. Because reports seemed to indicate the need for an army was pressing. After the Treaty of Cateau Cambresis gave the promise to give Calais back to England, France was licking its wounded pride, with a fleet laid ready in Honfleur, and watching over their shoulder, imperial Spain was waiting, and wishing.

Like Cecil, he worried which of their foreign enemies had initiated the drama at St. Katherine's and almost robbed them of their Queen. But a drama closer at hand had defeated his work tonight. While consumed by the short-fall in hackbuts, the glaring deficiency of working field cannons, and utter lack of proper accounts throughout the country's armouries, he fell suddenly foul of his wife's tear-stained temper. And quite deservedly so.

Their London house was not immune to Meg's constant attendance at court, and she had returned late that evening to find their eldest child sick with a high fever. And her husband hadn't even noticed.

When an unanticipated caller came to the door, it had proved a welcome diversion, and he ordered his servant to bring the gentleman directly to the library. He knew the Master of St. Thomas by reputation, although they'd never met.

'Padruig Fitzgerald?' Bedford was politely surprised, not least by the man's great height.

'I must apologise for the lateness of hour, Lord Bedford. I have a dilemma, and it seems you might help its resolution?'

'If you're seeking Aalia, I'm afraid she isn't here.'

The man's long face held firm as any mask. Bedford settled him into a chair and brought a better lantern, setting it on his desk. St. Thomas was reputed to own the best library in London, and certain members of the Privy Council had expressed a recent interest in having this knowledge appraised, therefore it had always been in his mind to meet the man behind the illustrious Company.

'I've just learned of everything that has happened,' Padruig said softly, big voice curbed to a murmur.

'Indeed, I spoke to the girl this afternoon, but she left within the hour.'

The sombre eyes closed, and Bedford recognised the poor man's distress. The young woman was obviously far more than a servant. His thoughts went to his own son, lying sick upstairs.

'I didn't send her back into the streets without an escort,' Bedford continued levelly. 'Sebastian Trentham accompanied her. He was at the Legal wharf, too, spouting in apologies. A beggar was murdered, and Aalia's companion, the Indian soldier, seemed the likely suspect. Except Sebastian begged he was innocent.'

'The murdered man was Aalia's friend.' Padruig steadied his hands on the desk.

'Yet she'd just arrived in London.' He turned the facts in his mind. 'Come with *Cornucopia*, all the way from India. A fair-skinned girl who speaks good English, if you ignore the odd

Scottish phrase, and something of an enigma, even without the disturbing talents.'

'Aalia was raised in India and knew Tom throughout her childhood; he served for many years as a servant of St. Thomas.' The level eyes cut like steel. 'He returned to his homeland last year.'

'And, together, they saved her majesty from harm. But then, I ask why this man, who has served your Company and showed such concern for his sovereign, was begging on London streets? And why, more crucially, was he murdered? I put this question to you, Master Padruig, in the hope you may know what the hell is going on?' He raised his voice deliberately.

'I'm sorry to have troubled you.' Padruig was on his feet and already at the door, when Meg flew into the room, pale as winter and shaking.

'Husband... John's so sick... the physician doesn't offer much hope.'

'What's wrong with the child?' Padruig took her hand, but the Countess couldn't speak. Only her eyes gave answer.

The fever was high, radiating through the child, so his body felt like fire, and the doctor tending the infant relied on those practises Padruig feared most. He ordered the fool outside before throwing off the covers and stopping away the leeches. Padruig's cures held less drama; a rotation of cold-compresses, sips of boiled water, and prayers. The white-haired nurse did everything he asked, touching his hand each time she returned to sit at the child's bedside.

By mid-morning, he knew they'd succeeded. The boy's heart beat stronger, more regular, like a drum, which made him think of Aalia, who knew every rhythm possessed its own special song.

Just before mid-day, after his son's fever broke and Meg sat sleeping in the hall, the Earl of Bedford left Padruig at his home and went to search for Aalia. Checking the precious Chrism Bowl before setting it safely inside his wife's travel chest, he weighed what he remembered of his meeting with the girl and set out for Sebastian's lodgings. He owed that small service to the Master.

The city streets were molten. He rode through back streets, avoiding the busy lanes packed with market stalls, merchants who knew him by sight. Sebastian's rented house faced St. Paul's crowded green, ideal for keeping watch on the dissenting preachers and printers who stalked the cathedral's great shadow. The servant who came to the door said he hadn't seen his master that day, though his horse was still in the stables.

Bedford demanded they check, and the servant led him dourly through the grime-filled courtyard. The horse was in its stall, and a mule, kicking at their intrusion. Thanking the servant for letting him look, Bedford decided Aalia must have raced off to find Sybil Penne straight after their meeting yesterday. The girl was born in India; she couldn't know the Palace of Hampton Court was half a day's ride from London. Although, surely Sebastian might warn her. Mrs. Penne had watched over the royal nursery during King Henry's day. Kind-faced but proud, she'd be distraught to learn her brother had been reduced to beggary. But perhaps she might explain how he came to own the royal Chrism Bowl.

Bedford remounted his horse and made his way home. There was little more he could do today, but felt comfort in trusting Sebastian travelled with Aalia. The lad was no fool, and his uncle, for all his faults, had rounded his nephew's education with every expert he could afford. And Scythan could afford the very best. In fact, there had been rumours, giggled at court, Sebastian had never lost a fight. And Meg suggested his conquests weren't confined to swordplay. Bedford hardly trusted the Trentham measure of chivalry, knowing their ambition, knowing their spite, and was more than certain something other than coincidence was at play. What made Sebastian so protective of the girl, or perhaps more pertinently, what did he expect to gain?

SANCTUARY – 17th Disclosure

Rivalry is mere jealousy, cloaked in a game lacking rules.

Dawn was spilling into the room when Aalia next opened her eyes. She could hear the trebled pitch of birdsong and a pheasant's ugly squawk. Her head hurt. And then, she remembered.

Lying at her feet, just within arm's reach, her native clothes were piled clean and dry. On top was her knife, its sheer steel blade mirroring sunlight. She was reaching for her tunic when someone said her name, softly.

To not sense someone watching was unpardonable.

'Good morning, Aalia.'

A voice hollowed of sympathy, not the physician of yesterday.

'Your costume awaits its next scene. Sebastian begged my housekeeper to wash and dry your rags before sunrise.'

'I may be a player, but my star is fixed.' She pulled on her trousers, knotting the cords effectively, balanced on one foot unsteadily.

'But you play dangerous games, young lady.'

The voice came from behind the molten sweep of tapestries.

'And I'm never ever dull.' She sat down heavily. It was hard to do anything with her head pounding like a war-drum.

'I think you are well-conceived but, nonetheless, a fantasy. Do you sing, I wonder, to harness praise, or because it pleases you to bend weaker souls to your bidding?'

'How cynical you are, Lord Scythan. I promise your nephew has yet to hear me sing.' She felt him move closer and waited, not daring to turn her head. 'Are you afraid of me? No wonder you hide.'

'Why were you attacked?'

He moved into the bay of windows, a silhouette framed in sunlight. She couldn't see his face but sensed his air of mockery.

'Of course, the dimensions are far more complex when deciding who to trust.'

She was surrounded by his possessions, yet found it hard to measure his taste amongst the searing extravagance. He didn't answer, but waited where the diamond panes bellied into gardens. Half-blown lanterns burnished the elegance with a golden light, and white as crystal above her head, the ceiling hung with brightly painted bosses, carved Tudor roses, and shielded crests. Empty-eyed portraits lined the panelled walls, fabled in tempura, and there was a brooding statue near the fireplace, a bronze Hermes, wings clipped, face vacant. Snow-like marble surrounded the carved fireplace and supported a colossal, mercury mirror. In that window to faithless infinity, she met Scythan's hooded eyes reflected. Damn. The man was gloating.

She must focus on what he couldn't know.

'Do you always pursue perfection?' She matched his gaze in the mirror.

He smiled and came close enough to touch, smelling of lavender and fresh flowing water and, surely not, Indian musk.

'Only you can decide who to trust.'

She closed her eyes, sensing his mind, the way she'd been taught. *Come with me, and we shall taste Paradise.* Someone had whispered those words just as she fell from the boat. Had she made a novice mistake, been utterly stupid? The river flowed stronger than she could have ever anticipated. It would have been easier to drown.

'As far as I know, you might be our attacker?'

'That would deem me rather ruthless.' He laughed.

'And vanity insists you succeed by intellect alone?' It suddenly occurred he would have searched all her belongings. Tom's ring? She'd tied it on a cord around her neck. It was gone.

Scythan bent close, warm breath soft on her cheek. 'I might teach you to trust me.'

'Never... but I see you'd savour the challenge.' She must keep her temper. *One day, I will own you.* Deep, thudding pain distorted every thought. She could feel him waiting for her to flounder, to fail.

'I am not trying to seduce you.'

She opened her eyes.

He was close enough to kiss, frozen as the Hermes in quilted dove-grey damask. The jacket was covered in a trellis of tiny onyx beads, each diamond-frame fitted with a blood-red table ruby inscribed in swirling Arabic... *There is only one God, Allah.*

Piatro would be impressed.

'I'm listening.' Her voice at least behaved.

'You possess a rare and natural gift, though presently raw-edged and wanting. I delight in perfection and have means to hone your talent. My resources are limitless, and I will not haggle the fee.'

It would be wrong to think he was bargaining merely for her music.

'My friends and protectors might feel betrayed. Besides, I happen to enjoy what I am.'

'Really? And what happened yesterday is acceptable? You have half a talent, and I can offer tutors who will clarify your ability. You know you possess an exceptional voice.'

The room stopped spinning. He went to a table and filled a tiny crystal goblet with honey-coloured liquid. When he returned, he levelled the glass at her lips.

She shook her head. 'Would you place me on a pedestal like the bronze, or line me beside the paintings... something to entertain your friends? Will I be discussed, dissected and then discarded when found wanting?'

'Is it wrong to want your talent?' He offered the glass again, emerald eyes searing.

'Or worse... it becomes intimate.'

He ran his eyes luridly over her face, her body, as though she was a whore. Then laughed unkindly. 'That would be your choice. I'm offering a banquet, and you choose to beg?'

'I prefer to starve.' Pushing the glass aside, she wrapped her belt tight round her waist and took a deep breath. She must get to the door. But which door? There were too many.

'You can't leave. You're far too weak to ride, and I have no escort to spare.' He did not offer his hand.

She tried to walk, but her feet felt like dead-weights.

'My friends need to know where I am, and I very much doubt they'll trust your... any intermediary.' She stumbled, trying for the nearest door. 'Thank you for your kind hospitality. I shall ask blessings from your favoured god... do you actually have a preference?'

'That could be conceived as blasphemy, young lady.'

His voice bit hard, but the jade eyes had softened.

'You're a collector. Surely faith motivates better than beauty? Or who will hold a candle to your soul?'

'A minstrel who dabbles in metaphysics?' He roared with laughter. 'Perhaps I need to discover who created this fantasy called Aalia?' He stood squarely in her path.

She stood very still. 'They usually ask *what* not *who*.'

But this time, she was misconceived. Grabbing both her hands, Scythan squeezed to the point of pain. But before she could fight, a door flew open, and Guy blustered into the room. She wondered how long he'd been listening.

'She needs to rest, Simon, or must I repeat how this young lady was struck on the head and very nearly drowned?'

The physician took her arm and led her back to the couch, smoothing the water-stained pillows. 'Sebastian brought you here so you could recover. Is there anything else you need?'

At last, someone without motive. 'Perhaps a bowl of porridge?' She felt her mind fading, but the room had stopped spinning. 'Served with a very long spoon.'

SANCTUARY – 18th Disclosure

Truth is not always self-evident, or pleasing.

Dawn was lighting the long bend of river when Sebastian returned. As he searched the sandy banks where he'd brought Aalia to safety, a soft mist hung over the surrounding fields, and he could hear the drag of oars as a wherry slipped upstream. With help from his uncle's servants, he'd recovered most of Tom's possessions. Rags they might be, but they were attacked for a reason, and he heard the man who struck him whisper in Spanish, '*Anillo.*' Ring.

Last night, while the girl was retching up half the river, he had expected their attackers to follow. But no-one had appeared, except Drake, clinging to the wreck of *Lydia*. Sebastian had spent much of his childhood along this stretch of Thames, but, confused by darkness, decided they'd landed further down-stream, until moonlight had revealed the jetty. There was no mistaking the livery shield with its bold porcupine crest. He prayed his uncle was sleeping.

Turning to the broken hull of *Lydia*, Sebastian remembered the young pilot's despair. Though he promised to settle the repairs, Drake remained more than fearful of Solomon's wrath. The beggar's dog lay sleeping under the wreck, and as he approached, it barked and wagged what was left of its tail. An ugly little cur, but Aalia would be glad to see it safe. Trapped beneath the hull, he also found Tom's leather jack, and his sack, blackened and slimed with mud. If Aalia still insisted on visiting Tom's sister, everything would need to be washed, though from what he knew of Sybil Penne, he doubted the lady would want anything to do with such a brother. There seemed little sense in taking her the beggar's paltry belongings when Bedford retained the one thing worth a mention. The beautiful and precious Chrism Bowl.

The irony was, had Aalia not arrived at the Mermaid Inn, he would most certainly have learned Alvaro's plans and served his duty better. It had taken many weeks to earn the Spaniard's confidence, but whatever they were plotting, William seemed just as bull-headed and unpredictable as the girl. Sebastian recalled Aalia's taunt, "Siblings come two a penny," and the sheer bloody rage on William's face. He aimed that knife deliberately, and the men accompanying him had been shocked, too shocked to come to his defence when Georgiou had brought him down.

And that brought to mind Aalia's dark skinned companion's absolute and utter skill. Sebastian's meticulous training bore little in common with his methods, or his pace. Small wonder Aalia felt safe in his care, and from the appalling events at St. Katherine's to the confrontation with her so-called brother, it seemed clear they were snared in every scene. Though he knew for certain neither Aalia nor Georgiou were responsible for Tom's murder, he would gamble his horse they knew far more than were telling. He just hoped this sodden sack would bring him better truth, or he was bound to lose his commission.

SANCTUARY – 19th Disclosure

Rational thought is often the first victim of disaster.

When Bedford heard the knock on his library door, he feared his son had taken a turn for the worse. It wasn't long after noon, and his moon-eyed servant apologised, but the caller was extremely distressed and begged an immediate audience. The disturbance also brought Padruig downstairs, but Bedford hardly needed the Master of St. Thomas to convince him the messenger was entirely trustworthy; Francis Drake was his godson, though with all the business he needed to attend, he'd barely seen the lad since Princess Elizabeth was crowned.

'Is your father well?'

The poor lad looked harried, grey-blue eyes glazed from lack of sleep. And his linen shirt was stained, boots damp and muddied.

'Last time I saw him, my lord, he was at Gillingham, baring his fists in the service of God.' He readjusted his cap, but couldn't contain his shivering.

'His heart is in his faith.' Bedford laughed. 'Don't despise him for it. Now, Francis, what message is so important you stir the whole household?'

'I'm sorry? Master Trentham sent me, though I would have sought out Master Padruig next by any means.'

Bedford steered them into the kitchen and set Drake beside the fire. With a blanket clutched to his chest, the lad spurted out his news, answering every question in brief and breathless sentences. At the end, he requested Lord Bedford should send for

Aalia, with all the weight of his authority, in order she should be released from Lord Scythan's care.

'At your earliest convenience, sir, please.' He stood close to the hearth, absorbing the serried heat.

'By now, if she has tongue, his lordship would likely be thankful for any reason to set her loose.' Padruig pinned Drake with calm, steel-grey eyes. 'Aalia made it clear how much she disliked the man.'

'But Sebastian is worried his uncle wishes to spoil her ambitions before they ruin his position at court.' Drake quoted his part, nursing a cup of ale. 'Because he fully intends to place his chore of musicians at the palace tonight.'

'Instead of Aalia! I'd forgotten the royal summons amongst all this drama.' Padruig turned to Lord Bedford and bowed. 'I will stay here with your son until you return, but I would be in your debt, my lord, if you could find Aalia and release her from Scythan's care.'

Taking leave of London, Bedford rode in the direction of Isleworth, accompanied by the meanest of escorts. Afternoon sunlight spliced the sand-filled lanes in long, graceful shadows. The summer had begun so well. His appointment to the Privy Council meant the new Queen was willing to ignore his family's lapses in faith. A Protestant to the core, his father had placed loyalty to his country above the call of religion and lent his political nouse to the Catholic Queen Mary. Francis had been less forgiving and spent most of that bitter reign in self-imposed and expedient exile, but just before he died, his father had warned he was on the eve of an extraordinary mission. Though shrouded in secrecy, he wrote the barest of explanations; the Spanish had commissioned him to search for a lost son of King Henry VIII.

Francis was familiar with the old rumour Jane Seymour gave birth to twins, but like everyone of sense, thought it a mere scheme created by dissenters and aimed to stir the country closer to civil war. However, it was hard to dispel a rumour when one suspected one's father of having a hand in its creation. Francis recognised the Chrism Bowl immediately when Aalia had lifted it from Tom's sordid rags, because it had been commissioned by his father. Except the bowl he had held at Prince Edward's christening, the one he passed to a four-year-old princess to present at her brother's feet, had the name Edward pricked deep inside the rim. And the name scored into the matching bowl he'd placed in Meg's travel chest, the name he checked again and again, was undeniably William.

He kicked his horse into a gallop. Less than five miles to reach Sawyer's Fold, but he had yet to negotiate with Scythan and then ride back to the city. His wife had warned the Queen would expect the entertainment to begin before sunset and Meg's instincts were seldom wrong. In fact, her first impression of Aalia was that her talents were unusually diverse. He should have guessed then the burden of his office might be tested by the girl. And a foreigner at that.

SANCTUARY – 20th Disclosure

To sustain legal trade every officer of St. Thomas
must respect local customs.

The court was in high spirits. Extraordinary as summer snow, the minstrels from *Cornucopia* were expected after the banquet, and those who didn't dare venture to the legal wharf wanted to judge if the legend met in truth. And those who crept down to the quay remained ever hungry for more.

Lady Bedford clung to the shadows in the Palace of Whitehall's entrance hall. Though duty-bound to serve her royal mistress, her heart, her soul, remained with her ailing son. In the great hall, the Queen was dancing, her favourite sport, and courtiers scurried to join her like bees around a hive. Meg had slipped out from the dancing and stayed hidden, watching them play, while trying not to fold her arms and put creases in her extravagantly bold, silk sleeves.

When Henry Tudor restored York Place, to create a palace worthy of a Renaissance prince, he had the minstrel's gallery moved into the rafters, music being a feast for the ear not the eye. That was in the days when the King had composed the pageants and placed himself at centre stage. Younger, and far shrewder, Elizabeth chose differently from her father, although the feasting still began at noon, and there was an undignified crush for seats. Brompton, Master of the Queen's Table, had made ribbons of the Flanders carpet even before the dancing had begun. Watching him flustering in front of the open door, Meg hung back, knowing the odious man would be seeking a confederate. But he'd already noted her hiding place.

'Where are these foreign musicians?' Anxiety shrilled his voice. 'Countess, what am I meant to do?'

She drew him into her eerie. 'There are other musicians. The acting Master of Revels will have the matter in hand, I am sure.' She soothed, without lending anything of empathy.

'Oh, Lord Scythan arrived with his players long before the first dishes were served. Who do you think performs the pavane and galliard? But they are not to the Queen's taste tonight. She expected some rare voice called Aalia, and I don't know where to look.' The lace of his ruff quivered under his bulbous chin.

'And Lord Scythan hasn't offered to find her?' Meg had been asleep when Drake arrived with his news, but while her husband prepared to leave, he had reeled off an account of what had happened, begging her opinion, as he always did. She had agreed it would be to Scythan's advantage to prevent the girl attending.

'His Lordship informs me the matter is in hand, but Her Majesty is furious, because the singer has not yet arrived.'

'Let Lord Scythan have responsibility, Brompton, then I'm sure no-one will hold you to blame.'

From the corner of her eye, she caught sight of Sebastian Trentham, herding a line of drums, lutes, and viols up the tiny passage which led onto the overhanging gallery. More than one of them appeared to be wearing a turban. Patently, her husband's errand had been a failure, and they were about to be lullabied by Turks.

Retreating to the farthest bay of windows, she turned to look outside. A thousand torches illuminated the gardens, ghosting the hedges and the patterned lattice of chalk-white paths where flounced damasks and patterned silks paraded like mating peacocks.

Still no word of Aalia.

Her husband thought the girl bewildering, and yet, he hadn't witnessed her timely actions at St. Katherine's. Nor was he there the next morning when Meg had visited the injured man at the Hospital of the Savoy. The physician had been so impressed by the stemming of Paulo's wounds, he demanded to know which doctor had been in attendance. Aalia was beyond bewildering. However, when Meg considered her look of sheer horror when Tom had blurted out just who they'd rescued, Meg wondered what brought such a girl to England when she clearly didn't seek fame.

She caught sight of her mistress, the young, oval face flushed from dancing. Looking up to the gallery, Her Majesty waved a signal to Brompton, and he immediately clapped his hands for silence. Meg nestled into her hiding place, resting her gabled headdress against the drapes. In the upper gallery, a turbaned head stepped forward and, raising the lute in his hand, smiled directly at the Queen. As the room rippled with disapproval, he bowed and gently, without accompaniment, sang a lullaby so tenderly, it stilled every restless tongue.

Meg watched the pampered faces melt as the singer fingered his lute and rippled out the chords of an Italian madrigal. His voice had a quality she'd rarely heard bettered, and the audience inside the room soon began to swell. Only then was his harmony sweetened by the purest of sopranos. Meg recognised it was Aalia. The girl's voice wove seamlessly with the tenor, marrying the melody to create a sound which was better than enchanting. Next, she sang a piety in solo with the lute. And nothing else seemed to matter.

The gardens emptied as men and women came to gather inside. Watching them drawn like moths to a flame, Meg leaned deeper into the curtains and closed her eyes. How long would it take before they turned this magic to stone?

It ended as it had begun. In silence. But the silence hung desolate, while the packed chamber waited on an encore. Aalia stepped up to the rim of the gallery and bowed. Then, gently, in a voice that soared with larks, she sang a final verse alone. The cheering broke wild, and pompous as any new father, Brompton ordered the servants to bring more sweetmeats and wine, gathering his harvest from the teeming glut of praise.

As the court dispersed, the minstrels were presented to the Queen; knees folded, turbans unbound. Hovering about the Queen were Meg's good-friends, the ladies of the inner chamber, reminding her she was shunning her part.

'Why is a jewel like the Countess of Bedford hiding in the drapery?' Lord Scythan was standing beside her, dressed in a bitter-sweet smile.

'I can't abide gushing,' she said. 'Were you hoping to feed her to the lions?'

'Not lions, dear lady, but sycophants, with no concept of her gift. They'll liken her to others and think the compliment fits. You and I know better. What we're seeing is an original.'

His praise was unexpected.

'She has them by the heart-strings; they'll forgive her being late.'

'But will Her Majesty? That's the question. I trust your husband received Drake's message?' His eyes were focused elsewhere.

'Just in time to act.'

'Lord Bedford is a man of honour.' He smiled.

'And a loyal servant to the Queen.' She sparked.

'I do as I see fit, Lady Bedford, but Her Majesty is never far from my thoughts. I believe you've already met Aalia?'

She wondered how much he knew about St. Katherine's, but curbed her first reply. 'A woman of many talents.'

'As I have discovered.'

She turned her gaze aside, mindful of Scythan's talent for tricking less wary dotes into breaking private confidences. Catching her reflection in the candle-mirrored window, she straightened the crooked headdress. *Damn!* Scythan was never anything but flawless.

SANCTUARY – 21st Disclosure

A performance must endure until the final bow.

Sebastian was steering Aalia wide of the favourites fanning the royal dais and had almost reached the outer hall, when the painted coterie of women huddled beneath the patterned tapestries called out her name. He daren't let Aalia out of sight and wanted to avoid meeting the lesser court, mindful of her injuries, of his uncle's wrath, but there seemed no way of escaping without giving offence. These women found pleasure in baiting the defenceless. Softly, he warned Aalia to curb her tongue, because servants did not bite. But she knew, always knew, whatever was achieved tonight mustn't flounder on her pride.

'Tell the singer she may attend me.' The oldest doyen threw her a squinted gaze and gestured to a place at her side.

It was an absurd tryst. An obscure, low-born singer and the sharpest tongue at court, Lady Maria Rayner was incapable of being civil to anyone of minor consequence. Age and spite had done little to temper her bite, but her reputation meant they still invited her to banquets, if merely for entertainment.

'Girl, you own a captivating voice, but in this company, you'd do well to employ better restraint.'

Lady Rayner was composed like a child's wooden doll, her ruff, her sleeves and layered skirts billowing around her like a cowl. Sebastian expected Aalia to walk swiftly past, but instead, kneeling dutifully at the old doyen's feet, she held the glass-worn eyes without flinching.

'I presume you are Lady Rayner? Then I place my restraint at your command.' Bending her turbaned head, Aalia kissed the spidery fingers.

'Never promise what you can't deliver, young lady.' Studying Aalia's bowed frame, Lady Rayner didn't move.

Sebastian shuffled, unsure of his duty. Aalia caught his eye and smiled.

'I'm of the opinion a promise isn't a command,' she said. 'Or perhaps I should lay my future in your hands.'

Caught in Aalia's lissom fingers, the liver-stained hand relaxed.

Sebastian couldn't fathom why Aalia met the old harridan so meekly. His confusion only mounted when Lady Rayner unfolded from her seat and, taking Aalia by the arm, smoothly steered her into a side chamber. He followed, but didn't enter the room, thinking his charge would do better to face Lady Rayner's inquisition alone. Leaning casually against the door-jamb, he watched where he couldn't be seen.

'Where did you beg the rags?' Lady Rayner pinched the cuff of Aalia's tailored sleeve.

Sebastian had gone with Aalia to collect her costume from *Cornucopia*'s store. From the perfect bulb of her turban to the sweep of her ankle-length coat, the scarlet velvet was couched in sunbursts of purest gold. Though its style favoured the Orient, the effect was simply breathtaking.

Aalia laughed, holding her arms to show better the costly threads. 'Jamie sends his love.'

As she spoke, the old lady buckled.

Aalia caught her by the arm and led towards a chair. When the woman was set comfortably, the singer knelt on the tiled floor, pressing against the silk brocade skirts.

'You shouldn't be so confident with your lies, young lady. My vagabond son never wasted a moment's thought on his family, therefore, we do not embrace his sentiments.' She traced a finger along Aalia's cheek, pausing at the curve of her lip.

'I found another profession, as you suggested.'

'It wasn't your profession I found wanting… you really should work on your English. You are, I see, the new sensation.'

'I do seem to struggle with the language… is it sensation or spectacle? You must be the judge.'

The old woman closed her eyes and rested her wrinkled cheek on Aalia's soft, turbaned head.

The sharp tap on his shoulder took Sebastian by surprise.

'What are you doing here, Sebastian? I thought you despised the court and its corps of careful deceivers.'

Sebastian knew to be cautious; his work depended on divining the dross from the flame. This petite and very pregnant lady had recently married the former Ambassador of Spain, but as plain Jane Dormer, she'd shared Edward Tudor's nursery while her father was tutor to the prince. And being raised in that rarefied circle brought her to the attention of Queen Mary. From the age of sixteen, she had faithfully served the mistress she soon came to worship. It was said the Duke of Feria begged Jane's hand in marriage, because he was enchanted by her simple piety. But gossip at court suggested charm wasn't entirely spiritual, Feria being of such an age she could readily be his daughter.

'Countess! I'm obliged to my uncle for putting me amongst the pigeons.' He tried to draw the young woman towards the outer hall, but she shook her head determinedly.

'Are they whispering?' She wore a composed form of smile.

Being wed to a noble Spaniard, who had made no secret why he abandoned Elizabeth's court as soon as his successor De Quadra had reached his posting, Jane had many motives for despising her new Queen. Now six months pregnant, she had begged almost daily to be released from her duties so she could join her husband abroad, but Elizabeth was dragging her heels. One of many reasons Sebastian knew he must be wary of this intrusion.

'I don't know what you mean!' He led her away from the door.

'Lady Rayner is a pedantic witch, who shows small concern for anyone lacking a title, yet here she is, placating the favours of a base-born troubadour. Next, she'll be cavorting with Romanies, mark my words.'

'You're very observant tonight, Countess,' he whispered.

'And you are very discreet. At least your uncle is loyal to the faith, shoring our cause on home ground.'

That the Countess was a dedicated Catholic was barely secret at court, but he didn't want to peddle his loyalty. 'Lord Scythan taught me to know my enemy, a motto which, I believe, proved useful during the last queen's reign.'

'You've grown almost as shrewd as your uncle. I can't imagine why he thought you'd never make headway as a diplomat.'

'What diplomat?' Lady Rayner was behind them, steered on Aalia's arm.

The Countess nodded at the old woman, her voice sour. 'I'm surprised to find you in company with this chantress from India?'

Sebastian had always judged Jane Dormer a dutiful tongue-tied mouse, but her manner had changed since her mistress died. It had even been rumoured Elizabeth tried to have her arrested during the first week of her reign, a rumour he'd never been able to substantiate. However, it might explain the bitterness.

'My uncle had hopes I might aspire to such duties,' he lied.

The old lady took his arm, tiny fingers grasping at his elbow. 'Not with your reputation, young man! Handsome as your father but equally adept at hawking favours. Had I a daughter, I'd warn her to run.'

'Thank you, my lady, but any daughter of yours would likely inherit the Rayner spite; I'd need to sharpen my tongue every morning.'

'Boy! You do not own the wit to keep my house entertained.' And without waiting on his response, put out her twisted hand to be kissed.

He could hardly refuse, not with half her cronies whipping up a tempest with their fans. He bent dutifully. And briefly, in the flicker of candlelight, caught a glimpse of the carved beauty for which she was once famed.

The Countess de Feria hooked his other arm. 'It must be difficult to know where your true loyalties lay. Weren't you wounded at St. Quentin?'

He slipped her hold, not wanting to be drawn by the Countess's malice. He might say something he'd regret.

Turning to Lady Rayner, he bowed. 'I believe my father was once acquainted with your son, James Rayner? I hear he's carved an extraordinary career since joining the Company of St. Thomas.'

Aalia smiled. If she thought he didn't know, there was little in her eyes to reveal it. Lady Rayner pinched his arm. He mustn't forget who else was listening.

'On those rare occasions he corresponds, it's generally to beg gold from the family coffers. James rarely finds time for irrelevancies.' The wise eyes crinkled.

The Countess stepped back, shimmering in fury and over-starched lace.

'But he has built such an enviable reputation for conveying rare goods from the East.' She squinted at Aalia, desperate for some response.

Sebastian bit down an urge to march Aalia outside and leave the women to their differences. But then again, he wanted to learn more of James Rayner. He knew the merchant could likely triple his mother's great fortune just with the treasures he sent to London. However, it was widely supposed his business sprung from Istanbul, not India, and Sebastian couldn't wait to see his uncle's face when he brought that news to his door.

'Jamie loves to bargain.' The look Aalia threw him was not entirely serious. 'Yet, he rarely has time for friends, never mind writing letters, not even to his mother. We were going to see the Queen's pigeons. Would you like to join us?'

Sebastian thought he saw her wink. 'They're doves...' he started to argue.

'You two have met before?' The Countess glared at Aalia.

'Never before tonight,' Lady Rayner rimed.

Sebastian was convinced she lied, but she held onto his arm like a child.

'I was once introduced to your father, long before your simpering mother dropped you into the world. Which of his sins turned you away? I know the liberty of exile marks those of us who are left behind, and pray the men who bartered your father's life will never own a place in heaven.'

'You are marking the wrong target, madam, but pass my good wishes to father on the next occasion you meet.' He bowed and, turning on his heel, stormed off, spurred only by the shimmer of Aalia's smile.

SANCTUARY – 22nd Disclosure

Examine the motive before you argue the quest.

Piatro wasn't concerned by his long wait outside. The night air was sultry, and the palace gardens enchanting. He enjoyed the precisely laid borders, with their stubbled lattice frames, the heady scent of roses and the groan of illicit liaisons. People of rank were no different in their desires. Padruig had ordered him to bring Aalia to the Old Temple as soon as her performance ended, but when he arrived at the water gate, it was quickly made clear he had no permission to enter inside the palace. Unthwarted, he settled in a discreet hollow, near the entrance to the busy kitchens, teasing a delightful kitchen maid and stealing sweetmeats as she passed to and fro, whilst always keeping watch for Aalia.

'Those who dwell in doorways are either wanton or misplaced.'

The cultured voice was Spanish and spun from the shadow of a cropped topiary tree. But Piatro never doubted who was speaking.

'At court, the world is divided into those who are invited and their sycophants.' Piatro focused on the darkness, waiting for the man to stir. It seemed an age before the Jesuit took the bait and stepped into the light. The fine cut of his costume told Piatro he'd come as one of the invited. No expense spared for a loyal servant of Spain. Such a tailored doublet, brazil-dyed and edged in filigree lace and silver, would leave most gentlemen's funds in debit. And God's elegant soldier was armed, despite court protocol, with a type of sword which wasn't meant to be ornamental.

'A worthy observation, Kopernik, because that's exactly what you've become—a sycophant, smoothing the Company's indiscretions. How does that marry with your ambitions, with the merchant who bankrupted Danzig? You aspire to better, surely?'

'How well my reputation grows! I hardly need guess who informs you; William always embellished on the truth. However, if you've a price in mind, I'm quite prepared to listen.'

'Your loyalty does you justice.'

'I presume you're here on behalf of William?'

'I serve De Quadra, Spain's Ambassador to the court of Queen Elizabeth, as his secretary, but I serve first as a soldier of God.' He turned, looking towards the doors where a couple robed in black had just emerged. 'I see the girl has become the Court's favourite muse, but they will soon tire of her talents. The English are shy of such passion.'

'And what do you do on the days you're not acting the gentleman, Alvaro? Days when you seem to entertain very different morals.'

'Much like you, Piatro, I take good care of my friends.'

'And being a gentleman precludes the need for labour.'

'Unlike Aalia's musicians, who flaunt their talents around the streets? Late of the Italian school, I think?'

The Jesuit's eyes were guarded by the wide brim of his hat, but his smile was wide and scathing.

'I've never enquired after references. Aalia summoned them all without my advice.'

'But a female soprano? Quite certainly she risks her reputation as a woman alone in such company?'

'That falls within the premise there's a reputation to protect! Measuring our conscripts against your ingratiating standards, Alvaro?'

'A godly woman must guard her reputation, if she hopes to secure good prospects.' His broad smile didn't falter.

'And this prospect provides a hearth and home and several mauling infants at the heels. That's somewhere out of tune with my ambitions.'

Alvaro removed his cap and, head polished like obsidian, tried to kiss her cheek.

Except Aalia ducked out of reach, laughing.

'William surely warned you I was born under an adverse star. Domestic creature I am not.'

She attempted to step further away, except Alvaro grabbed her arm.

Piatro intervened. 'I've come to take her to Padruig and he was hoping to meet before breakfast.'

'Which rather deflates any sense of euphoria... my apologies, it seems another interview awaits. I trust you enjoyed the baptism?'

Before the Spaniard could answer, the kitchen door flew open, and the flighty maid giggled and kicked up her skirts as she flounced past.

Soft mist clung to the river like a shroud. Dipping beside the water-steps, the four-oared Company boat held ready. Gull sat beside another cauled oarsman, and Piatro held his temper until the boat pulled out into the current, and they were well out of earshot of the palace.

He dropped Aalia's arm and set his resentment loose.

'When, in all your wanderings, have you had time to attend a baptism?'

She was bent over the side, running her fingers through treacle-brown water.

'Didn't you speak with the messenger?' Aalia didn't turn her head as she spoke. 'I wanted to warn Padruig... Alvaro tried to stop me on my way to find Tom's sister.'

Gull drew on the oar and looked up hesitantly. 'I met with Drake because the Master wasn't at the Old Temple when he came with your message...'

She didn't allow his excuses. 'Isn't it curious how Alvaro was at the Palace tonight? How did he know I would come? I shouldn't be tempted to play dice with him, Piatro. Just be thankful I arrived before he could match your price.'

Piatro allowed her spite, putting up his finger to defer Gull's response. 'Tonight, I'm unimpeachable. Besides, I've nowhere else to be with *Cornucopia* gone.'

Then she turned and met his gaze. 'Gone where? Aren't we paying Marron enough?'

'Padruig's orders. He wanted *Cornucopia* hidden because he fears the city might impound her. Young Drake's acting as pilot; said he knew a good place to hide.'

Gull looked at Piatro with a question in his eyes, but said nothing, and for a long time, the only sound was the sculling of oars.

Piatro was half-asleep when Aalia spoke again.

'Do you ever pine for home, Meester Kopernik? For the sound of Polish tongues and remembered dreams of childhood?'

She used his formal title, and the breach left him disturbed.

'Padruig wasn't to be dissuaded.' He tried to apologise.

'Such very schemes of magic ignited,' she whispered, staring into the water, her fingers white in the spray. And when she looked up, he was suddenly afraid.

'I never felt I belonged anywhere,' he said truthfully.

'But your family would take you back.'

'Otar once said you are what you believe you can be, no more and no less.'

'He also said we must pay the price for our dreams, which appears rather apt tonight.' And lifting her fingers, she shook them dry and smiled.

'We could get lost downriver, if Mister Gull would oblige?'

'Thank you. When next I need excuses, I shall remember to apply elsewhere.'

They arrived at the Old Temple's arched water-gate within the hour, despite a turning tide. Gull guided the boat into the vaulted boathouse which let inside the river wall. While he stowed the oars, Piatro hammered on the bolted inner door. It seemed an age before he heard footsteps approach, and it was only when he turned to voice his frustration, he discovered

Aalia had fainted. He checked her pulse, astonished to realise she wasn't pretending.

Padruig opened the door. Without a word, he placed his lantern on the wet flagstones and gently pulled at Aalia's hood. The glazed light revealed deeply bruised shadows.

'You let her continue in this state?'

'I'm not her keeper!' It had been a very long day.

'Surely you can judge such matters? I expect better from you, Kopernik. Pick her up and follow me.'

He led through a damp, curved tunnel, which emerged in the small courtyard where Gull kept his garden. They crossed into a long corridor, before climbing a short flight of stairs. At the top was a simple, white-washed room, almost square, with a bleached wooden floor and several bed-frames lined against the wall.

'This is our infirmary.' The Master unrolled a mattress, and, taking linen from a cupboard, efficiently made-up a bed.

Piatro laid Aalia down gently. 'I was told you wanted to see her as soon as she finished her performance, and that you would take no excuses.'

The Master didn't answer. He pulled off her head-dress and ran his fingers gently through Aalia's hair, then lifted and squeezed her hand, watching for any reaction. Finally, he unhooked the tight-buttoned neck of her tunic and pulled the lawn shirt open.

'The injury doesn't appear serious. There's a swelling the size of a duck egg on the back of her head. She probably expected her turban would hide any blood.'

'I thought she only had a ducking.'

'Can't she swim?'

'Like a fish.'

'Drake said Sebastian saved her from drowning, which hardly makes sense, if she can swim.'

He removed her tunic, gently unlacing the shirt, when he stopped and brought the light closer.

'Do you have any idea when was she stabbed?'

The blood on her sleeve was fresh.

'God no! Except… when she came back to the boat yesterday, she asked for Andreas… then said the cut didn't warrant a bandage.' Remembering her anger, Piatro realised the deception. *Damn the precious dice.*

Then, the Irishman hauled him outside by the collar and ordered him to wait in his study.

It was two daunting hours before Piatro was dismissed. Padruig demanded to know every detail of their actions from the moment *Cornucopia* had arrived. Aalia had always delighted in making diversions, but during this headlong chase to catch her brother, something crucial had changed. And they'd all failed to notice her recklessness. Padruig made it clear how her actions had threatened the Company and placed them all in danger. Tom was dead, and although they had no proof, they must suspect it was on Alvaro's order. And if he was capable of murdering William's oldest friend, there was clearly no boundary to his ambition.

Dissecting their incompetence, weighing their failings, Padruig ruled until Aalia was completely recovered, nobody left the Old Temple. Skulking towards his new quarters, Piatro considered the Master's measures and wondered if he really believed he could harness her vagrant spirit. But then, he'd never lived in India.

Padruig spent the rest of the night in vigil, although latterly, his head nodded with fatigue. After dismissing the merchant, he sent Gull to the Savoy to engage one of the sisters to wash and care for the girl. Such needs required a woman's touch.

Through it all, the girl remained senseless. And Padruig was concerned, knowing some wounds never heal. She'd been surrounded by men chosen for their abilities, yet not one of them recognised how far she'd over-reached her limit.

While the sister dressed the girl's wound, he stood outside the door. But the old woman called him back, gentle eyes grave, when she found the old scars. Did Scythan see them; was that why he wanted to prevent her performance? During the night, as he sat in vigil beside the bed, Aalia cried out, child-like in her sleep. Except the time had passed when he could afford to behave like an anxious father, otherwise the girl would never learn to accept his authority.

Georgiou, or Blemydes, depending on acquaintance, was waiting in the refectory sprawled along a bench. A wooden platter piled with bread and cheese was balanced on his knees.

He'd woken hungry.

The candle guttered as the Master passed into the room, grey eyes hooded from lack of sleep.

'Her middle name is never,' Georgiou said.

'I understand. But while she continues to fly headlong into trouble, without notifying anyone else of her plans, what can I do, other than lock her inside the Old Temple?'

'That's very ambitious. It's worth remembering she smiles before she bites.'

'Thank you, but I'm not a fool. Can you tell me anything which might curb her disobedience?'

Taking an apple from the store, Padruig squatted beside Georgiou, quartering the fruit with his pocket-knife.

'You understand she came because blood is thicker than water, but having deserted her dreams, her life, she learns this boy is not truly her brother. I think she continues, out of love. And love, they tell me, is blind. But you knew these things already.' He stabbed the knife into the table. 'Knew he was a bastard; knew he was tainted.'

'You think she didn't suspect this already?' He met Georgiou's angry eyes. 'You know her far better than me. Who is Aalia? What does she want? Then you may convince me not to keep her confined!'

'When I first joined St. Thomas, she was still a child. Sometimes, I'd see her when I visited Otar, but then, he took away her to Padua… they were gone almost a year. Until *Cornucopia* was chartered, I wasn't even sure she was back in India.'

'You know William better?'

'We trained together. He was a good… an exceptional swordsman, nearly took my arm off once in practise. He can be brutal…' Georgiou re-filled his cup. 'Not someone who enjoys book learning, he always left his sister… I mean, Aalia… to speak for him. They were inseparable, until Otar took her away.'

'You suspect he wanted to separate them?'

Georgiou's head came up. 'Otar knew they were not blood-kin?'

'And was sworn to secrecy. The Company takes in many orphans, but William is different. And now, he's become a pawn in a deadly game. If we do not stop him soon, we could also lose Aalia, and I cannot allow that to happen.'

Padruig returned to Aalia's bedside a little after dawn. She lay on top of the covers, fragile as snow, glaring at the sister.

'Did you offer last rites?' she snapped, as soon as he entered the room.

Always a need to shock. He sent the poor nurse away, leaving Gull to plead their apologies. Taking the woman's place, Padruig felt the girl's rebellious eyes. But he was learning; her intellect was instinctive, and the need to hurt disquieting, but both were used like armour, hiding her inner hurt.

'Don't push me, child. I've been forced to extend my tolerance ever since you arrived. Any further charity will require a higher cost.'

'For you, perhaps… as the guilty party, I remain free of charge.'

He needed a means of restraint which didn't forfeit her trust entirely. 'You think that's a fair epitaph for your grave? Or, perhaps, it better suits Tom's?'

It was meant to hurt. And she blinked back tears, glaring at the wall behind his head, and he regretted the plain, wooden cross pinned there.

'Despite what you believe, I have never acted randomly,' she spoke quietly.

'You think so? Death steals many legends.'

To control emotion was possible, with discipline, but containing every hurt… that he couldn't condone. She'd been devoted to Tom. He wasn't merely William's friend. This void, this lack of feeling, was a plain indication of her instability. He must shake her from this isolation, and he could not afford to be kind.

'I made it clear I was to be consulted on every facet of this enterprise. I am assuming, judging by the state of the wound, it happened during your meeting with William? Not merely did you chase your own interests, but you enrolled the help of two young men, who've no obligation other than your bidding. For that alone, I would hold you here in chains! But you compound your actions by drawing the attention of one of England's ablest statesman. If Lord Bedford knew our secrets, he could condemn every member of this Company and earn the reward of a royal pension.'

'I am acquainted with the facts; it is you who applies the conditions.'

He would have struck her then, except her fingers tightened on the linen sheet, one slight proof she was listening.

'You let Piatro and Georgiou suffer the consequences, while nothing was achieved, except your warned our enemy of your presence and made him wise to our plans. Is that how Otar taught you?'

She propped herself up slowly in an effort to meet his gaze. 'I was under the impression you needed me for bait. William didn't intend to hurt me. It was meant as a warning that he couldn't show weakness in front of his men. Scythan's physician provided ample dressings.' She stumbled on her brother's name but otherwise showed no remorse.

Padruig was losing. The rebel eyes told him that.

She leaned closer, shaking with the effort. 'I had to speak to Tom's sister. To ask what she knows of his past… a small hope, but surely worth trying. I didn't realise Alvaro wanted the ring… that must be why Tom was killed.'

Padruig kept his voice steady. 'What ring?'

The sheet stirred from her tightened grip. 'It was a gift from William's mother. Tom wore it on a cord round his neck. He said it had no value; it was just a signet ring. But I teased William, not thinking…'

'Alvaro would kill for it!' He grabbed her hands, every facet of his mind racing. 'Did you ever see this ring?'

'Tom gave it to me, after St. Katherine's. I was wearing it when I fell from the boat, and now, it's gone. And don't ask me where, because I really don't know.'

'Aalia, that isn't your fault.' Gently, he curled her hands inside his own. 'But if you can remember what the ring looked like, enough for Gull to draw an image, it might help our cause.'

She flinched, tearing her hands away. 'Why not draw Tom, too! Something to carve on his grave. I'm sure his sister would appreciate the gesture.'

'A thoroughly infantile response deserves an equally infantile punishment. You will remain here, in this room, until I give permission for you to leave. As the only patient in our infirmary, you will have constant supervision, of that, I can promise.'

He stood so quickly his hem disturbed the dust, and it danced like a wraith round his feet. And soft against his chest, he felt his own silver cross stir. Almost, for the first time in many years… he'd very nearly lost his temper.

'Can you not judge me on my own resources?' Her eyes were closed.

'What do you mean? As a woman? You set these terms by your actions.' He made a point of watching her hands. 'Shall we recount these honestly, one at a time?' It was a mistake, offering her a challenge, and he knew it immediately.

Aalia jumped from the bed.

The linen fell softly, pooling on the floor, just in time to cushion her fall. Studying her motionless form, he made no effort to lift Aalia, but went and woke Gull to attend. Only, and much later, did he forgive himself. The girl had been anything other than meek.

SANCTUARY – 23rd Disclosure

It is a sin to defy the law, because law is the principal function of state, but the interpretation of law is subject to reasonable debate.

I t was to his wife's displeasure the Earl of Bedford was meting out his anger on the servants. The bells of St. Dunstan's rang noon as he passed through the front door on his return from the legal wharf and, stepping inside his house, his children were running wild on the stairs and not a servant in sight thought to stay them. Of course, it had frayed what remained of his temper.

Closing the library door, Francis set out to weigh what he'd learned during his busy morning. He'd attended a fractious meeting, as demanded by the idiot in charge of taxes and tithes, following complaints about *Cornucopia*. Only when he arrived did he learn the ship in question had gone, and although he had to agree it was unlawful for her to sail without permit, there was little he could do when the vessel was nowhere in sight. More than a little annoyed that he'd been summoned to such an impotent meeting when he had such little time to spare, he was making his excuses to leave when he caught sight of the name which had brought the damning charges. That the Spaniard Alvaro wanted Mortimer to impose the full weight of law was worth Bedford's closer interest, and he promised to look into the matter, though it wasn't to appease Sir Andrew.

On making enquiries along the wharf, he discovered another potent fact. Namely, the measure of loyalty *Cornucopia*'s musicians had inspired in everyone he met. If it came to gathering evidence, and any laws had been broken, they would struggle to find a witness outside Spanish pay. Not a soul who worked the quay was willing to offer an insight into the affray or point any blame towards the Company of St. Thomas.

He was departing from the Custom House when he met his godson Drake searching for Pilot Solomon. The lad had nothing but praise for *Cornucopia* and, propped against the forged quay gates, took time to explain what made her so unique. Much of the engineering was new to his understanding, such as the housing on the fore-deck which held a magnetic compass. The lad also commented how there was little ordnance on board, which seemed most improbable, given the great distance they'd travelled. Could they have sold their guns up river before entering London? Watching his godson's eyes burn with enthusiasm merely compounded his suspicions. Were they missing something critical?

Mortimer had also been impressed by the sumptuous living quarters, thinking it went some way to explaining why her officers stayed with the ship. Although sailing under the banner of St Thomas, he suspected Padruig wasn't fully informed about everything they had brought. Otherwise, they would have carried barrels of pepper and spice. And according to Mortimer, who earned his keep through meddling, Sir Martin Bowes, Master of Goldsmiths, shared his concerns, because the merchant Kopernik couldn't clarify who owned the exceptional diamonds he wanted to sell. For all he knew, they could be dealing with a very sophisticated band of thieves.

Being a meticulous man, Bedford penned detailed lists of these ambiguities before cautiously burning them. Having committed the most pressing points to memory, he made yet another list deciding what actions to best take. Then, seeking a more qualified head, he penned a coded missive to Thomas Gresham, English agent in the Low Countries, because if anyone could supply him with details about trade in diamonds Gresham was likely his best source, but he could hardly expect a swift answer.

Perhaps the real question was whether the unusual girl called Aalia was actually sanctioned by St. Thomas. Putting everything in perspective, this one point required better clarity. Pushing his list inside his pocket, he decided to go for a short walk to enjoy the fine summer morning, and meantime, call by the Old Temple.

The dry heat of midsummer burnished the sand-covered Strand. Bedford was thankful the house of St. Thomas wasn't far from his home in Covent Garden. He'd passed many times without once being curious what lay behind the crumbling grey walls, but the entrance proved evasive, and it was only after a second circumference he discovered a low-beamed door hidden behind an ivy veil. He thought the building had likely been a monastery, but then wondered how it had avoided old King Henry's plunderers. He knew St. Thomas was highly regarded in the city, and not merely for the exceptional goods they traded. He needed little persuading of their medicinal skills, Padruig had become his wife's new hero, but the Company had long provided free lessons in writing and grammar to help ambitious apprentices. In fact, it was likely not a few high-ranking guildsmen owed their success to St. Thomas. But the Company were eminently cautious, like many who steered through difficult times. Tentative in its achievements, his family also followed the path of jurisprudence.

Bending his head to descend the shallow steps, he pulled on the bell chain firmly. Being a private mission, he'd dismissed his usual retainers and taken the precaution of dressing in modest travelling gear. His leather jerkin had hardened through lack of recent wear, although his wife suggested the discomfort could be better attributed to lack of exercise, which was harsh but probably fair.

'Sir?' A young man's face peered through the door's iron grid.

'I would like to see Padruig Fitzgerald? My name is Francis Russell.' He felt embarrassed, having come without invitation.

The heavy door swung open smoothly. 'My Lord Bedford, it is our honour. My name is Gull, please follow me.'

While Bedford waited for the young man to bolt the door, he had a slight concern his visit was anticipated, but then he needed to hurry to keep up with Gull's brisk pace as he followed through a warren of cold, empty passages. Despite being clothed like a lawyer's clerk, the lad had the decisive stride of an experienced man-at-arms.

They came to an open courtyard, and were half-way across the sun-drenched grass, when Bedford stopped to remark on a curious structure surrounding the well. The large, hexagonal tower was formed of metal cogs and pulleys, and a fantastical bronze pelican sat at the top. Gull smiled but didn't offer any explanation, as he ushered Bedford quickly to the opposite side of the green. There, they entered the shade of a vaulted cloister where ancient carvings twisted around every portal and pillar, but again, he wasn't allowed time to examine the workmanship before being rushed into another corridor. Eventually, they arrived at a small kitchen garden where his guide stopped to open a tall, metal-strapped door.

Bedford found himself inside a white-walled chamber, bathed in searing light and furnished sparingly with a heavy oak table and two unbroken settles extending the length of the room. On the far end of the table, balled like a cushion, a marmalade cat was sleeping, but otherwise, the room was empty. He walked over to the window and was admiring the exceptional view across the river when Aalia appeared.

'You fear a conspiracy? Don't be concerned. You have reached sanctity. St. Thomas's brokers failed sins... have you stroked Delos? He's blessed with excellent manners... for a feline.' Bare of foot and wraithlike, she could have been a street urchin, except she smelled of summer rain.

'Aalia, what an unexpected pleasure. I trust you are completely recovered? I came...' Before Bedford could finish, a rainbow-hued whirlwind swept into the room.

'Lord Bedford, I believe? Please ignore our oracle. She thrives on dismantling mortals. Delos understands. He spits whenever she comes near, and we do well to emulate the beast.'

The whirlwind dropped a mountain of rolled parchments onto the table, and with his arms free of their burden, looked up, showing a moon-like face equated by a pair of spectacles. Despite the limited stature, his presence filled the room, but any introduction was unnecessary, because his legend had preceded him.

'You are Doctor Steynbergh? I'd hoped to make your acquaintance. Thomas Thurland at the Savoy was keen to trumpet your praise. I believe you met him recently? He thinks you possess the kind of expertise currently wanting in England.'

Sweeping Delos from the table, Andreas Steynbergh pulled a bench from the wall and offered Bedford a seat.

'Really, sir, I must dispute his praise. Thurland, indeed, has vision, but my simple knowledge has limitations. He congratulated your foresight and believes anything is possible when you have a populace boasting a bevy of skills merely wanting purpose.' Pulling a chord deep inside his cloak, he discharged a further set of papers onto the table.

'That's entirely my point. We have time-served craftsmen lacking industry who can learn better means of manufacture. I've long been seeking an authority of your stature.' Bedford found it hard to conceal his enthusiasm.

Aalia sat between them and, smiling soulfully, placed one hand on Steynbergh's balding crown and the other on Bedford's cap, measuring the difference.

'You see, Andreas, they are wanting a man of your stature. Have the grace to accept before they grasp your deficiencies… or worse, they might even think to chart them?'

As she laid her hands on the table, Andreas reached deep inside his cloak and pulled out a measuring tape, then counted the distance between her fingers.

'I make it about half a chain?' Screwing up his eyes, he looked to Bedford.

'I think you could be right.' He nodded. 'Providing this chain is soundly forged from metals mined in this country.'

'You have my measure, sir, well-perceived. There is no question we can do business.'

It was better than a triumph for Bedford. For months, he'd been concerned England must rely on her continental allies to furnish iron for her foundries. To be truly independent, they needed to learn better means of mining native metals, and in a bid to gain such autonomy, he'd been making widespread enquiries. And the name Andreas Steynbergh had been the most frequent response.

SANCTUARY – 24ᵗʰ Disclosure

Know your weaknesses and favour your strengths.

It was very much later when Bedford was brought before the Master. He'd lost all sense of time until a servant arrived and laid out a simple meal of bread, cold meats, and cheeses. Steynbergh attempted to lead him to Padruig's chamber, but on reaching the grassy quadrangle, declared he wasn't sure which was the right way, having never made sense of the building's maze. Fortunately, Gull, who had first admitted him, happened to be nearby.

Padruig's room was as simple as the one he had just left, except far smaller, and its trio of stone-rimmed windows lay in the shadows of the courtyard. There were many books, piled in islands on the flag-stone floor, and a painted Venetian chair stood next to a square, wooden desk, which was pitted and stained with black ink.

Bedford sat in the chair while Gull served wine. After his steward had left the room, Padruig went sombre-faced to the door and turned the key, then fetched a three-legged stool and placed it beside the desk. As he squatted down, Bedford half expected a school-masterly reprimand from the gaunt Irishman.

'I met your father once.' Padruig's tone was disquieting. 'When you were a child at his feet.'

'I'm sorry, I don't remember. My father was a loyal servant to the Crown… as I try to be.'

'A man of honour and faith, he served during trying times.' Padruig put his hand to his heart, and his voice softened. 'Your son is growing stronger?'

'Thank you, yes. Today, you would hardly know he'd been sick. And Aalia seems to have recovered…'

'I've confined her to the Old Temple for the present. She's spirited, and strong enough to hide the effects of her injuries. I believe you directed her to Tom's sister. I wonder how you knew the woman.'

'When Aalia told me, his full name was Thomas Hampden and his sister called Sybil Penne, I might have thought it coincidence, but taken alongside the Chrism Bowl, I could hardly make any other assumption.'

'What Chrism Bowl?'

'She didn't tell you? Aalia found it hidden amongst this man Tom's belongings. Obviously, she recognised its value but not its pedigree. Beggar or thief, he had no right to it.'

'Again, if I may clarify, what Chrism Bowl, Lord Bedford?'

'The Chrism Bowl my father commissioned for the christening of Prince Edward. Sybil Penne was his nurse, so it's likely her brother stole it.'

The Irishman's composure flickered. 'Have you shown this bowl to anyone else?'

'Only my wife. Meg noticed how the engraving had been altered.'

Padruig leaned forward and touched Bedford's hand. 'I would like to tell you a story. It's a strange tale, about a man who was charged with doing the impossible.'

Bedford drew closer.

'A rich man's wife bore him a fine baby boy with healthy lungs and a strong heart. For many years, the rich man had prayed for an heir who could take charge of his vast estates. Although he had two daughters, his family were divided, and he hoped a son would bind them together. Imagine the celebrations when this first boy was born, the entire household gathered together as wine flowed freely.

'Few gave thought to his wife, as she lay in her chamber recovering from a long and difficult labour. But the birth pains didn't weaken. Soon after, his brother was born, healthy and strong as the first. The only witnesses to this second birth were a newly qualified physician and the dry-nurse.

'Truly, the mother was overjoyed but also full of fear. A second and equal heir would mean the estate must be divided. So, she begged the nurse to hide the newborn and tell no-one of his birth.'

'That's a remarkable story.' Bedford sat motionless.

'Now, by chance, the nurse had a brother nearby. A warden who had served the same master. She told him to hide the boy, and he refused, but then, he was brought to see the child's mother, and she begged him to take the child. That same night, he hid the baby with the dirty linen and brought him to a house of charity, hoping the mother would change her mind once recovered from the birth. But the mother died, and those who knew of the birth dare not reveal their secret.'

'Not to anyone?' Bedford was standing, his hands on the desk.

'No living soul shared the burden.' Padruig lowered his voice. 'For fear it would destroy the whole estate.'

'What happened to the child?'

'Fearing for both their lives, the soldier took him far away. He was a man of duty and wanted to serve his country well.'

'I see. And you are going to tell me this boy is now a man.'

'Head-strong as a young lion, he has his father's blood. But I'm not sure how the story will end, because this is merely his beginning.'

There was silence while Bedford absorbed Padruig's words. Then, 'You've met this young man?'

Padruig shook his head slowly. 'Not yet. I know he received a good education, equalling that of his sibling at home. But he was never given an account of his birth, nor can he possibly prove it.'

'I see.'

'I've said too much.' Padruig unfurled awkwardly. 'But the reason I've told this story is so you recognise the need for caution.'

'And why is Aalia concerned?'

The Irishman's voice was less steady. 'The two children were raised together, as though brother and sister. She will not allow him to be hurt.'

Bedford's heart was thumping like a drum. 'Where's the boy now?'

'Somewhere in London, last time I had news of him. He bears St. Thomas no loyalty.'

'What should I do with the Chrism Bowl…'

'Destroy it, Lord Bedford.'

Bedford's mind knitted with Padruig's gravity. 'You think the boy has learned of his birthright?'

Padruig shrugged his shoulders. 'I've told you what I know.'

The rumour Jane Seymour bore King Henry twins had simmered throughout Bedford's childhood, and his father never laughed when the servant's carolled those ditties. A loyal servant of the crown, he'd been preparing to leave the country when Edward Tudor had died, barely out of his childhood. The exigency of that mission had been clouded over by time.

His heart heavy, Bedford was glad to assist the Master of St. Thomas in finishing the finest jug of burgundy he'd tasted since his time in Geneva. He'd come to the Old Temple seeking clarity, but just like Pandora, wished he could return the contents into the jar and re-seal the broken wax. His wife had warned, before he left the house, trouble always dropped from the least expected source.

For the young gentleman keeping casual watch on the Old Temple, Lord Bedford's visit proved the only matter worth recounting. Calling at his uncle's London house later that evening, Sebastian held his tongue while Scythan ranted at not being informed sooner.

'You haven't seen the girl since Whitehall?' His voice levelled. 'You're certain she stays inside the Old Temple?'

'Guy told you she needed rest, and it makes sense… this is where she's safest. That building is like a fortress.'

'And the Indian soldier accused of the beggar's murder, where is he?' His uncle was re-lacing his ties; fingers nimble as a lace-maker's.

'At the Old Temple, along with the Polish merchant and that little German doctor.'

'They didn't sail with the boat?' His uncle turned sharply.

'No, *Cornucopia* sailed without them. Didn't you get my message?'

'No! You think the Spanish keep watch, too? Who do you think killed the beggar? Sir Andrew Mortimer couldn't see his nose in a looking glass never mind root out a murderer.'

'Sir Andrew muddles along. He sent officers to ask around the wharf without learning much, except a good number of beggars occupy the foreign quays, and until this month, the one-legged soldier wasn't one of them.'

Scythan had finished dressing and, picking up his gloves, went to the door.

'I suspect you have a point?' he said.

'Amongst the beggar's belongings, I noticed a uniform stitched with the livery of King Henry's personal guard. I showed it to the wardens at the Tower, and they told me a story about a sergeant of the guard called Tom Hampden, who disappeared in the middle of the night... left his post at Hampton Court without a word, and was never seen again. Anyway, I'll try and discover more.'

His uncle stood posed. 'Is that all?'

'You look delicious. Her Majesty will be ravished.' Sebastian winked. 'I'm going back to the city. Is there anything you need?'

'Not unless you can conjure a Eurydice for my Orpheus? The boy I've honed for the part is taken with fever.'

'I'm sure you can improvise.' Sebastian picked up a wide-brimmed cap and pulled it hard over his brow. 'I know of one soprano with a glowing reputation? Shame she's a woman.'

SANCTUARY – 25th Disclosure

Trade does not drive wisdom but provides purpose and possibilities.

The first deep rumble shook the pavilion like a clap of thunder. A diaphanous bellow of black powder hovered above the guns, as seconds later, another line fired, and then the next, shrouding the heath before sifting over the heavy-leafed hedges. Hanging like figures in a great Flanders tapestry, cosseted nobility watched from the gallery. London's Great Muster had begun.

The Earl of Bedford gave the signal for his captain to ride forward with the royal standard. It might not be a battle, but by God, he meant to impress. Europe would see that this "weak and unprepared" nation would not easily be trampled underfoot.

The Queen was speaking to her Master of Horse, and their laughter caught in the wind. Standing to her right was William Cecil, one hand shielding his eyes from the sun as he watched the ordered lines march downhill. Bedford had gathered every man of arms within two days' march of London, housed them overnight, fed them, and provided each with more than a ploughshare. The Tower arsenal was empty; in fact, every armoury within a hundred miles was empty, by order of Her Majesty, the Queen.

Discussing the shortfall in helmets, Meg suggested he look to Blackfriars, court storehouse for costume and pageantry. At this distance, the ambassadors would hardly know the difference, and the bright noon sun would do the rest.

Beyond the field, where the boundary was marked by red-coated wardens, a sea of restless heads gathered to watch the spectacle of England bearing arms.

Bedford's horse sneezed, catching the bit in its teeth. He drew the reins tighter and felt the beast relax. It wouldn't do to be thrown this early in the day, although it might amuse his wife.

Before the parade began, each corps was ordered to lead forward and present their arms to the gallery. The militia passing in front of the royal stand were clothed in buff-leather jerkins. He'd placed the Southwark faithfuls between a professional corps of hack-butters, more than adequately financed by the Guild of Clothiers, and his own blue-coated guard, steel helmets polished like silver.

The single, dull line turned to face the Queen in fading jacks and crusted boots, shoulder to shoulder, pikes pointing up like masts to the sun. And meticulous as the drum beat to a man, they bowed. Except one bold head, who raised his leather helmet, shook out his amber mane, and smiled.

Bedford spotted the contempt at fifty paces, but before he could act, the soldier bowed and stepped back into line. And the Queen had failed to notice; at least she turned to Cecil's comment and smiled, holding a fan to her face. By the time she looked back, the line had formed into squares, eight men across, marching to the beat of pipe and drum.

Looking up at the gallery, Bedford wondered who other might have noted the insolence. Cecil, without question, would store the observation without making any comment. Beside him, round face florid, Bacon was leaning from the gallery, his eyes following the line of pikes as they moved up through the field. Only Lord Scythan was looking directly at the Queen. Had anyone else noticed how the soldier, despite his lowly rank, was the very likeness of young King Edward? It was as if his ghost had come to haunt them on this auspicious day.

Bored, underrated, and unusually rebellious, Georgiou prised Kopernik from his bed early that same morning and badgered him into an outing. All the fears of Padruig begged better study; London had a reputation to prove, and they'd contained curiosity too long.

With the whole day given to do as they pleased, they recruited Gull for guide. It was his suggestion they made for Greenwich, where, apparently, an important muster was taking place.

A morning mist softened the water's edge, as they abandoned a city pricked like a pin-cushion in tall, masted spires. Church bells had been pealing since first light and lent their discordant melody to the sound of a thousand oars beating the mirrored water, as a flotilla of river-craft rowed on the Thames. By the time Gull drew up to the jetty near Greenwich, in the round-bellied skip they'd commandeered from the boathouse, sunlight was blanching the muddy shore, and the low hills of the horizon were ringed by an indigo sky.

The narrow pathway to the field was packed. Those newly arrived were being herded by crimson-coated wardens waving their long, silver-headed pikes, but the mood was generally affable, and the crowd buzzing in expectation. Few had seen a battle, never mind practised war.

While waiting for Gull to secure the boat, Georgiou and Piatro watched a small company of green-liveried archers practise firing at straw targets. The archer's banter carried from the field, arguing their prowess. Georgiou lifted the edge of his cloak and smiled.

Piatro glanced at his belt jealously. 'When did Aalia lend you her knife?'

'She said she had no need of it.' Georgiou fingered the hilt, making its vivid gems spark. 'William threw it at her when we met at the inn.'

'You thought he missed, but he didn't.' Piatro smiled at Georgiou's expression. 'No wonder she doesn't want it back. Did you know it has its own legend? The emeralds came from Russia; you could barter each stone for a ship.'

'Master Padruig doesn't approve of her wearing a weapon.'

'It isn't the weapon but the fact she's trained to use it the Master finds objectionable. Whatever weapon she chose would be equally unacceptable.'

'He is right; women do not make good soldiers.'

'I didn't expect you to side with the Master.'

'But Aalia wasn't raised to be a woman.' He drew in his breath at the look on Piatro's face. 'Otar never saw any reason to train his charges differently. The key to a rounded education, he said, is in giving opportunity to hone natural talents.'

'But Padruig hasn't yet had chance to witness Aalia's unwomanly skills. Did she ever challenge her brother?'

'They are evenly matched, I think, but sentiment hobbles her ability.'

'Which is why she surrendered the weapon to you? When, I ask, did Aalia learn humility?' Piatro's green eyes narrowed.

'She has been very dutiful of late… perhaps it's the blow to the head?'

'The Master worries the injury wasn't slight.' Gull had joined them, wet to the knees.

Georgiou married Piatro's glare. 'Aalia is strong. But while she is recovering, I think we've earned our day at leisure. There'll be little time to rest when Padruig discovers her true capacity for mayhem.'

Piatro and Georgiou squeezed through the crowd, as Gull led slowly towards the top of the ridge. His young face brimmed with pride at sight of the boldly coloured parade marching across the heath sparred by the stalwart beat of drums. This was to be the greatest gathering of soldiery England had ever witnessed during times of peace. But Georgiou and Piatro, not being Londoners, not being Englishmen, failed to engage with his excitement. Politely, they applauded the crackle of hackbuts and complimented the archer's skill. They didn't recognise the noble crests or famous pennants which marked the mounted officers or distinguish the regular uniforms of the proud militias.

Neither could they see the reason when a louder cheer rippled through the crowd, although someone near them cried, '*God Bless the King.*' Gull cramming his neck, went to ask those at the front. Coming back soon afterwards, his face was glowing redder than a royal warden's jacket, but he kept whatever he'd learned from Georgiou and Piatro. That news must keep for the Master.

SANCTUARY – 26th Disclosure

Owning the ability to read does not make you wise.

After three days of pleading, Padruig had finally allowed Aalia to enter inside the library. Enclosed like a beating heart within the rambling Old Temple, its vaults of ranked wisdom seemed fair compensation to her enforced confinement. Except half-way through the afternoon, Padruig felt the pangs of remorse and decided he must join her.

'I appreciate this is not an easy surrender.' He softly closed the heavy oak door.

She'd thrown open the shutters, a woman's touch, and golden sunlight exposed the voracity of St. Thomas's storehouse. The orderly shelves appeared less daunting when bathed, as they were, in natural light. But it also exposed the dust and decay. This testimony to his life's work where Padruig preferred to spend his days would be first victim if he failed.

She was crouched on the flag-stones, despite their coldness, a large and pristine folio blanketing her knees. Fractured beams of sunlight danced across the floating pages as she looked up unwillingly, not masking her frustration.

Padruig felt the intruder. She gently closed the book and slid it onto the floor. Then, drawing her knees to her chest, sighed solemnly.

'But this is an armistice, surely! I've learned to grab comfort wherever I may find it.' Her smile was strange and awkward.

'You've been trying to achieve the impossible; don't be disappointed when you fail.' He squatted down beside her, ignoring the distress in his ancient bones.

'I'm not frustrated, just unwilling to fix my limits by your measure, Doctor Fitzgerald.' She watched him closely, eyes shining like sapphires.

He looked up to the lectern which towered above her head, carved with a host of ecstatic-faced angels. By his own rules, encouragement must take precedent over discipline.

'You occupy a remarkable position, Aalia, being the most gifted woman, I know.' He knew to study her hands not her face. 'You have talent and ability in abundance, but Otar advised I do as I see best! I cannot allow William to harm you again.'

She sat motionless. Her hair like molten butter, finger-tips pressed white against the precious bindings of his Mercator. And he continued, very gently.

'At every stage of life, you've been supported by the faculties of our sympathetic and, I believe, enlightened Company, but I need to stress nothing so far has prepared you for the enmity and envy of an English court. Rank is their driving force, and that is incontestably male and preferably inherited. It is on this premise, your nest-mate builds his hopes, and on this presumption, he will ultimately flounder.'

She tucked her hands from his sight and lifted her eyes. 'Otar warned you would deal premises with sweetmeats. How am I supposed to feel encouraged when you discharge me on account of my gender?' She pressed her lips into an artificial smile.

'You are acting the spoilt child! You are neither excluded nor rejected, but the nature of this venture has altered considerably since Otar gave you charge.'

'I,' she stood up smoothly, 'am acting not at all. If I appear spoilt, then assuredly it betrays my standards. Why put a good education to waste? I am what I am, a working model created by your ancient fraternity. But unlike these precious manuscripts, I do have the capacity to feel. William is my brother, and nothing else matters than drawing him out from the ruthless ambitions of Spain.' She turned to face the window, but Padruig had already seen what she wanted to hide.

'I will not administer your death warrant!' he bellowed.

She swung to face him, eyes wild with tears. And he steeled his heart, forcing his mind to obey, otherwise he had lost.

'My death sentence? Isn't that rather dramatic for a stoic soul like yours? Don't fret. I'll forgive your impossible standards, but Otar will receive twenty lashes in my prayers.' And she stretched like a cat before re-opening the Mercator. 'Interesting, his use of geometry... Otar wasn't specially impressed by his manners... But then, Duisburg is a lifetime away from India.'

SANCTUARY – 27th Disclosure

Understanding is honed by putting knowledge to the test.

The heady scent of musk-rose pervaded every breath in Mrs. Penne's borrowed garden. Sticky with bees and humming with summer, the Countess of Bedford sat with her back to the sun, wishing she could shake off her gabled headdress and run barefoot over the smooth, hand-cut grass. It was a fabled garden; sewn from the seeds of Italian fantasies. King Henry had no doubt wooed his latest love under the self-same arbour, but that thought was hardly helpful today.

The graceful apartment behind the royal Palace of Hampton Court had been provided to the king's old nurse for the remainder of her natural life. She didn't use the rooms in winter, preferring her own small residence in Little Missenden, but during high summer, she could enjoy the gardens and combine her knitting with her memories.

Sybil Penne, a round-bodied matron with warm, chestnut eyes, had not been ungracious. A creature of the court, she knew her place. But neither had she been very forthcoming. In the heat of an airless afternoon, they took several turns around the dry fountains while Meg listened patiently as the gentle-mannered woman counted her many blessings. Princess Elizabeth had been the sweetest, gentlest child, she repeated. As servant to her current whims, Meg wasn't truly convinced of her memories.

On the subject of her brother Tom, she was more than reticent. He'd been gone away so long, a stranger he remained. Then, Meg unwrapped the Chrism Bowl, and sunlight spurred the windows of enamel to spark its colours. The woman fell silent and traced the line of engraving, *To Obey and Serve,* moving her finger slowly along the rim. She placed it in her lap and smothered the precious silver under skeins of bright green wool. Her kind eyes narrowed.

'Why did Tom bring it back? What a silly thing to do.' And she described her brother, such a sentimental soul, gracious, handsome even, if you'd met him as a young man. He could have married well, had he married.

Meg allowed the woman her tears. There was no urgency to her mission, and her oarsmen were no doubt enjoying their rest.

A servant brought them wine. A tall, bluff-faced young man, he clung to the gate until Meg marched firmly across and dismissed him. He was bold for a house-servant, throwing a mischievous smile, which she found disrespectful. But it wasn't time to make a scene, and the old nurse didn't seem to take note.

'No kinder lady graced these rooms... I never heard her speak a bad word, not against anyone. And pious, she praised God on her death-bed for giving her riches she never deserved. Jane Seymour was the finest queen England never knew.'

'You served her here, at the palace?'

'I was engaged during her confinement by my cousin, Lady Sidney.' She touched the Bowl as though it came fresh from the oven. 'Not an easy birth, she had too many days of torment while physicians gathered at her bed, mumbling their concerns... It wouldn't do to lose both the queen and prince! But one of the younger doctors had been recently schooled in Padua... he showed so much compassion, I thought he might be a priest. He said they must ease the birth; even suggested there might be more than one baby. But the others wouldn't consider their failings, and he lacked for authority.'

'You were present at the birth?' Meg touched her hand, willing out each word.

'No! I wasn't permitted. They brought me the tiny prince to wash and dress... he was fair as his mother, perfect... I'd not yet finished, when the king burst through the door and took him in his arms, bellowing down the hall like a rutting stag. He couldn't wait to show his new son to the world.'

'And the queen's physicians followed, all except the young one... he worried for the queen. I was in the nursery when he came and put his head round the door and asked for my assistance. When I entered the queen's chamber, I thought the very worst; she was white as a newborn lamb. But the second baby came easy.' Sybil palmed her hands around the bowl. 'This was her gift, his Chrism Bowl.'

'It's very beautiful.' Meg exhaled deeply.

'You see… if it had been a girl, there wouldn't have been such dilemma. But another boy? An equal to rival the throne? The queen begged us that the king should never know.'

'So, you took the second babe and hid him?'

'Of course, we refused, at first. The poor woman was weak… but her mind never waivered. She said the king would have the newborn smothered, and she must save his soul that burden. We were to name him William.' She squeezed Meg's hand hard. 'We hid him before anyone else came. Never have I been so afraid… we packed him in the laundry basket and went by way of the servant's passages. We didn't know what to do next, so I went to find my brother. Tom's duties as a warden meant he often came into the royal apartments. Tom was horrified. He sent the young doctor immediately to plead again with the queen, to try to alter her heart. Except it was too late; the king was at her bedside.'

Meg's heart beat against her bodice like a drum. 'What was this young doctor's name?'

Sybil's wimple flew up, brown eyes rimed with fear. 'I had my duties to attend, and by morning, they were gone. Not a day passes when I don't wish they'd left me my Tom.'

'The young doctor's name, Mrs. Penne, can you remember?'

'Would that I could forget, Lady Bedford. His name was Jon Chambre, and he came from the North Country, but I couldn't say what town or place.'

SANCTUARY – 28th Disclosure

Mark new discoveries, but do not bellow them aloud.

The London house of Lady Maria Rayner was in utter disarray. Jaffa, jowled mastiff and tabletop poacher, had been absent from his post behind the kitchen door for the better part of the day, but it was only after Ella, Maria's devoted house-maid, searched the patterned gardens for "a third and final time," she truly began to panic. She sent the gardener to beat the outer grounds and ordered the groom to check inside the stables. Finally, she went down to the cellars, getting plastered in cobwebs and dust to no avail. The brute had simply vanished. By the time she came to her mistress's door in order to confess, Ella was close to tears. Taking a long breath, she was further mortified to hear someone on the other side was singing. It was a fact her mistress hated all forms of music.

The singing was interrupted by Lady Maria's crackled voice. 'I take it they pay well for these diversions?'

'I've never had to look for my keep, if that's what you're suggesting.' While the singer spoke, the lute continued playfully.

'I can't think Padruig approves. Perhaps you use witchcraft?'

'Now, there's a thought… but if guile can outwit your enemy, why risk using enchantments?'

'You count St. Thomas as your enemy?'

'The Company raised me. How can I possibly turn against them?' The bright tone deepened. 'Someone seems to be simpering at the door.'

Lady Maria crackled. 'Yes, Ella?'

Pushing open the heavy door, she peered from its shadow. 'Jaffa is gone. We've been looking everywhere…'

'He is here, Ella, under Mistress Aalia's feet.'

'But he hates…' Ella's freckled nose began to glow. 'That is… he doesn't like anyone except her ladyship. He bites, you know?' She glared disapprovingly at her ladyship's visitor.

Aalia's agile fingers caressed Jaffa's heavy jowls, and the feckless animal showed complete abdication of duty by rolling onto his back.

'Greetings, Ella. It seems Jaffa and I share a like temperament, except I only bite people I know.'

The singer's bare head was cropped, just like a boy's, but her gentle voice was definitely that of a woman. Still, with her ragamuffin clothes, Ella didn't think she could be suitable company for Lady Maria. Then, Aalia took her hand and kissed her calloused fingers. Like Ella was the lady. She looked to her mistress for guidance, but the singer ignored her ladyship's disagreeable expression.

'Oh dear! I think Ella sees through my disguise… I'm an infamous dog-napper, and your mistress and I were debating Jaffa's ransom. How much did we agree per paw?' Pulling a fine silver knife from her belt, she lifted one of Jaffa's huge pads while the silly great mastiff rolled at her feet and gazed on with dark, sanguine eyes.

Lady Maria lifted the point of her chin. 'Don't distress my servants, Aalia; I can't maintain this house without them.' And turning to the stricken Ella, added, 'Of course she's teasing you! That saintly face masks a mischievous spirit.'

The dowager went to the open door and beckoned her servant to leave.

'You may charm the very gods, Aalia, alongside my turncoat of a guard-dog, but unless you learn to respect lesser minds, we shall all suffer the consequences.'

Ella fled back downstairs to the kitchens, and wasted the better half of the day pouring her disapproval on the groom, the gardener, and finally the hens, locking them one and all inside their coop.

Since Aalia climbed like a common thief through her bedroom window, interrupting her afternoon nap, Maria Rayner had, by turn, been charmed and irritated. The girl had a remarkable talent for disturbing the tranquillity on which she based her days.

'Tell me again how you intend to lure William back to the fold?'

'If I could recover the lure, I would most certainly use it.' Aalia was wedged inside the window-seat, legs arched over the lute, looking down at the garden below. 'But I lost it in the river, and William is proving neither predictable nor meek.'

Rose bowers hung with memories were Maria's private indulgence, and the lavender borders were at their purple best. Her son James provided the rare cuttings.

'Padruig seems to think your brother has grown immune to your charms. You must find better bait and leave the others to do their duty; those less sensitive of the turncoat's heart.'

'Clearly you haven't had the pleasure of meeting William.'

'Padruig tells me he lacks for morals but has looks in plenty. Mark my words, when a man becomes hungry for power, he soon turns into a despot.'

'William doesn't want power. He wants England, and is currently incapable of understanding how the post came to be filled... such despicable hand of fate... by a woman. William holds a low opinion of women in general, but a woman as monarch, that's against nature and an utter disgrace... do you follow the poets?' She paused, waiting for an answer, but Lady Maria's face was set like stone. 'All right, we set aside the poets... if he'd arrived when his Spanish masters had hoped last year, he might even have succeeded. Therein lies the enemy... time... who possesses no higher master. Therefore, William's epitaph shall be written in blood. If I do little else, I must stop this madness before more people die. Did Piatro show you his diamonds? He is so conceited of his little gems.'

Maria Rayner wasn't fooled. Aalia's hands were hidden, and her study of the garden most convincing, but a deeper knowledge held true. Jamie had shown her the girl he adored through his frequent and unsparingly detailed letters.

'You love him, even when he destroys everything you hold sacred.'

Aalia didn't reply straightway but rippled her fingers across the lute, sifting the chords of a sad melody.

'You have a son who deserted his home and stole your heart to live abroad, yet gives you each day a reason to breath.'

Maria had long ago convinced her friends, her peers, she'd grown impervious to Jamie's exile. Aalia sliced through her armour without restraint, because when she spoke, she used his words and every careful action came laden with Jamie's mindful resolve, as though he sat in the room, guiding her hand.

'Jamie gave me you… and I do not intend to disregard your behaviour because...' She placed each word without the mask. 'You are the closest I will ever come to owning a grandchild.'

Through tears, she watched her meaning bite, revulsion fill Aalia's ashen face.

'I will not be loved!' She leapt from the window seat, splaying the lute on the floor. 'Don't you see? It threatens me more than a blade. Reserve these feelings for your true kin… while I convict Jamie for writing me into your sympathies.'

Aalia ran to the door, nearly throwing it from its hinges in her haste to escape. Maria listened as she fled along the gallery, footsteps soft as falling leaves. When the garden gate screeched shut, it wasn't merely Jaffa who pined.

SANCTUARY – 29th Disclosure

Be wary of ignorance and never cast swift judgement.

Aalia was being obstinate, and there was little point employing flattery. Not only was she immune, it would likely send her hissing from the room, just like Delos. Andreas had found her eventually, curled beneath the middle bay of windows in the Old Temple library. The lattice of patterned shadows spilled onto her head, hands, and the raw-skeined tunic which took his mind to India. He'd been sent to negotiate, a mark of Padruig's failure.

'Ask me again nicely,' she said, touching her tongue to her nose.

'I am always nice.' He gave a small pretence of being offended.

Knowing her mood, he'd brought his latest model of a pump engine, and setting it loose on the flagstones set the little cogs to whirl faster at each precise touch.

'As am I! Why spend your time making such toys?'

'To solve problems.'

He was proud of his model. It was easier to understand mechanisms in miniature. Aalia wasn't complicated, either, but the key to both was patience.

'So… where does all the water go after your engine pumps it upwards?' Her interest surprised him more than his vanity liked to admit.

'Where water always goes, back down… but not if we set an aqueduct to take it towards the nearest stream.'

'Then, surely, it diverts back inside your mine?' The machinery stopped with the obstruction of her smallest finger.

'Eventually… it's true we cannot stop nature following its course, but we can use the opportunity to dislodge God's bounty.' He moved his glasses back onto his nose.

'And if we rile against nature? Will God judge kindly?' With a flick of her finger, the cogs spun in reverse.

'No, Aalia. That you cannot change.' He took firm hold of both able hands.

'When Piatro went to the wharf yesterday, he saw William leaving on the *Santa Maria*, the same Spanish boat whose captain had lodged complaints about *Cornucopia*. Piatro discovers much by watching and listening. Yet while every instinct tells me we should be following behind William, Padruig demands we must remain in London. There's no sense to it.' Staring dry-eyed, she loosed her shivering hands. 'I thought I'd come to catch my brother, but Padruig refuses the chase.'

Andrea understood, and wrapping her tightly in his arms gave the only comfort required, one which came without words.

The dark blue liveried messenger would suffer no excuses; Doctor Padruig must attend on the Earl of Bedford directly. Padruig looked for his pack, but the servant assured him the child's fever hadn't returned. There were no instructions other than to bring him immediately to his master. In the brief time spent with Bedford, he'd learned the man was not given to hysterics. Such an abrupt command had to follow on the heels of reason.

The Countess of Bedford was at court, preparing her royal mistress for the latest sequence of feasting and diplomacy. The officious servant brought Padruig into a square, wood-panelled room hung with a low-beamed ceiling. A shelf was furnished with a selection of books of a kind most frequently published in Geneva, but pegged out on a panelled oblong table, prepared for frequent study, was a copy of one of the priceless charts Aalia had recklessly borrowed. On learning of Bedford's interest, Andreas had suggested they present him with the first completed map as a private thank you for his support. Padruig sincerely hoped it hadn't been misconstrued. It was never meant for a bribe.

While he waited, browsing the books, he realised the place of meeting had been chosen with absolute care—Bedford's methodical consideration being another symptom of his practical good sense. They seemed to share much in common.

'I must apologise for bringing you here so urgently, Master Padruig. Thank you for coming, I know you have much to attend.' Bedford, face drawn and bullish eyes troubled, came to stand next to Padruig. 'I'm expected at Greenwich this evening, but I need to discuss a rather critical dilemma which needs immediate response.'

Pacing the room deliberately, Bedford described in brief the essence of his wife's visit to Sybil Penne. As he finished his explanation, he returned to Padruig's side and nodded. 'I thought, and the Countess agreed, a woman's approach would be less troubling.'

'Mrs. Penne seems to have been very forthcoming after so many years of silence.' Padruig wondered what inducement was offered to make the nurse admit her secret, although certain the Countess would not threaten or intimidate. Then, perhaps, it was Tom's murder which had shaken his sister's resolve. Clearly Bedford believed her story; he looked like a man under sentence.

'I'm not questioning Mrs. Penne's loyalty, she acted in the heat of the moment and, perhaps, Queen Jane was not naïve in thinking Henry might murder a rival prince. But I need to know how was this secret discovered. And by Spain?'

Padruig had no answer. 'I have asked myself the same question since the boy arrived in London.'

'As you rightly warned me, William grows more brazen by the day. At the Great Muster, he made bold in front of the Queen.'

'Did Her Majesty acknowledge him?'

'Thankfully, she failed to notice.' Bedford sat down suddenly. 'You are certain there is no real evidence to support his claim.'

'Until you recognised the Chrism Bowl being exactly the same as that which your father presented to Prince Edward, I was certain nothing could prove the boy's past. May I see it?'

'That's my dilemma, Doctor Padruig. My wife took the Bowl to show Mrs. Penne. Unfortunately, while they were walking in the gardens, a young thief grabbed it from her hands and managed to escape.'

'You think the Countess was followed to Hampton Court?'

'No. The thief was already in attendance, disguised as a servant... from Meg's description, I believe it might have been William. He must have learned Sybil Penne was Tom's sister and taken a servant's part at Hampton Court. The other servants told Meg he'd only been there a couple of days, showing great interest in the king's old nurse. My wife raised the alarm, but...'

Padruig's mind was racing. Last night, during supper, when Kopernik blandly informed everyone he had seen William boarding a Spanish boat, he couldn't imagine what circumstance would make the lad leave the city. But here was such a reason; he'd found a means to prove his birth. He was searching for the doctor, Jon Chambre.

Bedford continued, 'I'm only thankful Sebastian Trentham escorted my wife to the palace, though he failed to catch the thief. You likely know the lad works under my orders? Spain simmers with conspiracy, but we couldn't fathom what schemes they were planning until you explained the story behind William. However, I never forget Sebastian is also his uncle's ward and, I suspect, balances the needs of two masters.'

'You don't trust Lord Scythan?' Padruig met Bedford's grave expression.

'I trust him as much as I'd trust any fox... but my wife has suggested Seb's smitten by your girl.'

'Aalia? I could warn him her charms wear thin on better acquaintance.'

'Just be grateful he came to me first. Mark my words; William is steered by men who grow ever more desperate. Irrefutable proof will draw him closer to the throne.'

'What do you want me to do?' Padruig closed his eyes, weighing his choices.

'Tomorrow, I will issue a warrant to arrest this "pretender." I wanted to give you time to send the girl away, back to India if you have means. I presume your boat can be made ready?' Bedford's heavy face was in earnest.

'Your godson, Drake, found us hidden moorings, but, yes, I believe *Cornucopia* can sail as soon as I give the order. But Aalia will not leave without William.'

'The boy is held in Spain's firm grasp, and while few suspect the measure of their conspiracy, Scythan's made a career by staying one boat ahead of the tide.'

'I'm grateful for your concern, Lord Bedford. And your trust, which I take with every risk perceived. I will begin preparations, and Aalia shall be sent away as soon as the caravel can be made ready.'

'In a couple of days, I leave for Berwick, but I've sent able men to make discreet enquiries about Jon Chambre. If he is alive, I will find him.'

'And silence him?' Padruig wasn't prepared to shoulder another death.

Bedford shook his head. 'We will hide him where Spain can never reach him.'

True to his word, and despite the late hour, Padruig dispatched Gull to Captain Marron immediately after returning to the Old Temple. The creeks of Kent would echo to Aalia's objections, but there was no longer any choice. The alternatives dared not be considered. He was back in the infirmary, packing phials of distilled oils to send for Otar's use, when he heard the river bell jangling. Gull hadn't yet returned and most of the household was asleep, so he sent Georgiou to unlock the gates, despite his failings with the language.

Waiting in the common-room, Padruig anticipated greeting Sebastian Trentham, brimming with feigned goodwill, but the crimson livery was born of golden unicorns and pampered lions. A sour-faced herald, Her Majesty's envoy, blithe with royal commands.

He demanded to speak with Mistress Aalia.

Padruig sent for wine and had Georgiou fetch the lacquer-wood chairs with their elegant cushions of damask silk. At least they could embrace formality without St. Thomas losing honour. But the tabard wouldn't be creased. The herald stood waiting with his face set in steel. When Aalia was eventually brought to the chamber, eyes heavy with sleep, she was dressed in the fine velvet tunic worn to ample effect at Whitehall, but instead of a turban, a simple skull-cap calmed her hair.

'Pretty, pretty.' Aalia came in spitting. 'Can we keep him?'

'Tush, child!' Padruig took her hand. 'He has a duty to perform.'

'Does it come in Latin… they like the dead tongues here. *Semper Eadem* gives any sin the seal of authority. Or why not quote regal France? *Dieu et mon droit;* they're fond of claiming England as one of their own lands.'

Georgiou laughed.

Padruig threw him a silent reprimand. 'The poor man wants his sleep as much as you. Behave, or I will call for a stick.'

'I'll lend you my sword,' she said, unrepentantly.

'You don't know why he's here yet, Aalia. The herald might bear good news.' He did not say, although it was in his heart, that bad news would have brought wardens.

The Queen's servant bowed, removed his cap, and bowed again. 'I am commanded to invite the minstrel named Aalia to attend Her Majesty's pleasure at Greenwich tomorrow noon, where she will perform in the company of Lord Scythan.'

Padruig had his hand over her mouth, before she could broadcast an answer. It hardly fitted with his plans either, but the herald came from the highest authority and could not be denied. Still, it was unfortunate they couldn't beg illness as an excuse. The Queen's herald had both eyes and ears, and would report the girl entirely recovered from her recent injury.

So, it was agreed. Despite Bedford's warning, despite Padruig's dark fears, Aalia would remain in England. And the scheming Lord Scythan be damned.

SANCTUARY – 30ᵗʰ Disclosure

In that there is always a beginning there must also be an end.

Henry VIII had favoured his Palace at Greenwich not least because it smothered the brunt of Tudor tantrums. The high surrounding walls concealed a tiltyard, where the king could pursue his favourite sports, and a wooded arbour stocked with songbirds, where he could pursue his favourite whores. Elizabeth, his youngest daughter, enjoyed its comforts, not least because it was where she was born, and amongst the sprawling parkland and clipped patterned gardens, she could meekly snub the foreign embassies intent on wooing her hand.

Pertinent of her treasury's resources, Elizabeth sent an army of carpenters to build a transitory banqueting hall from green-wood and canvas, replete with kitchens and grazing suites, where the diplomats and ambassadors could be duped of England's wealth. There was just time to commend the Master of Labour on his perspicacity before her first guests stepped into the bower-house later that July afternoon.

William Cecil had spent the morning trying his best to deflect her critical gaze. They walked side-by-side, examining the long, linen canopy decked inside and out with delicate pink wild roses.

'Didn't I stress the roses must be white or red.' Elizabeth's voice pitched uncomfortably high, and several palace servants, knowing her habits, scurried quickly past in their urgent desire to be elsewhere.

'Evidently, red is proving impossible.' He bowed.

As they passed, a row of young apprentices stood to attention in front of a tall yew hedge. Catching their master's eye, Cecil nodded and one lad came forward, dropped awkwardly onto his knees, and presented Her Majesty with a small, hide-skin box. Long regal fingers wrestled with the lid until, revealed in a nest of shavings, she discovered a gilded silver rose, perfectly true to nature except each curl of petal reflected the midday sun. Delighted, she gathered the masterpiece to her breast and patted the boy's mousey head.

Barely had the Queen and her minister passed beyond the yew boundary, when a whoop of sheer relief was heard, and from the corner of his eye, Cecil caught a cascade of caps rise above the hedge. In that same moment, a lute played and married with a bell-bright voice. A supple voice, distinguishable by its clarity.

'Aalia?' said the Queen, squinting at the rose. Engraved on the back of each solid petal were tiny curlicue letters.

'Lord Scythan insisted on testing her range. Apparently, he daren't trust she has sufficient practise of Italian form.'

'Does he truly think her a savage? Anyone with an ear may recognise a voice that's been honed by training. Tush…they've spelt my name wrong.' She waved the silver flower underneath his nose.

'Your Majesty knows I cannot read such tiny letters without spectacles.'

'E, L, I, S…or maybe Z is back to front?'

They'd reached a crossroads. Below them, at the farthest extent of the path, the steel-grey Thames flowed, fretted with myriad boats. Weighting the long thin jetty, where many of the invited would soon land, heady swags of marigold, lavender, and borage swayed on transitory arches. Content to see her instructions had been meticulously administered, Elizabeth turned and walked towards the palace. Strewing flowers and sweet herbs covered the winding path with bruised colours, and a mellow scent hung heavy in the warm humid air. Taking a diversion behind the high boundary hedge, they could listen to Scythan's rehearsal without being seen.

Aalia was carolling Proserpine's lament.

> *'Dear consort, since, compelled by love of thee,*
> *I left the light of Heaven serene,*
> *And came to reign in Hell, a sombre queen;*
> *The charm of tenderest sympathy*
> *Hath never yet had power to turn*
> *My stubborn heart, or draw forth tears from me.*
> *Now with desire for yon sweet voice I yearn;*
> *Nor is there aught so dear*
> *As that delight. Nay, be not stern*
> *To this one prayer! Relax they brows severe,*
> *And rest awhile with me that song to hear!'*

Without any obvious pause, Aalia spoke. 'Are you Orpheus or Pluto? Am I being raped or propositioned?'

Toned like a knife-blade, Scythan snapped a reply. 'Orpheus. I'm your husband. Try to remember you are the Goddess of Innocence.'

'I'll flutter my eyelashes and simper.'

There was a short silence, before Aalia sang another verse. Then, she stopped again. 'Or I could swoon; I've had good practise of late.'

'But can you sing and swoon? That takes particular skill! I'm concerned your costume doesn't fit properly. Perhaps we could pack it with cushions?'

'That's an engaging thought. Do you prefer your wife promiscuous?'

'Must you take pleasure in giving offence?'

There was another short silence, then the lute hummed, and Aalia chanted a verse in a higher key. *'Back, back to hell I'm drawn. My Orpheus, fare thee well!'*

Silence. The air hung as though drawing breath. Aalia continued speaking. 'Eurydice's remarkably erudite for a woman engulfed by the Underworld.'

'Turn back a page… to where your own solo begins.'

'This is ridiculous. What thinking creature would elect to screech through hell on any man's behalf?'

'I spend weeks rehearsing choristers to absolute perfection and a bout of summer fever reduces me to hire an ill-educated savage.'

'Sebastian said I came cheaper than a castrato. We could arrange things differently… I think I brought my knife.'

'You own a wicked tongue, young lady!' The Queen of England swept into the yew-framed theatre, heavy skirts trailing a sigh of lost summer.

"Your highness" and "My Lady" registered in close harmony, but only Scythan knelt, Aalia being squat on the grass with the belly of a lute resting on her knees.

'You are recovered well enough to perform this evening?' Elizabeth scrutinized the girl's face, while Aalia obligingly threw back her head. Except the movement dislodged the elaborate crown which had been balancing on her brow. The maze of silver wires, weighty with black-glass beads, sank slowly down her face and caught on her nose.

Aalia squinted through the filigree. 'The truth is…my head's the wrong shape for a crown… Perhaps Her Majesty knows the answer to my dilemma? How can the Queen of Hell also be Mistress of Innocence?'

'You're not expected to judge.' Scythan looked to Cecil for support, but being born cautious, particularly of poets, he shrugged at adding a comment.

'But then… how can I express Proserpine's emotion?' Aalia stroked the lute, looking down at the script. 'When all is said and done, and hell has frozen over, the whole cast join together for a jig. Who writes this rubbish?'

'I wrote this rub…performance.' Scythan rolled his eyes. 'You are required to sing, not question the morality.'

'What I sing I feel. How can I sing Proserpine's part if her part is perverted?'

'It's hardly your place to deride what greater minds respect.' Elizabeth took Scythan's side.

'Perhaps it helps to be Roman?' Aalia stated with absolute truth.

'Evidently, you are not.' Cecil laughed. 'What theme would you choose to entertain our guests?'

Aalia stroked the strings until they gathered in a tune. None of them knew the composer, but the poem was entirely familiar.

> *'Blame not my lute, for he must sound*
> *Of this or that as liketh me:*
> *For lack of wit the lute is bound*
> *To give such tunes as pleaseth me.*
> *Though my songs be somewhat strange,*
> *And speaks such words as touch thy change,*
> *Blame not my lute.*
> *Farewell, unknown, for though thou break*
> *My strings in spite with great disdain,*
> *Yet have I found out for thy sake*
> *Strings for to string my lute again.*
> *And if perchance this foolish rhyme*
> *Do make thee blush at any time,*
> *Blame not my lute.'*

Cecil poised in hard-learned discretion for the Queen's axe to fall.

'I expected exotic, never homespun.' Elizabeth's eyes burned like embers.

'Homespun maybe, but the poet has a passion that speaks to any heart.' And bending her head to re-tune the strings, Aalia failed to notice their absolute astonishment.

'How do you know Wyatt's work?' Scythan enquired, level-tongued.

'Through letters… Lady Rayner to her son James. He used them when he tutored us in English.' At last, catching their humour, she glanced up. 'Is the poet out of favour?'

'At court, he is rarely quoted.' The Queen's temper simmered. 'Although his words do not lack beauty.' And turning on her heel, she marched away so quickly, Cecil was obliged to run.

Scythan didn't speak until long after they'd gone. 'It's unfortunate Jamie didn't teach you discretion. Don't you know anything of Wyatt's life?'

'Only his words, and they are termed in loss.'

'And dedicated to the Queen's late mother.'

'Oh… blatantly indiscreet. I seem to have a knack for dredging up bad memories!' She was genuinely sorry.

'Learn to tread carefully, Aalia, or indiscretion will destroy you.'

Taking the wire crown in two firm hands, he lifted it gently from her face and balanced it on her head. She met his eyes, but before she could reply, they were interrupted again, this time by a party of children dressed as flowers of the field. Each carried a basket full of fruit and flowers, and they ran past strewing rose petals, marigolds, and lavender, infecting every step with their laughter.

Aalia removed the impossible crown and, leaning over the lute, sang Proserpine again, suffused in the rhythms she understood best. Scythan closed his eyes and did not open them again until she finished.

The morning had long passed noon, and he had many duties pressing. Taking the lute, he offered his hand without thinking.

'Why do you wear my ring?' Her grip was stubborn.

Slipped onto his little finger, it had remained fixed and, almost, forgotten. 'This was not, nor ever will be, your ring, young lady.' Tearing his hand from her grasp, he placed it behind his back. 'Can you even tell me what is written there?'

'Inside the band are entwined the letters H & I, and written either side the names, Edward and William. There is a motto, but I don't have the Latin to translate… and there are numbers I think, in the Roman style.'

'Do you know the crest?'

'It's a phoenix, rising out of flames.'

'Now, convince me why should you own it?' he barked.

She was close enough to touch. Close enough to feel the storm simmering in her soul.

'Because it belonged to a very dear friend.'

'Tom Hampden?' he pronounced the name with distaste.

'Sebastian told you that?' She had no reason to trust him.

'No! I went to see Lady Bedford, and she told me about St. Katherine's. But I know the Hampdens of old.' He held her eyes, looking for deceit. Or anger? Or perhaps Sebastian was right; she acted from the purest of motives.

Attempting to rise quickly, her feet became trapped in the plethora of skirts. Trapped, she held her head high.

'Why do you think he gave you the ring?' He thought it a simple question.

Drifting through the hedge came the frothy chanting of flower children.

Aalia looked away, biting her lip. 'What do you gain from owning it?'

Brindled in shadows her hair shone like golden silk.

'I'm curious, and… you… puzzle me, Aalia… I might even be concerned for your welfare.'

Her head turned back then, sea-blue eyes bewildered.

'Tom never wore it on his hand, that much I know. He came to London in search of my brother, and I followed. The ring has little value, except it belonged to someone I loved. Even if I argue my William is the same whose name is engraved on the band, I have nothing to prove it because Tom, who owned it, is dead.' Each word was bitten in earnest.

'The ring has no other provenance?'

'Any goldsmith could make such a ring. But since Tom's death, it seems to have gained substance, at least with the men who attacked me. I wonder if Lord Bedford has suffered as much by the Bowl.'

Scythan studied her carefully. 'What Bowl?'

'I wonder Sebastian didn't mention it? After Tom's death, I found an enamelled bowl hidden amongst his belongings. Lord Bedford said it was a Chrism Bowl.'

'You took this Bowl to the Earl?'

'No! He took it from me.' She was shaking. 'And whatever else remains for Tom's eulogy is lost in the River Thames.'

They'd already missed the first call. A messenger burst through the hedge, waving his arms in distress.

'Duty, they say, is a jealous mistress.' She took up the lute and gathered up the long skirts as if they were a shroud.

Scythan lifted the crown from the grass and suspended it over her head. 'And must be served in prudence. You do not have to pursue this course alone.'

Reaching for the crown, she laughed. 'What is a kingdom except for a crown? I'll make the costume fit, just direct me to your cushions. You'll have a Queen of Hell fit for Orpheus, but don't condemn me for being cynical. I was born under the light of an obstinate star.'

As evening settled beneath a wide, blushing sky, Elizabeth's untamed court gathered in the damascene arbours of Greenwich Palace. Dressed in their finery, they'd spent the best part of the afternoon at the tiltyard, watching the Queen's champion prove his worth. Emerging from the dust of that enclosure, the entire gathering mounted as one onto powdered snow-white horses and chased through the woods in an arc of fantastical splendour, arriving at the makeshift banqueting house with an edge to their appetites. The Queen, gowned in purple velvet, glowed bright as her coppery hair. No-one doubted her radiance as she walked among her guests, delighting them with her wit, and surprising them with her wisdom. Thus, the seeds of myth were sown. And when the trumpets sounded for dinner, she led her retinue under bowers of wild pink roses still heady with dew-born scent. There weren't enough tables, but her ladies-in-waiting could hardly object to sitting on the grass, bending the rims of their farthingales for the purpose of chastity.

While silver platters were delivered by yeoman guards, bareheaded and clothed in scarlet and gold, Scythan's musicians performed madrigals to an audience still sweating from the chase. And afterwards, before daylight faded completely, the gentlemen were invited to prove their skill at the marks. Instead of arrows, they opted for hackbuts. The ladies covered their ears and begged for gentler entertainment. They were not to be disappointed.

Scythan understood every essence of their needs, every nuance of their hunger. Into a bower illuminated by a thousand gilt torches, he brought tenors and contraltos, and Orpheus married Eurydice. It was fortunate Tragedy's part could be played from the shadows, where no-one might see Aalia read from the script. It was hardly her fault, having been elected the role solely by request of Her Majesty after hearing the rehearsal.

Harp, lute, and viol collaborated in mellow harmony as the ancient story unfurled. And with the ladies of the court cushioned on grass, it was prudent the youth playing Eurydice refused Aalia's offer of a tame snake. 'Georgiou's favourite pet; she keeps *Cornucopia* free of vermin.' Only Scythan comprehended she wasn't actually teasing.

The girl was in excellent voice; she could touch the highest notes with searing perfection, although she informed him at the outset the real challenge was keeping a straight face. Before the first act ended, the shepherds and nymphs were following her lead, despite the look he gave them. It was only when the second act began, and the Queen of the Underworld swept under the bower, that a different legend was born. The Aalia who emerged, swathed in night-black velvet, owned more than a seductive voice. The dresser they'd employed to pin the dress to fit, had drawn her rebellious hair into a chignon, and unveiled a very different muse.

The audience, practised, spoilt, and urbane, melted in her performance. Watching the courtly masks slip away, watching their hunger at play, Scythan understood how far Aalia's soul was betrayed. She'd meant the lackaday disguise, the boyish clothes, to always be her armour.

Whatever the cost, whatever the morality, he knew he had to find this brother she loved. Or the girl would be obliged to sacrifice her future, too.

SANCTUARY – 31st Disclosure

It is the responsibility of the Master of St. Thomas to warrant that his officers are given every opportunity to refute any allegation of disobedience before taking action.

As soon as the performance ended, Aalia had been meant to slip quietly away. Padruig had paid Francis Drake handsomely to ferry her down-river to the hidden creek where *Cornucopia* waited, fore-warned and ready to sail.

When the tide turned, the pilot's apprentice held tight to his mooring, despite the rush of departing guests. But Aalia did not come. The Master of St. Thomas had ordered him to wait all night, if he must, but dawn was breaking, and he didn't have another course to steer. He was deciding what he should do, when the Spanish ambassador's servant casually shouted the news that the King of France lay dying, scored in the eye by a lance. Not a soul at the palace would be sleeping tonight.

Finding a warden guarding the path which led out from the gardens, he asked if he could pass a message to his friend. On describing Aalia, the man laughed, refusing to take any payment, and told Drake to get home to his bed. It seemed the only solution, except he would head straight back to the Old Temple and hope Master Padruig didn't beat him for a fool.

The news from France had shaken the night of pleasure. Elizabeth hadn't yet been crowned a year and needed every friend she could muster in order to survive. Even Scythan feared the thought of Mary, adolescent Queen of Scots, ruling as Queen from the proud, and infinitely wealthy, house of France. Cecil, whose penitent heart found war a sin, might even be stirred into taking the field. They'd both served the crown from the shadows and learned to read the current as it changed.

The news that the King of France lay dying, felled by a loyal Scot, meant a new game was set to begin. All those sleepless nights spent on prising terms and treaties out of England's rivals would be tossed in disarray, because, as everyone knew, the Scottish Queen's uncles, proud and ambitious De Guises, had been writhing at the bit in their efforts to rule France. Now they had the crown within their grasp, with an anxious Pope nodding agreement. For every ambassador in London, the remainder of the night would be spent in composing expedient letters home.

Cecil could handle the politics; the man was like a chameleon. But he didn't have Scythan's instincts, didn't indulge his heart, if his head couldn't picture its reach. Aalia, who had breathed life into the dross of his creation, was the flaw he couldn't afford to set free. Given wind of an alternative, the French might willingly back William and have him crowned King of England, providing his Spanish backers could guarantee he'd stay loyal to the Catholic cause. Scythan's men, ordered to be discreet, caught the girl in a blanket and, trussed like a hunter's lure, kept her locked in his chamber. At what cost to their health, he only later discovered.

It took Scythan far longer than he anticipated to track down William Cecil. And then, the Queen's right hand was secluded in a moonlit arbour with Lord Bedford and his nephew, Sebastian. Not wishing to be accused of spying, Scythan called to announce his presence.

Bedford and Sebastian turned to leave but Cecil held them back.

'My Lord Scythan…you've delighted a remarkable assembly, my congratulations.' It was a rare compliment from a man known to dislike frippery.

'Her Highness was right to insist on Aalia for Proserpine,' he said.

'Her Majesty is seldom wrong. And even if she were, few would take pains to correct her.' The Queen's secretary smiled. 'But it has been suggested you didn't want this "troubadour" anywhere near your company?'

Scythan's nephew coughed.

'My principal's voice broke last week, leaving me in need of a soprano.' Scythan was carefully polite. 'What I refused to mentor was a woman for the part.'

'And Aalia would never serve willingly. What drew the bait, Scythan?' Bedford rubbed his chin and smiled.

'You've met her… perhaps I merely offered gold?'

'Enough, gentlemen.' Cecil put up his hands. 'You've obviously heard the news? There's a crisis looming. King Henri's death will place a pawn on the throne of France, and there is little doubt who will assume the mantle of power.'

'Surely we're ready to mount a strong defence. Isn't that why you ordered the Great Muster?' Scythan felt Bedford's eyes resting on his hand, and slipped the ring inside his pocket.

'It's hardly secret the French have readied their fleet. King Henri had been making veiled threats to challenge Elizabeth's legitimacy, but was waiting on Rome's blessing before announcing his daughter-in-law as rightful Queen of England.' Cecil spoke with gravity.

'But if they break the treaty recently conceded at Cateau-Cambrésis, Spain will be obliged to protect England, and Calais must be surrendered.' Scythan proved his understanding by specifying the flaw. He also knew the solution, but wanted to hear the facts from Cecil's lips.

'Not if they force us to take troops into Scotland,' Bedford answered, looking to Cecil for acknowledgement. 'The regent Queen Dowager is determined to crush reform, and the Lords of the Congregation are not equipped to defeat her French commander, d'Oysel. It takes more than ploughshares to match his mercenaries. As fellow Protestants, we'd prefer Scotland free of papists… but if we act openly, we invite the French fleet to set sail.'

Cecil drew them close. 'I'm told the people of Scotland want reform. They've grown weary of French garrisons and their costly demands. The Dowager is virtually a prisoner, while John Knox inflames the people to burn and pillage the monasteries. And driving Catholics out of Scotland might help secure the English Borderlands.'

Scythan played his hand impeccably. 'Which is why Lord Bedford is leaving for Berwick?'

Cecil nodded, his steady eyes implacable. 'To inspect the new defences. Lee has completed his commission and warns of particular concerns. He trusts Bedford will inspect the works honestly and report his findings to the Privy Council.'

'I wonder if I might seek Her Majesty's permission to join him in this review?' Scythan ignored Bedford's blatant stare. It wasn't the private interview he wanted, but given Cecil's consent, his motive for joining Bedford's party needn't be addressed.

'What will you do, Scythan, entertain the garrison in Berwick?' It was flippant, but proved Bedford might actually be ignorant of his true purpose. His nephew merely smiled.

Scythan shook out the lace of his cuffs with every indication of bored impatience. 'I promised Percy I'd pay him a visit, but if it should become necessary, I'll happily chant lullabies to the Scots.'

William Cecil watched them with a seasoned lawyer's fortitude. 'I will arrange the necessary permits, if you follow me to my chambers, Lord Scythan. The new Spanish ambassador is roaming somewhere in the orchard, I left him being entertained by Lady Sidney and her brother... perhaps you could honour them with your presence, Lord Bedford?'

THE BLOOD OF KINGS

ESCAPE – 1ˢᵗ Disclosure

Northumberland · July 1559

It fell about the Lammas-tide,

When the muir-men win their hay.

From the square roof of the keep, Nigel had his best view of the harbour. Of course, he kept vigil on the low hills surrounding the castle walls and made sure he knew every man within view. Ward Hinckley, chestnut head bare, was laying sandstone hedges up beside the river, and leaning on his crook beside him, Jobby Tait was jabbering for Warkworth.

Out of duty, Nigel counted every head of the Earl of Northumberland's great white cattle as they grazed on the lower pastures and scrutinised all herdsman as they brought up the new-mown hay. No Scot or Kerr was going to fool him with that old trick. Nigel knew the comings and goings of every resident in town, marking as he did each crossing of the stone-arched bridge spanning the glistening river. But he much preferred to watch the boats coursing in and out of the harbour, and there wasn't a day which passed where he didn't dream of sailing away with them.

Nigel could name every ship moored and guess its likely cargo. Jacky Wright had just returned on his dad's big hulk *The Doris* and brought his mam an orange. She'd set it in her window bay where anyone passing could see. Jacky said they tasted sweet, even better than the pippins which ripened on the baillie wall. Nigel often weighed his days on-guard at the keep as squandered, except that blissful morning a golden galleass limped up the estuary and steered into the harbour.

Stretching over the battlements, Nigel marked her from the moment she dropped her main-sails and steered towards land. She was obviously a foreigner, flying pennants brighter than church windows on every mast and easily three times the size of Master Wright's best carrack.

He sent Carter with the news but told him not to hurry. Father would be at his lunch, and the boat had yet to anchor. He had a moment's panic when he counted her gleaming bronze guns, but decided against ringing the bell, which was just as well, because his father came stomping up the back stairs yelling to anyone within earshot as far as he knew, Warkworth wasn't presently engaged in a war with Spain.

By the time they'd learned better, the level of hospitality meted out to the men of the *Santa Maria* had to be deftly underplayed. Despite his father's orders, Nigel's animated telling of the affair kept Alnwick entertained for weeks. But then, he was barely thirteen years old.

The Spanish had departed a scant three days when the next foreign party arrived. This time, Nigel's father went to greet them, noting a liberal pocket was at play by the sheer quantity of post horses. It was proving a remarkable week for Nigel.

Despite their exotic appearance, these foreigners hailed from London. Nigel watched his father study their papers, thinking they must be written in blood, such was his expression. It was the first time they'd seen the new royal crest. The Queen of England's special envoy stamped his feet on the stone tiles impatiently. Nigel had never seen a man dressed so fancy, but just as the novelty tickled his thoughts, the envoy's yellow-haired aide winked. And Nigel blushed from head to toe.

Even before his father could decipher their letters, the envoy began firing off questions.

'Tell me, boy… did any of the gentlemen who came off the Spanish boat offer you their name or title?'

The Royal envoy wore such a glut of flounces, they held Nigel's full attention, until his father coughed.

'Yes, most certainly, sir. The Captain was called Alvaro de Manríquez, and he had four noble quarterings on his family crest and spoke English "huelle." He said he was "highly exalted" in the service of his most Catholic Majesty King Philip of Spain, and that his master was well-disposed to his "poor compatriots in faith."'

Nigel's gift for mimicry was better received by the rest of his company. While the envoy stood sternly, with his hands behind his back, his youngest aide, the one who later sang like an angel, laughed, and shook his hand, saying it was better than an artist's sketch.

'What kind of gifts did they offer? Sweet wine, perhaps?' The aide seemed barely older than Nigel, and his voice was gentle and his manners kind.

'Father said it was too good for the men, anyway. They drink ale.'

'And they brought beer, too, I suppose?'

'Yes, sir! The quarter-master hasn't stood up straight since Sunday, and Father's up in arms 'cos he sold them half our rations.' He glanced towards his father. Looking like a man condemned, he nodded very slowly.

'You will have to purchase more provisions?' The envoy's tone was not kind.

'Oh, we've plenty, if you're fond of fish. There's a smokery in town, and Father has no problem drawing favour. Father says we can feed an army on fish; it's the granary that's wanting and…' This time, he avoided his father's eye.

'Do you know if there were any Englishmen in the party?' the aide interrupted.

Nigel's blush deepened. 'No! At least, I didn't meet anyone you'd say was English, but Becky at the Sun said she served a red-headed Scotsman who came ashore with the crew. She was that chuffed with his generosity, she telled it all about town. We rarely see Spanish gold here in Warkworth.'

And that was all they wanted. Nigel pleaded with his father to let him go as well, when the party left for Berwick next day. But his father said he was needed at Warkworth, being he was the next best person to entertain visitors while he was away.

It was the best news they'd heard since crossing the length of England. By sheer bloody chance, they'd almost netted William, despite not knowing where he was finally headed.

It had been a difficult journey even before Bedford's early departure at York. Scythan had kept his retinue small so they could travel north even faster. Riding sometimes at breakneck speed, never resting during daylight hours, Georgiou kept Aalia constantly in sight, just as Master Padruig ordered. Mostly, she behaved, though she couldn't resist sparring with Scythan whenever he came near. Even then, Georgiou wasn't warned.

Since the night a distraught Francis Drake had returned to the Old Temple without Aalia in hand, Georgiou's feet had barely touched the ground. Master Padruig had raced straight down to Greenwich and managed to get a servant to wake Bedford, although it was the middle of the night. That was when they discovered who was responsible for detaining Aalia. The Earl had immediately offered to approach Scythan on St. Thomas's behalf, but unfortunately, the disturbance had brought William Cecil running, and the Queen's secretary demanded to know why everyone was so concerned for a mere base-born minstrel. It was Bedford who pertinently explained his wife was absolutely convinced Her Majesty would hardly wish to lose a songstress of such rare talent.

But Scythan had proved beyond sense, and standing in front of the highest legal mind in England, they could hardly state their real reason, that Aalia was key to binding William's ambition.

That would betray all their secrets. Whatever Scythan's motive, Bedford doubted it was sincere, but he also had means to meddle and found a post for Georgiou, guarding the baggage train.

Before leaving London the following morning, Padruig had warned Georgiou to garner friends amongst Scythan's retinue, because Aalia would be impossible, of that he could be sure. He listened hard to their gossip at every turnpike and inn, learning little, except the land north of Newcastle was wholly infested with bandits the locals named *reivers,* and their reputation was such they'd as likely execute strangers as enquire about their business. It went some way to explaining why the hand-picked retinue carried such a wealth of arms. But while Scythan's relentless standards wore every man to the bone, Georgiou discovered they mostly respected him, despite the flounces and frippery, because he never ordered any one of them to do something he couldn't do himself.

Riding out of Warkworth in the first hour after sunrise, the small party, headed by Scythan, comprised of twenty-one men at arms, apart from the Keeper of Warkworth Castle. Georgiou took up the rear, while Aalia chose to ride close to Scythan but setting out onto the low, rolling hills, he paced his mount with something near pleasure. Better the wide blue Northumbrian skies than the narrow confinement of London. The rough road led as far from London as any could lead, but Georgiou had come to distrust that city, better the saddle and endless horizons.

Bedford had been reluctant to return to London.

They'd arrived in York during late afternoon, and Georgiou had been ordered to wait at the farriers while they prepared fresh horses. The hammering and dust of blacksmiths at work led him to opt for the yard, so he noticed Bedford hail the messenger as soon as he rode through the arch. Of course, they didn't discuss anything out in the street, but that hardly mattered; news spread like fire through York's narrow streets. Scotland was close to civil war. The Lords of the Congregation had attacked the Dowager's French garrisons and now openly begged Queen Elizabeth's help. Although the Scots might hate the English, these reformers hated Catholics more. Bedford's chief worry was the dispute would boil across the Border. He knew he must ensure the messenger reached Cecil quickly, however Scythan refused to oblige. Bedford was forced to leave them at York, handing his sealed orders to Scythan, and trusting Georgiou to protect the girl.

A ring of deep pink clouds girdled the round hills of the horizon when Scythan finally pulled up his horse and waited for Aalia. She'd made a point of trailing behind, and his patience was ready to snap. He'd warned already how they must reach Berwick before day-light faded completely. A competent rider, she'd never complained at the unrelenting pace, yet found delight in questioning his every command. They'd reached a ford on a stone-bedded river, which, despite being low, was treacherous with dark green moss. The rest of his party had crossed without mishap, but Aalia was biding her time, sitting on the opposite bank slowly unlacing her boots while Georgiou, her dark-skinned cohort, sat over her like a shadow.

'Why do you think his lordship turns pale whenever I mention Scotsmen?' Aalia kicked off her boots, and though Georgiou bent to take them, he didn't reply to her question. She continued anyway.

'Perhaps they, like us, are savages because they neither think nor act like an Englishman. Doesn't he look a little like Lord Kali on a feast day?'

Scythan caught Georgiou's eye, while Aalia fixed her attention on a pair of golden-winged buzzards wheeling overhead.

Surveying him from the opposite bank, Georgiou finally answered. 'You should know Lord Scythan was once Captain of King Edward's personal royal escort and highly experienced in matters military.'

Scythan shifted in his saddle just as Aalia kicked her mount to ford the river, splashing enough water to spray his clothes.

'And you trust the words of his lordship's paid lackeys?' She slid from her horse to paddle in the water.

'The river is deeper this side; shall I order one of my men to carry you?' Scythan turned to find the tail-end of his party waiting for his call.

'Should've spoken Spanish,' Georgiou said.

She spun to splash him as he crossed behind. 'But Lord Scythan is perfectly fluent in Spanish,' she said firmly, mounting the stirrups with her wet feet bare.

Scythan's horse skipped sideways, as Aalia kicked her horse forward, and jumped the bank in a single leap. Then, she reined in beside him.

Georgiou was still considering the revelation. 'But he didn't understand…' Breeching the river with similar skill, he fell silent at her frown.

'How you cursed him in London? He comprehended every dark insinuation, however the Queen's Acting Master of Revels has better things to attend to than prosecute your whims, Spanish or otherwise.' Ignoring the impatient frown of both men, she pulled up her hood and stifled the dandelion hair.

Scythan turned his horse and started towards his retinue. 'Berwick remains more than ten miles north, and I'd prefer we weren't caught out after dark. There are too many Scotsmen who forget where the Border ends and real law begins.'

As he cantered to the back of the line, he considered the girl had no option but to follow. She had nowhere to go, no friends in this wild country. And he would hand his coded orders to Ralph Sadler as soon as he reached Berwick and be free of the burden of duty. Sadler could be trusted and, with luck, might have gleaned news of Aalia's brother. It wasn't easy to hide a Spanish galleon along these shores. Apart from Berwick, the only other port which could service such a vessel lay in Scotland's waters.

'I wonder they'll have room to board us in Berwick? I hear the garrison lives in fear of being breached from within following the rumours of invasion.' Aalia was riding at his elbow.

'I trust they'll find space for Her Majesty's envoy, but you might have to bed down with the common soldiery, or seek privacy in a water-closet?'

'Don't be concerned on my behalf. Georgiou brought a tent.'

'A tent?' He turned, but she was perfectly serious.

'Canvas walls spare blushes. Not mine. Any vanity I owned has long been ground to dust, but Georgiou hates performing his ablutions in public. You've travelled this road before?'

Scythan didn't want to lose patience this late in the day. Nor did he turn his head.

'Far too often! You're very well-informed child. Have my servants been gossiping? Scotland has squabbled with England for as long as anyone remembers, but the situation is little improved by a local disregard for law. Border loyalties lay with whoever pays the highest ransom, and reivers require careful handling.'

'I thought you despised diplomacy.'

Snatching her bridle, he lowered his voice. 'You know why I've come to Berwick. Once your brother is found, I'll tear him apart.'

'Then, I will have to stop you.' Her eyes bled steel.

There wasn't time to argue. Twenty or more horses were thundering down the road from the north. He snapped a string of orders, as Nigel's father yelled out greetings. The standard at the front of the party held a greater authority than royalty here on the Borders. The proud Percy lion.

'Did we bring anything other than a flag of truce?' Aalia clung to his flank.

'I have rather a comely tabard to spare, if you'd like to take your turn as herald?' he hissed.

'Your porcupine crest doesn't do justice to my colouring.' She held his eye. 'What about Georgiou? He has a nice broad chest.'

'Does he have the necessary manners?'

'Trust him with anything but diplomacy… unless you want a fight?'

'The Earl of Northumberland prefers hunting to fighting, but let us gauge his mood; he might even invite us to the party.'

'What makes you think he's going to a party?' She held his eye, not slightly troubled by the ring of heavily armed men who surrounded them.

'Because Tom's wearing his best party clothes... See? He's polished his sword and sharpened his helmet.' Scythan greeted the square-faced man wearing a fur-lined cloak who was riding towards him. 'I presume Croft passed on our message?'

'And a fine time I've had finding you. Lucky for you, every rogue in the Borders is currently trading his spurs for the harvest.'

'Surely a mark of your success as Warden? Old Tunstall was keen to get to London and promote his part in the new treaty. Bedford decided he'd better give him an escort.'

'The Bishop has every need to prove his loyalty; he's a bloody two-faced crow. But Cecil will give him the reception he deserves. Is the Court maudlin? You haven't ventured this far north since my favourite auntie died.' The tough wiry face of the Earl of Northumberland grinned from ear to ear.

'Your auntie had a big heart, and it was a fine feast you laid, although mourning was never her colour. How is Anne? Blooming, I hear, and when is this baby due?'

Night had drawn in by the time Scythan's entourage came to the broad obsidian sweep of the River Tweed and clattered across the long wooden bridge under torchlight. It had been another tiring day in the saddle and the hour was close to midnight before the party of men gathered inside the sturdy fortress. With the outer gates firmly locked they were ordered to attend a final muster. Scythan's Captain, anxiously checking a third time, had the unfortunate duty of informing his lordship that Aalia, and her black-haired shadow, were currently missing from their ranks.

ESCAPE – 2nd Disclosure

The dir runs wild on hill and dale,
The birds fly wild from tree to tree;
But there is neither bread nor kale,
To fend my men and me.

That same night, Aalia and Georgiou spent pitched beneath the stars. Drawn to the light of a fire, and the distant rhythm of music, they found guarded hospitality amongst a tribe of Little Egyptians who were also journeying north using less travelled byways.

It had been easy to slip away from Scythan's grasp while his men were distracted, and their numbers swollen, by the arrival of the Earl of Northumberland. Shielded under the cloak of dusk, Aalia had driven her little mount into the heather-bound hills to the echo of Percy's greetings, and Georgiou didn't dare argue as they stumbled blindly through wiry heather and thorn.

But nobody followed. Soon, they slowed to a saner pace, and a marble-moon lit the wild hills like a lantern as they had trotted over rough pack trails, brushing aside the bracken and gorse. Half a night's hard riding, and their horses' hooves stumbling more and more frequently by the time they met the gypsy encampment.

The canvas hooped benders were set in a circle on the fringe of a coppiced wood and the acrid smell of smoke drew Aalia and Georgiou from the drover's path down towards the clearing. Although the headsman was wary, he let them share the fire. Then, Aalia flavoured his curiosity by tuning her voice to their songs. Unfurled by the heat of the fire, Georgiou dreamed of India. Indeed, the gypsy tongue had phrases which sounded very like Sanskrit, something he never expected to hear amongst these desolate hills. Yet, he worried their hosts were only waiting opportunity to slit their throats and made a solemn promise he would stay awake the remainder of the night.

A promise he failed to keep.

'Time to move, sleepyhead. A fox must run clear of the chase.' Water was dripping onto his face. Aalia's poised above him like a huntress, hair gleaming wet.

Georgiou sat up and immediately regretted the movement. 'My head's broken! Remind me what poison we were drinking last night?'

Cushioned on bog-moss, he hadn't lacked for comfort, but the cloak he'd used for a blanket smelt like an alehouse. He was considering the practicality of standing without floundering when he recognised a voice calling from the woods. No! It couldn't be.

In the cobalt sky above his head, a flock of ragged black crows swooped and cawed.

'No games, Aalia! My skull is split in two.'

She laid her ice-cold hand on his brow. 'You were imbibing the water-of-life.'

The same voice called again, but he didn't dare turn his head.

'They've made you an honorary gypsy based on that frown.' She laughed. 'Our hosts are on their way to crown some noble soul King of the Gypsies. It would have been rude to refuse such hospitality.'

He wiped water from his face. 'Have you been swimming?'

'As Eve once said to Adam, it is like Paradise here. These gypsies know most everything... wisdom born from aeons of wandering. I'm sure they'll have a cure for your broken head.' She straightened, combing her fingers through sodden fronds of hair. He'd learned never to trust that smile.

'You are bursting to tell me something.'

'Better we find friends in lowly places... and by the way, Piatro's here.'

ESCAPE – 3ʳᵈ Disclosure

I will not yield to a bracken bush,

Nor will I yet yield to a brier;

The fortress town of Berwick was seething. From the officer at the gate to the men-at-arms attending picket-duty, there spread an air of officious order rarely encountered, even in times of siege. Word passed through the town that some foreign spies had managed to pass through the Border city. No doubt they'd taken every opportunity to inspect Master Lee's newly-improved defences and sold their observations to Monsieur D'Oysel, marshal of the Queen Dowager's French army in Scotland. Now, the flamboyant gentleman, newly arrived from London, the one who had arrived long after dark the previous night, was stomping across the flagstones in the old commander's quarters, spewing a damning reproach on the whole exalted assembly.

Tom, being the present Earl of Northumberland, was raised in Border anarchy. Swiftly tried, and cheeks aflame, he directed the blame squarely to Berwick Fort's commander, an offcomer, being Herefordshire born. Sir James Croft, at forty, was blunt, unpretentious, and impatient to keep Scottish and English rivalries under military law. He wasn't prepared to have his abilities undermined by a young Percy, even if he was bloody *noblilis genere natus.*

Lord Scythan, elegantly poised in front of the hooded hearth, had yet to finish relaying the summary of his charges.

'It did not occur to either your guards or gate-keeper someone using privileges signed by His Most Catholic Majesty of Spain should first be interviewed by his commander? This authority never being questioned they are allowed to proceed into Scotland. I'm surprised they weren't offered an escort! It beggars belief, when the Privy Council specifically decreed we take no action either for or against the Lords of the Congregation. You've allowed a foreign envoy to pass unmarked through the most fortified town in England. What if they mean to liaise with the French Dowager, replete with plans of Berwick's latest defences!'

Croft narrowed his eyes and fixed on his accuser. 'Simon, we have no orders to detain Spanish couriers, and anyway, it's pure hearsay these gentlemen were carrying documents from the King of Spain to the Queen Dowager. They possessed lawful permits appertaining to their authority to trade. And besides that, as Northumberland has already argued, refusing safe passage might insult His Majesty King Philip.'

Sir James didn't add that Percy had gathered them round his table, sharing wine and victuals. Though he had many doubts regarding Percy's reliability, he drew the line at spelling them out to someone with Scythan's reputation.

'I'm sure you keep yourself well informed, James.' Scythan threw off his gloves. 'And, clearly, recognise the need for civil discretion, but I'd expect you to delay them at least a day or two; it's generally anticipated by such men.'

Scythan kept his fury barely sheathed as he berated their incompetence. It was the form of command he least enjoyed, raising his voice and yelling like a miscast fool. Lack of discipline he could forgive but not rank stupidity. However, he never let his temper burn out of control. Taming his emotions had taken many years of practice.

Tom Percy smarted at the humiliation, having never been tongue-whipped in a room packed with inferiors.

'Then again, Simon, we don't have any evidence to suggest these men were not who they claimed to be? Unless there's something you haven't told us.'

Scythan turned on his heel and paced slowly back to Percy. 'Why do you suppose the Privy Council felt it necessary to dispatch a special envoy? You think I came on a whim? I know you were expecting the Earl of Bedford, but that shouldn't mean you question my authority. God knows I would much prefer to be spoiling at court in good company. But...' He surveyed the room until his eye fixed on the mess of papers weighting the commander's desk. 'We know these men came north on the tail of news that Henri of France would soon reach his Maker. What brand of mischief should we expect if Philip enters an alliance with the French Dowager and her brothers?'

'Which makes it more likely these men were drawn by profit? Being first to bring news that the Dowager's daughter reigns in France would surely mean gold for the messenger.' Northumberland refused to back down.

'We are talking of power not vanity.' Simon deliberately dropped his voice low. 'Mary Stuart was destined to become queen from the moment she was born. Never forget she is the grandchild of Henry VIII's sister. In the eyes of every Catholic abroad, she has more than legitimate claim to England's throne. The De Guise family engineered every step of her ambition, and with Henri's death, have right and means to use Scotland as the sluice-gate to invasion.'

The room closed into silence. Scythan retrieved his cup from the desk and drained the bitter contents. Studying Percy's face, he wondered how far he was actually implicated. It had been decided, even before leaving London, that William might be steering towards a meeting with Northumberland. The family's allegiance to Rome had hardly gone un-noted. Meanwhile Scythan had no intention of confiding these suspicions to anyone in Berwick, particularly when its commanders were so clearly at loggerheads. His young Queen had declared she would learn from her father's mistakes and never trust the northern nobility. Faith was patently one thing these men did not have in common.

Blunt as his reputation, Sir James determined to chime his loyalty.

'We heard reports that King Henri of France had been struck in the eye during a tournament but there seemed every confidence he'd recover. If my Lord Northumberland received superior news, he did not choose to share it.'

The allegation made Percy's cheeks burn even brighter. Throwing himself into the commander's chair, he focused entirely on Scythan. 'Do you really think the Dowager's brothers will bring a greater army into Scotland?'

'The Dauphin dotes on his Scottish wife, and he's fifteen years old and weak. I'm told he treats Mary like an older sister. It wouldn't be difficult to take control of France; with the death of Henri, they have the crown under their fingertips.'

'Which is why the Habsburgs will be looking for means to stop their influence? For all we know, we've just sent the Dowager Queen of Scotland her assassin.' Percy's suggestion took Croft by surprise.

But Scythan had already considered the possibility. 'Really, Tom? The Habsburgs do not fear French rivalries, but they might use everything in their power to fan the flames; it suits Spain to have the French nobility fighting against each other... but murdering Marie de Guise of Scotland? I think not. Our orders are quite clear; do nothing to the detriment of Protestants in Scotland, but do not be seen to be helping them either. Whatever we may suspect about these Spaniards, we absolutely know them to be true Catholics.'

ESCAPE – 4th Disclosure

Johne cum kis me now, Johne cum kis me now,

Johne cum kis me by and by, And mak no mair adow.

Travelling north, disguised as a tinker, Piatro trailed two hundred dismal miles in Aalia and Georgiou's footsteps. Following Bedford's retinue, as instructed by Master Padruig, he tracked behind his friends without anyone suspecting he was near That he succeeded to do so efficiently was due in no small part to the perspicacity of his guide.

Scythan's abduction of Aalia had thrown St. Thomas into frenzy. Having waited on board *Cornucopia* all the long night, Piatro had returned to the Old Temple next day to find the Company's four-man barge ready at oar and the sanctified halls humming like a hive. Gull was already there, arms full of papers, too busy to answer his questions, but Padruig was in his chamber with Georgiou.

The Indian soldier was pacing the room, spitting out his fury in Urdu, while Padruig was packing books into banded wooden crates, his usually ordered desk strewn with torn papers and broken seals.

'We have a crisis.' Padruig's grey eyes flickered anxiously.

'That would be blatantly obvious.' Piatro said.

'I thought Scythan was merely ambitious for royal favour, but clearly he wants to meddle in our affairs. Did you inform any other living soul that William had left London?'

'No!' he had shouted. Then, remembering precisely what was at risk, he mended his humour. 'But it was hardly a secret along the wharf, and that sharp-eyed nephew of Scythan's hangs there daily for news.'

'I need you to follow them, Kopernik. Bedford has secured Georgiou a place in his retinue, but apart from lacking fluency in English, he doesn't know the land, and Andreas left the city yesterday.'

'I know. Bedford asked him to survey some old mine workings.' He managed to level the Master's look without flinching. 'Andreas told me what he was about, even gave me a copy of his maps in case he… got lost. It's a moot point, really, but we need to have some level of trust.'

'Steynbergh's undertaking is for the State, Piatro. It's hardly open for discussion, and his secrecy is not of my making!'

Piatro had wanted to argue, to tell him he bore no loyalty to this particular State, but Padruig's eye silenced his first answer.

'I will go and pack,' he said meekly.

Gull took Piatro to an inn called The Lion. It lay half a day's ride out of London on the Great North Road at a crossroads with a scattering of houses. The three-storied inn was perfectly placed for travellers, and by early evening, its chambers were packed, and there was barely room to breathe in the low-beamed room where bread and eels were being served. Behind the main building was a cobbled yard where a blacksmith was working, and line of carts and horses spilled into the lane as they waited to be stabled. Servants dodged between, cupping pots of ale and wooden plates of steaming food.

Gull took Padruig to wait on the grass-lined bank which faced the inn, beyond the grind of bustle. It was dusk before a lank-maned gypsy, stooped by a twisted shoulder, hobbled across the lane and slipped Gull a silver token bearing the Company of St. Thomas's seal. Gull confirmed the mark was true.

They squatted in the hay-store for privacy. During the panic which had followed Scythan taking Aalia, Padruig had found and instructed a crippled tinker to act as Piatro's guide. Gull explained the gypsy owed St. Thomas a blood-bond, but Romany tradition meant you didn't ask a man his name. Piatro studied his pitted face. The hooded eyes were wary, and his clothes and manner feral. He knew he had no choice except to trust him.

By noon the following day, Piatro was tired of making one-sided observations and almost reconciled to silence, when the gypsy started to sing. It began with mumbled verses, the choruses ripe with profanities, but better that than another mile of brooding silence. At the end of the day, he even offered his name, Toff, and by the middle of the third day, when the pace of Bedford's party unexpectedly slowed, Piatro taught him a Polish drinking song. While he wouldn't trust the tinker to mind his purse, he had to grant the man was tenacious and managed to keep close enough so Piatro could sometimes see his two friends but never so near they were noticed.

The road north was well-used and led through villages and towns which had grown prosperous from the trade of servicing travellers and baggage chains with their well-maintained bridges and over-priced inns. Toff had a gift for seeking out broken barns and empty buildings where they could rest overnight unseen, showing an initiative Piatro, and his bones, sometimes wished was lacking.

It was on the fourth afternoon they arrived in the city of York. Piatro anticipated they could spend the night at an inn, because Bedford's party would surely take a day or two to rest. As they crossed the stone-arched bridge and entered the city, he heard the first anxious whispers. A party had arrived from the Border with news that the North had reached a fevered pitch, and Scotland was close to civil war.

Toff discovered a soldier who was supping free at an inn in Gillygate by giving account of the troubles. He'd ridden post from Haddington in the retinue of the Most Worshipful Bishop Tunstall, and his opinion was nobody of sound mind should be heading towards the Border.

Piatro wasted no time in searching the cramped streets until he discovered the Earl of Bedford's billet. Finding King's Manor guarded like a fortress, he made a nuisance at the door until a guard escorted him inside. With the carved Lion of England dangling above his head, he managed to get an audience with Bedford.

'Scythan will not reconsider. The man thinks Aalia will entertain his friend, Northumberland. And Cecil knows this isn't the time to upset any nobles on the Border; he needs their alliance to keep the peace.'

'But, assuredly, you can't consider keeping your appointment in Berwick?' Piatro's head was boiling.

Speaking as if to a child, Bedford explained, 'No, I've already decided my duty lies with the Very Reverend Bishop. I must ensure Tunstall reaches Cecil without delay. I'm passing my orders to Lord Scythan.'

Standing in the high-beamed, polished hall, surrounded by the faded shields of every guild in York, Piatro felt his heart sink.

'You trust the Acting Master of Revels to shore up trouble? The man's a peacock. He lacks the wherewithal to control his servants, never mind organise an orderly defence of the realm.'

'You overstep the mark, sir! I hardly think you have the right to question my authority.' Bedford looked up and down the hollow hall. 'Lord Scythan has left York already, with a lesser retinue so they can travel north more quickly. He will meet the commander at Berwick and carry out my instructions, but his private arrangements are none of my affair. However, you can inform Master Padruig I gave Aalia the opportunity to return with my party, and she refused. Make of that what you will.'

After that terse meeting, Piatro was forced to abandon any hopes of sleeping in a real bed. Politics, he understood. England must be seen to be neutral, or France would have the excuse they needed to invade. If the Earl of Bedford appeared in Berwick, the most fortified town on the Border, it would simply add weight to the rumour that Queen Elizabeth was ready to support the Lords of the Congregation, because nothing could be more to England's advantage than having Scotland embrace the Protestant cause. Overtly, Lord Scythan wasn't recognised as such a blatant threat.

Gathering Toff and their horses, Piatro left the city within the hour. They were already half a day behind, and Scythan's small retinue could travel at a much faster pace. It was dark, and they were ducking under a gate-way, which protected a small stone bridge, when Toff noticed the first patrin. The ring of white pebbles was divided by a fine twig tied with a strand of grey wool; the very same shade as the Company cape Piatro was wearing.

They both understood the fragile message. Wherever the road diverted, or there was any question which way they should follow, they would find a similar patrin, because Georgiou knew Piatro would be following and also knew his capacity for observation.

Next evening, they crossed the broad River Tyne. They took a local ferry and landed just west of Newcastle's sombre walls, skirting low-lying marsh in order to avoid passing through the city. The sky was black before they found a place to rest, but Piatro slept soundly in the knowledge that Scythan, and therefore Aalia, were tucked safely in the city.

When they rejoined the road next morning, crossing patchwork fields golden with corn, the first patrin they found precipitated a heated argument with Toff. It was their first quarrel, but Piatro was sure the sign had been altered, because it was directing them away from the Great North Road, east, towards the sea. Such a diversion hardly made sense. But the gypsy was proved right when, not an hour later, they almost netted Scythan's party returning along the very same road. Watching from behind a farm stoop, Piatro recognised Aalia's uncapped mane.

They spent the rest of the day stalking the retinue's dust, but just as the sun rested on the range of low western hills, Toff stopped and dismounted, crouching near another grey-spun patrin. Piatro could still see the line of helmets from Scythan's retinue moving north and bawked at Toff's suggestion his friends had left the party. Faced with the prospect of scrambling through gorse and bracken just as darkness was falling, he argued the gypsy's reading.

Toff agreed they were probably less than ten miles from Berwick, Scythan's destination, but pointing to each stick and stone, he barked until his voice cracked, until Piatro surrendered though sheer bloody fatigue. A defeat he'd never imagined against a gypsy of limited words.

Although not entirely convinced, they tracked into the night. Given the lantern of a glowing moon, they pricked their way along the flanks of wild, low hills and, as the first blush of dawn warmed an uncluttered sky, dropped into a green pastured valley where a silver ribbon of river flowed out of a thicket of scrubby trees. Toff pointed to a feather of black smoke spinning above the woods and, dismounting from his pony, led towards a well-laid Romany camp.

Piatro's first gut-wrenching thought was he'd been deceived. Thankfully, being more than tired, he held his tongue. Because the dark-eyed tinker, stamping the feeling back into his feet, pointed to a small but distinct canvas tent set slightly apart from the circle of the Roma's domed benders. Discovering Georgiou alone, though asleep and snoring blissfully, Piatro braced his heart. But it didn't take long for Toff to track down Aalia, highly incensed but perfectly unharmed, swimming almost naked in the river. She wasn't enchanted by his "rescue," but at least he had the satisfaction of knowing his latest news would make the long journey worth every sore and blister.

'What did you say about Andreas?' She sat at the edge of the river, wet hair dripping down her cloak.

He coughed, glaring up at the sky. 'That he'd already left London. You may be surprised to learn the Company has other schemes that beckon. Schemes of more prosperous nature. Padruig had word of Scythan's meddling from Bedford. Have you met his wife? I like these English ladies; they know how to charm.'

Aalia poked out her tongue.

Bones aching, Piatro stretched to his full height. 'Apparently, the Countess has also been busy with our affairs… it's unfortunate this problem erupted just when the Goldsmiths were ready to bite… they like my pretty stones, and we need to make a profit. Do you think my English has improved? I'm going to get a drink. I'm parched.'

'Sit down, look me in the eye, and repeat after me… I cannot drink if my throat is cut.' Somehow, she had a knife in her hand.

'There's a letter, in my inside pocket.' Piatro unbuttoned his coat and gestured to the place where he habitually concealed his gems.

Knife smoothly sheathed, she removed the letter without comment, and breaking the wax seal, read quickly to the end. He knew its content word-for-word, paper being easily destroyed, if he should be detained. He knew Lady Bedford had learned the name of a man who could give testament to William's birthright, and her husband had managed to get a hint to this witness's whereabouts. What did a ring or Chrism bowl matter when it was irrefutable proof William required? The sort of proof a priest could provide. The man called Jon Chambre had taken holy orders soon after leaving royal service. Tunstall himself had taken his vows.

'Time to wake my escort.' Aalia was shivering.

Raising her damp head, she considered him thoughtfully, and something in her eyes tore Piatro to his soul. He tried to smile, shrugging his heavy shoulders, knowing he'd forgotten she was a woman, and therefore, mortal.

'Aalia, the Master was quite firm in his instructions; we must wait until William is safely under lock and key before seeking an interview with this priest.'

'But why? Now, we know the likely reason William travelled north!'

'William can't know where to find Jon Chambre; he could be searching for months. Besides, Padruig doesn't want you anywhere near your brother.'

Her shoulders braced as she leant forward. 'What do you think Will's been doing, except gathering proof of his birth? The Spanish may have offered him an opportunity, but he was raised and trained by St. Thomas. He's no fool. He'd never act without proof, no matter how resolute his masters. And Padruig underrates my brother, if he thinks otherwise. Of course, he's been seeking out those who had happened to be present when England's last King was born, because he's been told categorically, by an ordained and self-righteous authority, that he is Edward's twin!'

'Why didn't you say all this to Master Padruig?'

'Because the great man has been treating me like a leper. Tom understood what William was about. He knew four physicians attended the queen during the birth of Prince Edward. He discovered two had long since died, but then, found one still living in London... unfortunately, the poor man's mind had gone. However, he also discovered, from his servants, that William had already visited this doctor. Tom couldn't understand how he'd found the names of these witnesses. Very few people knew, and they were all in the royal circle. Then, he told me about a woman called Jane Dormer, who married a duke of Spain. Where exactly is this Sweetheart Abbey?'

'Near a town called Dumfries, inside Scotland, where we are not permitted to travel. For a Company founded on reason and knowledge, we seem to have failed in our calling.' He was tired, and Aalia's revelations made his head spin.

'But Piatro... as everyone and his brother keep telling me... I'm not able to join your illustrious fraternity. Having the bad sense to be born a woman, I'm merely the Devil's spawn.'

ESCAPE – 5th Disclosure

He belted on his good braid sword,
And to the field he ran;
But he forgot the helmet good,
That should have kept his brain.

During a summer without rain, the real storm was wanting. The wide Border skies filled with gathering clouds until, black steeped in grey, every track and by-way, every folded hillside, spewed in tides of gravelled mud. Travelling in any direction became impractical, as the barren landscape of sparsely clad hills and moss-laden gullies merged into an impenetrable bog.

The previous day they'd ridden, alongside their Romany hosts, to the loose-strung hamlet of Kirk Yetholm, where they met to crown a new king. Tucked into a forgotten valley that married England and Scotland, the low-roofed town was filled to bursting with this gathering of roaming families.

Aalia had earned their hosts' respect. There was never any question the girl could sing. And Toff, lulled by her chanting, barely left her side on the ride from Yeavering to Yetholm. Entering the boundary to the Meet, he bagged a well-sought pitch not far from the glass-clear river. But she insisted they proceed to Dumfries without stopping. And Toff, unpredictable as the weather, refused to forgo the party to guide them.

Piatro argued, folding his arms and stamping his feet. At which point, the tinker was almost loquacious, warning how Border folk held small loyalty to common law, and wouldn't hesitate to kill, whether or not it gained them a profit.

Aalia wasn't deterred by his warning. And when Georgiou sided with Aalia, Piatro admitted defeat, dowsing his temper in a sweat of common-sense. Deep down, he wanted to know the truth, too, and if this priest was the only witness, they had at least a chance of taking his testimony. They headed into the bleak western hills with neither guide nor map.

Steel-grey skies clung to the craggy hills ringing their view, shuttering their path, hampering progress. They'd been riding hard through wild hill country, when the storm finally broke, and were still at least a day's ride short of their destination. However, they could hardly outrun this downpour.

'Now I know why everything here is so damned green.' Georgiou sat shivering in his saddle, his bow-necked pony shuddering on rocks and stones.

Turning her head to commiserate, Aalia suddenly laughed. Clinging limpet-like to his crown was a knitted woollen bonnet fenced from the gypsies, and rivulets of emerald dye were dribbling down his face.

'And you are greener than most!' she said. 'Had we seen a place to shelter, I'd have been first to stop... but now... well, we can hardly get much wetter. Neither tree nor bush lines this Godforsaken trail. Scrawny sheep and reckless goats... that's all we've met since dawn.'

Piatro listened, muffled in his cloak. Aalia wouldn't rest when he had suggested, wouldn't let up the pace, despite the stormy skies.

Aalia noted his silence.

'Did anyone warn Piatro about reivers?' She glared at him, lifting up the fold of her sodden hood.

'The locals lack any custom for hospitality, Kopernik!' Georgiou hissed. 'Another reason, should we need it, why we should have sheltered in that last broken barn.' He kicked his horse, pointing to a rift in the hillside. 'That could be a cave. It might be worth exploring.'

Aalia peered through the sump of her hood. 'Damn the rain. Just this once I thought we'd actually forestall William. How much further 'til we reach Dumfries?'

'I will do a sortie.' Piatro sighed. 'If I know William, he'll be settled in some airy corridor, idling the hours until he can ride in comfort.'

Aalia held up her hand and stood high in her stirrups. She was peering down into the valley. 'That's why we must hurry, despite the rain. Have you seen how Georgiou's face is stained greener than grass?'

The soldier snatched off his cap, wrung out a wash of emerald water, and then pulled the shapeless form firmly over his dripping black hair.

Piatro didn't laugh. 'Getting to this priest before your brother hardly means we stop his plans.'

'It does, if we can alter his testament.' She reigned so abruptly, her short-legged horse almost stumbled.

Distinct as a drum-beat, despite the pounding rain, was a steady throb of hoof-beats. Many hoof-beats. Like a charge of cavalry.

Georgiou jumped from his horse and put a hand hard on the ground. 'At least twenty riders.' He rolled his eyes at Aalia. 'And, I suspect, a smaller party is coming round the other side of the hill?'

'It appears we are caught in a trap, my friends. That broken byre would be most welcome now.' Aalia dismounted. There was nowhere they could run. The ground to their right dropped into a sodden, black bog, and the other side was banked in a shale of loose, grey scree.

'Piatro! You will pass as a foreign emissary bound for the Scottish Court; those letters you carry are weighted with enough stately seals to impress any layman. Georgiou is your escort, and I, a novice servant, will humbly follow your lead.'

'As if anyone would ever believe that,' Piatro snapped.

He would have liked to argue, but a ragged corps of moss-troops charged towards them along the path at a pace far faster than was sane. They were well-armed. Most carried spindled lances and, bobbing to the trot, every head was dotted with a round, rusty helmet. As they drew closer, he could see that few wore any mail, and none had obvious badge or banner to proclaim a master's name.

Georgiou gave a warning cry, and Piatro turned to see another pack swooping from the other side of the hill. Drawing up next to Piatro and Aalia, he gave every indication the trap was a complete surprise.

As the men circled, blocking the narrow path, Aalia rifled through her leather pack-bag then let out a cry. Waved gallantly in her thin, right hand, was a fine curved blade of Indian steel. She ripped off her hood and turned to face their attackers, mortified boyish face framed in sopping silken hair.

'Aye, lad, ye can put away your sword. I think we can safely say you'se are outnumbered.' Climbing down from his fat-bellied pony, the headsman strolled slowly towards them.

Piatro stretched to his full height and, better than a head and shoulders taller, regarded the robber indignantly. 'The boy was only carrying out my orders, sir. May we offer you a truce?'

Swarthy-framed above short, bowed legs, the raider's bowl-shaped helmet cut an oblique angle across his craggy face. Setting Piatro with pin-prick eyes, he loosened the buckle under his chin and took off the steel bonnet, revealing the lack of one ear.

Turning to his men, he roared, 'Two men and a boy against my fifty? You huv me there, sir, I'll just tell my men to turn tail and run, if they have a care.'

From the corner of his eye, Piatro could see Aalia desperately holding her nose. The girl was insufferable. These men were hardly playing games. He took a deep breath and tried to gather a sense of authority, hoping to fulfil the role which Aalia had prescribed.

'You appear a man of good-sense. We're travelling from Melrose with letters for our brothers at New Abbey. You'll no doubt have news of the troubles? We've little to trade, beside our mounts, and they are weary and ragged. We own nothing that will earn you a profit.' Piatro held out his hand and fixed the odious man with his best effort of a glare. 'If we have to resist you, and your men, will suffer injuries far beyond our worth, so surely it is wiser to settle in a truce.'

'You'se obviously a foreigner, so maybes huvnae the gist, but it gaes like this… we takes everything you'se own, including said mounts and them's feel lucky that we leave whole. Take the boy first, Pollie!' He pointed out Aalia, shaking his fist.

Piatro almost sympathised as the ungainly lump called Pollie slid obediently from his pony. Large-boned and awkward, the lad didn't see the manoeuvre which felled him to his knees, because he was still attempting to draw his rusty sword out from its rain-swollen sheath. And long before he could muster his wits, Aalia swung her blade again, cutting clean through the belly of his oiled-leather jack, moving with a turn of speed which clearly beggared anything in the reiver's experience.

Dismay in his wide, brown eyes, Pollie almost managed to block her next strike by grabbing his lance in square, sturdy hands. But his coarse triumph faded as the arc of Aalia's blade sliced through the stout wooden shaft as if it was made of wax.

Pollie dropped both ends in bewilderment. On his knees, with Aalia's zealous blade pricking a hole in his throat, he splayed his muscular arms and surrendered.

Piatro threw the headsman a look of pure contempt.

'If this were a fair fight, amongst gentlemen, we'd settle with a duel, but would you dare pitch your best man against mine?'

Georgiou squared his shoulders at Piatro's nod. He stepped firmly forward, arms boldly folded, face fixed in dark determination. There was no hope of rescue, but Georgiou was honed and trained by St. Thomas. They couldn't ask for a better man to defend them.

The one-eared headsman's face creased into an uncertain smile. His men expected easy victory, and he couldn't afford to judge wrong. Rough-handed men required decisive leaders. Piatro could see the beaded eyes judging Georgiou's mysterious skill against his need of glory. Perhaps he was bewildered none of them showed fear, but before he could make a decision, a sharp voice hollered from the rear.

'Nay, Jock! Start with the wee blond lad. We'll beat him no bother, if you set him against our best man.'

Pollie didn't join the sniggering. Shoulders drooping, he waited for the call, blood blotting the collar of his shirt and running crimson down his ruined leather jack.

Studying the soft-faced boy holding the steel against Pollie's throat, Jock held up his hand. The lad had just been lucky, taking the big dumpling off-guard.

'Aye, we choose the lad against Com Daly, God bless his mortal soul. Com rode out for King James at Solway Moss, but we've forgiven him that lapse. Fist-to-hand with his faither's great beastie, I've ne'er seen him bettered.'

Piatro scowled at the ring of eager faces, swearing brutally in every language they didn't know, while Georgiou stood without moving, almond eyes fixed only on Aalia.

The parcel of men shuffled to make a space on the narrow path. The man called Com stepped through them like a fighting bull, and their wild roar carried him forward. Taller than any man amongst the gang, his father's two-handed sword was even taller. And because his ancient sword was forged from native iron, he needed both tight-flexed arms to swing it into action, but there was little doubt his first strike would be fatal.

Aalia considered Com as she dropped her guard on Pollie. She didn't step forward but waited, laying down her sword and taking from her belt a thin, short bladed knife. Then, she looked to Piatro, hooded eyes unblinking. He'd seen that look before. It wasn't fear or courage which made her bloody dangerous but a total lack of emotion. That was why Georgiou worried. Aalia liked to dance with death.

As another roar ripped from his fifty companions, Com flexed his huge shoulders in readiness to swing the decisive blow. Swifter than a hare, Aalia ran under the arc of his swing and struck with an assassin's precision. Her blade sliced like a razor through both his angled wrists, stemming the attack, cutting taut flesh like butter.

Com never found opportunity to swing his father's sword again. Blood spurted out of his severed veins, forming scarlet puddles at his feet. He sank to the ground, eyes bloated in disbelief.

The cheering floundered with his fall.

Piatro felt for his own sword and locked his fingers on the hilt. This rabble would want swift revenge, but with Georgiou at his side, they'd wound and maim as many as possible before succumbing to sheer numbers.

Then, Aalia showed her instinct for genius. Pressing Com to lie completely flat on the rain-sodden ground, she tore strips from the hem of her cloak and tied them tight around his upper arms. This was something St. Thomas demanded from even the slowest-witted apprentice. How to save life.

The flow of Com's blood faltered.

'How infinite is the power of God…' Aalia said quietly. 'And how insane man's iniquities! If you've done negotiating, Piatro perhaps you can help by holding down this compress ?'

'Yon Laddie's gay fast.' Jock suddenly found his tongue. 'But I didnae have him marked as Scots. That was a sight to see.'

'I'm only Scots by mis…apprehension.' Aalia's attention was fixed on her patient. 'Being raised by an Annan man.'

'Is that so? Wha's his name?' Jock tipped his head to better hear.

'James Rayner, I believe his mother was a Maxwell.' Raising busy eyes, she beckoned to Georgiou, reeling out a string of instructions in his birth-tongue.

Growling like a bear, he stowed the weapon he held ready and backed along the path to snatch Aalia's horse from the ruffian gripping its reins.

'Right enough, Maxwells are Borders folk! My brother married one, God save his mortal soul.' Jock pointed towards Georgiou. 'But where's that de'il hail frae?'

'Georgiou comes from the other end of infinity… a country called India.' Kneeling in the puddled dirt, she prised open the tiny metal box Georgiou had fetched from her pack. Com's weathered cheeks paled to ash as she took out a fine-tipped needle and with calm efficiency, started to stitch his torn flesh together under the astonished jurisdiction of fifty-one pairs of spellbound eyes. The silence was deafening.

ESCAPE – 6ᵗʰ Disclosure

And he that had a bonnie boy, Sent out his horse to grass;
And he that had not a bonnie boy, His ain servant he was.

Padruig had been summoned to appear before Jamie Rayner's autocratic mother. He'd had no word of Aalia or the men he sent to support her, and it didn't help his mood to know the woman would rant about the girl and criticise his actions. But the messenger, a stubborn girl, had burdened him with tears when he first refused. He cherished life at St. Thomas, not least for keeping him remote from womankind. He would blame Otar for forging this relationship, except his good friend was lodged far away, so Aalia must bear his curses, though she didn't come willingly to England.

He tried to harness his displeasure as he stepped between the graceful marble pillars which marked the entrance to the Rayner's London home. The grumble of a large dog answered his knock and grew fierce as the carved door slid open. Peering through the crack was the same young maid who had demanded his attendance.

'You are late,' she said, keeping the mastiff at bay with her knee.

'And you are rude.' Padruig was beyond courtesy.

He was led to the upper floor by way of an oak partitioned staircase. The elegant house had hardly been altered from the last time he called, when James had taken charge of the property after his father died. As the maid shuffled him through the house, he realised it had become a mausoleum. Grandiose in its day, and furnished with excellent taste, the broadloom tapestries showing the story of Moses were faded and dull, and the paintings washed-out. Two carved elephants guarded the upper hall, rosewood polished to the soft sheen of silk. Padruig found them of interest only because Aalia had failed to mention them, and the house contained few other treasures from India.

The dowager was surrounded by travelling boxes. At seventy years, she possessed a silvered grace. She'd arrived in London a widow, serving a Scottish queen, and suffered the forfeit of her family's estates for daring to fall in love with an Englishman. The passage of time had merely honed her bite.

'She's not as headstrong as you think, but very afraid you'll sanction William's death.'

'I presume we're speaking of Aalia, Lady Rayner?' He stood framed by the doorway, not moving.

'I'm too old for procrastination, Padruig. How do you expect to protect her from the vanities of her brother?'

'Before Lord Scythan interfered, I was ready to send her away. But you already know this.' He spoke firmly, keeping his eyes on her paper-thin face. 'I'm sure Aalia is quite able to act for herself.'

'Nonsense. The girl's been isolated from this world; all your Company's doing, Padruig. She resists any familiarity, and I cannot shake her mind, but I expect you to act responsibly. You did promise her father.'

It was a detail he had never suspected she knew. Or perhaps she was merely guessing. Jamie certainly wouldn't inform his mother, but Padruig daren't press the truth, not here, not today.

'To my mind, your invitation to let her live with you offered the best solution. Unfortunately, I can no better predict Aalia than harvest the wind. So far, her voice has ruled her destiny.'

'Yet, you let Simon get his hands on her. Such a viperous man, God should strike you down for incompetence.' She sat abruptly on a large banded chest, her petticoats spinning the dust. But she lifted her lace-capped head and matched his eye. 'You know how much I love this child. Through the eyes of my only son, I have watched her grow… felt the joy of her first steps, suffered her

213

childhood fevers. Sitting in this very room, I delighted in her first stuttered words.' Her birdlike hands twisted in her lap. 'I know most of what she has been, good and bad. She is the candle of my darkness, and I fear men like Scythan will put out that flame.'

'You think I would allow that to happen?' He knelt, the better to see her face, and wrapped her fragile hands inside his own. 'I would die first.'

'Then, you must do more to protect her. Chase the moths away, or better, send her back to India.'

'If you know everything, then you know she cannot go back,' he said solemnly. 'Whether we like it or not, Aalia is compelled by William, and denying his ambition is the best means of saving them both. I'm using every talent of my Company.'

'Then it's time to go to Cecil and admit what has been done. Make the Privy Council afraid of William's ambition.'

'Bedford was preparing to issue a warrant for his arrest, except he's left London. The Earl knows almost everything.' He stopped, before he spoke of treason.

'But will he spare Aalia?'

'He gave me due to warning to get her away. An honourable man who serves his country first.'

'And whose father knew much about William's birth. Ask him—he cannot deny John Russell was involved, as surely as young Luke Trentham, Scythan's vainglorious brother. I know he was employed by St. Thomas.'

'Some secrets are not for the telling, Lady Maria. I hope you kept these things from Aalia.'

'Too many secrets mean too many lies. No, I would never tell this to the girl; she has troubles enough.'

'If we betray this promise… if I betray my promise to her father, Aalia will become another pawn of past inheritance. Please, Lady Rayner, you must trust my judgement.' He let go her hands and straightened. 'William has gone north. There is every chance he looks to gather support from Catholic nobles, those who dislike Queen Elizabeth's policies. Bedford has left to inspect the defences at Berwick at Cecil's bidding. But he also acts as a friend. It will be safer for us if William is captured where London eyes cannot hold witness.'

She considered his face for a long time. 'You think William has sufficient credence to gather a following?'

'There are certainly those among the cruder ranks on Bankside who'd willingly make him their king. His likeness to his father has been artfully manicured, but he garners support by promising a return to the old ways. There are many who doubt Elizabeth can rule in her own right, and fear she will choose an unsuitable husband like her sister Mary, a foreign prince looking to extend his own boundaries. William has set fire to the torch of dissent while the country's defences are weak, as Bedford has discovered. When Spain departed, they took with them the bulk of the armoury.'

The dowager's eyes burned like coals. Eventually, sighing deeply, she turned away. 'Tom used to write letters, too, telling me of India, a land he came to love. He was a good man, who stayed by his duty. It's just a shame his charge inherited all of his father's ambition and none of his mother's compassion. Then we may all have died happy.'

Padruig was dismissed without a need to make more promises. He stood outside the portico, embracing the warm, noon-day sun, incapable for a moment of taking any rational decisions. Maria Rayner had presented him with an unexpected dilemma. In fact, it was so unexpected, he daren't trust his senses.

On the opposite side of the road, he noticed Scythan's man keeping faithful watch and took an unusual decision. He crossed the street to join him.

'Robin, isn't it? You serve Scythan well.'

'Master Padruig, a beautiful day for a walk. Are you returning to the Old Temple?'

'You are welcome company, sir.'

It seemed the right choice, drawing his rival's watchman for company.

ESCAPE – 7ᵗʰ Disclosure

What wants yon knave that a king should have,

But the sword of honour and the crown?

Serene under a docile sun, Sweetheart Abbey was raised like a rose-hued island laid in a sea of golden wheat. A warm breeze rippled the ripening fields, stirring the smells of childhood summers which almost soothed the Polish merchant's worries.

Alongside Aalia and Georgiou, he'd spent another day in the saddle, and the riding was raw. Jock had bartered their worn but costly horses for bellicose short-legged ponies bred on a need for hardiness before comfort. Otherwise, the doughty headsman had proved honourable in defeat. Sending half his men "hame," he had insisted on escorting the "canny lad and his keepers" to shelter in a ruined priory. Little of the red sandstone building remained, except enough patched roof to shelter them from the rain.

Aalia ministered to her patient and held her tongue while they stabled the horses, thanking the single brown-robed priest who remained at the priory, serving God's holy vows in a landscape ruled by the devil. It was only after he'd withdrawn to the comfort of his prayers, and they were huddled around a blazing fire behind the abandoned altar, she began spitting out their failings in a confusion of languages even her companions struggled to comprehend. Then later, when the few remaining reivers came to share the fire, they drained their cups and laughed together. Aalia, eyes like sapphires, rhymed to their choruses, whilst Piatro garnered some pride by negotiating for the return of their possessions. Jock tried to barter for Aalia, but dismissed his last sniggered ransom without knowing Georgiou's hand was resting firmly on his knife.

By morning, they'd been allocated a guide. Hard-limbed as any reiver, face and hair worn grey, he came to the Priory in the heart of the night, plainly under duress. The local brand of industry might come laden with menaces, but at least it assured loyalty, or so Jock had them believe.

Travelling through Scotland brought its own risks; they couldn't afford to be taken for "foreign spies," yet had no map to help them negotiate the landscape. Their new companion understood this, and showed an incredible knowledge of the debatable lands which lay between the Border and Sweetheart Abbey. Lands which were brutally protected.

Jock's unshod ponies were sure-footed as goats, whether trotting rough-cut hills or plunging through rain-swelled marsh. But when they arrived at the stone-arched bridge spanning the powerful River Nith, their dour guide shook his head and muttered in despair. The toll-booth on the opposite side was peopled by guards wearing steel, and they were checking all who passed, man, beast, woman, and child.

'Maxwell's men!' The man drew up his hood and swore. 'Curs of few principles, and all of them founded on profit'.

Sweat pouring from the band of his bonnet, he pleaded his case. He daren't risk arrest, his family being outlawed over a debt they owed to Lord Maxwell. Turning his pony slickly, he waved at the fast-flowing river. 'The guards can barely read. Wave yon papers, and once you'se over the bridge, keep the Nith in yer sights. Yer cannae gae far wrang.' And he trotted off in the direction they'd just come, without waving goodbye.

For the first time in many days, there was no sight of rain, and riding along the flat salt-marshes, which skirted the shores of an ever-widening estuary, was almost a pleasure. Flocks of coarse-coated sheep grazed beside the road, and the few turf-roofed cottages they passed appeared abandoned. Rising to the west were high, round-peaked hills, splaying fields like petticoats frothing with ripe oats and barley.

A high, grey wall ringed the outer reach of Sweetheart Abbey, and when they found the door, set in a carved red-stone arch, it proved firmly locked. Even hammering with the butt of Georgiou's sword brought no answer.

Piatro trotted back along the boundary until he found a party of lay-brothers repairing a broken stone hedge, but they still had to wait an age before an indignant, white-robed porter came to open the entrance.

The merchant handed him their letter of introduction, prominent with the Company's seal. Puffed with resentment, the monk bid them stay in the outer courtyard while he disappeared inside a red, sandstone building. A lay-brother brought them warm bread and a flask of sweet ale as they sat in the sun and waited.

The bell rang for midday prayers, and still, they waited.

'We're sure this is the right place?' Georgiou leaned against the wall, playing with his empty cup.

Aalia was laying on a low wooden bench beside the door to the stable. 'Such a strange title for a house of God, I thought to question Jock. He said the Lady who founded it kept her husband's heart embalmed in a casket after he died fighting abroad. That's how New Abbey became known as Sweetheart.' She stretched lazily. 'If the Lords of the Congregation have their way, all these monks will be banished, and none left to pray for the departed. They seem to be dragging their feet… I wonder if William has been here already.'

Piatro drained his cup. 'Jock said his men would have sent word if any strangers had crossed their patch of the Border.'

'William came to Warkworth in a Spanish boat, and Scythan suspected he and his friends were making for Berwick… I overheard them whispering that they had a liaison with someone well-placed in the North, but unfortunately, Scythan didn't trust his thoughts with me.'

'Anyone can see you'd have a hard time crossing this country by ship,' Georgiou growled.

Aalia sat up and kicked the ground. 'I just hope this old priest will help us end William's delusions.'

She was stalking the enclosure walls when the porter finally returned.

'You've ridden direct from London?' Hands tucked under his apron, he stood facing Piatro, larded face grotesque.

'Yes! Unfortunately.' Piatro stretched stiffly. 'We bring letters to your Abbot. The Master of our Company kindly begs we offer his good wishes to an old friend.'

His expression unchanging, the monk pointed to the door. 'Abbot Brown would welcome the honour of greeting your party.' And without waiting for Piatro's answer, he herded them inside.

The tranquil beauty of the Abbey's carved interior wasn't lost on its guests. Perfect symmetry informed every tapered line in a temple born for an ascetic god. No brashness of colour, no bold tapestries or paintings, no outward celebration of faith. Cistercians demand abstinence from every human frailty, which meant the presence of women in any shape or form was absolutely forbidden. But Piatro wasn't overly concerned; Aalia masked her gender so well, he barely remembered the last time he thought her a woman.

The porter led them swiftly along a lime-washed hall until he reached an oak-banded door. He knocked hard, turned the handle, and pushed the heavy door open then stood aside.

They walked straight into blinding sunlight. A huge expanse of fretted windows encompassed the entire facing wall, bathing them in beams of harlequined hoar-glass. Instinctively, Georgiou put up his hands, while Piatro, one pace behind, gasped softly. This bore all the makings of an ambush.

Once his eyes had settled to the light, Piatro could see the room was actually no bigger than Padruig's study, and almost as sparse, except a life-like statue of the Virgin Mary stood near the door, and a simple wooden cross was pinned high on the wall above. The only furniture was a large table-like desk tucked beneath the window and shadowed by its light. Sitting behind it, unmoving as the statue, was the gross silhouette of a man.

The Abbot was writing, scratching a blunt nib across a sheet of parchment, and didn't raise his tonsured head or acknowledge their arrival, which disturbed Piatro more than he liked. Standing at his elbow, he sensed Aalia's frustration and reached to touch her hand, willing her not to speak.

They stood like errant novices lined in front of the desk, while the monk continued his letters. The desk was laden with loose-bound papers, each pile weighted with a smooth, grey river pebble. A large clay pot held a bouquet of goose-feathers and set beside it was a pewter dish full of broken nibs, but laid mid-table and facing them was a heavy leather-bound Bible, open on a page of psalms.

The Abbot reached the end of the page and started to reach for another sheet of paper when Piatro pressed his travel-stained hands onto the sacred book. Without looking up, the white-robed monk put down his pen and took up Padruig's letter.

He took an exceptional time to read its content then started over again.

Aalia, fingers hidden inside her cloak, finally stepped slowly forward. 'We come in peace, Father, as servants of the Company of St. Thomas.'

The monk put up his square, ink-stained hand. He squinted again at the letter and finally raised his head. The heavy-lidded eyes rested solely on Aalia.

'With all that that implies?' He spoke softly, but his voice wasn't kind.

'There was once an Order of St. Thomas, who, I believe, suffered a fate not unlike the Templars? Your Company was founded on their myth. I'm not obliged to acknowledge your letter of authority, young man… although I respect the Master's request. Regretfully, the Brother he would like you to meet has held a bond of silence for many years.'

The Abbot's mottled face lacked any compassion. 'There would be no sense in your staying, except to inform our concerns. During your journey north, you must have gathered news about the troubles?'

Aalia's voice was also soft. 'I doubt we can tell more than you probably know. We've spent little time in London and even less in Scotland.'

'This letter tells me you've come recently from the Orient. I might take you for a heathen, except your accent is Scots?' The Abbot held up Padruig's letter. 'It seems you serve as an informant?'

She opted, unexpectedly, for the truth. 'I'm not Scottish, but an Annan man taught me to speak. None of us serve England but represent St. Thomas in India, where the Company has recently started to trade. Master Kopernik here is a merchant who, for many years, has acted as interpreter to Father Ignatius' mission. Georgiou came as our guard; his family were refugees from Constantinople after it fell to the Ottomans. And I have no particular rank, except the priest we seek knows something of my childhood. I promise we intend no falsehood.'

Piatro didn't move or speak. There was something he didn't like or trust about the fat bastard, and, in such circumstances, he found Aalia's instincts better tuned.

The Abbot stood up, eclipsing the light. 'You are not the first messenger I received recently. Except Lord Scythan describes your mission less ambiguously.' He banged his fist squarely on the desk, spinning papers onto the stone floor.

Aalia tossed away her hood. 'That gentleman is a bluster when it involves other people's business. My fault, I failed to distinguish between peacocks and pelicans! I could argue Scythan is a man who doesn't engage in truth either, but blatantly, his credentials are better served than ours.'

The Abbot leaned across his desk until his nose almost touched her face. 'We may be a closed order, young lady, but that doesn't make us ill-informed. Lord Scythan's grandfather took communion here as a boy, and his mother's name still holds honour on this side of the border.'

Aalia smiled. 'We have nothing so eminent to barter... for the truth of an old servant's courage.'

The Abbot straightened. 'We are all penitents of the same God.'

'And Brother Jon's penitence is silence? How very convenient. Tell me, do you seek reward from God or Lord Scythan?'

The Abbot barked, 'The proofs you seek do not reside here. Only God knows what is true.'

Aalia's voice dropped to a whisper. 'Is that how you answer Him? There are others who want to know the same truth. They will not be so kind.'

'Nevertheless, the answer remains the same... you cannot meet Brother Jon.' The monk spat out his final words. 'Because you are a woman!'

Piatro held Georgiou back.

'And women are denied tongue, because men fear they'll be bested? No wonder you dread the coming crisis... the Lords of the Congregation hunger for change. They want freedom from the yoke of Rome… St. Johnston still burns from Knox's fire! Do you really think Scythan can protect you? Did he tell you the French won't be coming… that the King of France lies dead of wounds enacted by a Scotsman?'

It was clear he hadn't heard. 'I answer to God, not the State. You would do well to accept your limits, young lady.' He sat down heavily.

Aalia snatched the nearest pile of letters. 'Scythan didn't send a messenger? He came himself, breathless and fatigued. Oh, how did I miss that instalment?'

Laying her right hand flat on the open Bible, she began to chant the psalm. 'Have mercy on me, O God… according to your great compassion… blot out my transgressions...'

Then, turning to face her friends, she put her hands together as if to pray, and smiled a malicious smile. 'Otar was partial to

Psalm Fifty-One, particularly the verse of penitence. So useful in a crisis, don't you think?'

The Abbot slammed the Bible shut and herded them away from his desk. Holding the door open, he shouted for the porter.

They were to be expelled immediately, without debate, and could do nothing other than follow the round-bellied monk. He led them into a sunlit yard and past a line of crumbling outbuildings which stood in the shadows of their great ancient church. Piatro understood why Aalia had lost her temper. The Abbot was unworthy of his calling, but now they'd failed to achieve anything. From the church came the plaintive chant of Vespers. It was later than he'd realised. Behind him, Aalia stopped walking, and drawing Piatro's sleeve, whispered her thoughts in Urdu.

'Do you think you could engage the porter in one of your excellent diversions?' And running backwards nimbly, she threw him a beatific smile.

'Is this pertinent to Psalm Fifty-One?' he replied in English.

'How did you guess?' She nodded. 'I'm going to offer myself, like a lamb at the altar.'

'Not, I hope, like a lamb slaughtered...' But before he could finish, he tripped and lost his footing, and had to grab the porter's arm to steady his fall.

Not wishing to injure the monk unduly, Piatro rolled gently, spinning over the ground until they were both sealed in the net of his cloak. Even with Georgiou's help, it took a long time to unravel the generous folds. A long time before the monk realised Aalia was missing. Unfortunately, once he grasped the treachery, he tried to call for help.

Georgiou, one hand wrapped across the monk's mouth and the other snaring his arms, snapped, 'Trust me! This will end in tears.'

The porter refused to be silent. And without further regret, because he'd bitten clean through Georgiou's hand, Piatro sited a precise blow to the side of his head using the weighted hilt of his knife, and lowering the monk to the ground, finally turned to his confederate. 'Tell me where, in this well conceived plan, you suggest we should convene?'

'My friend, if there's one thing I've learnt where Aalia's concerned, you must always follow the music.'

A true apothecary's garden was stocked with many reasons to keep it carefully hidden. Secluded against the walls of the outer boundary, Aalia stopped at the unexpected scent of flowers blooming in summer abundance. Honeysuckle trailed across a high yew hedge and twisted over a broken gate, drawing her into the garden. Entering the serenity of its enclosure, she fingered the neatly tended rows of strewing herbs, clary sage, bitter wormwood, and sweet cicely, stirring their pungent aroma. She knew the merits of every herb from Otar's healing garden. But here were other, rarer plants, whose purposes the imbecile ward of that most eminent and wise physician couldn't presently recall, except poppy seeds cast eternal sleep when hyacinths fail in their calling.

Damn Scythan. Having failed to find any means of entering the Abbey's church, she huddled on the soft ground and trapped her shivering body in the comforting folds of her cloak.

'Are you lost? Not many visitors find their way to our physic garden. Perhaps I can lead you back to the gate?' An elderly brother bent over her awkwardly, warm with the scent of lavender and thyme.

Aalia studied his sandaled feet, clotted in red-brown earth. 'Lost in more than one sense… the truth is, I seem to have floundered.' She wiped her face on her sleeve. 'Isn't it rather early to harvest comfrey?'

The old man laughed and laid down his bundle. 'That depends on your purpose.' His voice was gentle, with an unusual accent, very like the boy, Nigel. The lilt of a Northumbrian. 'We've found comfrey cures our cattle of sickness when we mix it with their grass. Can I offer you some water? It's freshly drawn.' He lifted a horn beaker in hands twisted and swollen with rheum. Two fingers were missing from his right hand.

She looked up, disturbed by a memory. But the brother had a kind face, weathered and aged, but kind. 'You've made another Eden here? It's a very beautiful garden.'

'I wouldn't be anywhere else and count my blessings daily.' He squatted down awkwardly beside her.

'Isn't that what monks are supposed to do? Ensure the righteous earn their place in heaven and rescue sinners... such as me?'

'The best of God's recruits are sinners,' he said.

'I've never managed meek. It's like arguing metaphysics; I always end up on the losing side.'

The monk threw back his head and laughed. 'What have we here? Plain shod and fustian, hardly a rose! Perhaps we are closer to the truth with honeysuckle... or no, stronger, more like rowan. Birthed in ancient mysteries.'

'I know nothing of rowan, except its berries are bitter. Remind me, are they red or white?'

'In Scotland, the flowers are white, and the berries coloured like fire.' He took one of her hands and pressed it between his two palms. 'But there are no enchantments here; we walk in God's presence.'

Aalia leaned into the soft, damp earth. 'Are you the Brother Jon who was once physician to the English court? I've travelled a long way to find you. I'm meant to ask if you can tell me a secret, but now... now, I'm afraid of knowing.'

He nodded his head, and the blue eyes clouded. 'But still, you must ask.' He let go her hand.

'I once had a brother... that is, we grew up in the same house, but weren't born of the same blood. Strangers came and filled his head with stories... that he was born to be a king.' She closed her eyes, sunlight blanching her face.

'What is your brother's name?' He touched her hand.

'William Rose.' She felt his mind recoil.

The chanting in the church seemed to grow louder, as she listened for the monk to speak again.

'Where did you grow up?' His voice was hollow.

'Far from England. We travelled constantly, but settled in India. It was a Christian house.' She hardly dared to breathe.

'The Company of Saint Thomas?' His words touched her like a dream.

'You know?' She daren't move.

'And you love this brother?' He peered into her soul.

She opened her eyes. 'More than life itself... but this stupid dream has changed him.'

Brother Jon caught the wooden crucifix which swung from the end of his belt. Cupping it in his hands, he whispered, 'I once had a good friend, a soldier called Luke Trentham.'

Aalia's mind cleared. 'I've met Simon Trentham, a gentleman of the court, and he has a nephew called Sebastian. But they know nothing of William's birth, in fact... Lord Scythan stole my...' She looked up to find the monk weeping.

'Luke was his brother, and Sebastian his only son.' The Brother turned away. 'When I came to serve the court, Luke was Master of the Queen's Personal Guard. Except he disappeared the same night Prince Edward was born.'

'But Scythan knows nothing of William's birth... surely?'

The monk pressed his wooden cross into her open palm. 'Child, there is nothing to know... because everyone, not least that gentle queen, understood how our kingdom could be torn apart by two equal and legitimate heirs. Jane Seymour bore Henry Tudor one perfect son. I am an old man, and have lived to forget the past. There is nothing more I can tell you about your brother.' He laid his broken hand gently on her shoulder.

Aalia closed her fingers around the cross. 'Yes, I see. When things go wrong, it helps to close your heart and forget. Except I've never learned to accept when I fail!'

He leaned back, startled.

Aalia rolled onto her feet and pulled up her hood. 'Can you show me how to enter the church? I like to keep faith with my heart not my head.'

Damn William, damn Padruig, but mostly damn herself.

Cistercian voices raised in plainsong were fundamental, if not vital, to their form of pious worship and faith. The white monks justified this one profligacy, because they believed devotion is better versed in harmony. And, after a long period wondering just what he should do next, Piatro suddenly heard Aalia's sublime voice soar above the chanting monks. Leaving Georgiou to guard the porter, he braced his weight against the low beamed side-door and wondered, not for the first time, whether it was actually God or the devil who had gifted her that voice. Then, he took a deep breath and kicked.

The first thing he met inside the portico was Sebastian Trentham barring the way. Arms folded, face drawn like steel, he put a finger to his lips and pushed Piatro into the aisle behind the closeted choir. Leaning his back against a pillar, he spoke in a whisper. 'I could arrest you, or I can listen to your excuses and then arrest you.'

'Being in Scotland, and therefore without jurisdiction, I believe your threats are empty.' Piatro's knowledge of Scottish legalities had been recently revised by Jock.

'Breaking Border law doesn't fit my purpose either, but your arrival at Sweetheart makes you appear a spy. I expected William and instead, find his sister. How on earth did you carve a way through the Borders?'

'Friends. Which we garner daily. Having found the reason why William came north, Aalia had hoped to reach there first.'

The chanting closed to silence.

Sebastian glowered, not lowering his voice. 'William is heading for Sweetheart? But why?' His eyes fixed on the reeded screen which secluded the choir from the aisle.

'He is looking for a particular brother,' Piatro answered sullenly.

'I repeat the question, why?'

'Because he's desperate to know the truth about his birth, and it seems this monk was there.'

'And would it harm you to tell the monk's name? Despite the web of deceit your company weaves, I doubt that is a secret.' He shrugged and the hem of his cloak disturbed a shimmering of dust.

'Deceit deceiveth and shall be deceived… are you threatening my friend Sebastian?' Soft-footed as a hunter, Aalia slipped from the darkness of the porch, gilt head concealed by her hood.

Sebastian smiled, and in that moment, reminded Piatro of Aalia. 'The notion for trust is that it cuts both ways.' He stopped the casual swing of his sword. 'I thought you were heathen-bred, Aalia, but you chime Vespers virtually note perfect. Be warned, the monks will call it witchcraft. They're wary of women, particularly those who ignore their sacred rules!'

'Virtually note perfect?' She pretended hurt. 'I suppose for a Trentham that constitutes a compliment… did my absence frighten Uncle Simon? Some dainty thieves and vagabonds supplied us with good "craic" and very safe passage. We couldn't ask for better escorts.'

Sebastian caught her, gripping her arms, forcing her to look him in the eye. 'You are leaving empty-handed nevertheless.'

She didn't resist. 'The Miserere is my compensation. You have to respect the sheer majesty of Josquin's arrangement, but I wish it was his Magnificat; it's more in tune with my failings.'

The door to the rood-screen flew open, taking Sebastian's focus. He dropped his hold of Aalia just as the pattern of shadows shifted, and Abbot Brown came striding through.

'There you are, young lady; I hoped to find you. I don't know who trained your voice, but… I've never heard anyone sing with such… ecstasy.' His face was flushed, and his breathing awkward. Clearly, he'd been running.

Aalia stepped out of Sebastian's reach. 'Music is my refuge, too.'

'You didn't learn to sing like that in India?' Sebastian interrupted tersely.

'My step-father Otar took me with him when he taught at Padua. The first time I heard the papal choir, I was six years old.'

Piatro could see she was shaking and moved to catch her hand. Only then did he notice her tears.

'Master Padruig thinks her voice more a curse than a blessing, because she uses it arbitrarily… me… I trust it's a mark of God's consent.'

While she spoke, Piatro squeezed her hand, wondering what had happened.

The Abbot noticed as well, and turned to appeal to Sebastian. 'Your uncle, surely, would fit such rare talent to better purpose.'

Aalia pulled Piatro gently back until they were both clothed by the shadows. 'My choices have been rather limited of late. The Master of St. Thomas would likely suggest four solid walls and no obvious key.' She bowed her head to let her hood mask her face. 'He's wistful for the days when women lived in obedience and chastity, but most especially chastity. Talent being reserved for men.'

Sebastian coughed while Piatro turned away.

But the Abbot was fatally indulgent. 'Nevertheless, young lady, the quality of your voice betrays a deep sincerity. I think when you sing your emotions run almost too deep.'

Before anyone could reach to stop her, Aalia ran to the outer door. Throwing it open, she escaped into sunlight, which Piatro should have expected, being this was the first occasion he'd ever seen her cry.

If Sebastian was surprised, he didn't intend to show it. But the quality of his escort meant Aalia, Piatro, and Georgiou couldn't leave Sweetheart Abbey without being hosted by his company. His men had been hand-picked for the purpose, armed with the kind of arsenal more fitted to escorting royalty. Clearly, Lord Scythan had firm intentions and didn't want Aalia lost again.

Before they could leave the boundary walls, Sebastian had to soothe the furious porter. More than incensed by his injuries, the monk demanded they should send for Lord Maxwell's steward. The ensuing argument proved Sebastian's skills as a negotiator were almost the equal of Piatro's. Almost. By hinting the Abbey was caught in less than lawful activities, he smoothly silenced the bruised monk's fury. Looking at the long sweep of estuary looming on their doorstep, even Piatro could see the latent opportunities for smuggling, and the sour look on the Abbot's face seemed to confirm his theory.

An orange glow was melting the hills when the gateway was finally unbolted. The Abbot walked beside them as far as the stream which forded the Dumfries road. A water-mill churned the water, causing the troupe to cross in single file. Mounted on their short-legged ponies, Piatro watched Georgiou take his place beside Aalia. That she didn't argue or make any attempt to slip away from the ring of guards made him wonder what she'd learned in the Abbey which had had such effect to tame her. Piatro also noticed the Abbot place a sealed letter into Trentham's hands, probably a list of complaints, but it would make interesting reading should an opportunity arise.

Once the Abbot was out of sight, Sebastian leaned from his saddle and grabbed Aalia's pony by the mane. 'Just what did Brother Jon tell you?'

Her voice came muffled through her hood. 'That William was never born. Aren't you going to wait and arrest him when he comes?'

'No.'

'But he might harm the brothers, if he doesn't get his answers.'

'William isn't coming.'

At that, she turned. 'I thought… at least everyone seemed to believe, this is exactly where he'd be.'

'He's got other fish to land; at least that's what my uncle thinks.' He was smiling, teeth wide as a lion's kiss.

'Then why did you come to Sweetheart?'

'Didn't I say?' Something in his voice hinted at malevolence.

'I don't think you did.' Her voice was stretched, impatient.

'William asked me to find this priest and report his every word.'

Piatro, listening one step behind, kicked his horse's belly until he came alongside, expecting Aalia to strike. But she barely stirred in her saddle.

'I wonder what you did to earn my brother's trust.'

'Gave him the news you were still alive,' he said simply.

Aalia tipped back her head and laughed. 'Brother Jon said the truth is such it can never be known. As you obviously enjoy playing brother against sister, that must give you a profound sense of satisfaction.'

Piatro shrugged, wishing he understood what she meant. There had been no time to discuss what she'd learned from the monk, no time to discuss what they must do next. He wanted to trust Sebastian, but his men-at-arms weren't for show; she couldn't escape Scythan's net again.

Then, suddenly, Aalia kicked her mount hard, galloping ahead without thought for anyone's safety. Piatro had a moment's panic when he saw her jump into the shallows of a wide and swollen river, but the stalwart pony swam sturdily until it reached the opposite bank. Sebastian's bigger mount soon caught up, but he didn't drop the pace. In fact, Piatro decided, he wanted the chase as much as she did. Trotting alongside Georgiou, he spent the next hour cursing his pony's short gait and wishing he'd taken better heed when bartering their fine-boned horses.

SACRIFICE

Article One – 1ˢᵗ Disclosure

Fair is youth and void of sorrow; But it hourly flies away.

Master Wright's coal boat, with her fat hull skimming the sand-banks, sloughed into the Port of London like a beggar in the night. Sliding under the brooding walls of the Great Tower, stuttered sounds echoed from the slate-roofed sheds, a methodical clang of metal striking metal. The armoury was busy, or more likely, the Mint, producing the Privy Council's great hope of restoring faith in England's coinage.

Leaning his back against the forward mast, Piatro watched the filigree of lanterns prick the shore. He'd barely slept since they boarded *Doris*. Their journey to London had been uneventful, but the cramped boat had lacked any kind of comfort, and he worried constantly what was weighting Aalia's thoughts. But there'd been no chance to speak with her alone; Trentham made his company impossible to avoid and had clung like a limpet since Sweetheart. Yet, Piatro knew something critical had changed since her meeting with Jon Chambre.

It was barely a surprise Scythan was ready to greet them as soon as they arrived in Newcastle. Sebastian had sent a rider ahead, carrying his coded observations, informing who should be informed. They could thank the commander of Berwick for the fact they weren't harried by reivers, or even English troopers stalking the length of the Border. Croft had increased his patrols in case other foreign envoys tried to slip into Scotland and, more critically, to shelter the rush of Scots informers running south with potent news.

They suffered an excruciating interview with Scythan, something Piatro would rather forget, although to be fair and despite his fury, he didn't have them arrested. Perhaps it helped Aalia had held her manners; it was only afterwards, when Sebastian tried to imply he didn't trust his uncle any further than she did, Piatro had caught the flash of rebellion in her eyes.

Unusually, it was Georgiou who had suggested they abandon Aalia to Scythan's care and pursue his new-found passion for English ale. Newcastle's river harbour was very like London's—noisy, raw, and peopled by hoards of foreigners. Blond-boned seamen from the Northlands garbled their troubles in Flemish, Hanse-financed Germans held court amidst fishermen from the Low Countries, even a Calais Frenchman carolling, applauded by local boatmen. For the first time in weeks, they weren't noted for being strangers, not even Georgiou, although young Jacky Wright remembered him from Warkworth, and paraded him in front of all his mates.

Piatro couldn't remember how the actual deal was struck. Master Wright, keen to add funds to his piecemeal trade, was willing to ferry them to London, but nobody was more astonished than Piatro when Scythan agreed. They had boarded *Doris* next dawn, before the high morning tide.

It was Aalia who had explained his reasoning. With all the troubles in Scotland, there was a terrible dearth of post-horses; what with English troops moving north and Scottish lords fleeing south, the Great North Road was almost busier than Cheapside. Scythan had patiently closed his eyes and ignored her observations, but Piatro suspected his choice had more to do with thinking them less able to escape from a boat.

At the end of the first day's sailing, Aalia had given up baiting Trenthams and practised instead her talent for song. Before *Doris* swung her nose into the brackish waters of the

Thames, his lordship was referring to the hands as Aalia's lap-dogs, and Sebastian was using a less polite term, in private. *Just think*, Piatro mused as they waved goodbye to Master Wright and his crew, *what souls she might have charmed if they'd thought to pack a lute.*

As the steering board, ushered *Doris*'s bow to point finally towards the city, Aalia pulled on her cloak and shook Georgiou awake. But Scythan insisted on escorting them all the way back to the Old Temple. Dawn was sifting the shadows, and by the time they passed the grim cold walls of Baynard's Castle, the streets were busy with barrels and carts and market traders setting up stalls with their wares. It seemed anything could be legally traded during daylight hours, but no muezzins called the faithful to prayer, no saffron monks gathered at temple gates.

The limestone walls of the Old Temple, honed by four hundred seasons, were sealed and unwelcoming. Scythan banged hard on the ivy-strewn door, while Piatro brushed stranded cobwebs aside. As they heard the heavy bolts being drawn, the deep bass bell of St. Bride's began to chime a death toll. Piatro shuddered.

Gull opened the metal studded door. He looked Scythan up and down, sharp face impassive. Master Padruig was away. Summer fever was sweeping the city, and he was tending the sick. Gull had only returned that hour to collect more medicines from the store, though they couldn't steal every soul from death.

Bland face grounded in fatigue, Gull took the sealed letter Scythan handed him and gave solemn word Aalia would be kept inside the building until his Master returned. Piatro expected Scythan to leave his warden at the gate, and was mildly surprised he trusted in Gull's promise.

Striding through the maze of empty halls in his long, easy gait, Gull suggested another reason for his lordship's swift departure. Summer plague meant those with means had already fled the city, and his lordship was hardly immune. Briefly pointing out their rooms, he left them in the kitchen, noting there was freshly baked bread, rounds of cheese and ham, and good ale in the store.

As soon as he closed the door, Aalia shook off her cloak and smiled. 'I need to recover my integrity.'

By mid-morning, the air was sticky and hot. Having the shutters drawn and the banded door wedged open, Aalia's tiny room seemed airless, almost and very like her home in Goa. Georgiou perched at the foot of her bed, black hair polished and fresh blanched from bathing. Piatro dropped onto the only chair. He'd discussed, then argued, and finally refused to sanction her plans. But still, she pleaded.

'Don't you see? Scythan never had any intention of arresting William; he only took me along because he knew it would stay Bedford's hand. Jon Chambre said Scythan's brother Luke disappeared from the palace the same night the baby was born, which suggests he was likely involved in stealing William.'

'Then we'll take your concerns to Bedford, but only after we've discussed everything we've learned with Padruig.' Piatro shook his head.

'I don't see why we shouldn't go and find him now,' she snapped.

'Gull gave his oath,' Georgiou pressed.

'It might be days before the Master returns. Scythan is pursuing his plans while we are tucked up here.'

'What makes you think that?' Piatro failed to see any reason for urgency.

She threw back her head and groaned. 'Sebastian came to Sweetheart on William's behalf. What if they are all in league with Spain and working to supplant Elizabeth?'

It actually made sense. Piatro smothered his alarm. 'Still, we must wait and weigh these facts with Padruig.'

Aalia bit her lip. He could see frustration in her eyes. Scythan was deeply implicated, and everything she'd learned appeared to clarify his guilt. If Piatro had learned one rule in the years since Otar enlisted him, it was to strike while the iron was hot. He also understood the need for irrefutable proof. Later, when the outcome required an apology, he'd tell the Master he went merely to protect the Company. It didn't yet occur how much she would defy him.

It wasn't far to walk from the Old Temple to Three-Cranes Wharf. The mid-day heat had driven many of the booths to close early, but they soon found a wherry to carry them, and Piatro argued the fare. Laying his back against the boards next to Georgiou, he relaxed to the beat of oars. Despite owning a split tongue, the oarsman was keen to lisp his opinions, and while passing the shimmering façade of fabled riverside palaces, he raised the oars midstream.

'Thuch beauty the church commanded with all the monies it thtole. King Henry theized them all, but then let hith nobles have them cheap, and damn their thouls if they thtayed Catholic.'

Turning to study the buildings, Georgiou carefully avoided Piatro's eye. 'What's the building with the turret?' He nodded.

'Thurham Houthe!' The oarsman spat in the river. 'Where the Thpanith ambathador thtays.'

Aalia sat up and stretched. 'On such a beautiful afternoon, I think we should walk. Don't worry, sir, we'll not reduce the fare. Can you drop us there?' She smiled, pointing towards a narrow landing.

They alighted on a flight of narrow, moss-covered steps and climbed into a short, dank passage which reeked of stale urine. Emerging at its farthest end, they met a broad, sandy road which stretched from the walls of the city into open fields. Lining the road to the south were the high, brick walls and balustrades sheltering the palaces glimpsed from the river, but on the opposite side was an orchard, heavy with ripening fruit. As they walked along the road, Aalia started to count.

'Don't you know where Bedford lives?' Piatro asked lightly.

'Yes. I've been to his house in Ivy Lane; it's not far from here. I believe these orchards are part of his land. Sebastian said they were once the gardens of a convent, but that's hardly where I'm looking for.'

'I thought our plan was to inform the Earl of Bedford about everything you discovered.' Piatro caught hold of her arm.

'We'll find him later, if he's in town. But we've more urgent matters to attend. Such as stopping William, or have you forgotten that particular quest?'

Piatro looked to Georgiou, but he merely shrugged his broad shoulders.

'Still, we must speak to Bedford.' He tightened his grip on her arm.

'Please, Piatro. One last chance to separate my fool from his ambitions.'

'So, where are we going?' Georgiou asked curtly.

Aalia met Piatro's eye. 'Durham House, of course. Highly esteemed residence of His Majesty King Philip of Spain's most able ambassador, the Bishop of Aquila.'

She nodded towards a tall gated arch where the mitred spire of a bishop's arms was carved deep into the keystone.

'I wasn't aware we'd been invited for dinner.' Piatro frowned.

Aalia lowered her voice. 'What if we can prove Spain's involvement? Discover some tangible evidence linking William to the Ambassador… could it be Scythan who set Alvaro searching in India, knowing his brother's part? From the beginning, Otar wondered what spark lit this flame… wondered who spurred the Jesuits into believing King Henry had a legitimate heir hidden away from England's shores.'

Piatro placed his hands firmly on Aalia's shoulders. 'This is where we turn back, my friends.'

She slipped his hold and, making a skein of her cloak, ran towards the gates. 'You must agree the Jesuits possessed more knowledge than mere chitter-chatter.'

'And the Ambassador will leave this evidence on a calling plate for anyone to view? To enter his residence without permission would be foolish… even for you, Aalia.' Piatro tried to catch her again, but she slipped his hands with ease.

'All the niceties went out of the window long ago. We end this now, if we can reveal Scythan's dealings… because without Spain's support, William's claim is hopeless. A nameless beggar-boy wanting a crown?'

'We have nothing but your instinct to show he acts for Spain.' Piatro made another grab, but she twisted sideways. 'Believe me! The risk cancels any return.'

'She's right. William doesn't have a hope without support.' Georgiou stood with his arms folded, glaring at the closed metal gates.

'All the more reason we must return to the Old Temple and inform Padruig of these suspicions,' Piatro begged.

Georgiou looked at Aalia. 'We did give our word.'

'Yes! To Scythan… but the peacock has his own interests at heart. Think on it, Georgiou… just why did William go north? Not to find Jon Chambre, that was left to Sebastian. William must draw support from men who want Elizabeth stripped of her throne. Padruig said her recent Bill of Supremacy was despised by the old nobility. Who better to spur your coterie than those who rile against this woman's rule? And Henry Percy, current Earl of Northumberland, is bosom-friend to Scythan.'

Aalia leaned against the iron railings. Stranded through the bars was a range of grey-stone buildings with crenulated battlements, giving the look of a fortress.

'Have you discussed this with anyone else?' Piatro met Georgiou's frown.

'Of course not. It's merely a theory, but Scythan took great pains to join Bedford's escort once he discovered we might chase after William.' She shrugged, loosening the folds of her cloak.

'What else did the monk say? If you don't admit all, we go straight back to the Old Temple.'

He could see she wasn't listening. Her attention was fixed on an old woman filling her basket with fallen apples in the orchard across the road. Turning at last to face him, she smiled.

'What if Padruig already knows everything Brother Jon told me?'

'Why should he not confide in us?' Georgiou's gaze was steady.

'Because he understood if Aalia gathered these facts, she would take some mindless action,' Piatro concluded.

'While he sits on his hands and blinks?' she snapped.

'Unkind!' Piatro attempted a smile. 'The Master steers his course by subtler means and fears the consequences of your actions.'

'He would fear me more, if I were a man!' She raised her hood. 'Now, do we thieve, or do we flee?'

Finding the wrought gates of Durham House unlocked was certainly an advantage. More fortuitous, perhaps, was the fact, being Friday, the Ambassador's serving of fish was being delivered at precisely the moment Aalia and Georgiou started to creep inside. Nodding to the listless sentry, the fish-merchant wiped his thick, stubby hands on his apron and winked. 'I've heard this little songbird on manys an occasion.'

And without further comment, he let them share his slatted cart, dribbling across the cobbled courtyard on its regular route to the kitchen. It came as further blessing the cook and his servants were far too attentive of their chores to question the extra hands. Georgiou thanked them kindly, in Spanish, while he kept guard at the door.

Aalia went to find the Ambassador's chambers. Draped in her cloak, running soft-footed, she listened hard at every closed door before slipping inside. Searching the last room on the landing, she discovered a tiny side room filled with heavy, leather-bound travel chests. She was breaking the second lock when an argument spilled through the closed shutters. Recognising two of the voices, she went to the window and listened.

'I didn't expect you to come here; the Ambassador is at court,' came Alvaro's gritted tone.

'The girl has confused things,' Scythan answered. 'I can only hold her at bay if you keep your word and hide William outside London.'

'You promised you'd deliver her to me.'

'What would that achieve? My nephew informs me the monk she found in Scotland had nothing of consequence to tell, and just as we left Newcastle, a messenger arrived informing us he'd since died.'

'She killed him?' Alvaro barked.

'Would Aalia be capable?' A soft, woman's voice joined them.

Scythan continued evenly, 'More likely, his old heart failed. Her intrusion left him distressed… the Abbot penned a statement confirming the man had sought refuge at Sweetheart almost twenty years ago. Sebastian was allowed to meet him briefly, in the presence of the Abbot, and thought his testimony confused. You say he was your final witness to William's birth?'

'Bedford's hidden the nurse. She's locked in his estate at Chenies, but we still have the Chrism Bowl, which the beggar held such store by… and don't forget the letters.' The woman spoke, her accent clearly English.

'We need valid testimony, Countess, or King Philip will not be persuaded to intervene.' Alvaro's voice was shrill.

There was silence. Then, the woman spoke so softly, Aalia could barely hear.

'If only you'd recovered the ring, Alvaro…'

'What ring is this?' Scythan demanded.

'The ring Queen Jane Seymour entrusted to Tom Hampden,' the woman answered. 'Henry gifted each of his children a special ring to celebrate their birth. Queen Mary once showed me the ring which had belonged to her brother. She explained that her father had been furious because the first ring he commissioned was lost before the christening, and he had to order a second from the jeweller. If we could only place these two rings side-by-side, it would add credence to the story Jane had given birth to twins, and William is Henry's rightful heir.'

'What are you doing here?' A house servant, black-robed from head to foot, stood in the doorway, waving his arms.

Aalia backed mechanically. 'I came with the fishman.' She slipped past him, smiling. 'They didn't want salted fish in the kitchens, Cook says it stank, and someone told me to bring it up here… I put it on the chest next to those oranges.' She pointed inside the storeroom.

As the servant started to look, she ran through the hall, the kitchens, and outer courtyard, without engaging another soul.

Georgiou was already in the street, red-faced, with Piatro at his side.

'Lord Scythan…'

'I know,' she interrupted. 'Blaming me for Jon Chambre's death.'

'I didn't know the monk was dead.' Piatro, cap askew, turned from Georgiou to Aalia, hands weighting his hips.

'He was very much alive when I left him.' Aalia simmered. 'Why would Scythan say the monk had died, except… to prevent them bringing him down to London? It seems he likes to play both sides.' Her hand went to her neck, where she'd last touched the ring.

'That all went very well.' Piatro rolled his eyes. 'Now, can we go back and tell everything we've learned to Master Padruig?'

SACRIFICE – 2nd Disclosure

Padruig was standing on the Old Temple roof, staring out at a darkening sky. London squatted under clotted-grey clouds, while the sun hung shrouded like a candle at a wake. Soon, lightning would strike. He knew what was coming, knew it in his bones, despite putting every talent at his disposal towards preventing the inevitable storm. The letter he'd just deciphered exposed not merely William's folly. King Philip would quickly wash his hands of all involvement, should Alvaro fail, but if he did succeed, if those men intent on treason proceeded with their mischief, Spain promised to do everything in its power to ensure William was crowned King.

Thunder cracked like a field-gun overhead. He returned to his study by way of the narrow back-stairs. Unlacing his heavy boots, he pressed his bare feet on the flagstones. Before he condemned William to death, he must be certain there was no other way. Otar would surely concur. They could no longer risk the Company, its reputation, or its future, for the sake of one nameless girl, no matter what was promised.

As he folded the small sheet of paper and printed the Earl of Bedford's name, he recalled Luke Trentham's anger on that fateful night. Everything his good friend had warned had finally come to pass. It would have been far easier if they'd left the unwanted prince to his fate.

He'd barely time to conceal the letter, when Kopernik threw open the door. Striding across the narrow room, puddling rings on the floor, he slammed his hands hard on the desk. Kopernik, their sallow-faced merchant who lived to make a profit, brimming with revelations. Secrets, as Otar taught him, were never the best mordant for serenity.

'Would it not have been kinder to tell us everything you knew at the beginning?' he yelled.

Padruig put up his hands. 'Aalia never placed faith in me, so I remain blind to her loyalties. You understand what she is capable of doing, what she did in India? Otar may excuse her capacity for mayhem, but when it comes to William, I certainly will not trust her.'

Piatro raised one hand as though to strike. 'You banked on Aalia's defiance; otherwise, you'd have to break your promises and expose those secrets which bound up the truth. Whatever she discovered has merely made her reckless. We've just come from Durham House, the Spanish Ambassador's residence... they have gathered evidence...' He leaned across the desk, squeezing his hands into fists. 'You promised there was nothing to prove William's legitimacy, but they only want for a ring, and then, Spain will spur a rebellion.'

'I beg your pardon?' Padruig stepped back, mind spinning. Piatro didn't stop shouting. 'A ring... Scythan was there with Alvaro!'

Padruig seized on the facts. 'Scythan? Why would he visit Spain's Ambassador? As far as I'm informed, he went straight to Cecil after bringing Aalia here. I sent you to protect her, not to chase after ghosts. And I was right to worry... I hear she escaped Scythan's charge before he entered Berwick.'

'Did you suspect Sebastian from the beginning? Or were we supposed to bait some trap?'

'You are guessing at motives when you should be weighing facts. It was you who told me Sebastian had saved Aalia at the Mermaid and then later, on the river. Why would he do that, if his uncle wanted her dead? He works as informer for Bedford and wouldn't be drawn into a Papist plot.'

'Sebastian was waiting at Sweetheart Abbey. He said William sent him. If not involved in their treason, why steep himself in danger?'

'Because his uncle doesn't care what happens to William. He wants control of Aalia. I can't explain why, but I will put this right.'

Cornucopia had been a kind of home, despite its shortfalls, and Georgiou missed the steady rise and fall, the defined limits, of living on-board the boat. Leaving Piatro to fire his anger at the Master, he went in search of food. The storm had left him soaked to the skin, but hunger drove him to the kitchen.

Gull was in the courtyard garden as he passed through, harvesting herbs too heavy with rain. But there was a surprise waiting in the arched corridor, cloaked in berry red and stoppered by a yellow straw hat.

'Andreas! You finally remember your friends?'

'Georgiou, welcome back. I've not travelled far, unlike some?'

'We've chased to Scotland and back. Piatro said you were running errands for the Crown?'

'Extending my talents by serving St. Thomas and England in equal measure. This little kingdom is keen to be independent of Europe.' Behind his spectacles his brown eyes were shining.

'Come and tell me about it… I'm in need of ordinary conversation, Aalia's brother has us chasing around in circles.'

'Too much excitement for you?'

'Too much intrigue. Excitement, I can bear… remember, I'm one of the few who willingly plays Piatro at dice.'

'Never a better man.' Steynbergh pointed to the large hexagonal mechanism which sat in the middle of the grass quadrangle and waved. 'I brought a friend.'

A young, ruddy face peered over the long wooden beam which projected from the interlocking cogs.

'That's Aalia's friend, Drake.' Georgiou waved.

'Loves boats.'

'And serves his god-father well. Is that where you've been? Working for Bedford?'

'A more level-headed man I've never met. The Earl has great ambitions for his country, and I would like to help.'

'Trading engines?'

'Trading, understanding... more practical skills. Bedford would like his country to be less dependent on others, and I've been examining some possibilities.'

'Now who's playing with fire? Perhaps you shouldn't tell me, being I'm a foreigner.'

'If I can't trust you, Georgiou, I don't know who I may trust. But I wouldn't share this with Aalia.'

'Does Bedford know what took you to India?' His eyes remained on the young man clambering down the bracketed structure. 'Or is that something we mustn't discuss?'

'We've been most candid with the gentleman; after all, it distinguishes my credentials. I may not be a very good soldier, but I understand the mechanics of war.'

Drake swung to the ground only to meet Aalia. Gold head bent to chestnut, the sound of laughter carried to the passage, even before they ran from the rain.

'The engine is most extraordinary, Doctor Steynbergh. I've never seen such complex gearing.' The boy had the look of a faithful hound.

'We thought we'd lost you, Andreas. Judging by the hat, England has your approval?' Aalia patted the dome of his crown.

'They have children plait the straw; that's how they make it so fine. Each to our talents, dear lady. I've been extending the Company's good-will; Padruig would have us embracing all spheres. Apparently, your "borrowed" charts have been very highly praised.'

'You know I have the prescience of a butterfly when it comes to practical matters. Did you enjoy the company of Meester Geminus?'

He knew, none better, how far she relied on instinct, but still was shocked by her insight. He shuffled his spectacles, wiping the lenses clean. 'A fine mathematician and rich in all new learning, it's to its credit this country draws such capable men.'

Georgiou stuck to his point. 'What brings you back to the Old Temple?'

A fork of lightning ripped across the courtyard, splitting the beam where Drake had been standing not seconds before.

'Lord have mercy!' the young man said, putting his hands to his head.

'In this case, he did.' Aalia patted him gently. 'You must be in His good books. Whereas… I couldn't stop Piatro flying straight to Padruig… tell me, Andreas, what's to choose between a cauldron and its fire?'

Rain pelted down the slated roof, and molten curtains formed across the open arches, while Andreas examined her solemn face.

'I believe Padruig has your best welfare at heart,' he spoke gently. 'You must go to him and explain. Everything can be resolved with truth.'

'But what form of truth is he wanting,' Aalia answered sourly.

SACRIFICE – 3ʳᵈ Disclosure

Padruig sent Gull to fetch Aalia. Inscribing unusual reticence, his novice took an age to return, eventually tracking her to the kitchen, where she was gorging on bread and cheese in the company of friends.

Framed in the entrance to his study, she stood awkward at Padruig's door. Waiting on his reprimand, the wild cub contained. He remembered her birth and his promise. *Nothing done by chance.* Fearing for death he'd misjudged her. Now, he must redress that failure, gird his responsibility. The girl was not her mother.

In silence, he watched her move as though drawn, to the lectern. The single candle shimmered and settled on her face. He felt a shadow touch his heart.

'We both know you've run out of choices, Aalia.' His voice held steady.

'Brother Jon was kind. His memories hold more credence than yours. He made me understand there was no choice, not for Tom. If the queen hadn't died so soon… here's the crux… William would have been brought safely back to court.'

'That's what we all believed. Now, even after twenty years, many will be destroyed, if this secret is revealed. Good people. Who acted with the best of intentions, just as you have done.'

'Like Scythan?' Her eyes were emphatic. She was never afraid.

'Just like Lord Scythan. Tom had asked his brother Luke to help conceal William's birth.'

'Awkward, when Scythan has just charmed the Queen's ear.'

'It would be difficult to prove he wasn't implicated. Also, the Earl of Bedford, whose father likely knew everything. Otherwise, why would he have commissioned a second Chrism Bowl?'

'You think that's why he's been so earnest to help? And there was I, thinking it all came down to charm.'

'One benefit of this affair is Bedford has learned to appreciate St. Thomas's integrity. But we have nothing to barter with Scythan.'

'Except my voice.'

'For a ring?' He watched the colour drain from her face.

'You couldn't dress the truth with some meandering? Discuss the virtues of English policies—fix on Andreas and his engines?'

'Is that what you really want? The truth was buried to protect the innocent.'

'And like Pandora, I've opened the jar. Too late for excuses, we must hide what we know, and artfully mask the Company's guilt.'

He'd wanted to seek answers with an objective mind. 'William is outside the law. Had he come straight to me, I'd have been more considerate. This was never his fault.'

'What did you expect? Organise a welcome party, and he'll return here cap in hand? It's hardly his style, with or without the promise of a throne. Yes, Scythan has the ring, yet didn't offer to share it.'

'We can't accuse him without evidence.'

'Bedford might?'

'Not without proof. And I doubt he'd take your word. You've hardly proved your integrity and have good reason to wish Scythan ill.'

'So, William stands condemned by all his friends.'

'I will not expose this Company to treason; we would lose everything.'

At the look on her face, he recited his many reasons. And she listened patiently, standing beside his desk. Finally, she picked up a sheet of blank paper and waved it under his nose.

'Don't worry; I will not stain your principles.' She smiled. 'But give me one last chance to snare William, before you offer the Earl of Bedford your blessing.'

SACRIFICE – 4th Disclosure

The knocking on the street door grew steadily in persistence while Ella stomped down the length of the hall. Her mistress was far too old for such intrigue. There was no telling where it would end, and if anything should happen to her ladyship, where would Ella Jones be? Out on the street, that's where.

Jaffa, the house dog, was stroking his ribs against the door with a look in his eye she hadn't seen since that singer… what was her name… had enchanted the poor beast. Ella pulled open the door, too lazy to hold the dog in check, except he proved docile as a lamb. The bright-eyed songstress waited beside Doctor Padruig, and a less tall black-eyed foreigner, who smelt of musk, and dressed in rag-a-muffin clothes, just like the girl. At least the gently-spoken Irishman would sooth her ladyship's temper.

'It's Ella, isn't it?' Aalia said. 'Your poor feet with all this coming and going. What it is to be well-liked?' And then, the girl startled her by gently kissing both her cheeks.

'Nobody kisses servants, madam,' Ella blustered. 'Not in England, any-hows.'

'Aalia keeps her own rules.' Padruig shook his head. 'And finds small pleasure in discomfiting people.'

Padruig waited for Ella to bolt the heavy door while Aalia bent to scratch the dog's ear, his duties lost to her charms. Leading them up to her mistress's chamber, Ella couldn't disguise her frustration. Having one visitor was trouble enough, but filling the house put her routine in shreds. It unsettled the dust, making ever more work for the morrow.

Waiting in Lady Rayner's chamber was an exalted and invited coterie. The Earl of Bedford occupied the best chair, close to the hearth, and standing in front of the gilt-rimmed mirror, testing his reflection, was the Polish merchant, Kopernik. Waiting beside him, hued like a rainbow, stood the practical magician, Andreas Steynbergh, consoling a linen-capped Lady Maria. She was seated beside the window, feet tucked under a small, round table, hands busy wielding a needle, whiffling ochre silk through a sheet of cream-coloured linen.

Padruig waited until Ella had shuffled down the landing and returned downstairs, before closing the door and turning the metal key. Facing the room, he noted Aalia had withdrawn to a corner, leaning her back against the fine oak panelling. Marking the middle of the room, he squared his feet on the Turkey carpet and clasped his hands behind his back.

'I make no bones why I've asked you here. William Rose, a ward of our Company, came with one ambition—to seize England's throne. Whatever we suspect, whatever we may prove, there have been attempts on Queen Elizabeth's life, and I... we, cannot allow William's associates a chance to try again.'

Bedford nodded. 'Although we can't be absolutely certain William was allied to these attempts.'

Padruig kept his eyes resting on Aalia. 'Tom had no doubt the Jesuit called Alvaro was behind the attack at St. Katherine's, because he recognised his men.'

Bedford shook his big head slowly. 'My men scoured the streets looking for the two men he described, without success.'

'We are grateful for your support, Lord Bedford. I realise the crisis in Scotland weighs heavily on your time. And I'm extremely thankful to Lady Rayner for allowing us to gather here, hopefully unobserved by our enemies.' Drawing a long breath, Padruig settled his gaze on the empty grate. He'd practised his opening lines.

'First, I would like to remind everyone of St. Thomas's role, both past and present.' Padruig clasped and reclasped his hands, shifting the folds of his robe.

'I don't think there's any question of your Company's discretion, Master Padruig.' Bedford abandoned his chair and stood in front of the window. 'We've come together to discuss a means to avert tragedy, not for a lesson in history.'

'I merely wish to clarify.' Briefly, Padruig's eyes met Piatro's. 'There have been too many secrets.'

'Let him speak in his own way, sir… myself I welcome the clarity.' Lady Maria put down her needle-work.

'It was our quest for knowledge, or more particularly Otar Miran's pursuit of fabled cures and medicines, which first drew the Company to India. We soon established a successful house of trade, brokering precious goods between Portuguese and local merchants. So, it seemed pertinent to bring William and Aalia to India as children.'

'Bring from where?' Lady Rayner interrupted.

'Istanbul… we were obliged to move to move from our mother house because the French King had formed a treaty with Suleiman… We were perceived as rivals.' Padruig shrugged, putting out his ink-stained hands.

'How did the children arrive there in the first place?' The old lady kept watching Aalia, but the girl had set her face like stone.

'That, dear lady, is hardly the heart of the matter. When Tom Hampden came to my door with a new-born baby, he was terrified, almost to the point of madness. I allowed him to stay at the Old Temple, expecting he'd soon tell me what happened, however Tom only came to confess when he heard the news Queen Jane had died. I didn't know what to do. God help me, I even suggested we should smother the child. But the lady had put her trust in Tom, and he was a man of honour.

'Then I learned Tom had another confederate. Luke Trentham was Captain of the King's Guard. He'd made sure Tom escaped with the baby, and while we were unsure what to do, he organised passage on a ship bound for Danzig. I gave him a letter of introduction to Lady Rayner's son, James. He was responsible for managing our Company's trade along the Vistula.

'We thought the baby would be safe abroad, but the following month, Danzig fell to plague. James was about to leave for Istanbul, and it was decided Tom and Luke should accompany him with the baby.'

'I knew Luke in Geneva.' Bedford put his hand on Padruig's shoulder. 'Sebastian has his spirit. He was the very opposite of his brother Simon.'

'Why should this be secret?' Aalia stretched like a cat.

Padruig met Maria's brittle eyes. 'It wasn't meant to be secret. I'd almost forgotten Trentham's involvement. I had only met him once.'

'I think Brother Jon told Sebastian about his father.' Aalia looked away.

'And did this monk also inform him why his father and uncle didn't speak to one another?' Lady Rayner's frail hands were gripping the table.

Contrarily, Bedford was smiling. 'They said it was a woman… he had quite a reputation.'

'Lucji deserted Simon for his brother.' Lady Maria nodded to Padruig. 'We heard she died of plague… perhaps in Danzig?'

'How do these things explain our cause?' Andreas intervened.

'I'm sorry.' Maria closed her eyes. 'I merely wanted to provide good reason for Scythan's interference.'

'A Trentham seems at hand on every turn.' Piatro shook his head. 'Even at Durham House.'

Padruig stared out of the window. 'Yes, we would all like to hear about Durham House… Aalia?'

She moved forward, sunlight gilding her hair. 'I heard Scythan talking to Alvaro and an English woman.' She shuffled. 'They talked of Tom's Chrism Bowl and mentioned some letters, but, apparently, this isn't enough to tempt King Philip of Spain.'

She looked at the ceiling, avoiding their eyes.

'Drop your sulking, child.' Maria Rayner drew back her chair. 'Once a priest, always a priest… Padruig cannot break a contract he made before God.' She crossed the room, petticoats rustling, to stand beside Aalia, without touching. 'Everything he knows was given in confession.'

'Please, Lady Rayner, I don't want to open old wounds. This is difficult enough.' Padruig leant on the table.

'I will pay the ransom.' Maria stood between them. 'Since Luke abandoned us, I prefer to forget Lord Scythan is also my nephew.'

'Jamie is Scythan's cousin?' Aalia looked from Padruig to Lady Rayner and laughed. 'Why should that be unknowable?'

'Old wounds fester, child. Luke abandoned his wife for his brother's mistress.' Lady Rayner closed her eyes. 'And Simon has never forgiven him for bringing disgrace to their name.'

Bedford put down his glass and asked the question again. 'This letter clearly affirms Brother Jon's testimony—that only one child was born of Jane Seymour. But can we be sure there are no other witnesses willing to swear the truth of William's claim?'

The pair had adjourned to Bedford's compact study at Russell Place, the Abbot's finely drawn letter pressed open on the desk. A candle burned, and a lantern swung on the sconce; otherwise, darkness blanketed the room, the rest of the house being empty. He'd packed the servants with the rest of his household and sent them on to Chenies.

'Everything is hypothetical until we consider William's ambition.' He checked again, but the hall outside the door was black and silent. 'Once that seed was sown...'

Bedford held his glass above the candle, watching the burgundy dance. 'I think we can guess the identity of the woman at Durham House?'

'The Countess de Feria... Jane Dormer? Yes, it makes sense. She's a devoted Catholic, and served Queen Mary most loyally.'

'Did you know she was the last keeper of the royal jewels?'

'No! I'm hardly at ease with court appointments.' Padruig studied Bedford's broad face in the flickering candlelight.

'And that she was accused of stealing some piece before the chest was passed to Princess Elizabeth? Clearly, the Countess wanted one thing in particular.'

'Aalia sketched the ring, but I could see nothing remarkable. A signet ring with Seymour's crest. Anyone could make its like. She told me Tom gave her the ring, but she lost it after being attacked on the river. Later, she noticed Scythan wearing it. Actually, I didn't place much importance on the bauble, however, learning of its significance, isn't it rather intriguing Scythan didn't offer it to Alvaro?'

'Put alongside the Chrism Bowl, it links William to Jane Seymour. And what about these letters they discussed?'

'Unfortunately, we can hardly call on the Countess and ask to read them.' Padruig spelled the idea hoping the Earl would use his authority.

Bedford remained watching the candle flame. 'The Countess of Feria left London yesterday. The Queen finally granted her request to join her husband abroad. Poor Jane. Another month, and the baby might have dropped. It's no secret how much her Spanish husband hates Elizabeth. I would be inclined to believe them capable of doing anything to depose "this heretic queen."'

'They will continue to plot from outside the country. Cecil must have them watched.'

'But, surely, it is you, Master Padruig, who owns the best means of tracing them?'

'Lord Bedford, are you asking me to unveil their ring of subterfuge?'

'No, Master Padruig, I'm asking the whole bloody Company of St. Thomas to carry on doing what they're best at. There's barely a statesman in Europe who doesn't know St. Thomas's capacity for secrets. I'm merely suggesting you turn those means to your own benefit, for once.'

SACRIFICE – 5th Disclosure

Piatro was pressed against the rough inner wall of the Company's bow-roofed river-house, throwing empty nut shells into the slime-ringed water. Marron, on his way back from meeting Master Padruig with news of *Cornucopia*'s current moorings, was forced to stand and listen, his wherry being late.

'You know it takes seven years to master the art of engraving?' Piatro said.

'Drake said you'd visited the Mint.' Marron kicked at the step.

'Not any old Mint, dear Captain. The London Mint is set in the Tower, and there are obligations, oft quoted, upon those who enter that mighty fortress. I am among the rarest of individuals, singularly blessed.' The merchant was grinning from ear to ear.

'I can see you're bursting with the privilege.' Marron paced the length of the wall, hat mangled in plated hand. He'd told his men to be back within the hour, but having been at the remote Medway anchorage a month, they were glad to have a choice of city taverns.

He reached across and grabbed a handful of nuts.

'Hey! Shell your own. My fingers are raw.' The merchant swept up his store. 'The wardens like to give a tour.'

'What tour?' Marron was barely interested.

'The Tower... I was saying it's an honour to enter, if you're not charged with treason. The Master of the Assay took me to see where England's coinage is struck.'

'That's like showing a starving rat cake, surely?'

'True enough, my Captain, but they do not know my reputation as you do.'

'What reputation is that?' Aalia joined them, sloughing from the banded door which led inside the Old Temple.

'I thought you were detained by the Master?' Piatro smiled.

'After two weeks' penitence, I'm being trusted.' She returned his smile blandly. 'What are you eating?'

'Walnuts. Would you like some?' He opened his hand.

She shook her head. 'They smell musty… an ancient harvest. Didn't someone tell you not to accept gifts from strangers?'

'What makes you think these are a gift?'

'You wouldn't be fool enough to pay for old stock. They probably store them as a treat for the bears.'

Piatro spat into the water. 'There's a term for people who are always right, and it's not meant as a compliment.'

She laughed. 'Bedford explained his father's duties at the mint. Apparently, the Tower is also home to the royal menagerie.'

'I've heard Queen Elizabeth likes to watch the bear baiting,' Marron said, punching his hat.

'They do that elsewhere,' she said, stealing the mangled cap. 'What have you done with my musicians? For once, I've time to practise for St. Bart's Festival, and not a minstrel to be found.'

'They found a sponsor.' Piatro pointed across the river. 'Someone who pays by the hour.'

'Where, exactly?' She tossed the cap for Marron to catch. Soon, he'd be back on *Cornucopia* and thankful he didn't have to share the girl's company.

'The Castle on Bankside. I can take you.' Piatro smiled.

'I just need to find my voice… Does anyone remember where I left it?'

Leaving the captain in the boathouse, Piatro and Aalia passed through the covered vennel to reach the opposite pier, and there, they called a boatman, offering better than the usual fare. Crossing to the opposite shore, they could see the word, "Castle" painted boldly in black on a tall weather-boarded house overhanging the water's edge. The Castle upon the Hope was raised on wooden piers which shadowed the muddy shoreline, a towering, three storeys of lime-washed boards on a herringbone foundation of pressed red bricks.

The South Bank suffered less than the city from the dirge of summer plague. They'd cancelled most of the bear-baiting, but the stricken yap of fighting dogs, and those backing their bets, hung loud in the air as Piatro and Aalia dismounted from the wherry. Being Friday, the market had been busy, and its debris ran rancid on the jetty.

The inner courtyard of the tavern boasted two broad galleries where its patrons could leer down at the entertainments. Entering under its high-beamed gate, Piatro drew Aalia close. The crowd was tight-packed and ranked above their heads, men were banging on the rails. The uproar was being led by a round, canvas drum. It was strumming out of tune with the melody of Aalia's minstrels, who were playing from a dais set at the opposite end of the courtyard. The blond-haired lutist was making a brave attempt to lead the players in a madrigal, but the harmony suffered from the rebellious drum. The jeering crescendoed, just as Piatro pulled Aalia through the ring of observers.

'When the master's away... the servants wail like street hounds.' Aalia laughed, standing on tiptoe.

'Who the hell brought the drum?' Piatro pointed to the upper gallery. 'He's not one of ours.'

Aalia removed her cloak and dropped it onto the dais. 'No real tune or sense of rhythm... must be one of Scythan's. What do you think would settle them?'

'What about that Miserere you sang at Sweetheart? That should prove dulcet to the chorus of baying dogs.' Piatro swore as a flame-haired servant squeezed against him, sloping his silk coat with ale.

'Devotion? On this side of the river?' Aalia spat on her hands and used them to smooth down her hair. 'I'd prefer to survive the night whole.'

'Ouch.' The red-head laughed, and put out her hand. Piatro held up a coin, and she handed him a wooden cup.

'Don't worry; I'll fund your wake.' He raised the empty beaker, but Aalia was gone, squeezed onto the dais to join the huddle of musicians.

Every instrument, except the drum, fell silent. She smiled, catching Piatro's head as he ploughed through the crowd on a mission to silence the onerous drum. And then, she began to sing, a lurid song, bantered on the streets, and the lutist matched her as she chanted the first chorus. She followed with the most raucous song Piatro had ever heard her sing, at least in England. Guttural voices joined with the chorus, and then, the yard went wild.

Piatro didn't reach the drum before it stopped, but having found an excellent view, he remained on the upper gallery, re-filling his cup from the chamber behind. Aalia was in good voice and gave the audience whatever song they wanted. Piatro watched her teasing, laughing, tossing her golden head, and wondered what her admirers at court would make of this performance. As the applause grew longer, and louder, he wondered how she'd gathered such a store of English songs, and was considering the inn's takings, wishing he'd negotiated a share, when his eye went to a familiar copper-gold head steering through the crowd. William!

Reaching over the rail, he tried to catch Aalia's eye, but failed. Quivering like a feather, he raced down the gallery stairs, but splayed a gang of apprentices who grabbed at his coat and held him firm. He reached for his purse to pay for their ale, but they teased him until his temper snapped. Striking out, he jumped the stairs, three at a time, but by the time he reached the dais, Aalia was nowhere to be seen.

'Bloody William,' he swore.

The lutist, red-faced, said he'd warned her to stay, but he wasn't paid to act the bitch's fool when the men who took her were armed. Not for the first time, Piatro railed at Aalia's limp-wristed troubadours. Then, he remembered Padruig's last warning, and his entire being went cold.

SACRIFICE – 6th Disclosure

Piatro ran out of the inn, quickly realising there was only one way they could go, because he couldn't see any boats moving from the jetty. He chased up the cobbled lane, jumping gullies and gutters still muddy with yesterday's rain. Evening light pasted shadows between the muck-walled houses, but he ran on, hoping, expecting, he'd catch them soon. Coming to a crossroads, he was trying to decide which way to turn, and a raven-haired woman-child stepped into his path. Slowly she began to unlace her bodice.

'I'm missing a friend… tall, auburn hair, dragging his runaway sister?'

She tossed her head to indicate the way, and laughed, perfect little teeth like Arabian pearls. If only he had time… but he tossed a silver coin, promising he'd return.

The lane led to a market, and he recalled stuffed cherries and a reunion he'd rather forget. Dusk hung with the foetid stink of rotting vegetables, but the last stall was piled with bunches of herbs… lavender, sage, and lemon-balm. He pulled aside its canvas curtain to squeeze onto the narrow-paved path which went towards Paris Gardens.

Heavy-leafed trees rustled above his head. He was considering what to do next when he heard Aalia, swearing, in Urdu. Half hidden under the low hung branches of an ancient tree were two familiar figures, one tall and square, one slight and graceful. A stranger might think they were lovers. Piatro hung back, listening, veiled by a hedge, knife in hand.

'Isn't this what we both wanted?' William trapped Aalia's arm. 'Not to turn away from everything we… believed in?'

'I know who I am.'

'You once said we make our own destiny.' She stopped struggling.

'I never liked being nameless...'

'A name is like a prison. Look at the English... tied to the sins of the past. Without roots, we have freedom. Would you sell your spirit to this foolery, William, embrace their broken faiths, their passion for cruelty? Rebel, by all means, shout your name to the stars, but at least die for something you believe in.'

'There is no God, Aalia! Otar *knew* it, but hadn't enough courage to speak the truth. Don't you see, knowing the power of faith means I can use it to my advantage.'

'Otar knew it? Otar... is dead?' Aalia's voice faded.

Blind for words, Piatro stumbled towards them, just as William let go his hand. Aalia dropped to the ground.

William laughed. 'He burned with the Thomasines he was protecting. You want proof? Here's the amulet he wore.' He held out a small, blackened stone. 'Didn't Padruig pass you the news?'

'Have you finished?' Kneeling, Piatro held Aalia to his chest.

'Can we save the infant squabbles until we finish our business?' Alvaro seeped from the shadows, dressed in black from head to toe.

'What business?' Piatro stood to face him.

Aalia let go his hand and balanced unsteadily beside him.

'We should applaud the lady for her mischief; she's barely left a witness alive. I believe you have William's ring?'

'Not William's but Tom's. He said it was a gift from William's mother. Ironic you murdered your best witness, Alvaro. Tom might have shown you the crown.'

'There's the paradox, dear lady, I had nothing to do with Hampden's death. Just as you insist, he owned more value alive.'

Piatro saw the knife flare in Aalia's hand. Before he could move to stop her, she leapt onto Alvaro, spinning him to the ground. The Spaniard screamed then blotted his face with his hand. Blood spewing through his fingers, he jumped to his feet. Then, tearing at his belt, he drew his sword, except when he lunged at Aalia, William swiftly disarmed him, pinning the blade in the ground.

'Aalia!' William swung his fist. Aalia ducked, and instead, he caught Piatro. 'God damn you… I want to explain.'

'You just denied there was a God. Reason before you preach, or did you learn nothing from Otar?' She fired the words like arrows.

Piatro, head spinning from the blow, went to guard the sword, but the Spaniard stayed behind William. Black eyes glaring, he reached inside his jacket and pulled out a white square of linen, patting it against his cheek.

'Before you bite, I suggest you listen to our proposal.' Alvaro's voice came muffled through his handkerchief.

Piatro looked around, half-expecting a trap, but the gardens were empty. No company of soldiers, not even a drunken tinker leading his disgruntled mule.

Alvaro stepped forward and held Aalia tight by the shoulder. 'I want to propose a life for the ring,' he whispered in her ear.

Throwing out her arms, she twisted backwards, tripping over the gnarled roots underneath the tree.

Piatro spun on William. 'What did he say?'

'You're the master of trade, Kopernik. We have something of yours, and the price for its return is Tom Hampden's ring.'

Alvaro started to laugh viciously. Handkerchief masking his wound, he touched William's arm. Backing from sight, black faded to grey. Piatro watched until his eyes couldn't sift them from the shadows.

Aalia sat on the ground where she had fallen.

'What trade did he offer?' Piatro found his voice.

'They have Andreas.' Her hands gripped the earth. 'We must hand over the ring… or see Steynbergh dead.'

SACRIFICE – 7ᵗʰ Disclosure

The narrow street leading to Smithfield was impassable, being lined on either side with brightly painted booths and bracketed canvas stalls. Merchants bargained, bolts were unfurled, and anyone hoping to pass was funnelled into the melee until it was impossible to move without copious pushing and prodding, although Georgiou did his best. Padruig said the whole world came to St. Bartholomew's Fair, but lately, this most cosmopolitan market had degenerated into a feast of idolatry. Miracles came two a penny, and it was rumoured a hundred bands of minstrels would compete for the winner's purse. Twenty gold Angels, surely enough to please Piatro.

Long before Aalia had arrived in London, she'd heard Tom describe the Great Fair, seen it painted through homesick eyes. He'd remember the city officials in their glowing gowns and jewels, the mysteries of customs which always made him smile, the potent scents and feasting. Best of all, he recalled the music. That's why she knew William must come, and warned Bedford to be ready.

As they entered the fairground, she heard hand-bells proclaim the beginning. Looking down from their windows, the regular citizens waved. They'd likely bolted their doors against the mayhem. The travelling players and puppeteers, acrobats and tightrope walkers, the keepers of menageries, the fortune tellers, ballad-singers, card-sharps, prostitutes and pick-pockets. Thievery was rife, but the sergeant-at-arms kept close vigil, and any wrong-doers caught were tried and charged before nightfall, in the makepeace hall assigned to justice. The Pie-Powder Court would hear any plea, providing the plaintiff took oath the injury was sustained during the three-day fair.

Pushing through the stone gateway which bounded the priory, Aalia heard the Lord-Mayor begin his opening speech, but before he could finish, a peal of trumpets sounded, and a company of drums strummed an anthem. She laughed. Piatro warned he heard a rumour the Goldsmiths' apprentices, hated rivals of the Drapers, offered a fine reward to show the signal early.

Georgiou pulled Aalia onto a low, flint-faced wall where they could better view the proceedings. On a squat wooden platform stood a line of gentleman dressed in formal velvet, and one, robed in scarlet, was weighted by a huge gold collar which fired back the sun. Hand to his eyes, he was staring at the heralds, but just as the fanfare ended, a ribboned child ran onto the stage with a basket of gingerbread angels. The Lord Mayor started to push the infant aside, except the imp turned to the audience and lisped, 'God Bless Her Majesty.' With the crowd roaring approval, he duly bent to accept the gift, although the sugar-powdered smile hinted the donation had been sampled.

The chequered wall ringed a hubbub of entertainments, and it seemed the entire population of London were gathered inside. Aalia thought of Tom, who described the details so lovingly, the raw-faced apprentices and high-ranking guildsmen, the round-skirted ladies trailing servants at their elbows. And weaving like quickfire through the throng were ragged-boned children with busy, light fingers.

Making their way towards the allotted pavilion, Aalia stopped to finger a display of fine woollen worsteds. Cloth made for warmth, unlike her indigo tunic, woven for an Indian sun. India, where Otar was no longer waiting. Sensing a light hand touching her belt, she trapped the thin wrist, stopping the thief's razor-blade. The urchin looked up at her, grinning brazenly from ear to ear, daring she summon the sergeant. She released him, shaking her head, and he scampered into the crowd without looking back.

Piatro, dressed in a knee-length coat of finest bronze-watered silk, met them behind the pavilion's broad stage, bursting to mock English absurdities. 'These men of scissors and shears,' he said. 'At the final shout of "oyez," children rushed out screaming, and the lord-mayor set loose caged rabbits. The whole affair opens with the kind of rant more common at a boar hunt.' Piatro, collector of idiosyncrasies, laughter in his eyes, appeased his lack of trade.

People were piling inside the canvas walls, and Aalia sent Georgiou to call her musicians. The competition would run into the night, but they had to draw straws for the order of play. She'd told them to meet together when the clock on the tower struck ten, but they were distracted, and most of them pining for home. Passing through the crowd, she heard many unknown tongues and wondered how far they had come. Language, like music, was a mastering of sound.

Acrobats were performing on the canvas-covered stage. Red and yellow harlequins jumping through hoops and ropes, forming human towers. The smallest tumbler, who was not a child, leapt high into the air, performing several neat revolutions before dropping flat on his face. In a rim-pool of silence, the watching crowd held its breath, but he jumped up, apparently unhurt, and bowed stiffly to their applause. A hand touched Aalia, and William bowed his head, ignoring Piatro's hand on his shoulder.

'You have what I want?' he whispered.

'I will have it later. Be patient. I hope you haven't hurt Andreas.' She studied his face, measured his fox-hazel eyes. 'What have you done with Alvaro?'

'Do you think this a trap?'

'Thinking isn't very helpful where you're concerned, William. I must have left my wits in India, minding your common-sense. Deranged by summer madness, we both deserve to die young.'

'Did you think I wouldn't consider your future?' He tossed the threat idly, holding Piatro's eye.

A juggler had replaced the acrobats, but those watching near the stage became less attentive of the entertainments, and more interested in the man next to Aalia. William's copper hair, his richly embroidered clothes, made his likeness to a Tudor king difficult to mistake. He smiled his actor's smile and bowed to their applause.

'Andreas never harmed you, nor anyone I know. No more gentle soul ever walked this earth, yet you hold him hostage.' She damned him under her breath.

'You said our kind are able to choose their own destiny.'

'If ever there was a child of destiny, it is you, William, but I always hoped you'd choose right before wrong.'

'At least I know who I am.'

It was spoken too loud. Faces turned, interest spiked.

'And I'm the one who came to win this contest, and I've never reneged on a promise.' She caught his hand, wrenching the thumb in a cruel twist.

William wrestled free but didn't retaliate. The circle of curiosity shifted, as he walked majestically away. Here was another player, practising another scene.

Her musicians had gathered at the back of the stage, their blue and gold striped costumes burnished under the sun-bleached roof. Outside the pavilion, a crowd roared. The wrestling was about to begin. Aalia waited at the edge of the stage, as the juggler took his bow, then nodded to her lutist to begin. He stepped out to the tune of a jig, and the beat of a drum measured each phase deliberately, before bassoon and fiddle added their melody.

Georgiou stood with his arms crossed, guarding the end of the stage. Ignoring his glare of disapproval, she threw him her cloak, calmed her hair, and stepped up to join her troubadours. As the music swelled, her voice soared; the muse would keep her sane. But it took time to nurture the audience, to marry her songs to their passion. She felt their mood soften, just as someone called from the back. Would she sing to his request? She nodded carefully, expecting William's hand. However, when the crowd opened to make a path, there was Lord Scythan, a vision in his Sunday best.

'I thought you were bored with Orpheus's wanderings?' She bowed, leaning over the edge of the stage.

Scythan raised his voice, letting everyone hear. 'Most certainly the audience deserves your best... or do you beggar your songs for ignorance sake?'

She could feel her face glowing. Those within earshot were jeering already. Did he want to spoil her chances? She could see Georgiou and Piatro blundering forward, and then noticed

William, propped against the player's entrance, grinning. So, it was true; Scythan was his ally.

She sang the next lines without accompaniment, except Scythan, stealing the lute, married the chords to her voice.

> *'How pitiful is he who changes mind*
> *For Woman! For her love laments or grieves!*
> *Who suffers her in chains his will to bind,*
> *Or trusts her words lighter than withered leaves,*
> *Her loving looks more treacherous than the wind!'*
> *A thousand times she veers; to nothing cleaves;*
> *Follows who flies; from him who follows, flees;*
> *And comes and goes like waves on stormy seas!*

As the last notes faded, the applause was led by Scythan, whose eyes never left her face. He reached for her hand, knowing she couldn't refuse, and took her to the place where William had been standing.

'Master Padruig believed you were safely locked in your chamber. He seems to trust your word, even when everyone else sees otherwise.'

She didn't ask why he'd been to the Old Temple.

'We look at the same picture but see a different view.'

'Don't be flippant. Does Padruig know why you've come?' Scythan squeezed her hand so it hurt. 'I can see he doesn't. And despite all his commandments, you enticed Georgiou and Piatro to come here, too. How many must die to harness your whims?'

She bit her tongue on her first answer. He couldn't know everything, or he would have returned what he stole.

'I could argue I need the gold.' Twisting his hand, she smiled. 'You're not wearing Tom's ring?'

'I gave it away. Like you, I have no right to wear it.'

She opted to tell the truth. 'Alvaro asked me to bring it here today.'

'I hope you didn't promise... but you did, silly child!' He shook his head, sparking scarlet fire from the rubies on his chest.

He didn't know. Twisting from his grasp, she put a finger to her lips. Scythan, of all people, could negotiate her defences. Better say nothing than lie.

Before he could argue, they called her back to the stage. The audience had swelled, the canvas walls rolled up to accommodate the numbers. She gave her very best—the madrigals of a dead king, written out of love for his lady. A lady whose daughter reigned as Queen. It was meticulous and wholesale nostalgia, and they feted every chorus. Aalia carolled until her voice was hoarse, and Piatro sat drooling at thought of the prize.

It was late when Aalia made her way back to the pavilion to catch her brother's performance. He'd drawn the final place, which, by all accounts, gave him the best chance of winning. Dusk brought down the curtain of night, aided by smoke from the braziers. Closing her eyes only heightened the smells of burnt honey and roasting pork, of spiced wine and toasted nuts. Piatro, trailing behind, was filling his mouth with egg-sized marzipans, but she couldn't eat, hadn't eaten, since William had told her Otar was dead.

She didn't allow Georgiou to come back. She needed him safe. He spiked like a fighting cock, brown eyes burning. 'What's the point, when you can barely follow the language?' She pretended he was being unreasonable. And he stormed off, coal black head marking a trail as he ploughed towards the fair-ground and games he understood.

'Gingerbread angel?' William arrived at her side, splendid in ormolu velvet.

'Is it ripe?' She pressed the gift to her nose.

'Brought for your pleasure, from the fabled fields of Malabar, where ginger reeds are harvested with sickles formed from gold.' He kissed her cheek, while Piatro, anxious as a lap-dog, tried to catch his eye.

'Too rich, I think, for my simple tastes but tempting. The question is… can I take what is forbidden and not suffer hurt?'

'That's always the risk, sister… become my consort, and I'll make you immortal.'

She was almost afraid to answer. 'That reeks of incest, brother. I've flouted too many rules.'

'Then, there's nothing to lose and much to gain in flouting yet another. Come, we'll kiss on it.' Seizing a handful of yellow hair, he kissed her full on the lips.

Piatro tore him off.

'You ain't no right to grope the lady songbird.' One of the draper's in the crowd stepped forward, scissors swinging from his belt. Others around him were nodding. 'Shall we fetch the sergeant-at-arms?'

'What's a kiss amongst kin?' William laughed and pushed the man roughly so he fell into the crowd. And then, he stepped onto the stage.

The mood in the pavilion was perverted by copious amounts of ale. If William had sung a dirge, it would have been applauded. But he didn't sing a dirge, his voice propelled in perfect pitch. Aalia watched quietly, aware she was also being judged. He'd been practising, too. Music fit for a king.

William was starting his second song, when someone yelled he wanted a crown. Piatro paid the man to heckle, and Aalia stepped up to the cue.

'Would I had a crown for all the trouble he's caused me.' She came onto the stage, hoping her voice could be heard.

William raised his cap, and bowed. 'I think the girl's a poor loser.'

Some clapped, but the murmuring was louder.

'This girl's not lost.' She tossed her head and laughed. At the back of the pavilion, she could see Bedford's militia filing to ring the inner pavilion.

William followed her eyes. 'Have I introduced my sister?' He laughed, drawing her to his side. 'I thought she might have performed better, but that was early in the day. Perhaps you'd like a second chance to judge?'

She could hardly refuse.

Piatro was shaking his head. She drew a deep breath. What difference could a song make? Bedford's men were ready to arrest William. This was their plan; he couldn't escape.

'Better a duet than a duel.' She touched his cheek with her finger, and he smiled.

They'd learned the song in Padua; William was twelve and she two years less. A man of substance had stopped to listen, then applauded wildly, much as the audience did today. She turned to her brother before the ovation ended.

'What have you done with Alvaro?'

'He's nursing his face. You shouldn't have marked him, Aalia. He's burning for revenge.' Hazel eyes disdainful, he watched Bedford directing his men. 'If I'm arrested, you cannot save Andreas.'

Piatro beckoned a sergeant-at-arms at his side, brandishing a silver badge of office.

'My Lord Bedford has no jurisdiction here,' the sergeant yelled. 'While the Fair's in progress, any felonies must be tried by the Pie-Powder, and the complainant charged or discharged, whichever suits the court.'

Piatro pulled up to his full height. 'The Earl of Bedford is arresting this man for impersonating the king.'

'We ain't gotta king,' someone shouted, and a sea of heads nodded. 'Not at present, anyhows. You can't impersonate what ain't there.'

The sergeant-at-arms was joined by an under-sheriff. Banging his staff on the ground, he ordered they fetch the Lord-Mayor, or otherwise, place the "whole bloody pavilion" under arrest.

'If Lord Bedford insists on making a charge, I can't see any reason why the Pie-Powder shouldn't manage the trial. After all, the law remains the law.' The sergeant blanched as Bedford came up to them.

'Pie-Powder's about to begin. We'll have to hurry,' the under-sheriff growled. 'I've never arrested anyone for impersonating a king.'

'What about breaching the peace?' Bedford winked at Aalia. 'That's a felony, most assuredly?'

She swung before William realised, but the blow barely brought him to his knees, so she howled mischievously.

'But I was meant to win.'

Before her brother could argue, the under-sheriff grabbed his arm, and his sergeant arrested Aalia, despite the audience jeering and begging for another song.

SACRIFICE – 8th Disclosure

The Hand and Shears Tavern stood on the corner where Middle Street met Kinghorn. Reaching its open door, Piatro soon despaired. Filling the unpaved streets were boisterous crowds of people wanting inside, but, although the Pie-Powder Court was about to convene, guildsmen took precedence. The sergeant posted beside the chamber door shook his head when Piatro tried to pass. So, he slipped the man some weighty coins, smiling a callous smile. Finding the high-beamed hall bursting with aldermen, merchants, and clothiers brandishing the shears of their trade, Piatro's heart sank further. The pitch of anticipation was almost deafening as men shuffled to keep their places, baying for blood in their favourite sport, the game of lawyers not kings.

Bedford had warned how Englishmen loved to dispute law, reason he said they wouldn't accept any Dick or Harry, never mind William, for King, not without good and tangible proof. Piatro didn't have Tom's ring but, turned over and over in his pocket, a finite copy made from Aalia's sketch, formed and engraved by his friends at the assay. He hoped it would pass, at least until Andreas was safe. There could be nowhere more civil, more public, to exchange a life for a ring. He fingered Aalia's instructions again, handed with a scribbled map, her orders being absolutely clear. She wouldn't have Padruig told anything of Andreas's kidnap or even of Otar's death. He understood her reasoning, but standing here, a foreigner alone amongst Englishmen, he very much regretted abiding by that decision.

He was offered the share of a table by the very same tailor who had intervened at the Fair. A big man, firm-eyed, mousey hair tinged grey, Piatro shook him by the hand, acknowledging his gratitude, then perched on the opposite stool like a statue, mind hollowed of feeling.

The chief draper acting as steward held up a pair of outsized shears, hoping the room would fall to silence, but the signal went entirely ignored until the officer hitched up his robes and, jumping onto the same table which displayed the symbols of authority, waved his arms like the sails on a windmill.

'Go on, Billy, get the words out,' someone yelled.

The sergeant tried to clear a wider space in front of the table, forcing some men to abandon their places. All the while, Billy waited, holding up his shears, until gradually, the cries became mutterings, and every eye fixed on a solemn black-robed lawyer, who entered the room clutching half a dozen rolled papers under his arm. He removed the spectacles from his nose and bowed to a hail of applause before taking his place behind the table.

'Can the first complainant step up and be named?' the steward's deep bass voice boomed. Then, he jumped down from his temporary stage, looking daggers at the man who'd named him Billy.

A broad-shouldered tradesman wearing a badge of the city grocers' guild pinned to his cap was pushed into the room by the sergeant. It was a case of tipping weights, details being argued over the head of the perpetrator by those damaged through the fraud. The sentence was a fine of three shillings, though the crowd all bayed for a birching. There were two similar cases, before they brought down a luckless "fallen dove" found practising her "arts" behind the allotted tents. She stammered a lofty "Ta, mate," winking at the sergeant as they let her off with a token fine and a warning.

'Next case, please.' The steward looked to his sheriff. 'For causing an affray, a gentleman who refuses to give his name, and his sister, the lady songstress.'

William strode through the room, with Aalia following in his shadow, but neither looked slightly distressed as they took their places beside the table. William was robed like a prince, and Aalia more a pauper. She steadied her eyes on Piatro, just as every tongue in the room stopped its muttering.

'My brother asks to be called William Tudor, Lost King of England,' Aalia stated simply.

There was laughter, some jeers, and Piatro shifted in his seat.

Billy nodded to his sergeant. 'Thus, the pair caused an affray… we will hear the plaintiff's defence. Make your case, and be judged by those present, all good men and true.'

'I ask no better men to verify my name.' William glared slowly around the room, harnessing the laughter. Lifting his big copper head, he put both hands on his hips, setting his sumptuous cape in motion.

The candles on the table flickered. Billy stood up. 'Can you bring forth any witnesses who bare proof of your claim?'

Scythan swept up to the table, unusually sombre in fawn-coloured velvet, with Alvaro following close behind, dressed in black, his profile shrouded under a white linen bandage.

'I have asked this gentleman to present his proofs that William is the true-born son of Henry Tudor.' Scythan's heavy-lidded eyes fixed on Aalia's brother.

The room exploded again. Someone yelled from the farthest corner, 'The old king seeded a fair crop of bastards.' And tongues continued wagging long after Billy, face glowing red, put up his hands to calm them.

Alvaro placed a dull wooden box on the table and pulled out a parcel of letters. 'My name is Alvaro de Manríquez; I have irrefutable proofs.'

He presented the parcel to Billy.

It took a long time to unfold each letter and lay it flat. The lawyer read each word, shuffled the pile, and then read each word again. Face impassive, he handed the whole pile to Billy. Piatro uncrossed his fingers and swore.

Finally, someone shouted, 'What's it say, Billy?'

The lawyer whispered something in his ear. The documents were placed on the table, and Billy stood up to face the room.

'The first letter purports to be written by Queen Jane, the Seymour, to a gentleman named Luke Trentham, Officer of Her Majesty's Wardens.' He coughed. 'The letter bares her seal, and the date reads 20th October 1537. It thanks the gentleman for his services on the matter of her new sons' birth, and promises that he will be well rewarded for carrying out her wishes.'

'Where's the proof in that?' The tailor beside Piatro stood up.

'The letter distinctly writes "sons" in plural.' Billy pointed to the word.

'That's hardly proof,' the same man argued.

William shrugged away the laughter and copious waving of shears.

Alvaro smarted. 'It is evidence Jane Seymour gave birth to twins.'

The tailor wheezed to Piatro. 'That's a heavy load for one small letter. I'd hate to think any bugger would make as much of my plurals.'

'May I ask how you came by this letter?' a loud voice boomed from the doorway, and the crowd stirred to clear a path for the Earl of Bedford.

Alvaro picked up the sheet. 'The letter was discovered in Durham House.'

'Where the Count de Feria was accommodated while he served as Spain's ambassador to Queen Mary? Clearly, this letter was stolen and doesn't rightfully belong to you.' Bedford looked on gravely, while hoots and whistles distorted the room.

'Let us pass to the next letter, before we debate ownership,' Billy said importantly.

'This was also recovered by my Lord of Feria, but only recently has its relevance been understood.' Alvaro bowed to Bedford.

'Dated August 1551, it is signed by John Russell, First Earl of Bedford, Keeper of the Great Seal of King Edward VI of England. The letter commands Thomas Hampden, manservant, to return his charge to England on receipt of this document, along with a certain ring he holds in remembrance of his duty. It seems Hampden was given the ring in order to prove his charge's birthright.'

'And have you brought this ring to show the court?' Scythan asked casually.

'I have an imprint of its seal, the original being too precious to carry.' Alvaro, eyes burning into Aalia, held out his hand.

Scythan didn't examine the wax and ignored William's sneer.

'Spain has engineered this anarchy.' Bedford slammed his fists on the table. 'They sought a player with uncanny likeness to King Henry, and then fitted a puzzle which would unravel like the truth, no doubt hoping to fool weak-minded men.'

The room roared, hats spun into the air while lanterns gutted and sparked. Billy thumped on the table, and all eyes turned on William.

'You come, no doubt, Lord Bedford, to dismember your family's part. Surely both you and Lord Scythan are implicated in this conspiracy. It is true an agent of Spain discovered these letters, but nothing was ever fabricated to fit our purpose. This second letter dates to the time when King Edward was dying, and proves, I believe, that Bedford's father planned to find the twin and install him in place of his brother.'

William raised his rich baritone to greater effect. 'Tom served me loyally throughout my childhood, but never revealed any details of my birth. That is why you had him killed.' He pointed straight at Bedford.

The room burst uneasy, men pushed through the door, suffocating those already crushed within. Aalia stood without moving, but Piatro jumped from his seat, screaming out his opinion, but couldn't make his voice heard before Bedford replied.

'Hampden was murdered because he could identify men who plotted to kill our Queen. Men of your employ!' He laid his hand on Alvaro's shoulder.

William turned and bowed solemnly to the audience. 'When first told I was heir to England's throne, I laughed in the face of the messenger. Yet, I had to come to England, if merely to prove it was a lie. Tom was the only person who knew the whole truth. He took me to India, helped to hide my birthright. His testimony meant he had to die, they...' He turned on Aalia, shaking his fist. 'She knew Tom could prove who I was, but before he could hand me my mother's ring, she stole it, and had my oldest friend murdered. The Company of St. Thomas engineered her actions; they brought her to England so she could lure me into their hands.'

Every eye in the room fixed on Aalia. Ring-pooled by hatred, she put out her hand and touched William's arm. 'Tom remained your most loyal servant. He only wanted to protect you. You know that's why he gave me the ring.' She had never seemed so fragile. 'Tom loved you more than life.'

'That's not true,' Alvaro screamed.

William went to touch her face. 'You took it to show the Earl of Bedford?'

'No, I took it to show Tom's sister, but lost it when some fool tossed me in the river.' She glared at Alvaro.

'Such lies,' Alvaro spat.

'Such honesty,' Bedford intervened. 'It's true I planned to arrest the girl after Tom Hampden was murdered. A witness claimed she and her Indian guardian were guilty of slitting his throat, except I soon discovered the man was paid to speak her name. Never has she acted as your enemy.'

'I know she came to England just to destroy me,' William roared.

Piatro fought to be heard above the shouting. 'She didn't want to come... God knows we had to drag her away... all she has ever wanted was to save you...From being misled by these Jesuits. From being made a fool.'

Aalia, gazing back at her brother warily, climbed onto a stool. 'I am my own witness, Piatro.'

Scythan tried to steady her, but she pushed him away. 'Tell me, William… what is a king, except a star forced to shine perpetually? When did your ambitions stretch to courting tyranny? And this… in a country you've never known? Better a windowless prison than a crown… for miscreants such as we. Why throw away such freedom to sit in bondage to Spain? Because that would be their charge, to always be their pawn… discard your principles, William, but never sell your soul.' She stopped, and would have fallen except Scythan caught her.

'You can't prescribe my future anymore than you know my mind.' William's square jaw clenched.

'We were taught to question everything,' Aalia spoke softly.

'And have begged for our whole lives.' Amber eyes read her compassion.

'Where is freedom, except in the streets?' She put out her hands, knowing this time, he listened.

Outside, in the street, noise and movement exploded as men in half-armour flooded through the entrance door, forcing the crowd to shuffle aside, loading pressure on the tinderbox room. 'I charge you with treason,' Bedford shouted, as the soldiers moved to ring the central table.

Alvaro rounded on Bedford, having slipped Scythan's sword from its sheath. But Bedford was completely unarmed. The room held its breath. Before any troops could intervene, a disturbing number of the audience shook off their cloaks. Piatro recognised the buff-coloured jacks they wore. William's rough-handed militia.

William and Alvaro escaped through the door to the kitchens while Bedford's men were pinned back by the sheer weight of men. While the buff coats forged the path to the back of the hall, they didn't need to fight, having opened a way through the crowd The escape had been well-planned, and Aalia, a mere distraction.

SACRIFICE – 9ᵗʰ Disclosure

Aalia forced open the tall, outer shutters and climbed through the window to drop into the street. Padruig would understand. She had nothing more to give. The shouting, the jeering, the lure of the chase as panic spewed from the tavern into the streets, echoed down the narrow-walled lane which took her away from the rush of angry men. Bedford, trapped by the crush, couldn't reach William, couldn't stop him escaping. This was Scythan's doing; nothing left to chance.

She pulled up her cloak, strapping it tight at the neck, mechanically touching the raised badge of St. Thomas. The simple cross which stood for everything she aspired to be… once aspired to be. Her world had shifted its focus.

Piatro dropped into the street behind her, face drawn like a papist at prayer. She almost laughed. But he let her go without a quarrel, and she ran full pelt, before he could change his mind. William would go into hiding again until they were ready to play the next scene. Saviour or martyr? In the end, Spain didn't care if Tom's stories were true. There was once a beautiful, blameless lady… except she didn't make the connection, stupid child, not until today. What's in a name? Jane Seymour's first love, first promised husband, was a gentleman called William Dormer, father of another Jane, who married a Spanish count. Puzzled pieces moored in her head.

The steelyards were busy, despite the late hour. Ships must sail with the tide. The crane on the foreshore ducked like a braying donkey as she passed beneath, and another memory stirred, of Sebastian in his tinker's disguise. High above her head, a voice screeched out some blurred Teutonic warning, and she drew up her hood and pushed her legs faster. Piatro would have translated; a merchant must be fluent in many tongues. Poor Piatro. The profits weren't as predicted.

The boat sat moored where they'd promised. A clumsy vessel, wide-berthed, made for moving baser cargoes than bringing pawn to castle. She was betraying everything she loved, but Andreas should not die, not in a game of her making. She should have stopped them sooner, passed Bedford the truth, except she could not watch William die.

The oars cracked in unison, as they passed a string of barges steaming with their cargo of night dirt. London had a rhythm she was beginning to understand. Englishman preferred their world rooted in sense and order, not the brash chaos of India. What kind of ruler would William make? Between Agra and Kathmandu, he'd tested the brunt of petty kingdoms, yet the vain fool would set his sights on England. And it was all her fault.

Soon, it would be completely dark. No moon ghosting the velvet sky, and a heavy mist was seeping downriver with the tide. The landing where they took her was broken and decrepit; Alvaro dragged her from the boat, tempered by William's arm. Tucked beneath the overhanging beams of an inn, three men carried a rag-covered bundle. She walked across, turned back the folds, and touched Andreas's face. It was cold, but she felt the vein in his neck and found the pulse-beat strong. Whatever poison they fed, whatever harm they wreaked, Padruig would know the remedy. Poor Andreas. She pictured him slaking off his cap and spinning like a top, spewing observations. His was a brotherhood of intellect, unused to mitigating treason. St. Thomas had given her life without boundaries, but just as she realised her true gifts, they refused to trust in her gender. Padruig would learn to forgive her.

'You'll take him safe to the Old Temple?'

'You brought what I asked?' Alvaro trapped her arms.

'Everything, churned in a bucket alongside my pride.'

SACRIFICE – 10ᵗʰ Disclosure

Georgiou first noticed the gypsy while kicking a bladder ball surrounded by a knot of screaming children. Having retreated to the farthest corner of the fairground, he was running up and down chasing the ball, enjoying the chase and the laughter. Looking up, he recalled the man's limp before he caught any glimpse of his face. Goff, who no-one had seen since they had left Kirk Yetholm.

Leaving the field, he followed the gypsy, weaving carefully, but Goff never once glanced behind. Perhaps it shouldn't have been a surprise when he stopped at the Hand and Shears Tavern, but instead of steering inside the busy entrance, Goff waited outside the door. Georgiou held back, thinking what he should do next. Aalia hadn't thrown him off, but had chosen to take Piatro to the Pie-Powder Court, knowing the merchant's tongue held more power than a sword. Bedford was here, too, because the tavern doors spewed with men bearing his livery. In fact, the streets were bristling with armed men.

Georgiou knew a trap when he saw one. He melted into an alley, straight into the arms of a livid-faced Goff.

'I expected you to be with her.' Goff's accent was different, not the thick mottled burr he'd struggled to interpret but a tongue akin to Tom's.

'She said I'd be bored by the debating of law.'

'How many years have you known her?' Fury blazed his eyes. 'Yet, she dupes you into doing exactly the opposite of what is needed.'

'Piatro was with her.'

'God damn you all for fools… She wasn't meant to be here… Lord Scythan ordered the Master of St. Thomas to keep her under lock and key. He doesn't yet know the bastards have taken Doctor Steynbergh as hostage.'

Georgiou put his hand on his knife. 'How do you know this?'

'My name is Guy, not Goff, and I'm in the service of Lord Scythan.'

'You serve that peacock? Why?'

'He barely trusts you or your Company can protect the girl. I was meant to stay with her, whatever happened, but when she opted to aim for Scotland, I ran to warn Scythan. He almost had my head on a plate for abandoning you, said his orders were clear; the girl must not be harmed.'

'Did you know Bedford was coming here?'

'Of course not! Soon as I saw, I sent a message telling his lordship to get over to the Pie-Powder quick. William's gone and announced himself as rightful king. Didn't you hear the news? It's rife across the fairground.'

Georgiou turned towards the street, and caught sight of Piatro amongst the billow of people, running before he knew he was moving.

'Where's Aalia?' he said, catching the merchant's cloak.

Piatro didn't seem anxious. 'Georgiou, you found Goff. How clever.'

Georgiou's fist struck bone. 'What have you done, Kopernik?'

Then, his mask unravelled.

'They took Andreas as hostage, not that anyone in the Company noticed, and Alvaro will exchange him for the ring.' He stepped back, rubbing his cheek, smoothing his clothes.

'You let her go alone? Idiot. She doesn't have the ring, Scythan has it.'

Guy set his eyes on Piatro. 'You mean the one with Seymour's crest? I've not seen him wearing it since Berwick.'

Piatro sucked a loud breath. 'Don't worry; I had a copy made from Aalia's sketch. Remember, Alvaro has never seen the bloody ring, and probably neither has William. We had a serious plan.'

'And that makes you trust the Spaniard will keep his word?' Georgiou braced his fists to strike again.

'What choice did she have? That's why she wouldn't have Padruig informed.'

'But what did she tell Bedford?' Guy said. 'Because someone gave him the nod, and it wasn't Lord Scythan.'

'We must find Aalia.' Georgiou screamed in Urdu..

Piatro slowly nodded. A thin line of blood was dripping from his nose, and he mopped it on his sleeve. 'Which is just what I was doing... She made me a map, drawn on my shirt sleeve. Look, it marks where she was going.'

Guy peered over Georgiou's shoulder as Piatro shook his sleeve into the light. 'That's the German wharf; we might get there before her, if we run.'

Piatro hissed, pinching his nose. 'She expected me to follow… at a distance.'

'No, Piatro.' Georgiou pushed him back. 'You must go and tell the Master, because I don't want to be anywhere near when he finds out what you've done.'

SACRIFICE – 11th Disclosure

S ea mist swirled from the river, drawn by sticky night. Blanketing the town, seeping through brick and wood and stone, marling every patch of land, every cobbled thoroughfare. Fearing its witchery, wherrymen kept to their beds, trusting mid-morning's turn of tide would cleanse the fog and let them steer in safety.

A pair of riders halted at the barren wharf on Bankside, peering through the spooling blackness. It was close to sunrise, and their orders were most clear; their despatch from Ralph Sadler must pass to Cecil before anyone should glean a rumour of its news.

Riding post from Berwick, they'd made York before dusk, and given the light of a bald, July moon, managed footfall in Greenwich a bare two days later, only to find the Queen's secretary was not there. Nor was he in London.

They had to eat. But in the time, it took to swallow a mean supper and organise fresh horses, thick mist had swirled in from the sea. They'd ridden past the bridge in search of a wherry to row them to the Palace of Hampton Court, except this last stage of their journey was defeated by the lack of a boat.

'Bloody fog!' Sebastian Trentham spewed out his frustration.

'Hush!' Robin Yates, his second, peeled off his helmet in order to listen. 'What was that cry?' He trotted his horse into the darkness.

Hooking his saddle with one hand, Sebastian loosened the buckle on his hood, but his horse bucked, ears flattened in fear. Tightening his fist, he kicked hard, but the stupid beast reared and tossed him on the ground. Under the wharf, water slapped and spat as Sebastian swore at the night, wary of betraying his duty. Robin hadn't returned. And then, an unearthly scream ripped through the darkness.

He jumped up, but before he could re-mount, a handful of louts shuffled from the darkness, herded by Robin, standing tall in his stirrups. The half dozen ragged youths formed a hesitant huddle as the flare from their torch mirrored in Sebastian's drawn sword.

'What's happening here?' He pointed out a tall, thin-faced boy with thick, sandy hair.

But the lad was mutinous, staring at the ground.

'Me da sent me when we 'eard the fighting. We lives t'other side of pits. Me da thinks the watch was paid off.'

'Is he a Frenchie?' a thin voice yelled from the rear.

Someone slapped him silent.

'So, your father thinks there's money to be made?' Sebastian stepped forward, and six pairs of hungry eyes fixed on his raw blade.

'Aye, sir.' The reedy lad shrugged to his peers.

'Dobbin head, wha'da'y say that for?' another voice muttered.

'Show me the place, and you'll see real gold.' Sebastian held the urchin's chin. 'What's your name, boy?'

The glare became a broad grin. 'Jem, that is Jeremy Watts. I knows who you are, sir. Me da pointed you out pastimes… fought wiv' your uncle in France, lost a leg at St. Quentin, sir.'

'And does your father think it's the work of smugglers, Jem?' Sebastian dropped his hand.

'That's why me dad said I 'ad to fetch the guard, but Tommy 'ere fawht we should deal wiv it.'

Heads began nodding in unison. Brought up in the stews, they would doubtless carry knives and, spurred by danger, hungered for a fight. Sebastian's uncle had taught him to respect such instincts. Or exploit them, depending on the contingency.

'An Angel for whoever leads to our first arrest, lads! Or double, if we manage more!'

Robin nodded. These lads were better used to patrol their own territory. The horses skitted, as the gang slewed headlong into the mist. Sebastian followed on foot, leading his horse past the pike ponds. Following the balm of summer, they'd festered, but he suffered the stench, being more concerned the urchins could be trusted.

They trailed across pitted ground, with the lads keeping their torch low, exposing the path which circled the ponds. There had been no more cries, nor even the rumour of a brawl, but as they reached a low wall, some of the boys ran ahead, brandishing their coarse weaponry. The wall marked the boundary of a blacksmith's yard. Sebastian and Robin roped their horses to the gate before following the urchins inside.

Fog blanketed the cobbled courtyard and seeped inside the span of open-fronted buildings. The smoke-soured walls framed silence, and nothing, apart from their presence, seemed to stir the empty air.

Nevertheless, they moved cautiously. Robin unhooked and lit some lanterns, while Sebastian set one of the boys to work the bellows. As the fire began to glow beneath the broad hoop of its chimney, the full extent of the forge began to take form. The chimney was built against the highest of three brick walls protected by a huge peg-tiled roof supported by a tangle of heavy beams. A massive anvil stood next to the fire, and racked neatly along the walls on either side were rows of blackened tools; hammers ranged by shape and size, wood-handled files, and every manner of tongs. The lanterns caught glimmers of discarded metal ground into the hard clay floor.

They gathered in the fire's warm glow, all except Jem, who ratched around the shadows.

'Sir… here.' He waved his torch in front of a wood-partitioned stall set against the wall farthest from the hearth.

Robin took a lantern and led Sebastian to the stall.

Lying at Jem's feet was a dead man. Sebastian stooped to close the hollow eyes but then recoiled. A face of many seasons, a face he recognised.

'I know him! He worked for my uncle.'

'Are you sure?' Rob leaned across, holding the lantern closer. 'His face is deformed from beating.'

'God knows! I'm not mistaken… but why? What was Guy doing here?'

'And why did they cut off 'is fingers?' Jem's voice drained of bravado.

'This man… when I was about your age… taught me how to use a sword.' Sebastian knelt, ignoring the shuffled ignorance crowded round the stall.

'Was he a soldier like you, sir?' Jem crouched at his side.

'One of many reasons I wanted to serve. He gave his best years abroad… against an enemy less discriminating than the French!'

'Wot d'you mean, like Turks?'

Sebastian nodded. 'When I find the bastard who did this, I'll have his head on a plate.' Straightening, he spat out orders. 'Go and light more lanterns. We must search every inch of this smithy.'

He knew the murdering bastards were likely nearby, because Guy's body wasn't yet cold. Setting two lads to keep watch near the outer gates, he warned them not to speak unless to raise the alarm, then sent another to mind the fire, because they needed better light. Robin led a search of the sheds propped around the courtyard, while Jem took a lantern to check the rest of the stalls.

Barely a minute later, he shouted, 'I've found another one… I fink he's dead, too.'

Lying half-buried in filthy straw was Aalia's Indian friend, twisted awkwardly, because his arms were bound around a heavy, round-bellied cauldron, and slopped with coal-black tar.

'I fink this one's foreign.' Jem looked up at Sebastian, puzzled more than afraid.

Sebastian knelt. Under the flickering lantern, he examined Georgiou's wounds while Jem followed his actions closely. 'Bring the light closer,' he ordered. 'For God's sake, what's been happening here? I know this man, too.'

'Don't fink his own mother would recognise 'im wiv those bruises.' Jem started sawing at the bonds with his blade. 'Don't want to hurt 'im more than needs must. He's beaten rotten, sir. I 'fink he's lost a lot of blood… at least I don't 'fink this is water.' Jem held up red, sticky fingers and pointed to a thin stream of liquid seeping under the wooden partition.

Sebastian took the lantern from the boy and, brushing aside detritus and straw, started to trace the source. He'd checked inside the remaining two partitions before reaching the corner beyond the wooden stalls.

'Oh, my Lord… bring another lamp quickly,' he yelled.

Set into the floor behind a lesser anvil was a heavy iron bracket used to steady cart-wheels whilst the blacksmith beat the rim. Fixed inside the bracket was a metal-studded wheel and pinned to its spokes, stretched like a new-tanned hide, was another lifeless form, bound face down.

Sebastian ripped off the remnants of cloak which shrouded the broken body and pressed his shaking fingers into the cold hollow of neck, praying for a pulse. The skin was cold, too cold. As he began to cut the ropes, the scale of barbarity made him catch his breath. The bastards had nailed this one's wrist to the wood. Looking up at Jem, he whistled through his teeth. Then, he recognised the knife.

Desperately, he tried to draw the dagger out from its sheath of mangled flesh.

'The wood's swollen.' Robin was kneeling beside him. 'It might be easier to break the blade. I'll hold the arm steady.'

'That's some dandy dagger,' said Jem. 'Are those emeralds real?'

Sebastian was past knowing. Robin bent and loosed the boyish cap, spilling a mess of yellow-gold hair. But he already knew this was Aalia. Blind fury stopped the hammering of his heart.

They raided the blacksmith's store to free her lifeless body. And while he worked the tongs, Sebastian kept his anger in check, attending to what was needed without the agony of speaking. Jem, watching like a hawk, held the lantern steady. Finally, Sebastian heard someone say, 'Turn the body over.' But he already knew what was coming, knew what the pool of light would reveal.

'Oh my God, it's that songstress... the one wot...' Jem met his eyes and floundered.

Dawn came spinning through buttercloth, sieving the mantle of fog. Cordoned by Jem and his peers, the smithy was kept well guarded. But nobody came, not the blacksmith or his apprentices, not even the night-watch appeared, a bonus, as it happened, but it seemed to prove the truth of Jem's suggestion. Whoever was responsible, and he guessed his uncle would agree it was Spain, everyone had been paid. Perhaps it was better this way, keeping the dead anonymous.

Taking Jem aside, he asked if he could read.

'I don't do words, but I knows every church and alehouse between Southwark and Bishopsgate, if you sketch their signs. A cherry will do for the Drake and Berry, and a bell... well, that's easy I s'pose. You knows the rhyme? Oranges and lemons for the bells of St. Clements.'

Sebastian nodded. He liked the lad and wanted to trust him.

'I'll talk you through the route, then I need you to fetch a carter... I don't want to tell him the place where you're going. It's essential you lead him there.'

Drawing a map on a square of torn linen, he laid it on his hand.

'Whe're you going, Master Trentham?'

He was wrapping Aalia in his heavy travel cloak. Tearing a strip from what was left of his linen shirt, he started to wipe clean her face.

'The dead deserve respect,' he said.

And then, her eyes stirred.

'Make some bandages.' Sebastian hardly dared breathe. He slipped off his coat, untied his leather doublet, then tore off his jacket. Her body held no warmth, and the morning air was chilled; he had to give her life. They tied strips of linen around her wounded wrist, but Robin shook his head.

'She needs more than a prayer, Seb.'

'I'll take her to the old convent, near the Bishop's Palace. They'll know how to care for her.'

Robin studied his captain. 'Aye, I doubt she'll live 'til evening, anyhow.'

'What else can I do?'

'Fetch Maisie.' Robin squeezed his shoulder. 'She's to nursing what your uncle is to diplomacy. Let Maisie be the miracle. The girl needs a woman's touch.'

SACRIFICE – 12ᵗʰ Disclosure

Night fog buried the city beneath its spires. Watching from the roof, Padruig cursed the blanket which mired every street, wishing he wasn't so helpless. Gull had gone to search the river with every hand he could muster, using for guide the raw map Aalia had scribbled on the merchant's sleeve. Kopernik, their level-headed merchant, grey face drained of life, had returned like a beggar to confess his part in every damning fault and flaw. That was long before midnight, and Gull had not yet returned. There had been no word, nothing to succour his fears.

When Kopernik stormed into his study, proud face sculpted in remorse, Padruig didn't doubt the news was bad. Stooped in the white-walled chamber, twisting his hands, his rings, the merchant aged a good ten years, as he described each turn of his failings. That Aalia could deceive was hardly a revelation, but Kopernik's support underscored every stage of her defiance, and while Padruig believed she was safe in her room, trusting in her promises, she intended this futile sacrifice. Lady Rayner had warned him Aalia loved her brother too much to be trusted. Warned he must admit everything of the truth.

And what of his own failings? Since Bedford had sent Andreas to survey the iron works of Kent, it never occurred to Padruig he might have gone astray. Not their worldly magician. At every stage, they… no… *he* had underestimated William.

But then, Kopernik should have known better, seen the extent of William's greed. Power is a ruthless mistress. He should have recognised the mechanics of a trap as soon as William had pronounced Otar dead. If the efficient and dedicated network of spies serving the Company of St. Thomas were ignorant of this Master's death, how in damnation did Kopernik suppose a Spanish Jesuit in London could come by such news? Of course, it was a lie, effective in its treason. William knew exactly what steered his sister. And the cruelty of his lies turned over and over in Padruig's mind, sparking a form of rage he thought time had worn to dust.

Dawn smeared gloom through streets of mired shadows. Padruig, worn ragged with worry, went to stay sentry at the river-gate, hoping Gull, anyone, would bring some solid news. Voices sifted from the river, boatmen's cries, breached through the fog, and a metal-wheeled cart clattered down the vennel which led to the Old Temple jetty.

There was a shock of heavy-fisted hammering. He rushed to unlock the outer doors, but it was a stranger. A fierce-eyed youth, with blood and filth clotted all over his clothes. Padruig lifted a lantern from its peg, expecting he'd been told to fetch a physician.

'Are you the master of St. Thomas? Only the carter wants 'is fee.' The lad had an urchin smile. 'And Master Sebastian said you'd pay.'

'What need have I of a carter?' Padruig swung the lantern into the vennel.

Human form took shape from the fog. A carter, a big brute of a man, domed head sunk deep into his shoulders, shunted into the ringed lamplight, torn leather apron smeared in crimson gore. Padruig pulled the canvas cover from his cart and met, soused in blood, Georgiou's mangled form. The urchin's pale eyes married to his pity.

Padruig gave the carter an Angel for his labours, but dumbed by horror, spared no word of thanks. He expected the youth to go with the cart, but without another word, he helped lift Georgiou into the hall, shouldering his entire weight while Padruig closed the gates and slid the bolts home.

Padruig fought to quell his fears and concentrate on what he must do for the living. The lad was formed like a hank of string and looked in need of a good solid meal.

'Master Sebastian sent me 'ere. I'm to stay and wait for word, and answer all your questions wivout 'olding anyfing back.'

Again, the fearless stare. Padruig had no choice but to trust the guttersnipe.

The infirmary reeked of lavender. Symptom of Aalia's busy hands. At first light yesterday morning, she'd gathered flowers from the kitchen garden and set them into a jug. He'd been scathing of her frivolity, but then, she knew what was to happen and likely guessed it might come to this.

They laid Georgiou on a low wooden pallet. Through every action, the lad didn't stint, taking watch while Padruig ran to their apothecary store, doing everything he ordered until Georgiou's wounds were bound, and the broken bones set as best he could manage. And all the while he worked, the strange, pale eyes were watching. After Padruig washed away the last traces of blood and leaned back on his heels to pray, the lad was quietly respectful, unusual for his kind.

There was nothing more to be done. Straightening his aching spine, Padruig leaned against the wall, and the lad stood up beside him and asked what mended a broken bone. Padruig measured his interest and then quietly explained how bruises will fade without the use of medicine, but fractured bones may twist and bend if left unset, leaving the patient a cripple. All the medicine in the world couldn't help heal such scars. They could only wait and pray, hoping Georgiou was strong.

Padruig led the lad down to the kitchen. It wouldn't help to starve.

Taking out bread and a bowl of fresh curds, he set them on the table before fetching ale from the store.

The youth scooped the bread hungrily. 'We didn't see who dunnit.'

Padruig weighed his stare, wondering what he knew. 'What's your name?' 'Jeremy Watts, sir. Friends calls me Jem.'

Then, out poured his story, detailed like a play, and Padruig entered through hell's gate.

SACRIFICE – 13th Disclosure

Mid-evening, and a cockerel was crowing raucously, an excellent reason not to keep hens. Its banter disturbed Maisie's best measures for peace and quiet, and sent her scuttling to shut the window. A woman of grand proportions, and even vaster sympathies, her skirts caught on the bed, his bed, and she smiled, remembering that last time he'd taken her there.

She'd been furious when Sebastian had sent for her at such an early hour. Furious it wasn't Simon, needing her, after all these years. 'God, what have you done, Seb?' But as soon as she saw the girl, she understood his reasons. There wasn't time for pleasantries. She pulled the bloody cloths from his hand and sent him to kindle a fire. They'd need gallons of boiling water and fresh, clean bandages, in case their patient might live.

Maisie knew the waxen sheen of the poor girl's skin meant they were likely too late for anything but a wake. Yet, she set herself to do what must be done, diligent, despite her fears. Untying the crude compress - the lad did well - she probed deep into the wound to clean out the damage. And while she worked, Simon had come, lighting the tapers, ordering whatever was needed before the mantle of death filled the room.

Through it all, the girl never woke. Maisie bound the wound with linen, which Simon had brought. And only at the end did she dare look into his eyes, knowing her own were mired with the stains of yesterday's kohl.

For three days, Maisie barely left the girl but ate, drank, slept within call. Sebastian was obliged to return to his duties but Simon remained, taking Maisie aside, explaining he wouldn't leave until he knew if the girl would live, drawing her into his heart as never before, even when she'd been his mistress. There'd been a time she wanted him to love her more than life itself. She hoped the girl might live, if only for his sanity.

For the first time in many years, she actually knelt and prayed.

During daylight hours, Simon stalked the woods which bordered his estate, or swam in the sun-drenched river. On the second day, a herald arrived from Windsor, where the court was entrenched in pageants, and he sent him away with some meagre excuse, which Maisie thought unwise. Maybe he did despise them, but he'd never ignored a summons. Never letting anything stand before duty, obliging his sovereign's whims, except for this base-born misfit.

It was dark when she next heard his foot-fall on the stairs. He went straight to the bed, not daring to ask.

'She lives. I don't know how. She's stronger than she looks, this one.'

'But will she be strong enough?'

'She's hardly led a pampered life.' Maisie, discovering the scars, considered whether she should show him, trusting he'd believe it wasn't done out of spite. And she lifted the girl from the pillows just enough for him to see the raised bands.

'And the men of Saint Thomas promised to take good care of her.' He'd looked on, blank-eyed, as Maisie replaced the sheets.

By the evening of the third day, Maisie hoped the worst was done. At least the material pain; no amount of nursing could cure the hurt inside, not in her experience. And what if the abuse brought forth a child? Who'd love a runt born of such assault?

In one sense, they were blessed. Spending most of his days at court meant Simon hadn't opened the house in a year, so it contained no other servants than his steward. Whatever happened to the girl, it would pass un-reported.

During those long hours when the girl's life dangled on a spider's thread, he'd come to share the vigil and talked of what the girl had done, how she'd come from India. Maisie trounced out that such a thatch was surely made under English skies, and he'd blushed. Lord Scythan, who never showed emotion, which made her wonder why his passion ran so deep. Afterwards, Maisie tilted with better care when he demanded hourly reports. He'd never been tempered to sympathy, but it took much to gain his respect. And somehow this waif possessed more than that. Somehow, she'd harnessed his soul.

Maisie had tidied the bed-clothes, attended the fire, and settled back inside her chair before she sensed the girl was watching. Blanched like the pillows which framed her fragile face, she stared blankly at the windows. Such opulent eyes. And the hairs on the back of her neck suddenly marched to attention. Sebastian had those eyes, that same unnerving talent of looking right through you. But, surely, that couldn't be… Simon would never have taken one child and left another to its fate.

'Do I know you?' Her voice fell soft as a feather.

Damn the cockerel.

Maisie leant close, bending her wimpled head beneath the velvet bolt of curtain, but resisted the urge to act like a mother.

'You are safe, Aalia. Sebastian found you and brought you here… to Sawyer's Fold. He said you came here once before.'

The empty eyes looked past her.

'We are quite alone.' Maisie caught her gaze. 'I was Sebastian's nurse… he fetched me here to keep you safe.'

'Maisie,' she said. 'I heard someone say, "Send for Maisie."'

And then the tears came, wracking her frail body like a late summer storm. And Maisie wrapped her tightly in her heavy arms and rocked her to and fro, face turned to heaven, so the child couldn't see that she was weeping, too, knowing what the bastards had done.

Later, when the mirror-paned windows glowed crimson, Maisie changed the sodden bandages, and the girl barely stirred, hair soft on the pillow. She'd gathered up her knitting, when the girl spoke again.

'Maisie, is Simon your friend?' There was a trembling in her voice.

Maisie stayed seated in her chair. 'I was brought to nurse Sebastian when he was a babe and earned a mother's concerns.'

'Sebastian has no parents?'

'His father died abroad. His mother died in childbirth.'

'Sebastian was in Scotland recently?'

'They serve their country in different ways, but say nothing to me of their travels.'

'Lord Scythan has… private ambitions?'

'No-one is more loyal to his Queen than Simon Trentham.'

There was silence, and Maisie thought she'd fallen into sleep.

'Then, I challenge you to prove it.' Her voice scraped like a scratch. 'Teach me why I should trust this man.'

Eyes fixed on the candle flame, Maisie began to tell everything of her own childhood. Of growing up in the stews, and how Sebastian's uncle had taken her out of that hellhole and given her a life. And Maisie hoped it was enough.

SACRIFICE – 14th Disclosure

It felt good to be outside the Old Temple's bland walls and striding through streets bustling with commerce. Piatro stood for a moment, observing the cluster of people crowding into the market. The wide cross-roads which fronted old St. Dunstans Church were packed with men, women, and children, carrying baskets, pushing barrows, dragging sacks. The tented stalls across the square were laden with fresh-harvested fruit and vegetables. This was Piatro's world, not the devious stirring of secrets, not the threat of treason or the agonizing worry at any moment he might be arrested.

'Two pennies, I said.' A baker, apron tarred white by his wares, held out his hand impatiently. 'Weren't you there at the Pie-Powder? I 'ears we've got a king at last.'

There were those who laughed, but many more faces showed fear.

The man standing next to him handed the baker a coin. 'Load of worn out buskins, if you ask me.'

'Well, no-one's asking. Roger said they's giving odds of thirty to one on William being crowned before Christmas.'

'Same odds, if the Queen accepts the Archduke's proposal! Don't see me wasting my pennies on either.' The baker slapped floury hands on his apron and laughed.

'Well, I 'ears her passions lie nearer home.'

Piatro turned and walked away. There wasn't much Londoners didn't see.

Every form of tragedy began as a simple secret.

Gull had given him the directions. He must take the left fork when the road divided after the bridge. There should be an ancient orchard not far after the divide, but tall gabled buildings stood in long unbroken lines on either side of the street. He re-traced his steps and searched each cobbled door and over-hanging beam, hoping to find Bedford's singular crest.

For two days and nights, he hadn't slept. Two days of waiting for Georgiou to recover, at least enough to talk. Two days of watching Padruig going about his regular duties, doing nothing whatsoever to discover Aalia's fate.

Surely, it was time to raze her brother into dust.

He'd taken the Master aside and argued about what they should do. Piatro, the merchant, had accused their illustrious Master of being incompetent, screaming his convictions so loud, even the rats who inhabited the cellars searched for cover. The whole bloody Company was entirely inept. Time Piatro took the helm, because this storm would not diminish until William was struck from the living. So, he decided, he must go and stir Lord Bedford. Because he wanted his revenge, and Padruig was proving unobliging.

He finally found the Bedford crest carved on a small wooden shield above a neat, stable door. He asked for the master of the house and was waved to the opposite side of the road. A fine but unassuming brick tower was squeezed between the endless black and white gables. Not the grand palace he had expected, but there was no mistaking the painted crest set inside the compact porch.

The room where the servant led him was small and dusty, and lined with empty shelves, as if the family had left. No fresh rushes lay on the tiled floor or flowers set in the blue and white jug, which sat ready in front of the window.

The Earl of Bedford marched into the room, his servant jumping at his heels. 'I'm leaving for Hampton Court.' He waved the man away. 'Make it brief, Kopernik.'

'I demand you arrest William. You know where he will be… in the protection of Spain. Enter Durham House and destroy this plot once and for all.'

'And upset every legal protocol which keeps us from war with Spain? I think not.'

Piatro stepped closer, suddenly afraid. 'But we no longer have means…'

'To protect your Company? I think the Master lost that battle the day William landed in England. He should have trusted me.'

'Would you have taken William without harm? I think not. It should never have come to this, not if Aalia had had her way.'

'It's my belief your Company remained too frightened of the consequences until it was too late. A pretender to the throne is, by his very claim, a traitor.'

'But William isn't a pretender. He is the legitimate heir.'

'No, Kopernik! His birth was never testified, his very existence a lie.'

'His blood is true. The monk said Henry feared his country was about to descend into civil war. England couldn't risk two equal heirs.'

'What the monk said counts as treason.'

'Not treason but truth… the man delivered the queen of twins.'

'There can be no truth, because there is no proof.'

'He knew about the ring. That's why Alvaro wants it so badly; he knows it ties William to his mother.'

'I warn you, Kopernik, we cannot speak of these events without committing treason.' Bedford turned towards the door.

Piatro was beyond reason. 'The ring bears the crest of a phoenix and four names entwined, Henry and Jane, Edward and William. You heard what Aalia said at the Pie-Powder Court. After Tom gave her the ring, she thought it was lost in the river, but didn't tell anyone she saw Scythan wearing it.'

'You accuse Lord Scythan of stealing a pauper's ring?' Bedford held up his hand. On the smallest finger was a gold signet ring, bearing his crest. 'A good goldsmith can copy any ring. This is the third I've commissioned.'

'What if Alvaro can prove its provenance? The seal would surely verify it once belonged to Jane Seymour.'

'You want me to send for Scythan and ask him if he owns such a ring?'

'Isn't he already at court?'

'No! Scythan offered his excuses these past few days. His estate at Richmond requires attention. And, apparently, he's caught a cold.'

Piatro caught the measure of Bedford's grey eyes. Scythan's brand of ambition would never allow him to abandon the court in favour of a summer cold. Piatro knew he must tell Padruig, and together, they would visit Sawyer's Fold.

Lady Bedford, who was listening in the garden while pretending to fill a basket with herbs, embraced her husband as soon as the servant closed and bolted the outer door.

'Why the kiss, Meg?' Her husband smiled.

'Because sometimes your ingenuity surprises even me.'

SACRIFICE – 15th Disclosure

Sebastian arrived at Sawyer's Fold next morning, trailed by a ruffian who looked the very image of a street urchin, right down to his fustian breeches. Biding Maisie's stare, they both wiped their boots as they came through the door, and sat under her feet at the table.

'Meet Jem, Maisie,' Scythan's nephew said. 'Be kind. He's probably responsible for saving Aalia's life.'

Maisie was in a generous mood, Aalia had gained some strength overnight. One of her girls had brought fresh bread from Richmond, and it lay warm in the basket. Scythan had enjoyed a good breakfast.

Maisie let Sebastian mind her patient, and Jem was quick to help with chores, to such an extent she kept falling over him.

'I suppose you haven't eaten today?'

He was skinny as a galley slave, and his smile split his cheeks like ribbon. 'Thank you, miss,' he said cheekily, watching steadily as she prepared a plate. 'She sang beautiful, miss,' he chimed.

'So, I heard. When did you see her perform?'

'We sat on the wall at the Castle Inn off Bankside. Weren't room to swing a cat when we got there, but I never 'eard singing like that before. She was certain to win at Saint Bart's.'

'So, I heard.' Maisie laid out wooden bowls beside the eggs and ham.

'They say the Queen will be right mortified.' Jem was stuffing his mouth with warm bread.

Maisie didn't have an answer, but spotting the state of the boy's hands, dragged him outside to the pump. His screams echoed through the house and brought Scythan running from the garden.

'Sebastian arrived with this!' Maisie said, drying her hands on her apron.

'You must be Jeremy?'

The boy stood up straight with his hands behind his back. 'Yes, sir.'

'Is Seb upstairs?'

Maisie nodded. 'But there's breakfast to be had first.'

'Breakfast can be deferred, Maisie May. I need to speak with my nephew alone.'

Scythan left the bedroom door open, as he drew Sebastian to the top of the stairs. His nephew was creased from lack of sleep, and his eyes sunk into bruised roundels, but unless the lad complained, Scythan didn't intend to take him from his duties. There was little he didn't know of Sebastian's affairs but that little required defining.

'Has Robin returned to Scotland?' he snapped.

Sebastian raised his eyebrows and put his finger to his lips.

They'd barely spoken since leaving Newcastle.

Scythan shrugged. 'You've delivered your message? I hardly need guess. I have my own contacts in the north.'

'Sadler?' Sebastian nodded. 'I'd forgotten he's your friend. Robin was to leave from Cecil's Westminster house at dawn, and they plan to keep the escort small, enough to protect their charge but not enough to call attention.'

'God grant them safe passage. Cecil will be thankful when Hamilton is settled back in Scotland. He's had little peace of mind since we learned France is sending three thousand men to defend the Dowager. I only hope Arran keeps his promise and earns his place as leader of the Lords of the Congregation. Will Robin stay with the Earl?'

'I don't know, Uncle. He takes his orders from Cecil, and doesn't trust Arran's pledge.'

'Our wise young Queen didn't like him much either, but uses the promise of his suit to play the ambassadors against one another.'

'You think she might actually choose to marry the Archduke?'

'Never, but negotiations will hold Spain at bay for the time being. Is there any firm news of William or Alvaro?'

'Nothing, except Durham House has doubled its guard. Jem and his friends have been keeping watch in Southwark, too.'

'And Bedford? Have you spoken to your employer?'

'I reported to his office last night... listing everything I've seen and heard. He's searched London without unearthing any trace of William, although news of what had happened at the Pie Court has spread throughout the suburbs.'

'I've heard the odds on a new king are rising, while the Catholics dictate a woman is unfit to rule. Then, Knox blasts out his trumpet for the Protestants. Weak minds take heed of things they can't fathom.'

'But, Uncle, what I fear most is William's claim is legitimate.'

'In law, he never existed. Whatever proofs his supporters dig up, the man has nothing but rumour to validate his claim, and that debacle at St. Bart's showed how much they are grasping at straws. However, he gave us one advantage... I don't believe the letters shown at the Hand and Shears were forgeries, because Alvaro waited until both the Duke and his wife, Jane Dormer, were safely out of England, before deciding to use them.'

'Bedford thought the same, but openly accusing Spain of plotting is tantamount to declaring war. He's also of the opinion William and his friends probably had no knowledge of the attempt to assassinate the Queen at St. Katherine's. Lady Bedford overheard the injured young clerk called Paolo mumbling on his pallet... the Countess is very astute. It seems he helped to engineer the "accident," and by following those who had visited Paulo during his stay at the hospital of the Savoy, Bedford has pieced together more about the plot. The cleric belongs to a sect of Papists who preach that Queen Elizabeth is a witch, like her mother, and bringing about her death will reap heavenly rewards. Tom Hampden was killed, quite simply, because he could recognize the assassins, and they couldn't have him reporting that they'd arrived on a Spanish boat.'

'This certainly proves Alvaro the likely spur, does it not?'

'That's what Bedford thought, too, at first. However, I heard Alvaro order two of his countrymen flogged to death the morning after the attempt on the Queen.'

'Surely to hide his part?'

'No, he was furious they'd acted outside his command. That's why we've been seeking the "Monkey."'

'What can an animal prove?'

'Not an animal but a strange form of man… highly skilled at climbing. Alvaro was furious when he learned Hampden was dead but this "Monkey" still has such a critical role, he can't possibly be condemned.'

'How do you know this?' Aalia was propped against her bedroom door.

'Maisie will have my head for breakfast, if she finds you out of bed.' Scythan went to usher her back inside the room.

She didn't move. 'Seb knows because… the "Monkey" confessed what they'd done. That's why you argued with Alvaro… at the Mermaid. But who would Alvaro want to murder, if not England's Queen?'

After that, Maisie wouldn't let anyone upstairs, not even Scythan, unless she was installed in Aalia's room, pinning her to the sheets, if necessary. Scythan agreed to her conditions, rather more readily than expected, and fitted his visits about her routine.

It was another week before the girl gained enough strength to argue. Maisie merely increased her vigil, even sleeping near her charge. As soon as dawn fingered the curtains, she'd throw open the windows and let summer come calling from the garden. That morning, a woodpecker was attacking a tree, and bees were skimming the honeysuckle.

Maisie perched on the bed unwrapping Aalia's stained bandages, willing her fingers to be nimble and kind. Next, she went to fetch a kettle of fresh-boiled water and returned to find Simon sitting on the window-seat, playing with a gold hilted knife.

'Better while she's sleeping,' he said meekly.

Maisie wasn't used to seeing him concerned, nor could she scold him for breaking her rules.

Turning the blade in his hands, it danced in emerald fire.

'Worth a king's ransom?' Maisie asked.

'More likely a queen's?' He looked steadily into her surprise.

'Too pretty to be a weapon. Something to add to your collection?' She was brushing Aalia's hair, spun silk on the pillow.

'Perhaps it came from India? Certainly not crafted on this side of Stamboul. See how the blade has a look of water running through its steel? And the edge is quite exceptional, better than a surgeon's blade. Such workmanship is rare, not something you leave behind, unless, perhaps, you need to sign your deed?'

Maisie closed her eyes. 'Why let it be known you are capable of this?'

'Everyone thinks to blame Alvaro, but… I think the real master behind this conspiracy is the Count de Feria, Spain's former ambassador to England. Except I have no proof and can't afford to challenge Spain without some tractable form of evidence. Seb tells me Aalia's friend Georgiou survived, so we must wait and hope he can provide better witness.'

By Thursday, Maisie, never a doting nurse, felt the need to brandish the knife, if only to keep the girl bedbound. But it was for Simon she was really afraid. He'd always had a tongue like a sword and used it as he'd never done to any woman, not in Maisie's hearing. Storming down the corridor, he warned the girl was self-destructive, and whatever happened, Maisie must be sure to stay alert. That same day, he sent for Master Padruig.

It was Scythan's pleasure to swim, a pleasure he found impractical while his duties to the crown weighed heavy. Withdrawing from royal service meant he could indulge in those things he favoured, rather than those he was forced to practise.

He'd swum to the island and back, before he noticed the wherry rowing deliberately towards Sawyer's Fold. Thankfully, morning mist still clung to the river, screening his naked body. He watched from a sandbank, deciding it could hardly be someone of rank, because the boat displayed no pennant or badge, but he recognised the man's wrought accent immediately as he thanked the boatman, then waited until the wherry pulled out to midstream before sliding into the boathouse. Drawing his shirt and hose over cold, damp skin, he ran to enter his house by way of the kitchens.

Maisie, defending her charge like a mastiff, wouldn't let the gentleman pass beyond the entrance.

'Don't worry, Maisie. This one's invited,' he called. 'I'll see the Master in the gallery.' And, ignoring her frown, ordered her to bring honeyed wine.

Padruig stood braced in front of the white marble hearth, clearly ill at ease with the scope of treasures decorating the pampered room. Scythan had chosen deliberately, knowing the man preferred austerity. It had been little less than a month since Sebastian had brought Aalia to his door. A month of watching the essence of her being die, as the tapestry of her mind retreated into darkness. He couldn't allow them to destroy what she was, to silence that music forever.

'Georgiou has managed to describe some of what... what happened at the forge.' The Master's soft tone betrayed his reserve.

Scythan sat down and studied his long, ringless fingers. 'Guy acted on my orders to protect the girl. You knew she was a liability, but for a man who steers the most capable trading company in Europe, it seems a blundering oversight not to notice your German magician was missing.'

'There are many ways in which I've failed, but I'm not about to name them for your judgement, Lord Scythan.'

Scythan raised his voice deliberately. 'My nephew brought Aalia here because he didn't know where else she would be safe.' He sipped his wine, not smiling. 'Then, sent for Maisie in the faint hope she might live. You could have prevented this savagery.'

'You think I don't know that? But something changed your opinion, or why invite me here?'

The cold grey eyes did not blink. Scythan still wasn't sure. 'I lie.' He steadied his voice. 'She says nothing of what happened. In fact, she barely speaks at all, and that frightens me more than her unruliness.'

'You want my opinion?'

'I want you to end this madness, but we can't always have what is wanted. Your Company spins in a web of secrets, and tragedy is born from your lies.'

'I cannot break my solemn oath to hide William's identity.'

'Not even when you knew he was in London? You suspected what was coming, yet buried your head in the sand.'

'You cannot judge… cannot imagine how much we have to lose…'

'Secrets such as Aalia?'

'Aalia is different… her mother died in Stamboul. Otar was called to attend but the lady didn't survive the birth.'

Scythan felt his hand tremble. 'Then you must know her name?'

'Aalia has no need of the knowledge. Otar informed me her mother wasn't English.'

Scythan looked away. 'Nevertheless… doesn't she deserve the truth.'

'Aalia has never been curious of her parents. She doesn't live in the past. Otar raised her as his daughter. Loved her, taught her, and gave her everything he owned.'

'Then, why was she whipped? You needn't lie… I've seen the scars.'

'You must ask Aalia. Don't think of her as innocent… she came to England not merely to find her brother.'

'You're still angry?' Scythan smiled. 'That's why you cannot trust her?'

'If I were able I'd have locked her away… God knows Lady Rayner offered. I thought she was safer inside the Old Temple. Obviously, I thought wrongly.'

'She was the bait to bring William to your door. Most certainly you realised she ignores any rule that doesn't fit her motives? I'll take you to her room on the promise you'll be kind.'

'Of that, she'd be suspicious. I can only be myself.'

Scythan had promised Maisie could remain as chaperone, but Aalia was unattended when he brought Padruig through her door. She was perched in the window seat, staring into the garden. It had taken a parcel of salt and scrubbing to restore her tunic and leggings to their natural colour. Although giving every impression of a beggar's leavings, she refused to wear any clothes Maisie had brought. Sensing this wasn't spurred by pride, he'd had the room dressed not with fresh herbs but fragrant oils, sparing no expense to remind the girl of India.

Padruig walked straight to her side, unannounced. 'Who the devil are you saving now?' His voice held nothing of pity.

Scythan held Maisie back.

Aalia turned, as though cornered. Bowing her head, she moved her arms, thinking to conceal the bandages. 'Meaning?'

'You've been moping here while William remains at liberty, doing exactly what he pleases. You fail with more precision than you achieve. Just as I thought, an idler, who refuses to put aside her pride.'

'Each thread formed from a different hue. Personally, I relish the ambiguity.'

'You think this allows you a choice? You always suspected what William might become? Child, is it any wonder anyone can trust you, even Otar...'

She looked up then. Spare eyes haunted. 'Oh, especially not Otar. But we're not about trust here. Our role is born of talent... useful resources of an unrelenting master. Except William destroyed the dream. St. Thomas succeeds by curbing any taint of sentiment, thinking nature can be taught to abide by its principles. Only weak souls fall foul of temptation.'

'How did St. Thomas use you, Aalia? I remember a child who hid in the library, entranced by every word she read. Yes, we educate our novices and aim to prescribe their potential. We have the capacity to offer boundless gifts. But the best use of learning is to provide the knowledge to distinguish what is true and what is false. St. Thomas always defends the right to discover the truth. And, before you dispute that William's life is a lie, think what his life would have been if he was raised in England. What weighted my decision to deceive? His gentle mother didn't want him to become an instrument of destruction. St. Thomas gave you both the chance to extend your natural gifts...'

'Don't dare tell me they are divine!'

'The Company did not make you...'

'No. I agree the mistakes are all mine. The Company merely took flesh and blood and tuned them into something far more dangerous.'

'You despise yourself? I see a woman who has fought ignorance and bigotry with courage. Who has grace to defend the weak but lacks enough conviction to defend her honour.'

Aalia pulled up her knees, drawing them close to stifle her shivering.

Scythan let Maisie go, but Aalia pushed her aside.

'Why should I choose myself above others? What gives me that right?'

'I did not give you permission to sacrifice yourself.'

'Not even when pursuing my chosen path? Isn't this what you anticipated?'

'We both know you are perfectly capable of making decisions based on reason... Otar isn't dead. William knew exactly how that news would break you... drove you down his path. Would you let his malice succeed? Destroy the person you are?'

'A woman who prostituted her soul.'

'Go join the Papists, if that's what you believe.'

'I knew you'd be sympathetic.'

'Shall I inform the Holy Father you'll be disturbing the peace of the Vatican?'

She almost smiled. 'Levity... from Doctor Padruig? You didn't want me to come, so why dispute my failings now? I never meant to challenge you. William is the only brother I've known... there was a time... I didn't know where I ended and he began—our lives were so entwined. Yet, he didn't raise a hand to save me...'

He held her then, crushed in his arms. 'He must be stopped, you know that.'

'Am I standing in your way?'

'That's the trouble, child. You are standing in his, and Alvaro knows it.'

SACRIFICE – 16th Disclosure

Francis Drake was sprightly in his step. Master Solomon had sent him to deliver invitations. The Pilots of Trinity required a formal meeting with every barge-master of note, from fancy Goldsmiths' barque to Fishmongers' clinker-built wherry, to define the rules for the next annual apprentice's race. Last year, three apprentices drowned.

If the Master of the Barge would proceed in the honour…

Drake read the letter then re-set the seal with barely a trace he'd interfered. Since Lord Bedford asked him to keep both his eyes and ears open, he considered he had permit to take such liberties. His god-father explained there might be some kind of civil unrest, and they must be concerned for the Queen's safety, but Drake, along with all London, already knew what had happened at the Pie-Powder Court. Knew he could never bless "King" William.

Bedford had told Drake he'd best serve his country by continuing his duties as a pilot's apprentice. He had argued at first. What could he possibly do down in Deptford that might divert a rebellion? Then he remembered what had happened when they met Aalia's brother at the Mermaid, but daren't inform his god-father, for fear it might taint his future trust. Some decisions were complicated however pure the morality.

Yesterday, he'd called on Master Solomon with a warranted sense of guilt. The old man had succumbed to gout and looked for a cure in his cups. All summer long, Drake used the opportunity to shun away from his duties, troubling his father but fuelling his dreams. He found the pilot bitter, having dwelt too long on his troubles, but talk of war with France spurred his imminent return to Trinity. Drake had learned much of diplomacy while working in his god-father's service.

Keeping his ear to the ground meant Drake had heard the rumour early a clutch of royal watermen were holding secret meetings in the barge-house at Kew. Word was they wanted to raise river tariffs, and likely the truth was half the lie. But Solomon had it in his means to provide Drake with a legitimate reason to call at Kew, the invitation to Trinity lining his leather pocket.

The clay path along the river-bank was hard-baked and sharp underfoot. The musted tides of September had fused the river with a rim of stale fish, and the reeds were spilling feathered seeds. Dainty mottled dunlins were harvesting the debris while seagulls wheeled overhead. A swan flapped towards him, shielding a graceless pair of cygnets, forcing him to jump onto the low, broken jetty where an old State barge, lacklustre and grey, lay slowly rotting.

The great, hooded buildings, which housed the royal barges, each took the form of an upturned boat. Set on raised beams, they lay just above high-water, and as Drake jumped onto the jetty, he could see a freshly-gilded barque poking its nose into the river. He climbed over a locked metal gate, but further entry to the boat-house was guarded by a warden, red-breast bright with the new Queen's badge. He was young, by Tower standards, little more than twenty, Francis supposed, as the warden grabbed a pike and stood briskly to attention.

'Name and business,' he snapped.

'I'm come on Trinity business,' Drake said importantly. 'Is Master Bates here today?'

The barge-house smelt of new-sawn timber and crude molten tar. Under the broad shade of its curved mantle lay the smallest barge of the royal fleet, curtly powered by eight pairs of oars. There should have been an open dais raised near the bow, where Her Majesty would sit as she went along the river, but the dais was propped on the jetty with a pair of carpenters hammering at its joints.

One of the carpenters nodded but neither asked his business when Drake jumped inside the barge. Piled in the bow were the rich scarlet hangings used to clothe the dais, and a pile of plush, velvet cushions smutted in a shroud of sawdust. Finding nothing of consequence, Francis was preparing to return to the jetty, when he heard a familiar voice rattle out a stream of orders. He ducked into the bow and crawled beneath the heavy drapes and cushions.

'How long before you're finished?' William's artful voice silenced the steady hammering. 'We need to get to Richmond before the tide turns.'

SACRIFICE – 17th Disclosure

Piatro was confined, by his oath, to remain inside the Old Temple. Not merely had the Master forbidden him to travel to Scythan's house, he'd made him promise not to leave the Old Temple's outer walls. Since nothing he argued would ratify the ruling, he spent his daylight hours in comforting Andreas, taking his turn at Georgiou's bedside or brooding inside the library. He was in his room trying to compose a letter which didn't hint of remorse, when Gull came through the door trailed by two visitors.

One was Sebastian Trentham, boiled like a rag and blustering. Standing beside him was a lean street lad, equally distressed.

'Doctor Padruig is out.' Piatro didn't stand up to greet them.

'I know. Have you met Jem?' Sebastian said.

'Of course. He's been about the place helping the Master.'

'Jem has news. He and his friends have been keeping watch on the forge where Georgiou and Aalia were discovered. Last night, a man came asking if the smith had found a fancy dagger. From their description, I think it must be Alvaro.'

Piatro slammed down his pen. 'Where is Aalia?'

'Safe at my uncle's house, Sawyer's Fold.' Sebastian put up his hands.

'The Master's torn apart with grief,' Piatro lied. 'Didn't you think to tell us sooner?'

Sebastian's cobalt eyes studied him with pity. 'But Jem has brought messages almost daily. If you don't know, perhaps it is because the Master chooses not to tell you.'

Piatro stood up, folded his arms across the doe-skin of his doublet, and leaned over Sebastian. 'Then, what is so that important you run back here today?'

'The lads had the nous to follow the man. He went first to the Castle Inn, and then, to the old prior's hostel behind St. Mary's, where he was greeted at the door by a cripple with a tonsure. Soon after dark, they left together, going down to the old king's barge-house, where they gave a heavy purse to one of the guards. Then, they went to the Mermaid and drank for an hour or more with a gang of men wearing watermen's badges. Afterwards, the other man, the one who looked like a priest, took a wherry and asked for an address up-river.'

'Durham House?'

'No! Sawyer's Fold.'

'Shouldn't you report first to Lord Bedford? I thought he was your master.'

'Bedford's left London… the Queen ordered him to Hampton Court where she is presently entertaining.'

Piatro knew that was true.

Sebastian smiled and turned to the tousled boy standing silent at his side. 'Tell the man what else you heard.'

'Navy stores were broken into day before. Thieves cleaned out the powder stores. One of the guards is my cousin, and he says he saw a monkey.'

'A monkey?' Piatro looked down on the boy.

'Don't you remember, Piatro? The man with no ears was described as having a monkey?'

Gull, returning with wine, nodded towards the door. Piatro walked to the corridor to find Georgiou leaning against the wall, shoulders bare and shivering. He drew Piatro close and whispered, 'The Master has gone to see Lord Scythan. I was meant to tell you before.'

'Thank you, Georgiou, but we have visitors. Go back to your bed.'

'I overheard what they said. Padruig has been searching for this man they call "Monkey," but not only because he killed Tom…'

'This man links the plot to Feria and therefore, possibly, Spain,' Sebastian interrupted, peering round the doorway. 'Which evidence we require should we finally accuse them of regicide. I must go straight to my uncle on a promise and a prayer.' He lifted his cup. 'To music… and all pleasures that land from the East.'

SACRIFICE – 18ᵗʰ Disclosure

Drake watched and listened, peering from under the curtain of drapes. There were seven men with William, all dressed in the distinctive crimson and gold of royal boatmen. Someone loosened the ropes, and he felt the barge shift backwards without floating the whole keel. The men fetched squat, wooden barrels and carried them on-board. With the carpenters help, they were stowed beneath the dais, now raised slightly higher to accommodate the barrels. Drake couldn't decide on their contents, but recognised they were heavy, because the men struggled down the ladder. Brandy, he guessed, not shifting closer for fear of being seen. Then one man stumbled and dropped his load.

William stopped it rolling further with his foot. 'Don't get the powder wet, driddle-head.'

Francis's mind ran cold. They were packing the royal barge with gun-powder, and that could only mean one thing. Assassination. He knew he must get to Bedford, but first must escape without being seen. As the barge rocked with the weight of men moving into their places, he slipped off his clothes, down to his breeches, and waited, lying low in the bow, hidden under bolts of velvet. He had to jump before they hung the drapes back on the dais and hope the water deep enough to cover his escape.

He felt the boat float, heard the burr of a hawser being reeled, then the rope landed on his legs. There was a long pull on the oars and a rest while they lifted. This must be his best chance, before they reached mid-stream. He slipped off the blanket of fabric, slid over the side, and dived beneath the barge and held his breath. As his head broke the surface, he heard shouting, but instead of standing, the barge shot forward, powered by sixteen long oars breaking the water in unison. He didn't wait to know why they hadn't tried to catch him but waded to shore near the barge-house, then he ran as he had never run before.

He had no trouble hiring a wherry at Bankside; most river-men knew him by sight, and the skipper could see he was desperate. Even loaned him his shirt. He raced up the Strand, without thought of anything but what William was plotting, not apologising to those he knocked flying, or the friends he ignored. It was only as he thundered on the door of Bedford House he wondered what the hell he would do if the master wasn't at home. But, God bless England, Sebastian Trentham was standing at the door to the stables.

'Are you well, Francis?' Trentham called. He was dressed in Bedford livery and leading a big grey horse.

'I need to speak to my god-father,' he spouted, then looked to see if any of the people passing nearby had taken note.

'He's at Hampton Court, I'm just on my way there by way of my uncle's… Can I take him a message?'

Francis had enough sense to shift inside the stable. And as he reeled out what he'd witnessed, Sebastian's face paled. He slammed his hand on the stable door.

'I had word this morning about thieves breaking into the powder store, and was on my way to warn Lord Bedford. I hoped we'd have time in which to warn the court and arrest the culprits.' He walked his horse to the back of the stable and then to the door, looking into every stall before continuing. 'Can you go straight to Sawyer's Fold with a message for my uncle? It'll mean I can ride direct to Hampton Court. Tell Lord Scythan that… the messenger calling today is Bedford's traitor priest.'

'Beg pardon, sir!'

'My uncle will understand. Make sure you repeat my words exactly… and if the messenger has arrived, don't enter the house… ask for Maisie, and she'll find an excuse to bring my uncle to you.'

He kicked the doors open, and his horse skipped sideways. 'Fast as you can, Drake. Time is our enemy.'

Five minutes later, and Francis had run to Strond Bridge jetty and secured the loan of a wherry from a waterman who owed Solomon a favour. The middle-aged waterman was jaunty-eyed and laughed at Drake's emergency, teasing that he didn't usually take a man wearing another man's shirt. But he owned the shoulders of a bull and promised to reach Isleworth quick-time, provided Drake took his share of the pull. It was past mid-day, and the sun was high. Before they reached the wide bend at Lambeth, Francis was drawing huge breaths with every pull of his oars. Next time, he promised, he'd barter for a four-man crew.

SACRIFICE – 19th Disclosure

Maisie loved to see a dinner table loaded with good food, something recently lacking at Sawyer's Fold. Immediately after the Irishman who had upset Aalia left, she sent Scythan's steward to Isleworth market. The pantry was empty, and she'd given him a list with the warning there'd be no supper if he came home empty handed.

Then, the next visitor arrived.

A cripple. He called at the kitchen first, but when he couldn't get any answer, limped around the exterior wall until he reached the front door. Maisie, furious at his presumption, told him the master wasn't home. But he wouldn't be sent off. A sullen, dry-faced man, barely older than her Seb, he looked too much like a lawyer, broody and overly-pious.

'I must see Lord Scythan.' He raised his voice, demanding.

'And I've told you, he isn't here.' Maisie stood with her arms stretched, blocking his path through the door.

'Woman! He'll want to hear my words. Let me through.' He pushed forward.

Maisie grabbed his ear and twisted until he yelped. 'I don't think so,' she hissed softly.

She didn't hear Simon come behind, nor see him, except he touched her hand.

'Thank you, Maisie. If you think the whelp is house-trained, we might let him through.'

She stepped to one side, hands on her hips, pinning the visitor with a glare. She didn't like this one either. But Simon took him into the morning room, slamming the door behind, and she couldn't hear what they said.

Less than five minutes later, Simon found her in the kitchen.

'Where's my steward?' He'd changed into his riding clothes and carried a small leather satchel. 'I'm leaving for Hampton Court. I want you to lock the doors and allow no-body to enter… or leave… the house.'

'Gus has gone for food.' She balked at Simon's frown. 'We have to eat!'

He closed the kitchen door and threw the bolts, without saying a word. Then, he took her hand and led her through the house, checking every window and locking every door, before leading her up the flight of stairs which led to the upper hall.

'I want you to stay with Aalia. You will lock the bedroom door and let no-body through.'

'Should I be scared?'

'Why change your habits now?' He smiled, and her heart skipped a beat. 'I hope to return very quickly.'

'And if you don't return?' She faced him square, holding her breath.

'I have no choice… know that… the Queen is in danger.'

And then, he was gone. Thank goodness Aalia was sleeping.

SACRIFICE – 20th Disclosure

Padruig was passing the small town of Chiswick when he noticed the young man waving frantically from a passing wherry. The rhythmic movement of his own craft had almost sent him to sleep, and he thought for a moment he was dreaming, but, yes, the man waving from the other boat was young Master Drake, red-faced and florid yet definitely the same who was apprenticed to Dick Solomon. He'd barely seen him this past month; his god-father had likely warned him to keep away from the Old Temple. Bedford was full of good advice. He'd previously warned Padruig not to trust Scythan, but there was no denying what he'd done for Aalia.

With all that had happened, he'd forgotten he was going to invite Drake to join St. Thomas. He was seeking another apprentice and would have asked sooner, if he hadn't been run ragged of late.

'Master Padruig!' Drake shouted. 'Please… stop. I must speak to you.'

His oarsmen raised their oars, and Drake's boat rammed into their bow.

'Have you come from Sawyer's Fold?'

The lad's round face was distraught.

'Why don't you join us?' Padruig nodded to his steersman, and Drake jumped into the stern. Nor did his oarsman appear surprised when Padruig asked them to return in the same direction they'd been rowing.

Piatro was bringing food to Georgiou when he heard voices coming from the grass-covered courtyard. He looked outside and caught the flash of a rainbow cloak—Andreas. Where the hell had he been hiding? Furious with the little man, he slammed down the tray and ran outside. But the doctor wasn't alone.

'Lady Maria, I'm sorry, but the Master isn't here.'

'That's a blessing. I wasn't sure if I could face his mournful expression. Bring some of that… what do you call it… chai?' She perched on the stone mantle which surrounded the hexagonal well, and Andreas dropped onto the grass beside her, spreading his cloak like a blanket. His face was drained of colour, but otherwise, he seemed unhurt by his kidnap.

Piatro didn't move. 'Just where have you been?'

'Spilling my tale, Kopernik. Spilling it to all and sundry, hoping someone sits up and listens.'

Maria folded her twisted hands into her lap and frowned. 'We've had a busy morning I'd really like that drink.' She looked up and waved. 'Such a lovely man… why don't you invite him down?'

Piatro turned to see Georgiou's face peering down from a window. 'That doesn't answer my question. You must know how we've worried.'

'Now, boys, do not argue. Padruig has everything in hand. Silly that so many bones have been broken, but…' She stopped as Georgiou approached.

He'd wrapped up in a novice's robe and even tamed his hair, so looked almost whole and presentable, if you ignored his hands.

'A messenger arrived from Padruig, asking us to meet him here. I'm sure he can't be long wherever he was going.'

'He went to see Aalia.' Piatro studied their faces intently.

'There's nothing you could have done.' Maria held his eyes. 'She makes her own choices.'

'That's what everyone keeps saying, but it doesn't help. I should have stopped her.'

'We all think the same… except her knight in shining armour here.' Andreas smiled at Georgiou. 'Who very nearly died.'

'The ring she took to exchange for Andreas, I know it was a copy, but there was something missing, something they had expected to find.' Georgiou knelt on the grass.

'Aalia said it was perfect, identical to the original. The goldsmith knew the crest, a phoenix, said his guild had a book which contained every emblem. And Alvaro never saw the original.'

'Something in the detail wasn't right. William argued with Alvaro. He truly wanted to believe Aalia was telling the truth. But then, her brother left, and the brute let rip.' Georgiou looked away.

'Sebastian said Goff worked for his uncle… How did you meet him again?'

'At the fairground, he was sent to watch over Aalia. Scythan paid him to protect her, and he did… more than did his duty.'

Andreas patted his back, respectfully. And Piatro went to fetch the chai Maria had requested. The quiet reserve had melted by the time he returned, and Georgiou was laid on the grass, telling the tale of an Indian prince, and smiling for the first time in ages.

'We went to Bedford first,' Andreas said. 'Maria was worried he wouldn't act, being the father's son.'

'But the boys don't know the whole story.' She shook her head, putting down her empty cup. 'And I'm not sure if Padruig really understands. You see, Bedford's father is the key. Do you think it coincidence he received the gift of so many estates during Edward's reign? His father, John, the first earl, was a very close friend to the Seymours. He helped organise the king's marriage to Jane after the Boleyn queen was disgraced. To give John Bedford his due, he did try to find William after King Henry died, because he'd never agreed with the queen's decision to hide the child, and he wanted to put things right. But his fortunes changed when he informed Edward Seymour. As Protector to King Edward, he had maintained his sister had been right, and the boy should remain firmly hidden. Bedford was duly paid for his silence.'

'How does this help?' Georgiou looked up solemnly.

'Bedford can't have his family name mired in the mud when he's just found his feet in Elizabeth's court.'

'You mean, he's been slow to act?'

'Precisely, my boy. He's even hidden some critical evidence in the form of Tom's sister, Sybil. She's presently staying at Chenies, Bedford's estate in Buckinghamshire, apparently for her protection, but I doubt he wants anyone to hear her testimony. You know the woman was Jane Seymour's dry nurse?'

Piatro whistled through his teeth. 'And therefore, William's best witness?'

'So, I would judge.' Andreas nodded.

Piatro felt cogs turning in his head. 'When I went to see Bedford, he told me he couldn't interfere with such small proof, but this means he holds the best proof of all.'

'When did you see Bedford?' Georgiou sat up too quickly and scowled.

'Three days after Pie-Powder.' He shrugged. 'Padruig discovered I'd been and tied me to home comforts.'

Lady Maria smiled. 'Bedford only wants what's best for England. The good man knows William's blood-line is pure, and it hurts his Protestant soul to deny the boy his position, but we can't have Spain dictating this country's future. Not again. So, William and his Jesuit friends must be quietly destroyed. Bedford has gone to ask the Privy Council for permission, but I doubt he'll mention everything he knows.'

'What can we do?' Georgiou looked lost.

'Very little, except… well, we hoped Padruig would be here.'

'He left just before dawn.' Piatro levelled the look Georgiou gave him. 'We need to speak to him, too. Sebastian came with news an hour since; William is preparing a trap to finally murder the Queen.'

SACRIFICE – 21ˢᵗ Disclosure

The Queen's summer progress had emptied the stores of every palace from Eltham to Dartford, Cobham to Nonsuch, while a thousand pampered courtiers paraded through masques and banquets. The arrival of a lively young court had unsettled the peaceable household of the Palace of Hampton Court. Its kitchens were run bare, half the drains blocked, and most every cellar drunk dry of anything but peasant-ale—even the inner courtyard stank of urine and worse.

Ignoring the rack of complaints, the Queen and her new Master of Horse went racing their horses at dawn. Since Bedford arrived, he'd been waiting, sometimes patiently, to be granted a private audience with Her Majesty. September was turning to autumn, and soon, the court would return to the city. He'd rested with his conscience far too long. Someone had to inform this jealous Queen she owned a legitimate brother.

He had hoped to arrest William by using due process of law. Instead, his failings at the Pie-Powder had left him with limited choice. Before Elizabeth heard the gossip, he must take her aside and explain, while hopefully drawing a cover over his father's role in the affair. Having his father's private correspondence read out in a public court had been deeply humiliating.

It would have been so much easier if he'd managed to stir the men of St. Thomas to declare William's treason before Bedford felt compelled. His first unease had turned to shock when the pretender had shown his face, and his strength, during the Great Muster. No doubt the likeness was carefully manicured, but he was the very image of their last Tudor king, a true embodiment of his father's blood. Bedford saw the devoted passion of those bluff men-at-arms standing loyally at his side. Would that he'd warned that day how much they should be fearful.

The sun had burned away the mist, and the palace glowed like a jewel under the clear cerulean sky. While he waited for a hearing, Bedford wandered through the rose garden, where a late flush of pink damask blooms granted a musky sweetness to the air. That morning, almost at the hour he arrived, he snatched a moment with his wife before she hurried to her duties as Maid-of-Honour to the Queen. Meg grabbed his cloak and kissed his cheek, whispering how much her mistress was absorbed in womanly affairs. It didn't take long to gather the latest gossip and realise what Meg was warning. Elizabeth's dalliance with her Master of Horse had meant he probably wouldn't be called into the royal presence today.

But that wasn't the only gossip. Whoever set the seed should be taken outside and whipped, but someone had mentioned the little songstress was thought to be staying at Sawyer's Fold. Now, Elizabeth wouldn't rest until she got the girl to sing.

'Bedford.' Scythan's clever voice made him turn his head. 'I've been searching the grounds; you should really hoist a pennant to mark your progress.'

Francis would happily have given Sebastian his soul to mind, but wouldn't turn his back on the uncle, although he wished he had the peacock's gift with words.

'Seb keeps me informed of your affairs. How is the girl recovering?'

'Gaining in strength daily. Her brother, however… that priest called on me earlier this morning.'

'What priest?'

'I believe his name is Paulo… injured in the attack at St. Katherine's. The one you've been watching.' Scythan lowered his voice. 'Seb also keeps me informed! Alvaro seems to have drawn him into his coven, though it's hardly a feat to bend the will of a fanatic. He came warning me to be ready, because "William shall be named King before the Queen returns to London."'

'But Her Majesty is leaving later today. My wife Meg is organising the packing.'

'Then we must run and stop her.'

They chased back inside the palace, racing loud-footed across the cobbles without apologising to those they pushed aside. Entering the long hall, they reached the guarded door which led into the royal apartments.

Driving down his urgency, the Earl of Bedford demanded to see his wife, but the warden informed him grandly she'd recently left the palace. Bedford felt his colour rise and evoked his God's damnation twice, before the stupid man added the codicil that Her Majesty had left on horseback with a retinue which included Lady Bedford. Made garrulous by their fury, he then proceeded with the news that an order had been sent to dispatch the royal barge to collect the Queen and her party from the jetty at Sawyer's Fold. As they turned to race back to the stables, Scythan blandly enquired how many men-at-arms accompanied Her Majesty's retinue. And the answer came back—none.

SACRIFICE – 22nd Disclosure

The stupid woman wouldn't unlock the door, and Meg almost lost her voice, along with her temper, shouting up at the window. It took so long to gain an answer, her mistress finally came to find her, resplendent in purple, white, and gold. That forced the stubborn servant to give way. Meg was just thankful Elizabeth began the day in such high and buoyant spirits.

The ride across the heath had been exhilarating, galloping full pelt underneath a cloudless sky. While the Queen and her friends rested their horses on the heath, Meg had trotted her roan mount through the wrought iron gates and down the tree-lined drive to see if Scythan was home. Despite her curiosity, Elizabeth wanted this visit to remain very discreet.

Meg had seen the house from the river but never approached its doors. Her husband described it as Italian in style, but she considered it vulgar because the long red-brick fascia contained more windows than walls. Sunlight reflected from the panes of mirrored glass, and she suddenly felt an intruder, borne into another world.

After she had failed to get an answer at the steel-bound entrance doors, she trotted back around the building and entered a large paved courtyard. She was trying to decide which door to try next, when Scythan's steward arrived. He was returning from Isleworth market and insisted there was no-one else home, despite his cart being laden with food. He begged pardon for his master's absence and offered to prepare refreshments in his own quarters, insisting Lord Scythan would have his guts for garters, if he let anyone inside without permission. It was the first thing he'd said that she believed.

Meg had heard talk of Scythan's treasured collection; her husband even suggested it might rival the Queen's. But she'd seen that look on her mistress's face too often, on each and every occasion, it pre-empted some furtive assignation. She expected Elizabeth might have learned her lesson after the debacle of St. Katherine's, but the abrupt change to this morning's plans had left Meg highly suspicious. Something had spurred this sudden need to examine Sawyer's Fold, and Meg sincerely doubted the draw was Scythan's collected possessions, however fabled.

The steward said he would run and fetch a key, but knowing her mistress's temper, Meg started to bang at the windows. The sharp-faced woman poked her head from the upper floor, thinking to find the steward but still, until Her Majesty appeared, she continued to argue no-one was there. However, once she recognised the magnificence of Scythan's visitors, she came downstairs and sullenly let them inside.

The girl was curled asleep in a large carved chair when Meg went to tap her gently on the shoulder. She was dressed in the same raw clothes she'd worn that day they'd first met at St. Katherine's. Same cropped hair, smooth as silk. Except catching her bared in sleep, she seemed more child than woman.

The Queen waited a few paces behind. She must see Aalia was too fragile, too weak, to leave her sickbed to perform. But her cold amber eyes insisted. Meg shook the girl a second time, mindful of the hard-faced woman the steward was holding, with difficulty, at the bedroom door. The kind of woman she'd fear, if her mistress wasn't present.

'Aalia, Her Majesty begs your attendance.'

The eyes opened, and Meg smiled. Accusing eyes, those of a wild creature cornered. Taking careful span of her audience, Aalia stirred from her chair, and the coverlet slipped, revealing the soft, thick wrappings binding her wrists.

The girl wasn't sick; she was injured.

Meg turned to face her mistress and caught the truth in her eyes.

'Would you sing for me?' Elizabeth stood in stately arrogance. 'Songbirds are rare this side of the river.'

Aalia closed her eyes, and Meg prayed she'd have enough pride to refuse, but when the girl opened them again, she was almost smiling.

'I can't promise my best performance, but I'll order my voice to oblige.' Aalia was gripping the arm of the chair and seeing how much she was trembling, Meg reached to steady her arm. But Aalia shook her head.

'Goodness knows I've had poor practise of late. Maisie's deaf to my talents.'

At that, the woman pushed the steward away and rushed to her patient's side, hands set squarely on her hips.

'Does Lord Scythan own a lute?' Fox-eyes exultant, Elizabeth turned to face the woman.

'I don't scout round his belongings.' Maisie shrugged, kohl-rimmed eyes fitted to the girl. Meg read concern in her eyes, alongside something very like pain.

'He has a lute.' Aalia's voice brightened. 'In fact, there's very little Lord Scythan doesn't own.'

Maisie shrugged her shoulders and let out a loud sigh.

'Meg, go and find it! Take the steward to show you where.' Elizabeth laid her thin long hands on Aalia's shoulders. 'I've had my barge diverted to meet us at Sawyer's Fold. It's a long journey back to the city, but your songs will lighten the way.'

SACRIFICE – 23rd Disclosure

The Royal Barge of State sat over the tiny jetty at Sawyer's Fold, like a golden sun rising out of the river. Fresh-painted livery hung in a garrulous display above the tasselled curtains screening the dais. Crimson drapes which matched the coats, the dressings, the caps, of the eight liveried oarsmen lined at the stern clutching their oars. The sapphire river glistened, silver banks soft with willow.

Aalia stood watching, while the Queen and Lady Bedford stepped on-board the gilded boat. Then, she followed, stepping onto the carpet of crushed herbs and flowers strewn ankle deep across the wooden floor, releasing a bitter-sweet scent which reminded Aalia of another far distant, summer's day which also had smelt of lavender.

The Queen settled onto the dais, pillowed in sharp cloth of gold, framed in magnificence, as royalty should be. Aalia knelt at her feet inside the pampered cabin. The ropes were loosed, the oarsmen dipped their oars, and the precious boat slipped downriver sylphen as a fish. Like Jonah being borne by whale, Aalia decided wryly, as she studied the knotted shoulders of her one-time brother, William. There were no men-at-arms to protect the party, no supporting boat to call to their aid.

Aalia looked up at the Queen and smiled. The game was about to end, and she was entirely defenceless. Better sing her songs and do her duty and act, as she'd been taught, using every art and skill in her armoury. She fingered the strings of the lute, feeling its form, its latent tune, but her fingers were clumsy, shackled in pain. Damn, there was nothing she could do. But before she broke the strings, Lady Bedford gently came and stole away the instrument.

The Queen requested a song which Aalia had never heard. Lady Bedford strummed the chords, softer than a lullaby. And a different lullaby played inside Aalia's head, dire with the tongue of a Scotsman. Surely Jamie wouldn't mind.

'Tarry Oo, Tarry Oo,
Tarry Oo is ill to spin
Caird it weel, caird it weel
Caird it weel, ere ye begin
When 'tis cairded, row'd and spun
Then the work is halflins done
But when woven, drest and clean
It may be cleading for a queen.'

William lifted his head and held her eyes. He didn't dare to smile.

Elizabeth laughed. 'I want no more Scottish tunes.' And stealing the lute, she plucked out the chords of a famous madrigal.

Aalia sang softly, but her voice ran dry. Someone handed her a silver cup filled with burgundy wine. She drank deep and then tried a different form of song, shunning the use of strings.

'Shall reason rule where reason hath no right
Nor never had? Shall Cupid lose his lands?
His claim? His crown? His Kingdom?
In name of might?
And yield himself to be in reason's bands?
No, friend, thy ring doth will me thus in vain.
Reason and love have ever yet been twain.
They are by kind of such contrary mould
As one mislikes the other's lewd device;
What reason wills, Cupido never would;
Love never yet thought reason to be wise.
To Cupid I my homage erst have done,
Let reason rule the hearts that she hath won.'

Aalia's eyes never left William's sculpted face, but he gave no symptom he was listening. Her head was floating, too much wine and not enough reserve.

'Who contrived such words?' Elizabeth lifted the silent lute.

'A young lawyer I met on the road to Berwick. One of your majesty's intriguers in Scotland and faithful friend to Lord Scythan.'

There was no need to pretend the Queen didn't know. A rich man needed many masters, and Scythan was very rich. Suddenly, William was smiling, drawing back the oars, never missing his beat.

Elizabeth followed Aalia's look, hooded eyes cautious. '"Thy will doth ring me thus in vain…" I have many rings that bind me to my duty.'

Leaning forward, she put a gloved hand under Aalia's nose. Bold on her finger was a solitary ring, which made Aalia's blood run cold. A gold ring carved with the graceful crest of a phoenix rising from the flames. The ring Scythan had stolen.

Elizabeth slid the ring from her finger and, taking Aalia's broken hand, slipped it onto her middle finger. Sharp eyes bright with blatant pity, Her Majesty removed her white leather glove and lifted the edge of the oval mount with her fingernail. The top opened stiffly to reveal a pristine Tudor rose entwined with tiny letters H and I.

'My father gave each of his children a remembrance ring.' Elizabeth said carefully. 'And this one belonged to my brother, Edward.'

Her traitor fingers shaking, Aalia touched the hidden crest. Alvaro knew this, knew immediately her copy was a fake and struck, before she was ready. She didn't move, couldn't speak, as William's scorn seared through her mind.

Had no-one else noticed him watching?

'This is my own ring.' The Queen interrupted her agony, slipping another gold ring from her opposite hand. The oval crest was carved with a different bird, but when she tripped the lip, it contained an identical rose, this time laid with the letters H and A.'

'An excellent example of the goldsmiths' craft,' Aalia spoke cautiously.

Elizabeth laughed. 'But what I don't understand is how Lord Scythan discovered a spare?'

Aalia's head came up without thinking. And blanched in that amber glare she realised, too late, the Queen knew absolutely everything.

'Are the two rings identical?' Aalia put them together.

'Almost… the only difference being that one band is engraved with Edward and the other with William. Which begs the question, why? A forger would hardly make such an error.'

Aalia felt William stir from his seat and prayed his own nature would win, the child above the man, except a loud cry interrupted.

A black-timbered barge approached, propelled by eight strong oars. The stern was flying a formal crest, and at its dais and along its bow, hung a blaze of imperious pennants.

'Isn't that the Ambassador to Spain and his secretary?' Lady Bedford bridged the silence.

Someone had to speak.

'I invited him to join us.' The Queen smiled and waved to her Bargemaster.

Water shimmered under the bow as the sweep of royal oars was raised. Aalia sucked in her breath, studying Meg's frozen face. The lady had just remembered where she'd met the secretary before—Alvaro.

'Though we had invited him to greet us at Chiswick.' The Queen spoke lightly, laughter in her voice.

There was a flurry as the two boats locked together. The royal barge dipped and rocked while Bishop de Quadra and his secretary stepped onto the boards and made their way to the side of the dais. Aalia, still crouched on the floor, held Meg's warning eyes without answer. She hardly dared to move until the Ambassador and his secretary were seated. Only then did she trust her eyes to meet Alvaro's tempered stare.

Otar once said there are two forms of trap, the trap made for surprises and the honey trap, which is subtle but no less lethal. If confused, dissect the motive. The scar on the Jesuit's face was mending but had knit so badly, it dragged his eye. Twisting, disfiguring, particularly when he smiled. If only she had means to maim and destroy his heart.

The Queen was speaking in a voice too high for comfort. The barge began to move forward again, the rhythmic beat of oars drawing and resting, pulling the heavy vessel smoothly down-river. The Spanish barge was left trailing behind while the Ambassador, swathed like a raven in formal black robes, was a fluster of broken verbs. It was an extraordinary honour to be invited on the river with Her Majesty, he rambled, falling into Spanish when his broken English failed. But Aalia wasn't listening, every instinct strained towards her brother until Lady Bedford, Meg of the doe-soft eyes, touched her shoulder and nodded towards the dais.

'I have been praising your singing.' The Queen's amber eyes fired with fury. 'What will you sing for the Bishop?'

Aalia met the ambassador's heavy-browed stare. 'I haven't… would not presume my choice. Why not ask the Ambassador if he has a favoured tune?'

The look he returned was indifferent. She could almost believe the pious bishop was blind to his secretary's devices. Another useful pawn in Alvaro's deadly game.

'What about a carnival song?' Alvaro touched her sleeve, moving the fabric just enough to reveal the bandages.

Aalia didn't challenge his spite but looked instead towards the guarded eyes of her brother. "Two minds, one heart," Otar once said of them.

The Queen waved her hand, striking Alvaro's collar lightly with her fingers. Almost and as if by accident. Aalia lifted her head and looked again into Elizabeth's shrewd eyes and saw the measure of her understanding. Stupid, ignorant fool. Sebastian worked for Bedford, and his wife served as lady to the Queen. But how much had she been told, and why?

'Anything other than a dirge.' Elizabeth turned deliberately. 'Who will play the lute?'

'Alvaro, you're the master.' De Quadra passed the instrument, but Alvaro shook his head.

'I'm not even in the same sphere as another man here.'

William stood up and bowed, throwing his cap in the hull. His ruffled copper mane framed a broad and mischievous smile. The barge rocked as he stepped over his fellow oars to join those gathered round the dais. Taking the lute as offered, William perched on the side and tripped his fingers across the strings.

'What then, Aalia, do we quote Medici?' He laughed.

Aalia studied his hands. No hint of remorse, no thought of begging forgiveness. Otar raised a dragon, not a lion.

'It's hardly time for carnival.' She found her voice and gently whispered the first line.

'*In the infernal pit, Astolfo hears...*'

'No!' The Queen shook her head. 'I'd rather the part when he discovers Orlando's wits.'

William's rich voice rang.
'*It was as 'twere a liquor soft and thin,*
Which, save well corked, would from the vase have drained;
Laid up, and treasured various flasks within…'

Aalia joined him, and their voices married so seamlessly, it was hard to think they hadn't sat a month and practised every chord. Meg sat motionless beside her mistress, spellbound by their artistry. Two matchless voices entwined.

But the magic had to end.

'If only we could recover our wits so easily.' Elizabeth's cheeks glowed unusually red. 'Instead of resorting to treachery!'

Aalia bent awkwardly. 'Madam, may I introduce William.'

Her brother lifted the lute and smiled, dimples pinning his cheeks. 'Your Highness.' He bowed his head and knee.

'So, this is the one who would be king?' Elizabeth threw back her head and laughed.

Aalia saw the spark of William's pride and gently shook her head.

'Did you think I wouldn't recognise my own brother?' The Queen smiled, showing tiny teeth. 'Lord Scythan gave me this ring, Aalia, because he knew I had its twin. As I said, my father had one made for each of his children.'

William stared back at her triumphantly.

Alvaro growled, sweeping his bitter eyes across Aalia, William, and finally Elizabeth. Then, De Quadra stood up, confusion in his sullen face. But it was Meg, the gentle countess, who noticed Aalia flail, who jumped from her seat to rub her bloodless hands. Breathe, she must breathe. Elizabeth knew... everything... all they had done, all they had suffered. Was it for nothing?

Alvaro tried to grab William, rage boiling in his face. But shouldn't they be celebrating? Surely this was what they wanted, Her Majesty accepting William was her legitimate kin? But who pays the piper, when the piper is calling the tune?

William wasn't celebrating; the look he gave Aalia was... defiant, furious... She, who'd known him her whole life, knew that look too well. Revenge? He did care; his eyes spoke more than words could ever say. Nothing else mattered.

'Stop it... now!' Alvaro screamed.

Now, she could smell it—bad eggs and sulphur mixed. The scent of siege and battle; desolation, death, and fear.

Alvaro was waving his arms and screaming, 'I order it stopped, William!'

Aalia's head was spinning. Breathe. And then, she saw the "Monkey," bristle-round head poking briefly from the back of the dais. Why should William need to stop a monkey?

William's attention fixed on Alvaro. 'I told you I loved my sister,' he screamed.

'This isn't what we planned.' Alvaro jumped from his seat. 'Not on-board the barge, with my own Ambassador present.'

His hands went to William's throat, before he felt the knife.

Otar had trained each of his children to kill.

Aalia didn't wait to watch the Spaniard die, but crawled behind the dais to find the malformed man they called "Monkey." William, her brother, had meant to take revenge while she… she was weak and blazingly incompetent. Her head felt clotted, her hands stunned with pain. In Diu, she'd seen a monkey bite off a curious child's nose. William had laughed, while she mopped the blood.

Stifled beneath the dais, the scent of bitter smoke was overpowering, sulphur but no flames. Tearing aside the drapes sent light and air to the trail of stark black smoke, which was sparking and spitting as it threaded through the barrels. The "Monkey" was bearing down on her, steel blade shafting his fist. She twisted, pulling his knife arm forward as he lunged, delivering his weapon into her grasp. Her clumsy, impossible grasp.

The man attacked again, before she could turn, grabbing her arm and biting at the bandage. Except they were too thick. She raised the blade, irritated to see it was marred with rust. Never trust a man who fails to clean his weapons. Was it stained by Tom's blood?

A trained hand doesn't hesitate. She drove the blade hard against his neck and didn't recoil at his scream. The strange, brutish frame shivered in its death throes. She cut the canopy from the dais, following the black flare of powder.

The barge dipped and fell as men jumped over the side. William was laughing, a shadow at her side. Then, she found the reason. There was nothing more she could do. She couldn't count how many squat barrels were packed beneath the dais, plump as dumplings in an English stew. Flames were licking through the floor and round the wooden barrels, and they were far too heavy for her to lift.

'Jump… everyone, you must jump!' she screamed to the women, to the Ambassador. Why did they hesitate?

William was laughing, holding at her arm. 'They can't swim,' he yelled. 'And you can't save them all, Aalia.'

She twisted from his grip, disgusted at his triumph. 'But nonetheless I must try.'

She punched him full in the belly, a barren appeal. Laughing at her futility, he turned and dived into the water, vanishing under the glass-smooth surface in a shimmer of perfect ripples.

The Spanish barge was making headway half-a-league behind, but Aalia could see another boat racing to their bow. Flying bold at its stern was St. Thomas's bare cross. Padruig had come to witness her utter failure.

Meg was leading the Queen, dragging her as far away as possible from the sour, hissing smoke. The Ambassador was leaning over the bow, screaming at his barge, as though it could row any faster. Under Aalia's feet, the reeds were sticky and scarlet, stained with Alvaro's blood, but no lifeless body rested amongst the rushes. Surely William had struck true. Glancing across the water, she could see only crimson caps bobbing. No round onyx head, nor a perfect bronze one.

There wasn't time, she must help the Queen. Snatching Meg's gross sleeve, she dragged her over the side. They hit the water just as the first explosion lifted the dais into the air, turning its gilded magnificence into a thousand merciless splinters. Thunder roared in her head, as she sank into the cold, grey water. Her mind clung to her one, her only duty; she must save Meg and Elizabeth.

SACRIFICE – 24th Disclosure

A shattering riptide sent clouds of mismatched birds swirling into the air. Padruig hauled on the oars, beating the river in rhythm with Drake, rowing with all the power of men possessed. Half a league ahead, a heavy, black miasma hung round the burning barge, defiling the silver water like a stain of Indian ink. Another explosion burst their ears, stippling the water, splaying shards of debris into their path. Screams filled the air, as the broad wash creased the river, bracketing the crimson clad men clinging to the wreckage. Royal oarsmen, or William's men? Padruig counted seven as they rowed swiftly past, desperately skimming the shattered surface to find a copper-bright head.

They pulled the wherry so close, their faces were scorched by the flames. Drake reached out his oar to a black-clothed man caught in strands of wreckage. Pulling him into the wherry, Padruig asked of the Queen and her companions, but he shook his head, dark face clenched in fear.

It was Drake who sighted his god-father first, wading near the shore. He waved, shouting words they couldn't hear until they came near. But then, they could see the woman at his feet.

His Countess, Meg.

Bedford's face told them his wife was lost. Padruig jumped from the boat and waded to her side, feeling for some sign of life. Meg's long chestnut hair, loosed from its bindings, swirled round her thin throat. Her lips swollen blue.

Padruig rolled Meg's limp body until she lay on her side. The movement sent water trickling from her mouth and he knew there was still hope. Otar had taught him what he must do. Otar, master of wisdom and life.

Bedford touched his arm, tears rolling down his barren face. Kneeling beside the lifeless woman Padruig didn't hesitate a moment, but rolled the Countess onto her stomach and started to unloose the bindings of her bodice. Except his fingers were clumsy with the river-sodden silk. Someone handed him a knife but still it took all his strength, tearing at her tight-laced stays, ripping open the padded cage binding her chest. Suddenly Meg coughed and half the river burst from her mouth and she lay, sucking in breath, sucking in life, and Padruig understood what it was to see a miracle.

Elizabeth was brought soon after, trailing a bevy of saviours. She couldn't explain who had brought her ashore, because in the confusion of smoke and water, all she could remember was a broad, crimson coat and laughter while William held her head above the water, complaining of the abundance of skirts, coughing out blood. He'd saved her life then, let go, just as a wherry dragged her into its fold, and had anyone seen the songstress.

Padruig's heart stopped beating. 'Aalia was on the barge? But I left her at Sawyer's Fold, far too weak to travel.'

'The Queen…' Meg tried to speak.

Bedford, kneeling beside his wife, stroked her hands, her face, her lips. Then, he looked up at Padruig.

'Someone at court informed Her Majesty just where Aalia could be found… we knew some mischief was at play, but never this… Scythan and I rode straight to Sawyer's Fold, but arrived too late to stop them.'

'Where is Scythan?' Padruig screamed.

'Scythan dived into the river as soon as we drew level. He brought Meg… Where did you learn to bring back life?'

'I learned from Otar, the man Aalia calls Father. He charged me with her care.' Empty of words, he turned to walk away.

'The Queen… she knew everything.' Meg strained to speak.

'How could she know?' Padruig said gently.

'That bloody priest.' Bedford looked from his wife to Padruig. 'He called at Sawyer's Fold. Scythan thought it was brazen. Came to warn that the Queen was about to be murdered… today. Alvaro likely used him because he knew Aalia by sight, from St. Katherine's.'

'We were on the barge when it exploded.' Meg was sitting now, draped in her husband's heavy cloak. 'Aalia tried to hold me from drowning, but my… skirts became too weighted.'

'Scythan will keep searching. I saw him give orders to the Spanish barge.'

'Isn't that Sebastian?' Padruig pointed.

'We met him on the road. He was riding to warn the Royal Barge. Then, we heard the explosion.'

'What about William? Is he amongst the dead?' Padruig looked along the shore, where men sat hunched or lay without moving.

'Before they found… my wife, I only recognised one of the dead. Without doubt, it's the same they described as a monkey.'

Meg touched Padruig's hand. 'William was one of the oarsmen.'

The lesser Barge of State was driven by eight royal oarsmen. Padruig counted seven men in crimson robes on the bruised grass of the riverbank. The path which wound beside the river was filling with grooms in livery, servants carrying blankets and baskets, men scurrying about the Queen. He could see the black-coated man they rescued sitting under a tree. Bedford introduced him as De Quadra, the Spanish Ambassador. His barge had pulled to shore nearby, and Padruig went to ask if they'd seen anyone else. They pointed to a reed-bed on the opposite shore.

He was turning to leave when he noticed the body laid in the narrow stern.

'My secretary, Alvaro.' De Quadra was standing behind him, dripping puddles into the sand. 'Murdered! By one of the royal oarsmen.'

Watching the river, waiting on news, refusing to fall prey to despair, Padruig listened while Bedford confessed his part.

'One day, when our tears have dried, I will lend those of my father's letters which relate to his hand in the affair.' He lowered his voice. 'Though they hardly exonerate my part, I hope they'll better explain everything I've tried to hide.'

'I know. Your father was devoted to Jane Seymour. Tom told me as much.'

'Then, you will know why I hid his sister, Sybil, or they might have killed her, too.' He looked to his wife sitting shaded against a tree, detached from the chaos and bustle, but she nodded back, encouraging. Not for the first time, Padruig thought the woman a saint.

'Sybil's witness would have added much weight to William's claim. I understand, Lord Bedford, you serve Her Majesty well.'

Padruig felt a sudden need to sit and squatted on the sand.

'Spain will wash its hands of any involvement. Yet, I wonder how they ever found William?' Bedford lost his caution. 'My father always thought you kept the boy in Danzig. He sent me there to search, just before Edward died.'

Padruig weighed his confession. 'I'm afraid the source was Lady Rayner. Being proud of her son James, she boasted of his life in India. While she told her tales at court, a young maid-in-waiting listened—Jane Dormer, who'd grown up with the rumour Jane Seymour gave birth to twins.'

'I remember her father, William, had been engaged to marry Jane Seymour, until Henry intervened.' Bedford nodded.

'Her love for him never died. Surely that's why she wanted her son to be named William.' Padruig decided on the truth. 'Luke Trentham arranged everything. I didn't know who else to trust after Tom brought the baby from the palace.'

'After we failed to find any trace of the boy, my father supposed he must have died, but when Alvaro produced those letters at the Pie-Powder, I remembered Jane Dormer was accused last year of stealing a jewel box from Queen Mary's chamber, not long before her mistress died. We can only guess she told her lover about the lost child, and he suggested she find proof. Feria must have been delighted on discovering those letters. Perhaps that was when he decided to place an alternative heir on England's throne. Except their plans were mismanaged.'

Padruig smiled. 'And they hadn't accounted for Aalia.'

SACRIFICE – 25th Disclosure

I shall be low beneath the earth, and laid

On sleep, a phantom in the myrtle shade.

The long reeds parted to her touch. She caught a trailing branch of willow and pulled her useless body onto shore. Her arms were numb, and her legs too heavy, far too heavy to crawl. She steadied her breathing, lying in shallow water, letting stillness embrace her mind. The river spattered against the shore; a skylark sang overhead. At last, she'd abandoned the game.

In the distance, men were shouting, and an acrid smoke clung to the sky above the river. She pictured the devastation, the flustering servants, everyone pointing the finger of blame. The English had a peculiar need for knowing.

For an infinitesimal moment, she was free.

She thought it would be Padruig, bending into the reeds, touching her face. But when she opened her eyes, it was Scythan, arrogant eyes sapped of life.

'The Queen survives.' He seemed almost uncaring, except he stroked her skin.

'Have they found William?' Her voice felt distant, as if someone else was speaking. Breathing came hard.

'Not yet amongst the dead.' He gently brushed the hair from her face.

She tried to pull free of the reeds but flailed like a helpless wean. Scythan took her into his arms, lifting her clear of the water. Water stained with blood. She turned her head to see if anyone washed to shore beside her, then realised the blood must be her own. Her heart ached.

'I didn't want him dead.' She needed to explain, to be excused his murder.

Scythan put a finger to her lips. 'I know, Misfit, but the choice was never yours to make.'

'He was rightful king.' She couldn't find her voice. 'Those who mattered knew. He was the son of Queen Jane Seymour.'

'She wanted him to be forgotten.' He wrapped her tight in his cloak. 'But, yes, he was rightful king. And every inch his father's son.'

Her eyes closed. And as her mind slipped from the living world, she dreamed she heard him say, 'Just as you are your mother's daughter.'

The End

Lightning Source UK Ltd.
Milton Keynes UK
UKOW04f1633041017
310401UK00001B/23/P